CURE

CURE

Stories of
HEALING MIND
AND BODY

Edited by Kristen Couse
Series Editor, Thomas Dyja

ILLUMINA™

MARLOWE & COMPANY AND
BALLIETT & FITZGERALD INC.
NEW YORK

Compilation copyright © 2000 by Balliett & Fitzgerald Inc.
Introductions copyright © 2000 by Balliett & Fitzgerald Inc.

Illumina™ and the Illumina™ logo are trademarks of
Balliett & Fitzgerald Inc. New York, NY.

An Illumina Book ™

Published by
Marlowe & Company
A Division of Avalon Publishing Group Incorporated
841 Broadway, 4th Floor
New York, NY 10003

and

Balliett & Fitzgerald Inc.
66 West Broadway, Suite 602
New York, NY 10007

Distributed by Publishers Group West

Book design: Jennifer Daddio

Manufactured in the United States of America

ISBN: 1-56924-643-2

Library of Congress Catalog-in-Publication Data

Cure: twelve stories of the journey to healing the mind and body / edited by
Kristen Couse.
     p. cm. — (Illumina)
     ISBN 1-56924-643-2
     1. Medicine and psychology. 2. Healing—Case studies.
     3. Healing—Fiction. I. Couse, Kristen. II. Series.

R726.5.C87 2001
610'.1'9—dc21   00-048212

CONTENTS

LETTER FROM THE EDITORS

Many believe that literature cannot change the world, that it should be content to live between its covers, on the shelves, as a decoration to our lives.

But at the most difficult, challenging, complex moments, again and again we reach up to those shelves, finding guidance and solace and drive among the words of great writers. While a novel may not topple a government, it can change hearts, stiffen resolve, light fires, dry tears or cause them to flow and so affect the world along with the millions of other small motions, the seed-carrying breezes and rivulets, that make our planet work.

We have created Illumina Books in hopes of changing your life. Maybe not in earth-shattering ways, but in ways that comfort and inspire, in ways that help you to continue on.

Each Illumina anthology is a careful collection of extraordinary writing related to a very specific yet universal moment; bouncing back from a lost love, for example, or the journey to healing. With the greatest authors as your guides, you'll read the stories of those who have traveled the same road, learn what they did, see how they survived and moved on.

By offering you the focused beauty and wisdom of this literature, we think Illumina Books can have a powerful, even a therapeutic effect. They're meant not just to work on the mind, but in the heart and soul as well.

—The Editors

from

ANATOMY OF AN ILLNESS

NORMAN COUSINS

*Today, holistic healing and alternative medicine are
an accepted part of our culture. But in the 1960s,
when Norman Cousins was diagnosed with a rare
degenerative disease, they were virtually unheard of.
Rather than accepting the conventional wisdom,
Cousins became his own confident advocate,
engineering a cure which involved massive
doses of vitamin C and laughter.*

This [account] is about a serious illness that occurred in 1964. I was reluctant to write about it for many years because I was fearful of creating false hopes in others who were similarly afflicted. Moreover, I knew that a single case has small standing in the annals of medical research, having little more than "anecdotal" or "testimonial" value. However, references to the illness surfaced from time to time in the general and medical press. People wrote to ask whether it was true that I "laughed" my way out of a crippling disease that doctors believed to be irreversible. In view of those questions, I thought it useful to provide a fuller account than appeared in those early reports.

In August 1964, I flew home from a trip abroad with a slight fever. The malaise, which took the form of a general feeling of achiness, rapidly deepened. Within a week it became difficult to move my neck, arms, hands, fingers, and legs. My sedimentation rate was over 80. Of all the diagnostic tests, the "sed" rate is one of the most useful to the physician. The way it works is beautifully simple. The speed with which red blood cells settle in a test tube—measured in millimeters per hour—is generally proportionate to the severity of an inflammation or infection. A normal illness, such as grippe, might produce a sedimentation reading of, say, 30 or even 40. When the rate goes well beyond 60 or 70, however, the physician knows that he is dealing with more than a casual health problem. I was hospitalized when the sed rate hit 88. Within a week it was up to 115, generally considered to be a sign of a critical condition.

There were other tests, some of which seemed to me to be more an assertion of the clinical capability of the hospital than of concern for the well-being of the patient. I was astounded when four technicians from four different departments took four separate and substantial blood samples on the same day. That the hospital didn't take the trouble to coordinate the tests, using one blood specimen, seemed to me inexplicable and irresponsible. Taking four large slugs of blood the same day even from a healthy person is hardly to be recommended. When the technicians came the second day to fill their containers with blood for processing in separate laboratories, I turned them away and had a sign posted on my door saying that I would give just one specimen every three days and that I expected the different departments to draw from one vial for their individual needs.

I had a fast-growing conviction that a hospital is no place for a person who is seriously ill. The surprising lack of respect for basic sanitation; the rapidity with which staphylococci and other pathogenic organisms can run through an entire hospital; the extensive and sometimes promiscuous use of X-ray equipment; the seemingly indiscriminate administration of tranquilizers and powerful painkillers, sometimes more for the convenience of hospital staff in managing patients than for therapeutic needs; and the regularity with which hospital routine takes precedence over the rest requirements of the patient (slumber, when it comes for an ill person, is an uncommon blessing and is not to be wantonly interrupted)—all these and other practices seemed to me to be critical shortcomings of the modern hospital.

Perhaps the hospital's most serious failure was in the area of nutrition. It was not just that the meals were poorly balanced; what seemed inexcusable to me was the profusion of processed foods, some of which contained preservatives or harmful dyes. White bread, with its chemical softeners and bleached flour, was offered with every meal. Vegetables were often overcooked and thus deprived of much of their nutritional value. No wonder the 1969 White House Conference on Food, Nutrition, and Health made the melancholy observation that a great failure of medical schools is that they pay so little attention to the science of nutrition.

My doctor did not quarrel with my reservations about hospital procedures. I was fortunate to have as a physician a man who was able to put himself in the position of the patient. Dr. William Hitzig supported me in the measures I took to fend off the random sanguinary assaults of the hospital laboratory attendants.

We had been close friends for more than twenty years, and he knew of my own deep interest in medical matters. We had often discussed articles in the medical press, including the *New England Journal of Medicine (NEJM)*, and *Lancet*. He was candid with me about my case. He reviewed the reports of the various specialists he had called in as consultants. He said there was no agreement on a precise diagnosis. There was, however, a consensus that I was suffering from a serious collagen illness—a disease of the connective tissue. All arthritic and rheumatic diseases are in this category. Collagen is the fibrous substance that binds the cells together. In a sense, then, I was coming unstuck. I had considerable difficulty in moving my limbs and even in turning over in bed. Nodules appeared on my body, gravel-like substances under the skin, indicating the systemic nature of the disease. At the low point of my illness, my jaws were almost locked.

Dr. Hitzig called in experts from Dr. Howard Rusk's rehabilitation clinic in New York. They confirmed the general opinion, adding the more particularized diagnosis of ankylosing spondylitis, which would mean that the connective tissue in the spine was disintegrating.

I asked Dr. Hitzig about my chances for full recovery. He leveled with me, admitting that one of the specialists had told him I had one chance in five hundred. The specialist had also stated that he had not personally witnessed a recovery from this comprehensive condition.

All this gave me a great deal to think about. Up to that time, I had been more or less disposed to let the doctors worry about my condition. But now I felt a compulsion to get into the act. It seemed clear to me that if I was to be that one in five hundred I had better be something more than a passive observer.

I asked Dr. Hitzig about the possible origin of my condition. He said that it could have come from any one of a number of causes. It could have come, for example, from heavy-metal poisoning, or it could have been the aftereffect of a streptococcal infection.

I thought as hard as I could about the sequence of events immediately preceding the illness. I had gone to the Soviet Union in July 1964 as chairman of an American delegation to consider the problems of cultural exchange. The conference had been held in Leningrad, after which we went to Moscow for supplementary meetings. Our hotel was in a residential area. My room was on the second floor. Each night a procession of diesel trucks plied back and forth to a nearby housing project in the process of round-the-clock construction. It was summer, and our windows were wide open. I slept uneasily each night and felt somewhat nauseated on arising. On our last day in Moscow, at the airport, I caught the exhaust spew of a large jet at point-blank range as it swung around on the tarmac.

As I thought back on that Moscow experience, I wondered whether the exposure to the hydrocarbons from the diesel exhaust at the hotel and at the airport had anything to do with the underlying cause of the illness. If so, that might account for the speculations of the doctors concerning heavy-metal poisoning. The trouble with this theory, however, was that my wife, who had been with me on the trip, had no ill effects from the same exposure. How likely was it that only one of us would have reacted adversely?

It seemed to me, as I thought about it, that there were two possible explanations for the different reactions. One had to do with individual allergy. The second was that I could have been in a condition of adrenal exhaustion and less apt to tolerate a toxic experience than someone whose immunologic system was fully functional.

Was adrenal exhaustion a factor in my own illness?

Again, I thought carefully. The meetings in Leningrad and Moscow had not been casual. Paper work had kept me up late nights. I had ceremonial responsibilities. Our last evening in Moscow had been, at least for me, an exercise in almost total frustration. A reception had been arranged by the chairman of the Soviet delegation at his dacha, located thirty-five to forty miles outside the city. I had been asked if I could arrive an hour early so that I might tell the Soviet delegates something about the individual Americans who were coming to dinner. The Russians were eager to make the Americans feel at home, and they had thought such information would help them with the social amenities.

I was told that a car and driver from the government automobile pool in Moscow would pick me up at the hotel at

3:30 p.m. This would allow ample time for me to drive to the dacha by 5:00, when all our Russian conference colleagues would be gathered for the social briefing. The rest of the American delegation would arrive at the dacha at 6:00 p.m.

At 6:00, however, I found myself in open country on the wrong side of Moscow. There had been a misunderstanding in the transmission of directions to the driver, the result being that we were some eighty miles off course. We finally got our bearings and headed back to Moscow. Our chauffeur had been schooled in cautious driving; he was not disposed to make up lost time. I kept wishing for a driver with a compulsion to prove that auto racing, like baseball, originally came from the U.S.S.R.

We didn't arrive at the dacha until 9:00 p.m. My host's wife looked desolate. The soup had been heated and reheated. The veal was dried out. I felt pretty wrung out myself. It was a long flight back to the States the next day. The plane was overcrowded. By the time we arrived in New York, cleared through the packed customs counters, and got rolling back to Connecticut, I could feel an uneasiness deep in my bones. A week later I was hospitalized.

As I thought back on my experience abroad, I knew that I was probably on the right track in my search for a cause of the illness. I found myself increasingly convinced, as I said a moment ago, that the reason I was hit hard by the diesel and jet pollutants, whereas my wife was not, was that I had had a case of adrenal exhaustion, lowering my resistance.

Assuming this hypothesis was true, I had to get my adrenal glands functioning properly again and to restore what Walter B. Cannon, in his famous book, *The Wisdom of the Body,* called homeostasis.

I knew that the full functioning of my endocrine system—in particular the adrenal glands—was essential for combating severe arthritis or, for that matter, any other illness. A study I had read in the medical press reported that pregnant women frequently have remissions of arthritic or other rheumatic symptoms. The reason is that the endocrine system is fully activated during pregnancy.

How was I to get my adrenal glands and my endocrine system, in general, working well again?

I remembered having read, ten years or so earlier, Hans Selye's classic book, *The Stress of Life.* With great clarity, Selye showed that adrenal exhaustion could be caused by emotional tension, such as frustration or supressed rage. He detailed the negative effects of the negative emotions on body chemistry.

The inevitable question arose in my mind: what about the positive emotions? If negative emotions produce negative chemical changes in the body, wouldn't the positive emotions produce positive chemical changes? Is it possible that love, hope, faith, laughter, confidence, and the will to live have therapeutic value? Do chemical changes occur only on the downside?

Obviously, putting the positive emotions to work was

nothing so simple as turning on a garden hose. But even a reasonable degree of control over my emotions might have a salutary physiologic effect. Just replacing anxiety with a fair degree of confidence might be helpful.

A plan began to form in my mind for systematic pursuit of the salutary emotions, and I knew that I would want to discuss it with my doctor. Two preconditions, however, seemed obvious for the experiment. The first concerned my medication. If that medication were toxic to any degree, it was doubtful whether the plan would work. The second precondition concerned the hospital. I knew I would have to find a place somewhat more conducive to a positive outlook on life.

Let's consider these preconditions separately.

First, the medication. The emphasis had been on painkilling drugs—aspirin, phenylbutazone (butazolidine), codeine, colchicine, sleeping pills. The aspirin and phenylbutazone were antiinflammatory and thus were therapeutically justifiable. But I wasn't sure they weren't also toxic. It developed that I was hypersensitive to virtually all the medication I was receiving. The hospital had been giving me maximum dosages: twenty-six aspirin tablets and twelve phenylbutazone tablets a day. No wonder I had hives all over my body and felt as though my skin were being chewed up by millions of red ants.

It was unreasonable to expect positive chemical changes to take place so long as my body was being saturated with, and toxified by, pain-killing medications. I had one of my research assistants at the *Saturday Review* look up the pertinent references in the medical journals and found that drugs like phenylbutazone and even aspirin levy a heavy tax on the adrenal glands. I also learned that phenylbutazone is one of the most powerful drugs being manufactured. It can produce bloody stools, the result of its antagonism to fibrinogen. It can cause intolerable itching and sleeplessness. It can depress bone marrow.

Aspirin, of course, enjoys a more auspicious reputation, at least with the general public. The prevailing impression of aspirin is that it is not only the most harmless drug available but also one of the most effective. When I looked into research in the medical journals, however, I found that aspirin is quite powerful in its own right and warrants considerable care in its use. The fact that it can be bought in unlimited quantities without prescription or doctor's guidance seemed indefensible. Even in small amounts, it can cause internal bleeding. Articles in the medical press reported that the chemical composition of aspirin, like that of phenylbutazone, impairs the clotting function of platelets, disc-shaped substances in the blood.

It was a mind-boggling train of thought. Could it be, I asked myself, that aspirin, so universally accepted for so many years, was actually harmful in the treatment of collagen illnesses such as arthritis?

The history of medicine is replete with accounts of drugs and modes of treatment that were in use for many years before it was recognized that they did more harm than good. For centuries, for example, doctors believed that drawing blood from patients was essential for rapid recovery from virtually every illness. Then, midway through the nineteenth century, it was discovered that bleeding served only to weaken the patient. King Charles II's death is believed to have been caused in part by administered bleedings. George Washington's death was also hastened by the severe loss of blood resulting from this treatment.

Living in the second half of the twentieth century, I realized, confers no automatic protection against unwise or even dangerous drugs and methods. Each age has had to undergo its own special nostrums. Fortunately, the human body is a remarkably durable instrument and has been able to withstand all sorts of prescribed assaults over the centuries, from freezing to animal dung.

Suppose I stopped taking aspirin and phenylbutazone? What about the pain? The bones in my spine and practically every joint in my body felt as though I had been run over by a truck.

I knew that pain could be affected by attitudes. Most people become panicky about almost any pain. On all sides they have been so bombarded by advertisements about pain that they take this or that analgesic at the slightest sign of an ache. We are largely illiterate about pain and so are seldom able to deal with it rationally. Pain is part of the body's magic. It is the way the body transmits a sign to the brain that something is wrong. Leprous patients pray for the sensation of pain. What makes leprosy such a terrible disease is that the victim usually feels no pain when his extremities are being injured. He loses his fingers or toes because he receives no warning signal.

I could stand pain so long as I knew that progress was being made in meeting the basic need. That need, I felt, was to restore the body's capacity to halt the continuing breakdown of connective tissue.

There was also the problem of the severe inflammation. If we dispensed with the aspirin, how would we combat the inflammation? I recalled having read in the medical journals about the usefulness of ascorbic acid in combating a wide number of illnesses—all the way from bronchitis to some types of heart disease. Could it also combat inflammation? Did vitamin C act directly, or did it serve as a starter for the body's endocrine system—in particular, the adrenal glands? Was it possible, I asked myself, that ascorbic acid had a vital role to play in "feeding" the adrenal glands?

I had read in the medical press that vitamin C helps to oxygenate the blood. If inadequate or impaired oxygenation was a factor in collagen breakdown, couldn't this circumstance have been another argument for ascorbic acid? Also, according to some medical reports, people suffering from collagen diseases are deficient in vitamin C. Did this lack mean that the body uses up large amounts of vitamin C in the process of combating collagen breakdown?

I wanted to discuss some of these ruminations with Dr. Hitzig. He listened carefully as I told him of my speculations concerning the cause of the illness, as well as my layman's ideas for a course of action that might give me a chance to reduce the odds against my recovery.

Dr. Hitzig said it was clear to him that there was nothing undersized about my will to live. He said that what was most important was that I continue to believe in everything I had said. He shared my excitement about the possibilities of recovery and liked the idea of a partnership.

Even before we had completed arrangements for moving out of the hospital we began the part of the program calling for the full exercise of the affirmative emotions as a factor in enhancing body chemistry. It was easy enough to hope and love and have faith, but what about laughter? Nothing is less funny than being flat on your back with all the bones in your spine and joints hurting. A systematic program was indicated. A good place to begin, I thought, was with amusing movies. Allen Funt, producer of the spoofing television program "Candid Camera," sent films of some of his CC classics, along with a motion-picture projector. The nurse was instructed in its use. We were even able to get our hands on some old Marx Brothers films. We pulled down the blinds and turned on the machine.

It worked. I made the joyous discovery that ten minutes of genuine belly laughter had an anesthetic effect and would give me at least two hours of painfree sleep. When the pain-killing effect of the laughter wore off, we would switch on the motion-picture projector again, and, not infrequently, it would lead to another pain-free sleep interval. Sometimes, the nurse read to me out of a trove of humor books. Especially useful were E.B. and Katharine White's *Subtreasury of American Humor* and Max Eastman's *The Enjoyment of Laughter.*

How scientific was it to believe that laughter—as well as the positive emotions in general—was affecting my body chemistry for the better? If laughter did in fact have a salutary effect on the body's chemistry, it seemed at least theoretically likely that it would enhance the system's ability to fight the inflammation. So we took sedimentation rate readings just before as well as several hours after the laughter episodes. Each time, there was a drop of at least five points. The drop by itself was not substantial, but it held and was cumulative. I was greatly elated by the discovery that there is a physiologic basis for the ancient theory that laughter is good medicine.

There was, however, one negative side-effect of the laughter from the standpoint of the hospital. I was disturbing other patients. But that objection didn't last very long, for the arrangements were now complete for me to move my act to a hotel room.

One of the incidental advantages of the hotel room, I was delighted to find, was that it cost only about one-third as much as the hospital. The other benefits were incalculable. I would not be awakened for a bed bath or for meals or for medication or for a change of bed sheets or for tests or for examinations by hospital interns. The sense of serenity was delicious and would, I felt certain, contribute to a general improvement.

What about ascorbic acid and its place in the general program for recovery? In discussing my speculations about vitamin C with Dr. Hitzig, I found him completely open-minded on the subject, although he told me of serious questions that had been raised by scientific studies. He also cautioned me that heavy doses of ascorbic acid carried some risk of renal damage. The main problem right then, however, was not my kidneys; it seemed to me that, on balance, the risk was worth taking. I asked Dr. Hitzig about previous recorded experience with massive doses of vitamin C. He ascertained that at the hospital there had been cases in which patients had received up to 3 grams by intramuscular injection.

As I thought about the injection procedure, some questions came to mind. Introducing the ascorbic acid directly into the bloodstream might make more effective use of the vitamin, but I wondered about the body's ability to utilize a sudden, massive infusion. I knew that one of the great advantages of vitamin C is that the body takes only the amount necessary for its purposes and excretes the rest. Again, there came to mind Cannon's phrase—the wisdom of the body.

Was there a coefficient of time in the utilization of ascorbic acid? The more I thought about it, the more likely it seemed to me that the body would excrete a large quantity of the vitamin because it couldn't metabolize it fast enough. I wondered whether a better procedure than injection would be to administer the ascorbic acid through slow intravenous drip over a period of three or four hours. In this way we could go far beyond 3 grams. My hope was to start at 10 grams and then increase the dose daily until we reached 25 grams.

Dr. Hitzig's eyes widened when I mentioned 25 grams. This amount was far beyond any recorded dose. He said he had to caution me about the possible effect not just on the kidneys but on the veins in the arms. Moreover, he said he knew of no data to support the assumption that the body could handle 25 grams over a four-hour period, other than by excreting it rapidly through the urine.

As before, however, it seemed to me we were playing for bigger stakes: losing some veins was not of major importance alongside the need to combat whatever was eating at my connective tissue.

To know whether we were on the right track we took a sedimentation test before the first intravenous administration of 10 grams of ascorbic acid. Four hours later, we took another sedimentation test. There was a drop of nine full points.

Seldom had I known such elation. The ascorbic acid was working. So was laughter. The combination was cutting heavily into whatever poison was attacking the connective tissue. The fever was receding, and the pulse was no longer racing.

We stepped up the dosage. On the second day we went to 12.5 grams of ascorbic acid, on the third day, 15 grams, and so on until the end of the week, when we reached 25 grams. Meanwhile, the laughter routine was in full force. I was completely off drugs and sleeping pills. Sleep—blessed, natural sleep without pain—was becoming increasingly prolonged.

At the end of the eighth day I was able to move my thumbs without pain. By this time, the sedimentation rate was somewhere in the 80s and dropping fast. I couldn't be sure, but it seemed to me that the gravel-like nodules on my neck and the backs of my hands were beginning to shrink. There was no doubt in my mind that I was going to make it back all the way. I could function, and the feeling was indescribably beautiful.

I must not make it appear that all my infirmities disappeared overnight. For many months I couldn't get my arms up far enough to reach for a book on a high shelf. My fingers weren't agile enough to do what I wanted them to do on the organ keyboard. My neck had a limited turning radius. My knees were somewhat wobbly, and off and on, I have had to wear a metal brace.

Even so, I was sufficiently recovered to go back to my job at the *Saturday Review* full time again, and this was miracle enough for me.

Is the recovery a total one? Year by year the mobility has improved. I have become pain-free, except for one shoulder and my knees, although I have been able to discard the metal braces. I no longer feel a sharp twinge in my wrists when I hit a tennis ball or golf ball, as I did for such a long time. I can ride a horse flat out and hold a camera with a steady hand. And I have recaptured my ambition to play the Toccata and Fugue in D Minor, though I find the going slower and tougher than I had hoped. My neck has a full turning radius again, despite the statement of specialists as recently as 1971 that the condition was degenerative and that I would have to adjust to a quarter turn.

It was seven years after the onset of the illness before I had scientific confirmation about the dangers of using aspirin in the treatment of collagen diseases. In its May 8, 1971 issue, *Lancet* published a study by Drs. M. A. Sahud and R. J. Cohen showing that aspirin can be antagonistic to the retention of vitamin C in the body. The authors said that patients with rheumatoid arthritis should take vitamin C supplements, since it has often been noted that they have low levels of the vitamin in their blood. It was no surprise, then, that I had been able to absorb such massive amounts of ascorbic acid without kidney or other complications.

What conclusions do I draw from the entire experience?

The first is that the will to live is not a theoretical abstraction, but a physiologic reality with therapeutic characteristics. The second is that I was incredibly fortunate to have as my doctor a man who knew that his biggest job was to encourage to the fullest the patient's will to live and to mobilize all the natural resources of body and mind to combat disease. Dr. Hitzig was willing to set aside the large and often hazardous armamentarium of powerful drugs available to the modern physician when he became convinced that his patient might have something better to offer. He was also wise enough to know that the art of healing is still a frontier profession. And, though I can't be sure of this point, I have a hunch he believed that my own total involvement was a major factor in my recovery.

People have asked what I thought when I was told by the specialists that my disease was progressive and incurable.

The answer is simple. Since I didn't accept the verdict, I wasn't trapped in the cycle of fear, depression, and panic that frequently accompanies a supposedly incurable illness. I must not make it seem, however, that I was unmindful of the seriousness of the problem or that I was in a festive mood throughout. Being unable to move my body was all the evidence I needed that the specialists were dealing with real concerns. But deep down, I knew I had a good chance and relished the idea of bucking the odds.

Adam Smith, in his book, *Powers of the Mind*, says he discussed my recovery with some of his doctor friends, asking them to explain why the combination of laughter and ascorbic acid worked so well. The answer he got was that neither laughter nor ascorbic acid had anything to do with it and that I probably would have recovered if nothing had been done.

Maybe so, but that was not the opinion of the specialists at the time.

Two or three doctors, reflecting on the Adam Smith account, have commented that I was probably the beneficiary of a mammoth venture in self-administered placebos.

Such a hypothesis bothers me not at all. Respectable names in the history of medicine, like Paracelsus, Holmes, and Osler, have suggested that the history of medication is far more the history of the placebo effect than of intrinsically valuable and relevant drugs. Such modalities as bleeding (in a single year, 1827, France imported 33 million leeches after its domestic supplies had been depleted); purging through emetics; physical contact with unicorn horns, bezoar stones, mandrakes, or powdered mummies—all such treatments were no doubt regarded by physicians at the time as specifics with empirical sanction. But today's medical science recognizes that whatever efficacy these treatments may have had—and the records indicate that the results were often surprisingly in line with expectations—was probably related to the power of the placebo.

Until comparatively recently, medical literature on the phenomenon of the placebo has been rather sparse. But the past two decades have seen a pronounced interest in the subject. Indeed, three medical researchers at the University of California, Los Angeles, have compiled an entire volume on a bibliography of the placebo. (J. Turner, R. Gallimore, C. Fox *Placebo: An Annotated Bibliography*. The Neuropsychiatric Institute, University of California, Los Angeles, 1974.) Among the medical researchers who have been prominently engaged in such studies are Arthur K. Shapiro, Stewart Wolf, Henry K. Beecher, and Louis Lasagna. . . . In connection with my own experience, I was fascinated by a report citing a study by Dr. Thomas C. Chalmers, of the Mount Sinai Medical Center in New York, which compared two groups that were being used to test the theory that ascorbic acid is a cold preventative. "The group on placebo who thought they were on ascorbic acid," says Dr. Chalmers, "had fewer colds than the group on ascorbic acid who thought they were on placebo."

I was absolutely convinced, at the time I was deep in my illness, that intravenous doses of ascorbic acid could be ben-

eficial—and they were. It is quite possible that this treatment—like everything else I did—was a demonstration of the
placebo effect.

At this point, of course, we are opening a very wide door,
perhaps even a Pandora's box. The vaunted "miracle cures"
that abound in the literature of all the great religions all say
something about the ability of the patient, properly motivated
or stimulated, to participate actively in extraordinary reversals
of disease and disability. It is all too easy, of course, to raise
these possibilities and speculations to a monopoly status—in
which case the entire edifice of modern medicine would be
reduced to little more than the hut of an African witch doctor.
But we can at least reflect on William Halse Rivers's statement,
as quoted by Shapiro, that "the salient feature of the medicine
of today is that these psychical factors are no longer allowed to
play their part unwittingly, but are themselves becoming the
subject of study, so that the present age is serving the growth of
a rational system of psychotherapeutics."

What we are talking about essentially, I suppose, is the
chemistry of the will to live. In Bucharest in 1972, I visited the
clinic of Ana Aslan, described to me as one of Romania's
leading endocrinologists. She spoke of her belief that there is a
direct connection between a robust will to live and the chemical balances in the brain. She is convinced that creativity—one
aspect of the will to live—produces the vital brain impulses that
stimulate the pituitary gland, triggering effects on the pineal

gland and the whole of the endocrine system. Is it possible that placebos have a key role in this process? Shouldn't this entire area be worth serious and sustained attention?

If I had to guess, I would say that the principal contribution made by my doctor to the taming, and possibly the conquest, of my illness was that he encouraged me to believe I was a respected partner with him in the total undertaking. He fully engaged my subjective energies. He may not have been able to define or diagnose the process through which self-confidence (wild hunches securely believed) was somehow picked up by the body's immunologic mechanisms and translated into antimorbid effects, but he was acting, I believe, in the best tradition of medicine in recognizing that he had to reach out in my case beyond the usual verifiable modalities. In so doing, he was faithful to the first dictum in his medical education: above all, do not harm.

Something else I have learned. I have learned never to underestimate the capacity of the human mind and body to regenerate—even when the prospects seem most wretched. The life-force may be the least understood force on earth. William James said that human beings tend to live too far within self-imposed limits. It is possible that these limits will recede when we respect more fully the natural drive of the human mind and body toward perfectibility and regeneration. Protecting and cherishing that natural drive may well represent the finest exercise of human freedom.

from

MY YEAR OFF

ROBERT McCRUM

Robert McCrum, in the midst of a career as a distinguished literary editor, suffered a massive cerebral hemorrhage, a stroke that paralyzed his left side. McCrum's account of this ordeal and the difficult revelations of his recovery is laced with an everyman's casual courage and humor. The culmination is a surprising intervention, launching the last phase of his cure.

He looked about in that very place for his own image; but another man stood in his accustomed corner, and though the clock pointed to his usual time of day for being there, he saw no likeness of himself among the multitudes that poured in through the Porch. It gave him little surprise, however; for there had been revolving in his mind a change of life, and thought and hoped he saw his new-born resolutions carried out in this.

Charles Dickens, *A Christmas Carol*

The dream of leaving has always been such a powerful fantasy for the busy professional. How often, during my years at Faber, did I hear friends and colleagues express the desire to take time out from their overcrowded schedules and make the time to recharge their personal batteries? The dream of renewal, like the dream of leaving, remains the pipe-dream of the disgruntled professional. 'I just need time,' people will say, 'time to get my head together.' But of course, generally speaking, we carry on, because that's the way we're made, and because the commitments and responsibilities of life demand it.

When, however, you suffer a stroke, or an equivalent catastrophic physical breakdown, you experience the dream of leaving as a nightmare. But perhaps only such a crisis can precipitate change.

My shift of focus, from literary publishing to literary journalism, had been prefigured in my journalistic forays to places like Cambodia and East Timor. I was more than ready for the transition and, besides, there was a sense that the publishing world in which I'd grown up was changing. I no longer felt at home in a new literary environment dominated by the bottom line and the restrictive scrutiny of accountants and financial directors.

Everyone wanted to know if I'd changed. When I answered that, essentially, I thought I had not, I was aware that my old self had been left behind somewhere on the staircase of 41 St Peter's Street. Sometimes, in my more sentimental moments, I felt I was like Tom, the sweep's apprentice in Charles Kingsley's Victorian classic, *The Water Babies.* Perhaps I had left my sooty clothes on the riverbank and become purged and renewed by the waters of ill-health; perhaps—who knows?—my stroke had been a blessing in disguise.

The first year after illness struck was dominated by the struggle to become physically better. The second year—once I was back to an everyday existence—would be all about psychological well-being and the battle with the demons of despair and depression. But now, at least, I could begin to mix hope and optimism with sadness and gloom. In many ways, it was this mixture that would characterize the tone of much of the second year after my stroke.

Donal O'Kelly tells a nice story of the time he saw the great blues guitarist B.B. King at a live performance. B.B. King, the master of blues desolation, appeared on stage in an electric blue suit, with his hair coiffed in perfect ringlets, the effervescent picture of the successful star. He was, says Donal, obviously conscious that his audience would be not unaware of the contrast between his melancholy blues lyrics and his ebullient demeanour. Approaching the microphone, he addressed the front row of the stalls with a winning smile. 'To play the blues,' he said, 'you gotta know the bad times, but you gotta know the good times, too.'

So, of course, it wasn't just a year off. It could not, could never, be any such thing: the idea that, after a twelve-month break, one could seamlessly resume the life one had left behind was ridiculous. To illustrate this, I should enumerate the small but significant ways in which there can be no return.

First, and most obviously, I am typing this with the variously available fingers of my right hand; my left is intermittently useful to hold down the shift key, but it lacks the sprightly dexterity of old. Another thing: in the past, I used to enjoy holding a pen in my right hand. Now that pleasure has diminished, and (though my right side was not affected by the stroke) my handwriting is more difficult to read than ever.

Next, the left side of my face is still mildly frozen. To the untrained eye, I appear normal, but an expert can detect the slight paralysis of my left-side features. In the same category, my speech sounds normal to outsiders, but to me it is vulnerable to stuttering and slurring, and I now have regular speech therapy to correct the deficit. I still prefer to speak sitting down, where the weakness on my left side is less exposed, and find it difficult to stand upright and hold a sustained conversation. Interestingly, it was my speech therapists, whose skill lies in the art of communication, who were consistently the most helpful to me at every stage of recovery. It was they, for instance, who spoke most frankly about my 'deficits' and encouraged me none the less to believe in myself. What else?

I can walk for an hour or so, at a slow pace, with rests, but I cannot walk briskly, and the idea of running out to the shops for a pint of milk, or the newspaper, is unthinkable.

At the end of the day I can still feel profoundly fatigued, and in need of a rest.

My appetite for alcohol, formerly substantial and generally associated with much conversational late-night drinking, has dwindled almost to nothing. After about six months, my tastebuds returned to normal.

My interest in alternative therapies, and in the complementarity of Eastern and Western medical traditions, has become a significant part of my reading. In the absence of clear answers from conventional medicine, I am quite ready to take spin on the wheel of holistic treatment.

I still find that, although to outward appearances cured, I lack the sharpness and edge I believe I used to have. My confidence in many areas has not fully returned. I feel weaker, less competent, less commanding and more vulnerable. All of the above can equal the word that begins with D—depression. At times, I plunge into an abyss of depression, finding it difficult to emerge and then only with the greatest effort of will. For some months I experimented with Prozac and Zoloft. I also explored the potential benefits of several American drugs: Luvox, Xanax, Paxil, Navane, Valium, BuSpar, and Wellbutrin but found that I disliked the side-effects, and eventually switched to that gentle alternative, the herbal remedy, St John's wort (*hypericum*).

I no longer complain, as I had in the past, of the threat of boredom. Now, everything in the world seems precious, special and fascinating.

Outwardly, then, I am fine. I can meet people who do not know me, and pass for an unafflicted forty-four-year-old. Inwardly, I still have something missing. I believe, in time, that this inner sense of deficiency will fade. When I try to characterize it to people who ask about it, I say that sometimes I feel like the pilot of an aeroplane who on looking over his shoulder in the cockpit sees his tail-plane and the end of his fuselage suddenly blown away, but who finds, amazingly, that although his plane has gone into a 'graveyard spin', somehow it has not crashed. Today, I feel like a pilot who is nursing his crippled craft to a safe landing somewhere unfamiliar, but close at hand.

I take virtually no medication. My doctor tells me that a daily aspirin and a regular glass of red wine is probably the best kind of long-term treatment.

Like many forty-somethings, I wrestle with broken resolutions about taking exercise. In my case, the excuse I have is that swimming is the only activity in which I can achieve something like a normal exercise routine. So I swim. Not as often as I should, but perhaps at least once a week. Swimming has certainly helped to strengthen the muscles in my disabled left side.

I began the story of my stroke with a question, Who am I?, which I have attempted to answer, in my own way, through the stories that make up this narrative. As I have shown, a stroke will open up an almost unending vista of questions about yourself, and your significance. If your stroke was serious and you manage to survive, as I did, you become, as I've explained, shaken free of the concerns of everyday life. And yet the question Why? continues to hover over almost every day of your life, though before you can begin to get to Why? you have to ask yourself What? What was it that I went through? What exactly is its significance? What does it mean? These are questions, alas, which bring us inexorably back to Why?

In my case, since the doctors have failed to find a reliable explanation for my stroke, I like to think that I was profoundly lucky. If there is a God, he is remote, detached and impressively hands-off. I am inclined to say that at first I did not think there was anyone out there for me, and then that I had been cruelly punished without reason, and yet, finally, that there was an odd kind of purpose to everything that happened.

Even now, completing this chapter as the second anniversary of my stroke approaches, I can see that, much as I might hope to relegate this personal catastrophe to a file labelled 1995–96, in truth its effects will be with me for much longer. Two months after I came home I found myself wishing that I could somehow sustain the state of convalescence. I would read over my diary—noting how much progress I'd made—and feel almost nostalgic for the vulnerability and alertness of the first few weeks. When I was no longer a dramatically ill person and had become just a forty-four-year-old, nearly middle-aged man with a limp and a mild speech impediment I somehow wanted more. I wanted to retain my singularity. It was time to recognize that I was back in the world, but even here there were stages of rehabilitation.

At first I was glad to be home; then I felt imprisoned; then I became depressed; then I found myself reliving my first day again and again. I could not walk up the stairs without seeing my naked body curled foetally on the mezzanine. I could not lie in bed and escape retracing my confused journeys across the map of the ceiling that long ago Saturday. Whenever I stood on the front step, I saw my helpless body being stretchered out by the paramedics in the summer evening light. I watched TV a lot; I read familiar books; I sat in my armchair and entertained kind visitors. Otherwise, I did what I could to lead an ordinary life.

I have come to believe that by stressing normality and activity the stroke-sufferer has a better chance of recovery. The brain and its workings remain a mystery to doctors, but I am certain that adopting a vigorous and positive attitude to recovery actually assists the process of renewal. I cannot prove this; it's what I believe to have been true in my own case. Of course, there are countless sad examples of people who do not recover their faculties, but, as a youngish man, I'm inclined to believe that the more I use my brain in everyday life, the less likely I am to lose it. Sue, my physiotherapist, had a phrase for this. 'Use it, don't lose it!' she liked to say, cheerfully whacking my left leg with the flat of her hand. Gradually, I came to compile a personal list of Dos and Don'ts for the convalescent stroke-sufferer.

Under Dos, I listed the following:
1. Try alternative therapies like acupuncture.
2. Find out as much as you can about your illness.
3. Take the initiative.
4. Accept help from friends and relatives.
5. Trust your body.
6. Give yourself time.
7. Meet and talk with other stroke-sufferers.

My personal Don'ts were simpler and more fundamental:
1. Don't despair.
2. Don't imagine you are forgotten.
3. Don't surrender.

In hindsight, I believe that I've been 'away' to a prison, or a war, and come back, sadder and perhaps a little bit wiser. I'll probably not see the meaning of this event in my life for some years, but one thing is certain: even if, nearly two years after my stroke, the experience is beginning to seem just that, part of experience, still it has meant a lot, even as it is slowly becoming absorbed into the pattern of my personality.

Now, when I meet people for the first time, I no longer feel, as I did at first, that my stroke stands between me and the outside world like a pane of frosted glass. I can be myself again. When strangers ask me how I hurt my leg I can now say, without awkwardness, 'Oh, I had a stroke a couple of years ago,' and move on to other topics. 'What,' asks the *Mahabharata*, 'is the greatest miracle of all?' and then provides the inspiring answer: 'Each day death strikes, yet man lives as though he were immortal.'

I no longer think I am immortal (as I did in my twenties) but life has returned to normal, more or less. True, I have to plan my movements more carefully than before and I cannot spontaneously do things I'd like to do as of old: I cannot spontaneously go for a long walk, or run through the park on a bright Saturday morning, but as Sarah likes to chide when I wail about this, 'When did you ever do those things, anyway?' She christened this the 'Waterstone's sensation', after the bookstore on Islington Green, at the top of St Peter's Street, a distance of perhaps four hundred yards from my house.

Before my stroke, I had always loved to browse at leisure in our two small neighbourhood bookshops, Angel Books and the Village Bookshop. It so happened that when I was in hospital the bookselling chain Waterstone's opened a huge new store in a deserted building on the bad, neglected side of Islington Green, a two-minute walk from my house. In my 'old' life, I would have stopped in at the first opportunity and enjoyed browsing the shelves, buying paperbacks I'd never read and perhaps getting to know the staff. Now, frustrated that this simple detour on my way home had become an exhausting half-hour excursion fraught with difficulty and exhaustion, I regretted my lost freedom to do as I pleased.

Yet, as Sarah likes to point out, in my 'old' life, I would have sandwiched such a visit into the texture of an already over-crowded day, probably found fault with the selection and availability of the books and come home denouncing the way the book chains threatened the livelihoods of the independent bookshops. None the less, this 'Waterstone's sensation' occurs often enough each day to be worth noting. It offers an insight into the restrictions of old age, the dependency that comes with the loss of mobility.

Besides, for all the things I've lost, there's so much that's been gained. My stroke came as a punctuation mark in the course of a busy life. At the time, I thought it was a full stop, but it turned out to be a comma, or at worst an exclamation point. For a long time, I felt cursed. But then I would recognize that I had this consolation.

I suffered this blow, or calamity, less than two months after getting married. I had been absolutely sure of my love for Sarah in a way I had never been absolutely sure before, and yet who knows what the crisis might have done to our relationship as newlyweds? We knew and loved each other well, but no better than two people who had criss-crossed the Atlantic for a year in a highly charged romantic daze, and had spent barely one calendar month in each other's company. When Sarah was summoned back from San Francisco, she did not know what she might find at the other end of a long plane ride. Her new husband might be a vegetable. He might be dead. As it happened, I was conscious and alive and she, for her part, rose to the occasion with grace, humour and courage. Now, when I wake and find her breathing quietly next to me, every day seems like a blessing.

None the less, until I had reached 29 July 1996, I did not feel released from the malign aura of my stroke. After that anniversary I began to feel better. Besides there was someone other than myself to think about. By the end of July 1996, Sarah knew that she was expecting a baby.

She broke this news to me casually one evening as we were watching a video. Sarah, I remember, was eating a piece of fruit (one of Sarah's most endearing habits is the way she squirrels away food for hungry moments. You can be absorbed in a film at the movie house and suddenly find, from the rustling at your side, that Sarah is about to take a bite from a piece of cake or fruit she happened—just happened—to have in her pocket), and when I observed that this would be good for her, she replied, 'Good for both of us, I'd hope.'

The news of the baby in our lives came, I believe, not a minute too soon, before I turned into a monster of dependency. Now, suddenly, all the focus was on Sarah. Her welfare was top of the agenda, and it was now her well-being that mattered. In the next several months we went for the usual battery of tests and were relieved to be told that the baby (we had opted not to know its gender) was doing very well.

After the frustrations of stroke recovery, it was wonderfully reassuring to visit a clinic and to receive specific answers to simple questions, in other words to receive a diagnosis on which one could rely.

We would lie in bed and think about the future. We would lie in bed, read the papers, try to enjoy our freedom and imagine what life was going to be like when 'TK' (named after the journalistic abbreviation for copy 'to come') actually arrived.

Meanwhile, as we waited, we read in the newspapers that women's brains actually shrink during pregnancy. This, Sarah reported (for the Internet magazine, *Slate*), was why, as a pregnant woman, she felt 'so spaced out and inept'. So why haven't we mailed our Christmas cards yet? Because my brain is too small!

As the moment of TK's arrival drew nearer, traditionally a time of joyous anticipation, Sarah became more and more conventionally baby-centred. She told me one weekend in January that all she wanted to do was yell at me because the house was such a mess. This 'nesting instinct'—the time that you put charming little touches to your delightful home, floral borders in the baby's room, ruffled scraps of fabric glued to the windowframes—seemed so far from Sarah's nature that it was almost comical to behold. When, I teased, would she start needlepointing animal cushions or stencilling scenes of sweet wee fairies dwelling under toadstools? She replied that at least I should consider picking the mail off the floor. 'I think,' she observed on one occasion, 'that you're an even bigger slob than me, and you leave trails of paper behind you wherever you go, like a snail.' Well, quite so.

When Sarah went to the doctor, some two weeks before her due date, she was told that there was no sign of imminent labour. 'Perhaps,' she wrote in *Slate*, 'perhaps I'll be pregnant for the next fifty years, getting bigger and bigger and evolving from my current status (youngish, smallish water buffalo) through the really mammoth parts of the animal kingdom (aged enormous whale).'

These last weeks were so strange for both of us as we stood on the edge of this precipice, not knowing when exactly she would finally go over the edge into parenthood. It was like waiting for a guest who would be staying with you for the rest of your life, said Sarah, and—the joke is—YOU DON'T KNOW ANYTHING ABOUT HIM (or her).

And still, after what had seemed like years of outpatient visiting, we were attending hospital classes. My recovery from my stroke can be measured by the level of my disaffection on these occasions. In one survey of fathers' attitudes towards labour, most of the men questioned said they were thrilled to be present, looked forward to delivering one single-handedly at home, wished they could have a baby themselves, etc., etc. But 3 per cent replied that they got sick. My mood at these childbirth classes was somewhere between wanting to have the baby myself and feeling sick.

Sarah says that my attitude to these antenatal sessions was that of a political prisoner undergoing the torture of watching videos of other prisoners having electrodes attached to their private parts. My customary response was to lie on one of the beanbags provided for the mums (we were all supposed to sit on the floor) and fall asleep. Sarah likes to say that I would wake up when the po-faced instructor's flip-chart presentation moved from 'pain relief during labour' to 'parking near the hospital'.

The final session was especially gruelling. We were shown videos of several women actually going through child-birth. Stephanie, the first case, had decided only to take nitrous oxide and apparently spent half a day moaning and whimpering or laughing pointlessly as if she was insane. As the other cases unfolded, and we watched scenes of heaving and panting, unbearable pain and carnage, it occurred to me that, whatever else I'd gone through, it had been essentially pain-free.

Sarah was surprisingly tolerant of my response to the trauma of the antenatal class. She contrasted my behaviour with that of another man she'd heard about. This father-to-be arrived at his childbirth class and proceeded to sit stiffly in the only chair in the room, looking increasingly unhappy. The instructor noticed this and felt she should confront his repressed, but obviously intense emotions.

'What are you thinking?' she asked him gently.

'I was just thinking,' he replied, 'that I'd like to go skiing.'

At home, now, it was Sarah who was having the sleepless nights, caught in the antenatal limbo, that two-week border between the past and the future, lying in bed, as she put it, 'like a giant walrus marooned on the rocks'. When she confided her thoughts to her *Slate* diary at this time, it was an apt summary of our time together:

We've had a strange three years. I moved away from New York and into Robert's house in London just a year after we met. We got married six months later, and then he fell spectacularly ill, and while he's better now, I'm not sure I am—though I can usually push it down pretty far, I suspect I'll always feel unsettled and scared.

A few days after she'd written this, Sarah turned to me one Saturday morning, with a strange expression on her face. 'Time to get going,' she said. Now, for the first time in months, I was the one who was looking after her. It was a joyous moment. As I steered the car, with Sarah, the beloved whale, beside me, towards her maternity hospital, my view of the city streets was veiled with tears. No question about it: my year off was coming to a close.

BROKEN VESSELS

ANDRE DUBUS

*Andre Dubus, the late New England–based novelist
and essayist, was trying to help a fellow motorist one
night when he was struck by a passing car; he lost both
his legs. Dubus's attempts to maintain family rituals,
despite his disability, was heroism of the daily
variety. It also allowed him to look for his own
salvation in creating comfort for others.*

On the twenty-third of June, a Thursday afternoon in 1988, I lay on my bed and looked out the sliding glass doors at blue sky and green poplars and I wanted to die. I wanted to see You and cry out to You: *So You had three years of public life which probably weren't so bad, were probably even good most of the time, and You suffered for three days, from Gethsemane to Calvary, but You never had children taken away from You.* That is what I wanted to do when I died, but it is not why I wanted to die. I wanted to die because my little girls were in Montauk on Long Island, and had been there since Wednesday, and would be till Sunday; and I had last seen and held and heard them on Tuesday. Cadence is six, and Madeleine is seventeen months.

I wanted to die because it was summer again, and all summer and fall of 1987 I had dreaded the short light and long dark of winter, and now it was June: summer, my favorite season since boyhood, one of less clothes and more hours in the sun: on the beach and the fishing boats and at Fenway Park and on the roads I used to run then walk, after twenty-five years of running; and the five-mile conditioning walks were so much more pleasurable that I was glad I lost running because of sinus headaches in my forties. It was summer again and I wanted to die because last summer I was a shut-in, but with a wife and two daughters in the house, and last August I even wrote. Then with the fall came the end of the family, so of writing; and now the long winter is over and I am shut in still, and without my children in the house; and unable to write, as I have been nearly all the days since the thirteenth of November 1987 when, five days after the girls' mother left me, she came with a court order and a kind young Haverhill police officer, and took Cadence and Madeleine away.

On Tuesday evening, the twenty-first of June in 1988, I ate pizza and Greek salad with my girls and Jack Herlihy, who lives with me, who moved into my basement in January of 1988 to help me pay the mortgage; to help me. But Wednesday and Thursday I could not eat, or hardly could, as though I were not the same man who had lived on Tuesday: in early afternoon, with my son Andre helping me, I had worked out with bench presses and chin-ups in the dining room, where Andre had carried the bench and bar and plates from the library. He rested the chinning bar on its holders on the sides of the kitchen doorway and stood behind me and helped me pull up from the wheelchair, then he pushed the chair ahead of me, and after sets of chin-ups I pulled the chair back under me with my right leg and my stump, and he held me as I lowered my body into it. This was after I had shadowboxed in my chair on the sundeck, singing with Louis Armstrong on cassette, singing for deep breathing with my stomach, and to bring joy to a sitting workout that took me most of the summer of 1987 to devise, with gratitude to my friend Jane Strüss, who taught me in voice lessons in the winter and spring of 1984 that I had spent my adult life breathing unnaturally. The shadowboxing while singing gives me the catharsis I once gained from the conditioning walks and, before those, the running that I started when I was nineteen, after celebrating or, more accurately, realizing that birthday while riding before dawn with a busload of officer candidates to the rifle range at Quantico, Virginia, during my first six weeks of Marine Corps Platoon Leaders' Class, in August of 1955.

I came home from training to my sophomore year at McNeese State College in Lake Charles, Louisiana; and to better endure the second six weeks of Platoon Leaders' Class in 1957, then active duty as an officer after college, I ran on the roads near my home for the next three years, a time in America when no one worked out, not even athletes in their off-seasons, and anyone seen running on a road had the look of either a fugitive or a man gone mad in the noonday sun. When I left the Marines in 1964 I kept running, because it— and sometimes it alone—cleared my brain and gave peace to my soul. I never exercised for longevity or to have an attractive body and, strangely, my body showed that: I always had a paunch I assumed was a beer gut until the early spring of 1987 when my right leg was still in a cast, as it was for nearly eight months, and I drank no beer, only a very occasional vodka martini my wife made me, and I could not eat more than twice a day, but with Andre's help on the weight-lifting bench I started regaining the forty or so pounds I had lost in the hospital, and my stomach spread into its old mound and I told my physical therapist, Mary Winchell, that it never was a beer gut after all. Mary came to the house three times a week and endured with me the pain of nearly every session, and the other pain that was not of the body but the spirit: that deeper and more deleterious pain that rendered me on the twenty-second and twenty-third of June 1988 not the same man at all who, after my workout on the twenty-first of June, waited for Cadence and Madeleine to come to my house.

When they did, Jack was home doing his paperwork from the Phoenix Bookstore, and he hosed water into the plastic wading pool I had given Cadence for her sixth birthday on the eleventh of June. The pool is on the sundeck, which I can be on this summer because in March David Novak and a young man named Justin built ramps from the dining room to the sunken living room, and from the living room to the sundeck. I wanted to be with Cadence, so Jack placed the feet of the wooden chaise longue in the pool and I transferred from my chair to the chaise, then lowered myself into the cold water. I was wearing gym shorts, Cadence was in her bathing suit, and I had taken off Madeleine's dress, and rubbed sun screen on her skin, and in diapers and sandals she walked smiling on the sundeck, her light brown and curly hair more blonde now in summer; but she did not want to be in the water. Sometimes she reached out for me to hold her, and I did, sitting in the pool, and I kept her feet above water till she was ready to leave again, and turned and strained in my arms, and said *Eh*, to show me she was. But she watched Cadence and me playing with a rubber Little Pony that floated, her long mane and tail trailing, and a rubber tiger that did not float, and Madeleine's small inflatable caramel-colored bear Cadence had chosen for her at The Big Apple Circus we had gone to in Boston on the fourth of June, to begin celebrating Cadence's birthday: Jack and Cadence and me in one car, and Madeleine with my grown daughter Suzanne and her friend Tom in another.

Cadence is tall and lithe, and has long red hair, and hazel eyes that show the lights of intelligence. Always she imagines the games we play. I was the Little Pony and she was the tiger; we talked for the animals, and they swam and dived to the bottom and walked on my right leg that was a coral reef, and had a picnic with iced tea on the plastic bank. There was no tea, no food. Once Madeleine's bear was bad, coming over the water to kill and eat our pony and tiger, and they dispatched him by holding a rubber beach ball on the bottom of the pool and releasing it under the floating bear, driving him up and over the side, onto the sundeck. Lynda Novak, young friend and daughter of dear friends, was with us, watching Madeleine as Cadence and I sat in the water under a blue sky, in dry but very warm air, and the sun of late June was hot and high.

I had planned to barbecue pork chops, four of them, center cut, marinating since morning in sauce in the refrigerator. When Cadence and I tired of the sun and the pool and the games in it, we went inside to watch a National Geographic documentary on sharks, a video, and while Lynda and Cadence started the movie, and Madeleine walked about, smiling and talking with her few words, and the echolalia she and usually Cadence and sometimes Lynda and I understood, I wheeled up the ramp to the dining room, and toward the kitchen, but did not get there for the chops, and the vegetables, frozen ones to give me more time with the girls. A bottle of basil had fallen from the work table my friend Bill Webb built against the rear wall of the dining room; he built it two days after Christmas because, two days before Christmas, he came to see me, and I was sitting in the dining room, in my wheelchair, and chopping turkey giblets on a small cutting board resting across my lap. *You like to cook*, he said, *and you can't do a Goddamn thing in that little kitchen of yours; you need a work bench.* The basil was on the floor, in my path; I leaned down, picked it up, flipped it into my lap as I straightened, and its top came off and basil spread and piled on my leg and stump and lap and chair.

Nothing: only some spilled basil, but Cadence was calling: *Daddy, come see the great white*, and I was confronting not basil but the weekend of 17–19 June, one of my two June weekends with Cadence and Madeleine. So I replaced the top on the jar, and with a paper towel picked up the mounds of basil, and with a sponge wiped off the rest of it. Then on the phone (*The phone is your legs*, a friend said to me once) I ordered pizza and Greek salad to be delivered, and joined my girls and Lynda in the living room to watch sharks, and Valerie Taylor of Australia testing a steel mesh shark-proof suit by letting a shark bite her arm. The pizza and salad arrived when Jack had come home from the bookstore, and he and the girls and Lynda and I ate on the sundeck.

On Friday the seventeenth of June I had had Delmonico steaks, potatoes, and snap beans. Jack was picking up the girls on his way home from the store, at about six-thirty, so at five forty-five I started scrubbing potatoes in the kitchen sink, and snapping the ends off beans and washing them. I had just finished shadowboxing on the sundeck, and I believed I could have the potatoes boiling, the beans ready, and also shower and shave before six-thirty. Too often, perhaps most days and nights, my body is still on biped time, and I wheel and reach and turn the chair to the sink or stove and twist in the chair to reach and learn yet again what my friend David Mix said last January. David lost his left leg, below the knee, to a Bouncing Betty that did not bounce, and so probably saved his life, on the first of August in 1967, while doing his work one morning as a Marine lieutenant in Vietnam. His novel, *Intricate Scars*, which I read in manuscript, is the most tenderly merciful and brutal war novel I have ever read. Last winter he said to my son Andre: *There comes a time in the life of an amputee when he realizes that everything takes three times as long.*

He was precise. That Friday night I stopped working in the kitchen long enough to shower, sitting on the stool, using Cadence's hand mirror to shave beneath and above my beard; I dried myself with a towel while sitting and lying on my bed, then wrapped my stump with two ace bandages, and pulled over it a tight stump sleeve to prevent edema. Twenty, maybe even thirty minutes, to shave and shower and shampoo and bandage and dress, yet we sat at the table for steak and boiled potatoes and snap beans and a salad of cucumbers and lettuce at nine-fifteen. And Jack was helping, from the time he got home till the meal was ready; but the kitchen is very small, and with the back of my wheelchair against the sink, I can reach the stove and nearly get food from the refrigerator to my right. I occupied all the cooking space; Jack could only set the table and be with the girls. Cadence was teaching Madeleine to seesaw in the hall, and often she called for me to come see Madeleine holding on and grinning and making sounds of delight, and I wheeled out of the kitchen and looked at the girls on the seesaw, then backed into the kitchen and time moved, as David Mix said, three times as fast as the action that once used a third of it.

Saturday's dinner was easy: I simply had to heat the potatoes and beans left over from Friday, and finish frying the

steaks we had partially fried then, before we realized we had
more than we needed, and the only difficulty was wheeling
back and forth from the dining room table to the kitchen,
holding dishes and glasses and flatware in my lap, a few at a
time, then squirming and stretching in my chair to rinse them
in the sink behind me, and place them in the dishwasher
between the sink and refrigerator behind me. After dinner
Cadence went to a dance concert with Suzanne and Tom.

I bathed Madeleine in the sink. She was happy in the
bubbles from dish soap, and I hugged and dried her with a
towel, and powdered her body and put a diaper on her, then
buckled my seat belt around her and took her down the ramp
to the living room. The late June sun was setting in the northwest, beyond the wide and high glass at the front of the
house. I put her on the couch and got on it beside her, and
Jack sat in a rocking chair at its foot, and we watched *Barfly*
on VCR while Madeleine sat on my chest, smiling at me,
pulling my beard and lower lip, her brown eyes deep, as they
have been since she was a baby, when she would stare at each
person who entered the house, would appear to be thinking
about that man, that woman, would seem to be looking into
their souls. She is my sixth child, and I have never seen a
baby look at people that way. She still does.

That night on the couch she sometimes lay on my chest,
her fleshy little arms hugging my neck, her soft and sweet-
smelling cheek against mine. I felt her heart beating, and felt

from her chest the sounds she made at my face, a series of rising and falling *oohs*, in the rhythm of soothing: *ooh*ooh*ooh*ooh . . . . After sunset, in the cooling room beneath the fan, she puckered her lips and smacked them in a kiss, as Suzanne had taught her, then leaned toward my face, her eyes bright, and kissed me; over and over; then she turned and reached behind her toward Jack, pointing her right hand, with its shortened forefinger. The top knuckle was severed in the sprocket of an exercise bicycle when she was a year and twenty-one days old; she has a tiny stump that Cadence says she got so that when she is older she will understand my stump. I told her to go give Jack a kiss, and lifted her to her feet and held her arms as she stepped off my chest, onto the couch, and followed it back to the arm, where Jack's arms and face waited for her: she puckered and smacked as she walked, then she kissed her godfather. During most of the movie, before she grew sleepy and I put her in the chair with me and buckled the seat belt around her and took her up the ramp and to the refrigerator for her bottle of orange juice, then to the crib and sang "Smoke Gets in Your Eyes" while hers closed, she stayed on my chest, and I held her, drew from her little body and loving heart peace and hope, and gratitude for being spared death that night on the highway, or a brain so injured it could not know and love Madeleine Elise. I said: *Madeleine, I love you;* and she smiled and said: *I luh you.*

Once I paused the movie, and lifted her from me and got onto my chair and went past the television and down the short ramp to the sundeck, and I wheeled to the front railing to piss between its posts, out in the night air, under the stars. Madeleine followed me, with Jack behind her, saying: *She's coming after you, Brother.* I turned to see her coming down the ramp, balancing well, then she glanced up and saw what I had not; and still descending, her face excited, she pointed the stump of her finger to the northwest and said: *Moon.*

I looked ahead of me and up at a new moon, then watched her coming to me, pointing, looking skyward, saying: *Moon. Moon. Moon.*

About the next day, Sunday the nineteenth, I remember very little, save that I was tired, as if the long preparing of the meal on Friday had taken from me some energy that I suspect was spiritual, and that I did not regain. Suzanne spent the afternoon with me and the girls. At five o'clock, in accordance with the court order, she took them to their mother's.

Today, the sixth of July 1988, I read chapter nine of St. Luke. Since starting to write this, I have begun each day's work by reading a chapter of the New Testament. Today I read: *"If anyone wishes to come after me let him deny himself, and take up his cross daily, and follow me."* And: *"took a little child and set him at his side, and said to them: 'Whoever receives this little child for my sake, receives me'."*

In June of 1987 I graduated from physical therapy at home with Mary Winchell: she taught me to transfer from my wheel chair to the passenger seat of a car, meaning the Visiting Nurses Association and Blue Cross and Blue Shield would no longer pay her to come work with me. But it was time: for the physical therapy clinic at Hale Hospital in Haverhill; for Judith Tranberg, called Mrs. T by herself and almost everyone who knows her: a lady who worked at Walter Reed with amputees from the Korean War, a lady whose lined, brown, merry and profound face and hazel eyes and deep tobacco voice I loved at once. On the twenty-second of July I wheeled into her clinic and said to her: *They've always told me my left leg is my best one,* and she said: *Why did they tell you your left leg is your best one?* I said: *I like you. I had my spirit till June, then the surgeon took off the cast and I saw my right leg and I started listening to my body. But now my spirit is back.* Mrs. T said: *I never listen to the body; only the spirit.*

My right leg looked like one found on a battlefield, perhaps a day after its severance from the body it had grown with. Except it was not bloated. It was very thin and the flesh had red and yellow hues and the foot was often purple and nearly always the big toe was painful. I do not know why. On the end of my stump was what people thought then was a blister, though it was a stitch which would become infected and, a year later, require surgery, a debridement. So Mrs. T told me not to use the artificial leg. She started me on parallel bars with the atrophied right leg, whose knee probably bent thirty-two degrees, and was never supposed to bend over forty-five, because of the shattered femur and the scar tissue in my thigh muscles, and the hole under my knee where a bone is now grafted. The tibia was also shattered, and part of my calf muscle is grafted to the top of my shin. Because of muscle and nerve damage, my surgeon, Fulton Kornack, and Mary Winchell told me my leg would never hold my foot in a neutral position, and it still does not: without a brace, from the sole and heel up my calf, my foot droops, and curls. But Mary never gave up on the knee, nor has Mrs. T, nor have I, and it can now bend sixty-three degrees.

The best person for a crippled man to cry with is a good female physical therapist, and the best place to do that crying is in the area where she works. One morning in August of 1987, shuffling with my right leg and the walker, with Mrs. T in front of me and her kind younger assistants, Kathy and Betty, beside me, I began to cry. Moving across the long therapy room with beds, machines, parallel bars, and exercise bicycles, I said through my weeping: *I'm not a man among men anymore and I'm not a man among women either.* Kathy and Betty gently told me I was fine. Mrs. T said nothing, backing ahead of me, watching my leg, my face, my body. We kept working. I cried and talked all the way into the small room with two beds that are actually leather-cushioned tables with a sheet and pillow on each, and the women helped me onto my table, and Mrs. T went to the end of it, to my foot, and began working on my ankle and toes and calf with her gentle strong hands. Then she looked up at me. Her voice has much peace whose resonance is her own pain she has moved through and beyond. *It's in Jeremiah*, she said. *The potter is making a pot and it cracks. So he smashes it, and makes a new vessel. You can't make a new vessel out of a broken one. It's time to find the real you.*

Her words and their images rose through my chest like a warm vapor, and in it was the man shattering clay, and me at Platoon Leaders' Class at Quantico, a boy who had never made love, not when I turned nineteen there, not when I went back for the second six weeks just before becoming twenty-one; and memories of myself after my training at Quantico, those times in my life when I had instinctively moved toward action, to stop fights, to help the injured or stricken, and I saw myself on the highway that night, and I said: *Yes. It makes sense. It started as a Marine, when I was eighteen; and it ended on a highway when I was almost fifty years old.*

In the hospital one night when I was in very bad shape, I woke from a dream. In the dream I was in the hospital at Camp Pendleton, California, and I was waiting for Major Forrest Joe Hunt, one of the best commanding officers I ever served with, to come and tell me where I must go now, and

what I must do. But when I woke I was still at Camp
Pendleton and the twenty-nine years since I left there to go
on sea duty did not exist at all and I was a lieutenant waiting
for Major Hunt. I asked the nurse if we were at Camp
Pendleton and it took her a long time to bring me back to
where and who I was. Some time later my old friend, Mark
Costello, phoned me at the hospital; Mark and I met on the
rifle range in Officers' Basic School at Quantico in 1958. I
told him about the dream, and he said: *Marine Corps
training is why you were on the highway that night.* I said I
knew that, and he told me he had pulled a drowning man
from the surf one summer at Mazatlan and that a Mexican
man on the beach would not help him, would not go out in
the water with him, and he said: *Civilian training is more
conservative.* I had known that too, and had believed for a
long time that we too easily accuse people of apathy or cal-
lousness when they do not help victims of assault or accidents or other disasters. I believe most people want to help,
but are unable to because they have not been trained to act.
Then, afterward, they think of what they could have done
and they feel like physical or moral cowards or both. They
should not. When I came home from the hospital a state
trooper came to visit me; he told me that doctors, nurses, and
paramedics were usually the only people who stopped at
accidents. Sadly, he told me that people do stop when the
state troopers are there; they want to look at the bodies. I am

sure that the trooper's long experience has shown him a terrible truth about our species; and I am also sure that the doctors and nurses and paramedics who stop are not the only compassionate people who see an accident, but the only trained ones. *Don't just stand there, Lieutenant* they told us again and again at Officers' Basic School; *Do something, even if it's wrong.*

Until the summer and fall of 1987 I still believed that Marine training taught us to control our natural instincts to survive. But then, writing a long letter to a friend, night after night, I began to see the truth: the Marine Corps develops our natural instincts to risk ourselves for those we truly love, usually our families, for whom many human beings would risk or knowingly sacrifice their lives, and indeed many have. In a world whose inhabitants from their very beginning turned away from rather than toward each other, chose self over agape, war was a certainty; and soldiers learned that they could not endure war unless they loved each other. So I now believe that, among a species which has evolved more selfishly than lovingly, thus making soldiers an essential body of a society, there is this paradox: in order to fight wars, the Marine Corps develops in a recruit at Boot Camp, an officer candidate at Quantico, the instinct to surrender oneself for another; expands that instinct beyond families or mates or other beloveds to include all Marines. It is a Marine Corps tradition not to leave dead Marines on the battlefield, and

Marines have died trying to retrieve those dead. This means that after his training a young Marine has, without words, taken a vow to offer his life for another Marine. Which means, sadly, that the Marine Corps, in a way limited to military action, has in general instilled more love in its members than Christian churches have in theirs. The Marine Corps does this, as all good teachers do, by drawing from a person instincts that are already present, and developing them by giving each person the confidence to believe in those instincts, to follow where they lead. A Marine crawling under fire to reach a wounded Marine is performing a sacrament, an action whose essence is love, and the giving and receiving of grace.

The night before the day I cried with Mrs. T for the first time (I would cry many times during physical therapy that fall and winter and spring of 1987 and 1988, and she teases me about it still, her eyes bright and her grin crinkling her face), my wife took me to a movie. She sat in an aisle seat and I sat in my wheelchair beside her, with my plastic urinal on the floor beneath my chair leg that held my right foot elevated for better circulation of blood. Two young couples in their late teens sat directly in front of us. One of the boys was talking before the movie, then when it began he was still talking and he did not stop; the other three were not silent either, but he was the leader, the loud one. In my biped days, I was the one who asked or told people to be quiet. But in my chair I felt helpless, and said nothing. There was no rational cause for feeling that way. When you ask or tell people to be quiet in movies, they do not come rushing out of their seats, swinging at you. But a wheelchair is a spiritually pervasive seat. My wife asked the boy to please stop talking. He turned to her, looking over his left shoulder, and patronizingly harassed her, though without profanity. I said, *Cool it.* He looked at me as though he had not seen me till then; and maybe, indeed, he had not. Then he turned to the screen, and for the rest of the movie he and his friends were quiet.

I was not. I made no sounds, but I felt them inside of me. As the movie was ending, I breathed deeply and slowly with adrenaline, and relaxed as much as I could the muscles I meant to use. I would simply look at his eyes as he left his seat and turned toward me to walk around my chair and up the aisle. If he insulted me I would pull him down to me and punch him. During the closing credits he and his date and the other couple stood and left their row of seats. I watched him; he did not turn his eyes to mine. He stepped into the aisle and turned to me but did not face me; he looked instead at the carpet as he walked past me, then was gone. The adrenaline, the edge, went out of me, and seven demons worse than the first came in: sorrow and shame.

So next day, weeping, lying on my back on the table while Mrs. T worked on my body, I told her the story and said: *If you confront a man from a wheelchair you're bullying him. Only a coward would hit a man in a chair.*

That is part of what I told her; I told her, too, about making love: always on my back, unable to kneel, and if I lay on my stomach I could barely move my lower body and had to keep my upper body raised with a suspended pushup. I did not tell her the true sorrow of lovemaking but I am certain that she knew: it made me remember my legs as they once were, and to feel too deeply how crippled I had become.

You can't make a new vessel out of a broken one. I can see her now as she said it, hear her voice, soft but impassioned with certainty, as her face and eyes were. *It's time to find the real you.*

I was working on a novella in August, but then in September, a beautiful blue September with red and orange and yellow leaves, I could not work on it any longer, for I knew that soon my wife would leave. So did Cadence. We played now on my bed with two small bears, Papa Bear and Sister Bear. She brought them to the bed, and their house was my lap; Cadence had just started kindergarten, and Sister Bear went to school, at a spot across the bed, and came home, where she and Papa Bear cooked dinners. They fished from my right leg, the bank of a river, and walked in the forest of my green camouflage Marine poncho liner, and climbed the pillows and the headboard that were mountains. I knew the mother bear was alive, but I did not ask where she was, and Cadence never told me.

But what did she see, in her heart that had already borne so much? Her fourth birthday was on the eleventh of June 1986, then on the twenty-third of July the car hit me and I was in the hospital for nearly two months, her mother coming to see me from one in the afternoon till eight at night every day save one when I told her to stay home and rest, and Cadence was at play school and with a sitter or friends until her mother came home tired at nine o'clock or later at night.

Her mother had waked her around one-thirty in the morning of the twenty-third, to tell her Daddy had been in an accident and her brother Jeb, my younger grown son, was taking Mommy to the hospital and Jeb's friend Nickie would spend the night with her, and she had cried with fear, or terror: that sudden and absolute change in a child's life, this one coming at night too, the worst of times, its absence of light in the sky and on trees and earth and manmade objects rendering her a prisoner of only what she could see: the lighted bedroom, the faces of her mother and brother and the young woman, and so a prisoner of her imagination that showed her too much of danger and death and night. Her four years of life forced her physically to be passive, unable to phone the hospital or friends, unable even to conceive of tomorrow and tomorrow and tomorrow, of life and healing and peace. Over a year later, on a September afternoon in the sun, she told me of the first time her mother brought her to see me, in intensive care: *The little room*, she said, *with all the machines. I kept that in mind,* she said. *You had that thing in your mouth and it was hard for me to kiss you. What was it for?* I told her it was probably to let me breathe. Then she said: *I thought you were dead till then.* And I said that surely Mommy told her I was alive; she said: *Yes. But I thought you were dead till I saw you.*

She came to the hospital for short visits with her mother, then friends took her home; I talked to her on the phone from the hospital bed, and she was only with her mother in the morning and late at night. She did not mind that my leg would be cut off; *he'll be asleep and he won't feel it,* she told a friend who was with her for an afternoon in Boston while her mother sat with me. *When Daddy comes home,* she told her mother, *I'm going to help him learn to walk.* At the hospital her mother sat with me, and watched the clock with me, for the morphine that, twenty minutes after the injection, would ease the pain. Then I was home in a rented hospital bed in the library adjacent to our bedroom, and through its wide door I looked at the double bed, a mattress and boxsprings on the floor, where Cadence and her mother slept. In the mornings Cadence woke first and I woke to her voice and face, sitting up in the bed, on the side where I used to sleep, and looking out the glass door to the sundeck, looking out at the sky, the morning; and talking. That fall and winter she often talked about the baby growing in her mother's body; and one night, when she and I were on the couch in the living room, she said: *Once upon a time there was a father and mother and a little girl and then they had a baby and everything went crazy.*

She was only four. That summer of 1986 her mother and I believed Cadence would only have to be four and worry about a baby coming into her life, perhaps believing the baby would draw her parents' love away from her, or would simply be in the way. And her mother and I believed that, because I had a Guggenheim grant from June of 1986 to June of 1987, we would simply write and pay the bills and she would teach her fiction workshop at home on Wednesday nights and I would try to recover from burning out as a teacher, then becoming so tired visiting colleges for money from January till July of 1986 that I spent a night in intensive care at Montpelier, Vermont, on the fourth of July, with what the cardiologist thought was a heart attack but was exhaustion; and we would have a child.

Madeleine grew inside of my wife as she visited the hospital, then as she cared for me at home, changing bandages as they taught her in the hospital, emptying urinals, bringing food to the hospital bed in the library, and juice and water, and holding my leg when I transferred from bed to chair to couch and back again; Madeleine growing inside of her as she soothed the pain in my body and soul, as she put the bed pan under me then cleaned me and it, and she watched with me as the Red Sox beat the Angels in the playoffs and lost to the Mets in the World Series, sacrifice enough for her, to watch baseball till late at night, pregnant and caring for a four-year-old energetic girl and a crippled man. But she sacrificed more: for some time, I don't know how much time, maybe two weeks or three, because it remains suspended in memory as an ordeal that broke us, or broke part of us anyway and made laughter more difficult, I had diarrhea, but not like any I had ever had before. It not only flowed from me without warning, but it gave me no sign at all, so that I did not even know when it flowed, and did not know after it had, and for some reason we could not smell it either. So when a game ended she would stand over me on the couch and turn my body toward hers, and look, and always I was foul, so foul that it took thirty minutes to clean me and get me from the couch to the bed, after midnight then, the pregnant woman going tired and unheld to bed with Cadence, who would wake her in the morning.

Which would begin with cleaning me, and that remained such a part of each day and night that I remember little else, and have no memory of the Red Sox losing the seventh game I watched from the couch. *They saved your life and put you back together*, she said, *and they can't cure this.* Gene Harbilas, my doctor and friend here, cured it, and that time was over, and so was something else: a long time of grace given us in the hospital and at home, a time of love near death and with crippling, a time when my body could do little but lie still and receive, and when her every act was of the spirit, for every act was one of love, even the resting at night for the next long day of driving to and from the hospital to sit there; or, later, waking with me at home, to give me all the sustenance she could. In the fall, after the diarrhea, she was large with Madeleine, and exhaustion had its hold on her and would not let her go again, would not release her merely to gestate and give birth, and nurse and love her baby. The victim of injuries like mine is not always the apparent one. All that year I knew that she and Cadence were the true victims.

Cadence cried often. On a night in January, while Andre was staying with us for the month of Madeleine's birth, having come up from New York to take care of Cadence and mostly me (yes: the bed pan: my son) Cadence began loudly crying and screaming. She was in her bedroom. I was no longer in the hospital bed but our new one in the bedroom, and they brought her there: her eyes were open but she did not act as though she were awake. She was isolate, screaming with terror, and she could not see or hear us; or, if she could, whatever we did and said was not strong enough to break what held her. Andre called Massachusetts General Hospital and spoke to a pediatrician, a woman. He told her what Cadence was doing and she asked whether Cadence had been under any stress. He said her father was hit by a car in July and was in the hospital for two months and they cut off his leg, and her mother just had a baby and Cadence had chicken pox then so she couldn't visit her mother in the hospital, where she stayed for a week because she had a cesarean. The doctor gasped. Then she told Andre it was night terrors. I do not remember what she told us to do, because nothing we did soothed Cadence; she kept crying and screaming, and I lay helpless on my back, wanting to rise, and hold her in my arms, and walk with her, and I yelled at the ceiling, the night sky above it: *You come down from that cross and give this child some peace!* Then we played the cassette of *Porgy and Bess* by Louis Armstrong and Ella Fitzgerald that she often went to sleep to, and she was quiet and she lay beside me and slept.

In late spring of 1987 Cadence talked me into her room, in my wheelchair; I had not been able to do it till then, but she encouraged and directed me through the series of movements, forward and back and short turns, then I was there, beside her bed on the floor. After that I could go in and read to her. One night, still in the spring, I went into her room, where she sat on the bed. I looked at her face just below mine and said: "I want to tell you something. You're a very brave and strong girl. Not many four-year-olds have had the kind of year you've had. Some children have to be lied to sometimes, but Mommy and I never had to lie to you."

"What do you mean?"

"We could always tell you the truth. We could tell you they were going to cut off my leg, and that the right one wouldn't be good, and you understood everything, and when you felt happy you were happy, and when you felt sad, you cried. You always let us know how you felt and what was wrong. You didn't see Mommy much for two months while I was in the hospital, and then she was gone for a week to have Madeleine and you only saw her for a couple of minutes at the hospital till the nurse saw your chicken pox and said you had to leave. Then Mommy came home with a baby sister. Most little girls don't go through all of that. All this year has been harder on you than on anybody else, and when you grow up, somebody will have to work awfully hard to make you unhappy, because you're going to be a brave, strong woman."

Tears flowed down her cheeks, but she was quiet and her eyes were shining, and her face was like a woman's receiving love and praise.

Then in the summer and early fall of 1987, we did lie to her, but she knew the truth anyway, or the part of it that gave her pain and demanded, again, resilience; and she brought to my bed only the two bears, the father and the daughter; and her days must have drained her: she woke with the fear of kindergarten and the other fear and sorrow she must have escaped only in sleep and with new children and work at kindergarten, and with familiar friends at play school, in the same way adults are absorbed long enough by certain people and actions to gain respite from some deep fear or pain at the center of their lives. I could no longer work. When the house was empty I phoned Jack at the Phoenix Bookstore and asked for his prayers and counsel and comfort, and I went to physical therapy three times a week, going there and back in a wheelchair van, three hours each session with Mrs. T, and the physical work and pain gave me relief, and I prayed for patience and strength and love, and played with Cadence and Madeleine, and waited for the end.

The girls' mother left on the eighth of November, a Sunday night; and people who love us helped me care for my girls until after dark, around six o'clock, on Friday the thirteenth, when she came with the court order and the Haverhill police officer. That afternoon Cadence and I were lying on my bed. Beside her was her pincher, a strip of grey cloth from the apron of her first Raggedy Ann doll, before she was a year old. She goes to sleep with it held in her fist, her thumb in her mouth. When she is tired or sad she holds it and sucks her thumb, or simply holds it; and she holds it too when she rides in a car or watches cartoons. She held it that afternoon after my lawyer phoned; his name is Scotty, he is an old friend, and he was surprised and sad as he told me of my wife's lawyer calling from the courthouse, to say my wife was coming for my daughters. I wheeled from the kitchen phone, down the short hall to my bedroom where Cadence and I had been playing, where for nearly a year we had played with stuffed animals. I also played the giant who lay on his back, and had lost a leg, and his right one was in a cast. The giant has a deep voice, and he loves animals. Cadence is the red-haired giant, but we usually talk about her in the third person, the animals and I, for Cadence is the hearts and voices of animals with the giant; when Madeleine could sit up and be with me, she became the baby giant, cradled in my arm. Most days in the first year Cadence brought to the games an animal with a missing or wounded limb, an animal who needed healing and our love.

Next to the bed I braked the wheelchair and moved from it to my place beside Cadence. She was sitting. I sat close to her and put my left arm around her and told her that judges were people who made sure everyone was protected by the law, even little children, and Mommy had gone to see one because she believed it was better for Cadence and Madeleine not to be with me, and Mommy was coming now with a policeman, to take her and Madeleine. I told her Mommy was not doing anything wrong, she was doing what she felt was right, like a good Momma Bear. Cadence held her pincher and looked straight ahead and was quiet. Her body was taut.

"I don't want to go in the car with them."

"Who's them, sweetie?"

"The judge and the police."

"No, darling. The judge won't be in the car. Neither will the policeman. It'll just be Mommy."

One of our animals we had played with since I came

home from the hospital on the seventeenth of September 1986 is Oatmeal, a blond stuffed bear with pink ears and touches of pink on his cheeks and the top of his head and the back of his neck. On my birthday on the eleventh of August 1987, Cadence gave me shells and seaweed from the beach, and a prayer for a Japanese gingko tree she gave me with her mother, and Oatmeal. I am his voice; it is high. I am also the voice of his wife, Koala Bear; but after the marriage ended, Cadence stopped bringing Koala Bear to our games, save for one final night in December, while Madeleine was asleep and Cadence and I were playing in the dining room, and she said Oatmeal and Koala Bear were breaking up but maybe if Koala Bear had a baby they would love each other again; then she got a small bear from her room and put it with Koala Bear and Oatmeal and said they had a baby now and loved each other again. Then we watched Harry Dean Stanton as an angel in *One Magic Christmas*. After my birthday I kept Oatmeal on my bed; Cadence and I understand that he is a sign from her to me, when she is not here.

That afternoon she gazed in front of her; then quickly she moved: her face and upper body turned to me, her eyes darkly bright with grief and anger; and her arms and hands moved, one hand holding the pincher still, and she picked up Oatmeal and swung him backhanded into my lap. Then she turned away from me and was off the bed, circling its foot, and I watched the pallid right side of her face. When she turned at the bed's end and walked toward the hall, I saw her entire face, her right thumb in her mouth, the grey pincher hanging, moving with her strides; and in her eyes were tears. Her room is adjacent to mine, where I had slept with her mother, where I had watched all the seasons through the glass sliding door that faced northwest. Cadence walked past me, out my door, and into hers. She closed it.

My friend Joe Hurka and my oldest daughter Suzanne were in the house; Joe had been with us all week, driving back and forth, an hour and ten minutes each way, to his job in Peterborough, New Hampshire. I called to Cadence: "Sweetie? Do you want me in your room with you?"

I had never heard her voice from behind a door and a wall as well; always her door was open. Her voice was too old, too sorrowful for five; it was soft because she is a child, but its sound was that of a woman, suffering alone: "No."

I moved onto the wheelchair and turned it toward the door, the hall, her room. I wheeled at an angle through her doorway: she lay above me in her bunk on the left side of the room. She was on her back and sucking her right thumb and holding the pincher in her fist; she looked straight above her, and if she saw anything palpable it was the ceiling. She was pale, and tears were in her right eye, but not on her cheek. I moved to the bunk and looked up at her.

The bunk was only a few months old and, before that, she had a low bed and when she lay on it at night and I sat above her in my chair, she could not see the pictures in the books I read aloud. So we lay on my bed to read. But from the bunk she could look down over my shoulder at the pictures. She climbed a slanted wooden ladder to get on it, and I had told Mrs. T I wanted to learn to climb that ladder. *Not yet, Mr. Andre*, she had said; *not yet*. In that moment in Cadence's room, looking at her face, I said in my heart: *Fuck this cripple shit*, and I pushed the two levers that brake the wheels, and with my left hand I reached up and held the wooden side of the bunk and with my right I pushed up from the arm of the chair. I had learned from Mrs. T not to think about a new movement, but simply to do it. I rose, my extended right arm taking my weight on the padded arm of the chair, and my left trying to straighten, to lift my body up and to pivot onto the mattress beside Cadence. I called Joe and he came quickly down the hall and, standing behind me, he held me under my arms and lifted, and I was on the bunk. Cadence was sitting now, and blood colored her face; her wet eyes shone, and she was grinning.

"*Da*ddy. You got *up* here."

Joe left us, and I lay beside her, watching her face, listening to her voice raised by excitement, talking about me on the bunk. I said now we knew I could lie on the bunk at night and read to her. She crawled to the foot of the bed and faced me. Beyond her, two windows showed the grey sky in the southeast and the greyish white trunks of poplars without leaves. Cadence lowered her head and somersaulted, and her long bent legs arced above us, her feet struck the mattress, and her arms rose toward me, ahead of her face and chest. Her eyes were bright and dry, looking into mine, and she was laughing.

We were on the bunk for an hour or more. We did not talk about our sorrow, but Cadence's face paled, while Suzanne and Joe waited with Madeleine in the dining room for the car to come. When it did, Suzanne called me, and Joe came and stood behind the wheelchair and held my upper body as I moved down from the bunk. In the dining room Madeleine was in her high chair; Suzanne was feeding her cottage cheese. I talked with the young police officer, then hugged and kissed Madeleine and Cadence goodbye.

In Salem District Court I got shared but not physical custody. The girls would be with me two weekends a month, Thursday afternoons and alternate Monday afternoons through dinner, half a week during the week-long vacations from school, and two weeks in summer. *That's a lot of time,* people say. Until I tell them it is four nights a month with my two daughters, except for the two weeks in summer, and ask them if their own fathers spent only four nights a month with them when they were children (of course many say yes, or even less); or until I tell them that if I were making a living by traveling and earning a hundred thousand a year and spent only four nights a month with my family I would not be a good father. The family court system in Massachusetts appears to define a father as a sperm bank with a checkbook. But that is simply the way they make a father feel, and implicit in their dealings is an admonishment to the father to be grateful for any time at all with his children. The truth is that families are asunder, so the country is too, and no one knows what to do about this, or even why it is so. When the court receives one of these tragedies it naturally assigns the children to the mother's house, and makes the father's house a place for the children to visit. This is not fatherhood. My own view is that one house is not a home; our home has now become two houses.

On the tenth of January 1988, Madeleine was a year old. It was a Sunday, and one of my weekends with the girls, and we had balloons and a cake and small presents, and Cadence blew out the candle for her sister. During that time in winter I was still watching Cadence for signs of pain, as Suzanne and Andre and Jack were, and Marian and David Novak, and Joe Hurka and Tom. Madeleine was sometimes confused or frightened in her crib at night, but never for long. She is a happy little girl, and Cadence and Suzanne and Jack and I learned during the days of Christmas that "Silent Night" soothes her, and I sing it to her still, we all do, when she is troubled; and she stops crying. Usually she starts singing at *holy night, all is calm*, not with words but with the melody, and once this summer she sang the melody to Cadence when she was crying. We all knew that Madeleine, only ten months old when the family separated, was least touched, was the more fortunate of the children, if indeed anything about this can be fortunate for one of the children. So we watched Cadence, and let her be sad or angry, and talked with her; and we hugged and kissed Madeleine, and played with her, fed her, taught her words, and sang her to sleep.

The fifth of February was a Friday in 1988, and the first night of a weekend with the girls. Suzanne brought them into the house shortly after six o'clock in the evening; I was in the shower, sitting on the stool, and she brought them to the bathroom door to greet me. When I wheeled out of the bathroom into the dining room, a towel covering my lap, Cadence was in the living room, pedaling my exercise bicycle. A kind woman had given it to me when she saw me working on one at physical therapy, and learned from Mrs. T that I did not have the money to buy one. With my foot held by the pedal strap I could push the pedal down and pull it up, but my knee would not bend enough for me to push the wheel in a circle. In February I did not have the long ramp to the living room, against its rear wall, but a short steep one going straight down from the dining room, and I could not climb or descend it alone, because my chair would turn over. Madeleine was in the dining room, crawling, and Suzanne stood behind me, in the doorway between the dining room and kitchen, talking on the phone and looking at the girls. I was near the ramp, and Cadence was saying: *Watch this, Daddy*, and was standing on the right pedal with her right foot, stretching her left leg up behind her, holding with both hands the grip on the right end of the handlebar, and pushing the pedal around and around.

Then she was sitting on the seat and pedaling and Madeleine crawled down the ramp and toward her and the bicycle, and Cadence said: *Madeleine, no*, as Madeleine reached with her right hand to the chain guard at the wheel and her index finger went into a notch I had never seen, and a tooth of the sprocket cut her with a sound distinct among those of the moving chain and spinning wheel and Suzanne's voice: a *thunk*, followed at once by the sound of Madeleine's head striking the floor as she fell back from the pain, and screamed. She did not stop. Cadence's face was pale and frightened and ashamed, and I said: *She'll be all right, darling. Is it her head or her finger?* and Cadence said: *It's her finger and it's* bleed*ing*, and Suzanne was there, bending for Madeleine, reaching for her, saying: *It* is *her finger and it's cut* off. Three of my four daughters, and I see their faces now: the oldest bravely grieving, the youngest red with the screams that were as long as her breathing allowed, and above them the five-year-old, pale with the horror of the bleeding stump she saw and the belief that she alone was responsible.

Then Suzanne was rising with Madeleine in her arms

and saying: *I have to find the finger; they can sew it back on,* and bringing Madeleine up the ramp to me. She was screaming and kicking and writhing and I held her and looked at her tiny index and middle fingers of her right hand: the top knuckle of her index finger was severed, and so was the inside tip of her middle finger, at an angle going up and across her fingernail. In months, that part of her middle finger would grow back. Suzanne told Cadence to stop the chain because Madeleine's finger could be stuck in it, and she dialed 911, and the police officer told her to put the dismembered piece in ice. Cadence came up the ramp; I was frightened of bleeding and shock, and had only a towel, which does not stop bleeding. I said to Cadence: *Go get me a bandana.* She turned and sprinted down the hall toward my room, and I called after her: *In the second drawer of my chest,* and she ran back with a clean bandana she held out to me. Suzanne was searching the bicycle chain and the living room, and Cadence watched me wrap Madeleine's fingers. I held her kicking legs up but she did not go into shock and she did not stop screaming, while Suzanne found the rest of her finger lying on the floor, and wrapped it in ice and put it in the refrigerator, and twice I told Cadence it was not her fault and she must never think it was.

But she did not hear me. I imagine she heard very little but Madeleine's screaming, and perhaps her own voice saying *Madeleine, no,* before either Suzanne or I could see what was about to happen, an instant before that sound of the sprocket tooth cutting through flesh and bone; and she probably saw, besides her sister's screaming and tearful face and bandaged bleeding hand, and the blood on Madeleine's clothes and on the towel and chair and me, her own images: her minutes of pleasure on the bicycle before Madeleine crawled down the ramp toward her and then once again, and so quickly again, her life became fear and pain and sorrow, already and again demanding of her resilience and resolve. When a police officer and two paramedics arrived, she said she wanted to go in the ambulance with Madeleine and Suzanne.

By then Tom and Jack were there, and I was drying and dressing. The police officer found the small piece of Madeleine's middle finger in the chain and ran outside with it, and gave it to the paramedics before they drove to Lawrence General Hospital, because Hale Hospital has no trauma center. I asked Jack to phone David Novak, and by the time I dressed and gave the officer what he needed for his report, David was in the house. I phoned Andre at work and Jeb at home, then David and Tom and Jack and I drove in David's Bronco to the hospital, twenty-five minutes away. I had put into my knapsack what I would need to spend the night in the hospital with Madeleine. Her mother was in Vermont, to ski. But in the car, talking to David, I knew that Cadence would need me more.

In the ambulance Madeleine stopped screaming, and began the sounds she made that winter when she was near sleep: *ah* ah *ah* ah . . . At the hospital she cried steadily, because of the pain, but now she was afraid too and that was in her voice, even more than pain. A nurse gave her to me and I held her cheek to mine and sang "Silent Night," then Jeb was there. At Lawrence General they could not work on Madeleine's finger; they phoned Massachusetts General Hospital in Boston, then took her there. Suzanne rode with her, and Jeb and Tom followed. Suzanne dealt with the surgeons and, on the phone, reported to me; I talked to the girls' mother in Vermont; and Suzanne and Jeb and Tom stayed at the hospital until the operation was over, and Madeleine was asleep in bed. The surgeon could not sew on the part of Madeleine's finger, because of the angle of its amputation. Early next morning her mother drove to the hospital and brought her to my house; her hand was bandaged and she felt no pain; her mother had asked on the phone in Vermont if she could spend the weekend with Madeleine, and Cadence went with them for the afternoon, then in the evening her mother brought her back to me for the rest of the weekend.

When David and Jack and Cadence and I got home from Lawrence General, I put Cadence on my lap and wheeled to my bedroom and lifted her to my bed. She lay on her back and held her pincher and sucked her thumb. She watched me as I told her she had been very good when Madeleine was hurt, that she had not panicked; she asked me what that meant, and I told her, and said that some children and some grown-ups would not have been able to help Suzanne and me, and that would be very normal for a child, but I only had to tell her to get me a bandana and she had run down the hall to the drawer in my chest before I could even tell her which drawer to look in. She turned to me: "I heard you when I was running down the hall. You said the second drawer, but I already knew and I was running to it."

I told her that was true courage, that to be brave you had to be afraid, and I was very proud of her, and of Suzanne, because we were all afraid and everyone controlled it and did what had to be done. She said: "*You* were afraid?"

"Yes. That's why I was crying."

She looked at the ceiling as I told her she must never blame herself for Madeleine's finger, that no one had seen the notch in the chain guard, the bicycle had looked safe, and she had tried to stop Madeleine, had said *Madeleine, no*, and two grown-ups were right there watching and it happened too fast for anyone to stop it. She looked at me: "I started pedaling backwards when I saw her reaching for the wheel."

Then she looked up again, and I said she had done all she could to keep Madeleine from getting hurt, and it was very important for her never to feel responsible, never to blame herself, because that could hurt her soul, and its growth; and if she ever felt that way she must tell me or Mommy or Suzanne or Andre or Jeb. Her thumb was in her mouth and her pincher lay across her fingers, so part of it was at her nose, giving her the scent she loves. Finally I said: "Is there anything you want to ask me?"

Still gazing straight up, she lowered her thumb and said: "I only have one question. Why does it always happen to me? First you got hurt. Now Madeleine is hurt. Maybe next Mommy will get hurt. Or I will."

I closed my eyes and waited for images, for words, but no words rose from my heart; I saw only Cadence's face for over a year and a half now, suffering and enduring and claiming and claiming cheer and joy and harmony with her body and spirit, and so with her life, a child's life with so very few choices. I opened my eyes.

"I don't know," I said. "But you're getting awfully good at it."

It is what she would tell me now; or encourage me to do.

Today is the twenty-ninth of August 1988, and since the twenty-third of June, the second of two days when I wanted to die, I have not wanted my earthly life to end, have not wanted to confront You with anger and despair. I receive You in the Eucharist at daily Mass, and look at You on the cross, but mostly I watch the priest, and the old deacon, a widower, who brings me the Eucharist; and the people who walk past me to receive; and I know they have all endured their own agony, and prevailed in their own way, though not alone but drawing their hope and strength from those they love, those who love them; and from You, in the sometimes tactile, sometimes incomprehensible, sometimes seemingly lethal way that You give.

A week ago I read again *The Old Man and the Sea,* and learned from it that, above all, our bodies exist to perform the condition of our spirits: our choices, our desires, our loves. My physical mobility and my little girls have been taken from me; but I remain. So my crippling is a daily and living sculpture of certain truths: we receive and we lose, and we must try to achieve gratitude; and with that gratitude to embrace with whole hearts whatever of life that remains after the losses. No one can do this alone, for being absolutely alone finally means a life not only without people or God or both to love, but without love itself. In *The Old Man and the Sea,* Santiago is a widower and a man who prays; but the love that fills and sustains him is of life itself: living creatures, and the sky, and the sea. Without that love, he would be an old man alone in a boat.

One Sunday afternoon in July, Cadence asked Jack to bring up my reserve wheelchair from the basement, and she sat in it and wheeled about the house, and moved from it onto my bed then back to the chair, with her legs held straight, as I hold my right one when getting on and off the bed. She wheeled through the narrow bathroom door and got onto the toilet, her legs straight, her feet above the floor, and pushed her pants down; and when she pulled them up again she said it was hard to do, sitting down. She went down and up the ramp to the living room, and the one to the sundeck. *Now I know what it's like to be you,* she said. When she was ready to watch a VCR cartoon, she got onto the living room couch as I do, then pushed her chair away to make room for mine, and I moved onto the couch and she sat on my stump and nestled against my chest; and Madeleine came, walking, her arms reaching for me, and I lifted her and sat her between my leg and stump, and with both arms I held my girls.

1988–1989

from

ORDINARY PEOPLE

JUDITH GUEST

After seeing his idolized older brother drown in a boating accident, 16-year-old Conrad watches the bottom drop out of his own life. Following a suicide attempt and time spent in a sanitarium, he finds a fragile balance, only to have it shattered—which is when the real rebuilding begins.

After dinner he and his grandfather sit in the living room, reading the Sunday paper, while, in the kitchen, his grandmother does the dishes. He listens to the comforting sound of her bustling about, the cupboard doors banging loudly, the water going on and off with that peculiar, groaning wail as the pipes protest. Another memory that belongs to this old and comforting house. He waits patiently for the sports section. His grandfather reads every article, chuckling, rattling the paper at the stuff he likes; grumbling and crossing his legs when something annoys him. He leafs through his section casually, reading a dull article on riverfront-housing investments from beginning to end, testing his memory. He checks out his horoscope: *home, family, your life-style are spotlighted. Taurus and Libra individuals figure prominently.* He wonders about his life-style—what is it? He is becoming, Berger says.

An article, halfway down on page three suddenly leaps out at him. *Girl Takes Own Life.* Oh, God. He skips to the middle of it. ". . . carbon monoxide poisoning . . . nineteen-year-old Skokie girl . . . dead in her car early Saturday morning. She had been reported missing the night before by her father, Raymond Aldrich. . . ." He goes back to the beginning of the article. "Karen Susan Aldrich of 3133 Celeste, Skokie, Illinois . . . dead on arrival at Skokie General Hospital . . . hose attached to the car's exhaust pipe was drawn through a rear window. . . ."

His body is suddenly numb. The words thicken and swim before his eyes. *Oh God. Oh no. Oh God.* His head fills with strange sounds—a tuneless humming, like violin strings. His body trembles. ". . . we are in shock . . . father told reporters . . . everything going so well, I can't believe . . . I don't believe it . . . ."

He folds the newspaper carefully, holds it carefully on his lap, rocking slowly. He is dizzy and sick at his stomach.

"Conrad? What's the matter?"

His grandfather stands over him, the newspaper in his hand. "Are you all right?"

"I'm all right," he says. He can hardly hear himself, the sounds inside his head are so loud. His grandmother is there and there is more talking; broken pieces of conversation that he cannot follow. Her hand is on his forehead.

"You don't feel hot to me. Is it a headache?"

"A headache, yes," he says, getting up. "I need to go to bed. I'm tired."

"Let me get you some aspirin. You see? You don't get enough sleep, and then you work outside and get chilled and overtired."

"You're going to bed?" his grandfather asks. "At seven o'clock?"

"I'll get you the aspirin," she says.

"Never mind. I don't need it."

He heads for the stairway, holding himself stiffly upright. In his mind he sees himself putting his feet, one before the other, on the steps, carrying himself upward. His body feels nothing.

Fully awake, he lies on his side in the bed, memorizing the lines of the desktop, and above it, the half-inch ridge of desk pad, the chair beside the desk, the precise angles of his schoolbooks piled upon the chair. His eyelids feel dry and scratchy.

So safe so safe floating in the the calmest of seas what happened? What happened? A stone bench outside the hospital where they sat for hours soaking up spring and its sunshine Leo with them laughing and joking Karen's legs swinging back and forth back and forth and the blue cotton dress clings to her slim body her hair long and black freshly washed shines flatly against her skull smiling at him a dimple appears in her cheek what happened? "What happened?" Crawford you liar you promised you said you were never wrong oh Jesus God please I don't want to think about this let me sleep God let me sleep

Eyes closed a knee in his back hand at his neck forcing his face into the floor of the elevator rough under his cheek smell of vomit and matted fur "God don't hurt me" struggles against the indignity his pajamas pulled down around his knees a needle sunk deep into his thigh twists moans and all of it loose like water flowing salt tickles inner edges of his eyes into his mouth twists onto his back arms over his head raw wails of anguish break off in pieces hurt his ears "Baby, it's okay" Leo is over him lifts coaxing "Let's get up off the floor huh?" arm around his waist sags heavy his wrist aches where Leo holds him dragged along the watery dark he rolls off Leo's shoulder to the bed eyes closed hands folded in prayer between his legs can't look "God don't hurt me. Please."

Shock. His mind egg-shaped gray loose tracings of paths over it rat scratchlngs white hospital gown gentle Leo helps him into it never hurries him old friends in the steel-and-white room greet him with smiles "Here he is just lie back and relax head on the pillow that's it" get him ready shoot him up so he can't move can't get away Leo smiles down at him his face is purple in the light his teeth glitter "Easy now you know it doesn't hurt" no but afterward exhaustion fatigue that moves outward from the center of him flowing like warm oil in his veins can't lift arms or legs his ears ring his head light and empty all rat scratchings erased and Leo feeds him "Atta baby eat some peaches."

His body jerks awake. His hand reaches for the lamp. He turns it on; lies motionless in the sudden, bright light. He is in the narrow, twin bed in his grandmother's spare bedroom. Blue bedspread, blue-and-white-striped wallpaper, blue-and-white rag rug on the floor, everything in order. No good.

No good to think about it. About anything. It will not change. Just as before, it is done. He wills his mind to drop him under; to let him pass through into dreamless sleep.

Sits against the wall cool at his back in only his shorts the door locked testing only testing tension of skin sharpness of blade thin threads of blood well up from scratches his legs his arms have no feeling in them draws the blade down into his left wrist a deep vertical cut the artery bubbles up like a river widens does it again to his right arm warmth and color floods the room he is free at last comforted it crosses his mind to compose himself for dying awkward there is nowhere to put his hands the blood makes everything slippery lies on his side using one arm as a pillow he sleeps and then arms tied his jaw aches something hard pinches his mouth between his teeth "to keep him from swallowing his tongue" they say he knows better it is how they punish you for failure here and someone crying crying "Lord, what has he done? What has he done to himself?"

He awakens to fear again; his mouth dry. For terror-filled seconds he doesn't know if it is happening all over again. Or worse, that time has tipped backward and it is happening still. Numb with fear, he scrambles out of bed, pulling his clothes on over his pajamas.

The house is dark. It hovers around him as he fumbles for the stairway, fumbles for his jacket in the downstairs hall closet, quietly feeling for the handle of the front door, to let himself out.

He walks swiftly, without direction. To calm himself. To get away from dreams, because there are worse ones and he doesn't want to remember them, doesn't want to think at all, less intense, less intense, but how to do it? To concentrate on that is to at once accomplish the opposite. A phrase attaches itself to his mind: ". . . Why a kid would want to hurt himself . . ." a swift, sinking feeling in the pit of his stomach as he remembers another newspaper article. About him. The police chief was quoted. He couldn't understand why a kid would want to hurt himself like that. Crawford had let him read it afterward. He had tried to explain that he had not been trying to hurt himself, he had merely been trying to die.

No. You do not slash yourself in a dozen places if you are merely trying to die. Nor do you overlook the full bottle of Valium beside the razor blades in the medicine chest. Not for him that quiet, dream-drifted road outward on sleeping pills. Too easy. And too neat. *Oh, God, why, then?*

He stops walking. The sidewalk is shadowy; the air around him still and cold. Stiff, black limbs arch over his head. The black houses crouch, ready to spring. He is shivering, his skin clammy and wet underneath his pajama top, down his back, under his armpits. Freezing out here.

Ahead of him, a car approaches. It pulls to the curb opposite him. Police car. The door opens, and he has a sudden urge to run; swiftly he puts it down. He stands still, shoving his hands into his jacket pockets as the cop crosses the street.

"Where you headed?"

"Nowhere." He wets his lips nervously. "Just taking a walk."

"Pretty late, isn't it? After two. Where do you live?"

"Fourteen-thirty Heron Drive." He is surprised at how calm, how normal his voice sounds.

The cop frowns. "Long way from home, aren't you?"

He has given his home address. He takes his hands out of his jacket pockets; lets them hang limp at his sides. *See? I'm harmless. I'm okay.* "I'm staying with my grandparents. On Green Bay Road."

"Where do they live?"

For a moment, he panics. He cannot remember the number, and he stumbles over the words: "It's a gray house with black shutters. On the corner of Green Bay and Booth. Fifty-one thirty-five—"

"What's the name?"

"Butler. Howard Butler."

"Yeah, okay." The cop smiles, then. "I know the house. They know you're out?"

He shakes his head. His hands are sweating. His wallet is back on the dresser, in the bedroom. Suppose they should ask him to prove who he is. Will they take him to the station? Call his grandparents?

"What's your name?"

"Jarrett. Conrad Jarrett."

"Well, listen, Conrad, I wouldn't walk around here this late. Too many nuts in the world, these days. You want a ride back?"

"No, that's okay."

"You'd better head back, then. They might wake up. Be worried about you."

"Yeah, I will."

They drive off. He lets his breath out slowly, even manages a wave as they signal to him from the car window. *Too many nuts.* Meaning you aren't one of them. All the outer signs must be right, then: hair cut to the right length, polite answers, expensive suède jacket made in Mexico. *You're all right kid. Ordinary.* And this event, walking the streets at two o'clock is ordinary, too, but something is wrong about it, something not normal, what is it? He cannot remember. He is shivering again. He wipes his hands on his pants, zips his jacket up tight; turning, he follows the disappearing taillights, two red eyes in the darkness.

The door is unlatched, as he left it. He slips quietly inside; goes to the kitchen, to the sink, where he hunts in darkness for the faucet and a glass. He drinks greedily, then lets the cold water run over his hands. Still in the dark, he makes his way to the den at the back of the house. No lights. He doesn't

want to wake them. No going back to bed, either. Not safe
there. He sits upright in the chair beside the door, his arms
along the armrests, not leaning back.

*Unforgivable. It is unforgivable. They wrestle with the boat
together, the sails snapping like rifle cracks in the wind "Get it
down! Get the goddamn sail down!" grabbing at gray a bil-
lowing mass sticky and wet against his face it smothers him
with its weight a loud crack and the terrible rolling begins
everything out from under the water closing over his head he
fights his way back to the surface screaming emptied of everything but fear "Buck! Buck!" in front of him a hand stretching
out an arm along the upturned hull water crashing against
him pushing them apart Buck yells "Kick off your shoes!"
mindless he obeys chokes as water closes him off again from the
moon from everything they collide in the water Buck grabs his
shirt "Hang on, I'm gonna go under, have a look!" he screams
at him "Don't go Don't go!" and the wind takes it throws it
back into his face Buck is already gone and above him the sky
lumpy with clouds black it is painful to breathe terrifying he
must turn his head away from the dark shape of hull from
safety to do it Buck surfaces beside him shaking hair from his
eyes gasping "We screwed up this time, buddy! He's gonna haul
ass over this!" They stare at each other and Buck breaks into a
grin "Well? You got any ideas?" he shakes his head biting his
lips to keep back the terror "Always thinking, aren't you?" and*

he finds his voice then "It's not so goddamn funny, Buck!" he soothes him "Okay, okay. They'll be looking for us, they're looking now, for sure, just hang on, don't get tired, promise?" He says "Don't you either!" and they stop talking then address themselves to the dull, dogged task of enduring and the clouds level out it starts to rain hours into the night they hang two fish caught and strung off the sides of the boat arms straining hands numb with cold the water is icy laced with foam like root beer "How long you think it's been? I dunno. An hour? Two hours? Oh, hell, longer than that, don't you think?"

When did it happen? When did they stop calling to one another from opposite sides of the stern where they hung for better more even balance did he think it was over?

——"Man, why'd you let go?"

——"Because I got tired."

——"The hell! You never get tired, not before me, you don't! You tell me not to get tired, you tell me to hang on, and then you let go!"

——"I couldn't help it."

——"Well, screw you, then!"

Unforgivable and his grandmother crying at the funeral "Poor Jordan, poor baby, he didn't want to do it, he didn't want to leave us like this!" and he had answered her saying coldly "Why did he let go, then? Why didn't he hang on to the boat?"

And he was punished for that because afterward everything made him ill. Food and the sounds of people eating it crushing breaking slurping. Smells. He would lift a glass of orange juice to his mouth inhale the acrid odor of dirt and dying flowers even to think about eating made him gag and for weeks afterward not being able to sleep that was punishment too being forced to submit over and over to a hopeless rerun of that day to what could have been done to make the sum of it diferent. Nothing. That is the nature of hell, that it cannot be changed; that it is unalterable and forever.

Was it painful? He cannot believe so if it was he would have cried out he would have known it and he could have stopped him he could have said "Buck take me with you I don't want to do this alone."

He is awake again. *No more. No more.* He gets up quickly; goes to turn on the television set, kneeling beside it as it warms up. An old set; the images are snowy. The brightness hurts his eyes. He tunes the sound down and goes back to the chair, focusing his eyes in concentration on the screen. His hands smooth the worn denim of his Levi's methodically as tears fill his eyes, run down his cheeks. He feels the sudden, chill prick as they drop from his chin on to his jacket. Nearly morning now. Outside the window he can see faint streaks of light, separating the trees from their background of sky. Six-thirty already. On the television, a *Sunrise Semester* course in astronomy. Soon the light inside the room will match the grayness on the screen.

He gets up again, to go to the bathroom, taking a leak, washing his hands, staring at himself in the mirror. He can barely make out the contours of his face. His heart is pounding slow and full, keeping time with the cracking headache that has ignited behind his eyes. He leaves the bathroom, going to sit in the hallway, beside the telephone. It will be seven soon. People get up, then. It is not too early to call.

He looks up the number in the book: on Judson Avenue in Evanston, his home number. Waiting, he stares at the faded wallpaper, a pattern of eagles and stars in gold and blue and dull red. As he traces it with his eyes another pattern emerges. Wings and talons, a sideways stripe across the wall. It begins to move and his stomach heaves. He quickly dials the number.

It is Berger's voice at the other end: "Hullo."

"This is Conrad," he says. Tears blind him. His throat closes up.

"Conrad? Are you there?"

"I need to see you," he whispers.

"Yes. Okay. Can you make it to the office in half an hour? Come in through the back. The front doesn't open up until eight. I'll prop it for you."

"All right."

He replaces the receiver; goes upstairs for his wallet and his keys. He scribbles a note to his grandparents, leaving it on the telephone stand. *Had to leave early. See you tonight after school.* The writing looks stiff and jerky to him.

Nearly light as he gets into the car. He wipes his eyes, wipes his hands on his pants again. *This is how people get in accidents keep calm keep calm.* He grips the wheel tightly, his wrists aching, his head throbbing as the grayness around him washes away to chilly March sunshine. It is thin, without power. A huge truck, gears grinding, lurches past on the Edens and he fights the panic that engulfs him, trying to think of nothing but the mechanics of driving. *Now a red light, now stop, now watch the car in front of you turning left.* It feels like the very first time he has been behind the wheel. He tries to stay in his own lane, tries not to swerve, to keep his foot on the gas constant and even. He focuses his eyes carefully on nothing but the road ahead.

The light is on, and he pushes the door open. He stands a moment in the waiting room.

"You made good time."

He moves to the doorway. Berger is in the corner, filling the coffeepot. He says, over his shoulder, "You gonna come in and sit down?"

Outside the window, down below, a truck rattles slowly up the street. He is fumbling for the zipper on his jacket, but he cannot find it. There are pockets of tears behind his eyes. His throat aches. He stands, motionless in the doorway.

"It might help if you just let it out, Con."

Not the words but the use of his name that releases him, and he comes slowly forward to sit in front of the desk. The tears roll down his cheeks.

"I need something—"

"Okay," Berger says. "Tell me."

But old and powerful voices slam into him. He covers his face. *He is back in the hospital again back in B Ward the night of the burning Robbie Clay his friend a bachelor certified public accountant the joker always laughing his sister had committed him "First I was a certified public now I am publicly certified!" that night no jokes no laughter but an agony of sound the roaring of a bull Robbie had burned himself with matches a rag tied around his waist soaked in alcohol where had he gotten it? Nobody knew they knew only that he had hurled himself into the void it could happen to any of them it lay like a disease over the floor the nurses walking by talking late that night they passed his room he heard the words "penis, scrotum and thigh" and a wave of dizziness nausea sweeping over him he had gone to stand facing the corner of his room hands on the wall and Leo had found him "Baby he's okay you don't have to worry about Robbie" he had snarled "Stay the hell away from me!" but Leo would not he was the only one who could get close when he was begging loudest to be left alone laid his hand on his back "It isn't bad he's gonna be fine" but of course he wasn't fine moved that night up to Three and never seen again. Buck. Robbie. Karen. Everyone he touches he has a sudden vision of himself naked tied down on a table his penis scrotum and thigh cut away*

"I can't!" he cries. "I can't!" He drops his head on his arms. "You keep at me, make me talk about things I can't talk about, I can't!"

"Is that what you came here to tell me?"

He lifts his head, holding himself tight. Control. Control is all. He tries to clamp his throat shut over it, to stifle the sound, but he cannot and he begins to sob, a high, helpless coughing sound. There is no control any more, everything is lost, and his body heaves, drowning. His head is on his arms again, the smell of old wood is in his nostrils, the warmth of his own breath against his face.

"Ah, God, I don't know. I don't know, it just keeps coming, I can't make it stop!"

"Don't, then."

"I can't! I can't get through this! It's all hanging over my head!"

"What's hanging over your head?"

"I don't know!" He looks up, dazed, drawing a deep breath. "I need something, I want something—I want to get off the hook!"

"For what?"

He begins to cry again. "For killing him, don't you know that? For letting him drown!"

"And how did you do that?" Berger asks.

But it is coming from some part of him that is separate and unknown. He is helpless against it, hits his fist hard against the desktop. "I don't know, I just know that I did!" Head cradled on his arms again, he sobs. Cannot think, cannot think, no way out of this endless turning and twisting. Hopeless.

"You were on opposite sides of the boat," Berger says, "so you couldn't even see each other. Right?"

He nods his head as he sits up. He scratches his cheek, staring at Berger through the slits of his eyes. The itching creeps downward, under his pajama top.

"And he was a better swimmer than you. He was stronger, he had more endurance."

"Yes."

"So, what is it you think you could have done to keep him from drowning?"

Tears flood his eyes again. He wipes them roughly away with his hand.

"I don't know. Something."

It is always this way. His mind shuts down. He cannot get by this burden, so overpowering that it is useless to look for a source, a beginning point. There is none.

"You don't understand," he says. "It has to be some-body's fault. Or what was the whole goddamn point of it?"

"The point of it," Berger says, "is that it happened."

"No! That's not it! That is too simple—"

"Kiddo, let me tell you a story," Berger says. "A very simple story. About this perfect kid who had a younger brother. A not-so-perfect kid. And all the time they were growing up, this not-so-perfect kid tried to model himself after his brother, the perfect kid. It worked, too. After all, they were a lot alike, and the not-so-perfect kid was a very good actor. Then, along came this sailing accident, and the impossible happened. The not-so-perfect kid makes it. The other kid, the one he has patterned his whole life after, isn't so lucky. So, where is the sense in that, huh? Where is the justice?"

"There isn't any," he says dully.

Berger holds up his hand. "Wait a second, let me finish. The justice, obviously, is for the not-so-perfect kid to become that other, perfect kid. For everybody. For his parents and his grandparents, his friends, and, most of all, himself. Only, that is one hell of a burden, see? So, finally, he decides he can't carry it. But how to set it down? No way. A problem without a solution. And so, because he can't figure out how to solve the problem, he decides to destroy it." Berger leans forward. "Does any of this make sense to you?"

"I don't know," he says. "I don't know."

"It is a very far-out act of self-preservation, do you get that, Con? And you were right. Nobody needs you to be Buck. It's okay to just be you."

"I don't know who that is any more!" he cries.

"Yeah, you do," Berger says. "You do. Con, that guy is trying so hard to get out, and he's never gonna be the one to hurt you, believe me. Let him talk. Let him tell you what you did that was so bad. Listen, you know what you did? You hung on, kiddo. That's it. That's your guilt. You can live with that, can't you?"

He cannot answer, does not have an answer. He leans back against the chair. He feels as if he is seeing Berger through a curtain of mist. The air shimmers between them. He is lightheaded, his bones fragile, without substance, like scraps of paper.

"The thing that hurts you," Berger says, "is sitting on yourself. Not letting yourself connect with your own feelings. It is screwing you up, leading you off on chases that don't go anywhere. You get any sleep last night?"

He shakes his head.

"How about food? You had anything to eat since yesterday?"

"No—" He starts to say that he is not hungry, that he is too tired to eat, but Berger is on his feet and heading for the door, and he stumbles along behind him, unable to voice a protest, down the stairway and out into the street, dragged along by the force and flow of Berger's monologue.

"Geez, if I could get through to you, kiddo, that depression is not sobbing and crying and *giving vent*, it is plain and simple *reduction of feeling*. Reduction, see? Of all feeling. People who keep stiff upper lips find that it's damn hard to smile."

The restaurant is called Nick's. The lettering is spread, in red, block letters, across the front window. It has a dirty, neglected look about it, but inside it is clean and warm and cheerful. Berger picks out a table by the window. He pushes back the blue-and-white checked curtains so they can look out on the street. He orders for them both: orange juice, toast, bacon and eggs, coffee. He spreads his napkin across his lap, looking around, smiling at everyone—the two plump, dark-haired waitresses, Nick in the kitchen, a table of burly Greeks.

Conrad sits in the chair, hands between his legs. He is exhausted, his eyes swollen and tight. He looks down at his hands, at his fingernails, bitten to the quick again. He doesn't remember doing that. Narrowing his eyes, he blends every-thing to gray—the curtains, the walls painted with huge, atomic grapevines and leaves, the dark, gorilla-like man across the table from him.

"The little girl in Skokie is what started all this, am I right?" Berger asks quietly. "Crawford called me last night. He was pretty shook, too."

"Oh God," he says.

Berger hands him his handkerchief.

"Kiddo, you know the statistics. Out of every hundred, fifty are gonna try it again. Fifteen eventually make it."

He had thought himself empty of tears, but without

warning they start up again. He covers his face with his hands. "Don't," he says.

The waitress brings their breakfast, and he blows his nose, then props his elbows on the table. "She was okay," he says. "She was fine. Into everything at school, and happy. She told me to—to be less intense, and relax and enjoy life. Shit, it isn't fair!"

"You're right. It isn't fair," Berger says. "I'm sorry. I'm damn sorry for her, the poor kid. Crazy world. Or maybe it's just the crazy view we have of it, looking through a crack in the door, never being able to see the whole room, the whole picture, I don't know." He runs his hands through his hair. "Listen, eat," he says. "You'll feel better once you eat."

But he is too exhausted to eat; he takes a few tentative bites of the eggs; pushes the plate from him. No go. Too risky.

"Come on," Berger urges.

"I can't," he says. His legs feel as if they are weighted to the floor. "I don't know what I would have done if I couldn't have gotten you this morning. I felt so shaky."

"And now?"

He closes his eyes. "Still shaky."

Berger laughs. "That's what I like about you, kiddo. You got style. Listen, what happened this morning was that you let yourself feel some pain. Feeling is not selective, I keep telling you that. You can't feel pain, you aren't gonna feel anything else, either. And the world is full of pain. Also joy. Evil.

Goodness. Horror and love. You name it, it's there. Sealing yourself off is just going through the motions, get it?"

He opens his eyes to study the ceiling, too tired to comment, even to think of a comment.

"Go home and get some sleep. You look whipped."

"I can't. My grandmother would hassle me all day. I can't take the flak. She might even call my father and tell him I cut school."

"So, go to your own house. You've got a key, haven't you?"

He sits up. "Yeah, I do. I should have thought of that."

Berger laughs again. "You would have. When are your parents due back?"

"Not until Wednesday."

"Okay, go home, rest up, eat something, hear?"

"Should I come tomorrow? For my appointment?"

"Sure."

"It's okay for me to go, you think?"

"What d'you mean?"

"You don't think I'll do anything crazy?"

"Like what?" Berger asks. "Give yourself a haircut or something? You're a big boy. You're not gonna punish yourself for something you didn't do."

"All right."

"And anyway, punishment doesn't do a damn thing for the guilt, does it? It doesn't make it go away. And it doesn't earn you any forgiveness."

"No," he says wearily.

"So, what's the point of it, then?"

Berger walks him to the car. As he gets in, tears well up again behind his eyelids. For so long he has shielded himself from hurt, not letting it be inflicted upon him. Suddenly he is naked, unprotected, and the air is full of flying glass. All his senses are raw, open to wounding.

He wipes his eyes. "I'll see you tomorrow."

"Drive carefully."

He lets himself in through the kitchen. The air inside is heavy with the sweetish odor of too-ripe fruit. Or furniture polish? He goes upstairs to his bedroom, laying his keys and his wallet on the dresser, opening the window, slightly.

He turns on the shower and strips down, leaving his clothes in a pile on the floor. He gets in; adjusts the water to as hot as he can stand it. He does his best thinking in here. The heat relaxes the clots inside his brain, making the juices flow, and he leans his forehead against the wall, hands behind his back, as the warmth spreads downward from his neck to his shoulders, his buttocks, the backs of his knees.

He closes his eyes, sees Berger, a confident, sly gorilla riding a unicycle in a red felt jacket, eating a banana. Berger smiles and waves. Gorillas don't ride unicycles, though. The only one he has ever seen sat inside a huge truck tire suspended from a chain in his cage at the zoo. He rocked back and forth, sticking his tongue out at the world. Making judgments. He and Buck pondered the primitive intelligence of this gesture: *People laugh but maybe he knows something,* Buck said. *We wouldn't laugh if he gave us the finger, would we?*

Guilt. Is not punishment, Berger said. Guilt is simply guilt. A run-in he and Buck had years ago, with a clerk in a drugstore. He said they had not paid for two comic books, wouldn't believe them. He had threatened to call their father and expose them to the world as liars and thieves. *Go ahead* Buck said with scorn *My dad knows we don't lie and he knows we don't take things. What do I care what you think?* But he, Conrad, had cared desperately, and had felt, even as he knew he was innocent, guilty and shamed by it. Why?

Because it has always been easier to believe himself capable of evil than to accept evil in others. But that doesn't make sense. The clerk in the drugstore wasn't evil, just mistaken. Bad judgment doesn't make you evil—can he only see these two opposites—good and evil? Innocence and guilt? Is it necessary to believe others guilty in order for himself to be proved innocent? There is a way through this, an opening, if only he can find it. He stands very still, letting water sluice over his shoulders and river into the creases of his stomach to his crotch.

"——*C'mon!*"

"——*No. I changed my mind.*"

"——C'mon, you promised!"

"——Why do I always have to go first?"

They are eight and nine the leader and the follower as always in the garage that day with the door closed stuffy and hot in here and Buck is abruptly disgusted with him.

"——Ah, forget it, big-ass baby! I said you could do it to me after!"

Buck turns away tossing the clothesline to the floor and as always with freedom in sight he opts for prison it is easier to face than Buck's cool contempt he stands obediently still as Buck ties his hands behind his back sits then as the rope is lashed around his ankles Buck pulls a handkerchief from his pocket "How can you make me talk if you gag me?" and Buck considers "First we torture you. Then we make you talk" but he is no longer sure turns his head just as Buck discovers you don't need permission when you have the power forces him back against the cement floor sprawls across him while he ties the handkerchief around his mouth it is clean and smells faintly of his father abruptly for him the game is over terrified he struggles to free himself fights the gag choking a peculiar hollow clonging sound the garage door opening a shadow falls across them a cool breeze entering "What the hell is this?" he is pulled to his feet the ropes roughly loosened the gag snatched from his mouth not relief but horror as he sees Buck's pants jerked down to his knees his father's hand cracking across the bare ass Buck howls in protest while he stands in helpless terror waiting for his punishment only a game but they had both been playing it and then his father's anger is mysteriously spent and he kneels on the garage floor, an arm around Buck's shoulders Buck is sobbing his head down. "Don't you ever do a thing like that again, Bucky, you understand?"

"—*But I wasn't gonna hurt him, Daddy*—"

"—*People get hurt without anyone meaning it, don't you see?*"

For some inexplicable reason he was left out of this. Passed over. His shame and guilt ignored. It must have been too monstrous to mention. His crime, his part in it, and so he had to suffer alone. But what for? There is no evil there, after all. Just a boy's game, dangerous maybe, but not evil, and not Buck's fault, not his either. Nobody's fault. It happened, that's all. Not so frightening, is it? To believe them both innocent *Oh God.* His sinuses are packed with a spongy material. Tears leak out from beneath his eyelids. Resigned, he lets them come as he soaps himself carefully: his arms, his shoulders, and his back; his legs, between his legs. He stands and lets the water run over his head, washing his hair. When he is finished, he gets out, towels himself dry. Slowly and carefully he turns his arms up to look at the insides of his wrists.

In grade school a girl named Sally Willet sat next to him. She had taken his hand in hers one day, those strong, brown fingers tracing the creases in his palm, showing him his life-line, curving beside the heel of his hand almost to his wrist: a deep and definite mark. He draws a ragged breath, wondering about Karen, about her lifeline. Was it a long one, too?

Tears of grief this time *Not fair not fair!* no, but life is not fair always, or sane, or good, or anything. It just *is*.

He hangs up the towels in the bathroom and turns off the light. He puts on clean underwear, picking up his dirty clothes, throwing them down the clothes chute. All the while the hot oily liquid seeps out from beneath his eyelids. He continues to blink it back, to wipe it away.

Reduction of feeling. At least he is not guilty of that today. He sets the alarm on his clock-radio, stripping back the covers on his bed. He climbs in and cleanliness surrounds him, its smell cool and seductive. He rolls to his face and, without a sound, without a thought, he sleeps.

from

BLESS ME, ULTIMA

RUDOLFO ANAYA

Young Antonio Marez finds his life changed when Ultima, a curidad, or healer, comes to live with his family. In this striking excerpt, Tony not only witnesses Ultima's curative powers for the first time—but learns that he has power within himself as well.

The summer came and burned me brown with its energy, and the llano and the river filled me with their beauty. The story of the golden carp continued to haunt my dreams. I went to Samuel's house but it was boarded up. A neighbor, an old lady, told me that Samuel and his father had taken a job sheepherding for the rest of the summer. My only other avenue to the golden carp would be Cico, so every day I fished along the river, and watched and waited.

Andrew worked all day so I did not see him much, but it was reassuring at least to have him home. León and Gene hardly ever wrote. Ultima and I worked in the garden every morning, struggling against the llano to rescue good earth in which to plant. We spoke little, but we shared a great deal. In the afternoons I was free to roam along the river or in the blazing hills of the llano.

My father was dejected about his sons leaving, and he drank more than before. And my mother also was unhappy. That was because one of her brothers, my uncle Lucas, was sick. I heard them whispering at night that my uncle had been bewitched, a bruja had put a curse on him. He had been sick all winter, and he had not recovered with the coming of spring. Now he was on his deathbed.

My other uncles had tried everything to cure their youngest brother. But the doctor in town and even the great doctor in Las Vegas had been powerless to cure him. Even the holy priest at El Puerto had been asked to exorcise el encanto, the curse, and he had failed. It was truly the work of a bruja that was slowly killing my uncle!

I heard them say late at night, when they thought I was asleep, that my uncle Lucas had seen a group of witches do their evil dance for el Diablo, and that is why he had been cursed. In the end it was decided to hire the help of a curandera, and they came to Ultima for help.

It was a beautiful morning when the yucca buds were opening and the mocking birds were singing on the hill that my uncle Pedro drove up. I ran to meet him.

"Antonio," he shook my hand and hugged me, as was the custom.

"Buenos días le de Dios, tío," I answered. We walked into the house where my mother and Ultima greeted him.

"How is my papá?" she asked and served him coffee. My uncle Pedro had come to seek the help of Ultima and we all knew it, but there was a prescribed ceremony they had to go through.

"He is well, he sends his love," my uncle said and looked at Ultima.

"And my brother Lucas?"

"Ay," my uncle shrugged despairingly, "he is worse than when you saw him last. We are at the end of our rope, we do not know what to do—"

"My poor brother Lucas," my mother cried, "that this should happen to the youngest! He has such skill in his hands, his gift with the care and grafting of trees is unsurpassed." They both sighed. "Have you consulted a specialist?" she asked.

"Even to the great doctor in Las Vegas we took him, to no avail," my uncle said.

"Did you go to the priest?" my mother asked.

"The priest came and blessed the house, but you know that priest at El Puerto, he does not want to pit his power against those brujas! He washes his hands of the whole matter."

My uncle spoke as if he knew the witches who cursed Lucas. And I also wondered, why doesn't the priest fight against the evil of the brujas. He has the power of God, the Virgin, and all the saints of the Holy Mother Church behind him.

"Is there no one we can turn to!" my mother exclaimed. She and my uncle glanced at Ultima who had remained quiet and listened to their talk. Now she stood up and faced my uncle.

"Ay, Pedro Luna, you are like an old lady who sits and talks and wastes valuable time—"

"You will go," he smiled triumphantly.

"¡Gracias a Dios!" my mother cried. She ran to Ultima and hugged her.

"I will go with one understanding," Ultima cautioned. She raised her finger and pointed at both of them. The gaze of her clear eyes held them transfixed. "You must understand that when anybody, bruja or curandera, priest or sinner, tampers with the fate of a man that sometimes a chain of events is set into motion over which no one will have ultimate control. You must be willing to accept this responsibility."

My uncle looked at my mother. Their immediate concern was to save Lucas from the jaws of death, for that they would accept any responsibility.

"I will accept that responsibility on behalf of all my brothers," my uncle Pedro intoned.

"And I accept your help on behalf of my family," my mother added.

"Very well," Ultima nodded, "I will go and cure your brother." She went out of the kitchen to prepare the herbs and oils she would need to affect her cure. As she passed me she whispered, "Be ready Juan—"

I did not understand what she meant. Juan was my middle name, but it was never used.

"Ave María Purísima," my mother said and slumped into a chair. "She will cure Lucas."

"The curse is deep and strong," my uncle brooded.

"Ultima is stronger," my mother said, "I have seen her work miracles. She learned from the greatest healer of all time, the flying man from Las Pastures—"

"Ay," my uncle nodded. Even he acknowledged the great power of that ancient one from Las Pasturas.

"But tell me, who laid the evil curse?" my mother asked.

"It was the daughters of Tenorio," my uncle said.

"Ay! Those evil brujas!" My mother crossed her forehead and I followed suit. It was not wise to mention the names of witches without warding off their evil with the sign of the holy cross.

"Ay, Lucas told papá the story after he took sick, but it is not until now, that we have to resort to a curandera, that our father made the story known to us. It was in the bad month of February that Lucas crossed the river to look for a few stray milk cows that had wandered away. He met Manuelito, Alfredo's boy, you know the one that married the lame girl. Anyway, Manuelito told him he had seen the cows moving towards the bend of the river, where the cottonwoods make a thick bosque, the evil place."

Again my mother made the sign of the cross.

"Manuelito said he tried to turn the cows back, but they were already too near that evil place, and he was afraid. He tried to warn Lucas to stay away from that place. Dusk was falling and there were evil signs in the air, the owls were crying to the early horned moon—"

"¡Ay, Dios mío!" my mother exclaimed.

"But Lucas did not take Manuelito's warning to wait until the next morning, and besides our papá, Manuelito was the last person Lucas spoke to. Ay, that Lucas is so thick-headed, and so full of courage, he spurred his horse into the brush of the evil place—" He paused for my mother to serve him fresh coffee.

"I still remember when we were children, watching the evil fires dance in that same place," my mother said.

"Ay," my uncle agreed. "And that is what Lucas saw that night, except he was not sitting across the river like we used to. He dismounted and crept up to a clearing from where the light of the fireballs shone. He drew near and saw that it was no natural fire he witnessed, but rather the dance of the witches. They bounded among the trees, but their fire did not burn the dry brush—"

"¡Ave María Purísima!" my mother cried.

I had heard many stories of people who had seen the bright balls of fire. These fireballs were brujas on their way to their meeting places. There, it was said, they conducted the Black Mass in honor of the devil, and the devil appeared and danced with them.

Ay, and there were many other forms the witches took. Sometimes they traveled as coyotes or owls! Only last summer the story was told that at Cuervo a rancher had shot a coyote. He and his sons had followed the trail of blood to the house of an old woman of the village. There they found the old woman dead of a gunshot wound. The rancher swore that he had etched a cross on his bullet, and that proved that the old woman was a witch, and so he was let free. Under the old law there was no penalty for killing a witch.

"When he was up close," my uncle continued, "Lucas

saw that the fireballs began to acquire a form. Three women dressed in black appeared. They made a fire in the center of the clearing. One produced a pot and another an old rooster. They beheaded the rooster and poured its blood into the pots. Then they began to cook it, throwing in many other things while they danced and chanted their incantations. Lucas did not say what it was they cooked, but he said it made the most awful stench he had ever smelled—"

"The Black Mass!" my mother gasped.

"Sí," my uncle nodded. He paused to light a cigarette and refill his cup of coffee. "Lucas said they poured sulfur on the coals of the fire and that the flames rose up in devilish fashion. It must have been a sight to turn the blood cold, the dreariness of the wind and the cold night, the spot of ground so evil and so far from Christian help—"

"Yes, yes," my mother urged, "and then what happened?" The story had held us both spellbound.

"Well, you know Lucas. He could see the evil one himself and not be convinced. He thought the three witches were three old dirty women who deserved a Christian lashing, tongue or otherwise, so he stepped forth from behind the tree that hid him and he challenged them!"

"No!" my mother gasped.

"Sí," my uncle nodded. "And if I know Lucas, he probably said something like: ¡Oye! You ugly brujas, prepare to meet a Christian soul!"

RUDOLFO ANAYA

I was astounded at the courage of my uncle Lucas. No one in his right mind would confront the cohorts of the devil!

"It was then he recognized the Trementina sisters, Tenorio's three girls—"

"¡Ay Dios mío!" my mother cried.

"Ay, they have always been rumored to be brujas. They were very angry to be caught performing their devilish mass. He said they screamed like furies and were upon him, attacking him like wild animals—but he did the right thing. While he was behind the tree he had taken two dead branches and quickly tied them together with a shoe lace. He made a rude cross with the two sticks. Now he held up the holy cross in the face of those evil women and cried out, "Jesús, María, y José!" At the sight of the cross and at the sound of those holy words the three sisters fell to the ground in a fit of agony and pain. They rolled on the ground like wounded animals until he lowered the cross. Then they picked themselves up and fled into the darkness, cursing him as they went.

"Everything was silent then. Only Lucas remained by the light of the dying fire at that cursed spot. He found his frightened horse by the river, mounted it, and returned home. He told the story only to papá, who admonished him not to repeat it. But within the week Lucas was stricken. He speaks only to mutter of the revenge the Trementina sisters took on him for discovering their secret ceremony. The rest of the time his mouth is clamped so tight he cannot eat. He wastes away. He is dying—"

They were silent for a long time, each one thinking about the evil thing that befell their brother.

"But didn't you go to Tenorio?" my mother asked.

"Papá was against it. He would not believe in this witch-craft thing. But Juan and Pablo and myself went to Tenorio and confronted him, but we could not charge him with any-thing because we had no proof. He only laughed at us and told us he was within his right to shoot us if we made an accu-sation against him without proof. And he had his ring of coyotes around him in the saloon. He said he had witnesses if we tried anything, and so we had to leave. He laughed at us."

"Ay, he is an evil man," my mother shuddered.

"Evil begets evil," my uncle said. "His wife was known to make clay dolls and prick them with needles. She made many people of the valley sick, some died from her curses. She paid for her sins, but not before she delivered three brujas to carry on her work in our peaceful valley—"

"I am ready," Ultima interrupted.

I turned to see her standing, watching us. She carried only her small black satchel. She was dressed in black and her head scarf crossed over her face so that only her bright eyes shone. She bore herself with dignity, and although she was very small she was ready to do battle with all the terrible evil about which I had just heard.

"Grande," my mother went to her and hugged her, "it is such a difficult task we ask you to do, but you are our last hope."

Ultima remained motionless. "Evil is not easy to destroy," she said, "one needs all the help one can get." She looked at me and her gaze made me step forward. "The boy will have to go with me," she whispered.

"What?" My mother was startled.

"Antonio must go with me. I have need of him," Ultima repeated softly.

"I will go," I said.

"But why?" my mother asked.

My uncle answered the question. "He is a Juan—"

"Ay."

"And he has strong Luna blood—"

"Ave María Purísima," my mother muttered.

"It must be so if you want your brother cured," Ultima decreed.

My mother looked at her brother. My uncle only shrugged. "Whatever you say, Grande," my mother said. "It will be good for Anthony to see his uncles—"

"He does not go to visit," Ultima said solemnly.

"I will prepare some clothing—"

"He must go as he is," Ultima said. She turned to me. "Do you want to help your uncle, Antonio?" she asked.

"Yes," I replied.

"It will be hard," she said.

"I do not mind," I answered, "I want to help."

"And if people say you walk in the footsteps of a curandera, will you be ashamed?"

"No, I will be proud, Ultimo," I said emphatically.

She smiled. "Come, we waste precious time—" My uncle and I followed her outside and into the truck. Thus began our strange trip.

"Adiós," my mother called, "¡Cuidado! ¡Saludos a papá, y a todos! ¡Adiós!"

"¡Adiós!" I called. I turned and waved goodbye.

The drive to El Puerto was always a pleasant one, but today it was filled with strange portents. Across the river where lonely farms dotted the hills, whirlwinds and dust devils darkened the horizon. I had never seen anything like it, we seemed to travel a sea of calmness but all around the sky darkened. And when we arrived at the village we saw the horned day-moon fixed exactly between the two dark mesas at the southern end of the valley!

"The moon of the Lunas," my uncle remarked, breaking the silence of the entire trip.

"It is a good sign," Ultima nodded. "That is why they call this place El Puerto de la Luna," she said to me, "because this valley is the door through which the moon of each month passes on its journey from the east to the west—"

So it was fitting that these people, the Lunas, came to settle in this valley. They planted their crops and cared for their animals according to the cycles of the moon. They lived their lives, sang their songs, and died under the changing moon. The moon was their goddess.

But why was the weather so strange today? And why had Ultimo brought me? I wanted to help, but how was I to help? Just because my name was Juan? And what was it about my innocent Luna blood that was to help lift the curse from my uncle? I did not know then, but I was to find out.

A dust trail followed the truck down the dusty street. It was deathly quiet in El Puerto. Not even the dogs barked at the truck. And the men of the village were not working in the fields, they clung together in groups at the adobe corners of houses and whispered to each other as we drove by. My uncle drove straight to my grandfather's house. No one came to the truck for a long time and my uncle grew nervous. Women in black passed silently in and out of the house. We waited.

Finally my grandfather appeared. He walked slowly across the dirt patio and greeted Ultimo. "Médica," he said, "I have a son who is dying."

"Abuelo," she answered, "I have a cure for your son."

He smiled and reached through the open window to touch her hand. "It is like the old days," he said.

"Ay, we still have the power to fight this evil," she nodded.

"I will pay you in silver if you save my son's life," he said. He seemed unaware of me or my uncle. It seemed a ceremony they performed.

"Forty dollars to cheat la muerte," she mumbled.

"Agreed," he responded. He looked around to the nearby houses where, through parted curtains, curious eyes watched. "The people of the pueblo are nervous. It has been many years since a curandera came to cure—"

"Farmers should be farming," Ultima said simply. "Now, I have work to do." She stepped out of the truck.

"What will you need?" my grandfather asked.

"You know," she said. "A small room, bedsheets, water, stove, atole to eat—"

"I will prepare everything myself," he said.

"There are women already mourning in the house," Ultima said and gathered her shawl around her head, "get rid of them."

"As you say," my grandfather answered. I do not think he liked to empty his house of his sons' wives, but he knew that when a curandera was working a cure she was in charge.

"There will be animals sniffing around the house at night, the coyotes will howl at your door—inform your sons that no shots are to be fired. I will deal with those who come to spoil the cure myself—"

My grandfather nodded. "Will you enter my house now?" he asked.

"No. I must first speak to Tenorio. Is he in his dog hole, that place he calls a saloon?" she asked. My grandfather said yes. "I will speak to him," Ultima said. "I will first try to reason with him. He must know that those who tamper with fate are often swallowed by their own contrivance—"

"I will send Pedro and Juan with you," my grandfather began, but she interrupted him.

"Since when does a curandera need help to deal with dogs," she retorted. "Come, Antonio," she called and started down the street. I scurried after her.

"The boy is necessary?" my grandfather called.

"He is necessary," she answered. "You are not afraid, are you Antonio?" she asked me.

"No," I answered and took her hand. Many hidden eyes followed our progress up the dusty, vacant street. The saloon was at the end of the street, and opposite the church.

It was a small, run-down adobe house with a sign over the entrance. The sign said the saloon belonged to Tenorio Trementina. This man who doubled as the villagers' barber on Saturdays had a heart as black as the pit of hell!

Ultima did not seem to fear him, nor the evil powers of his three daughters. Without hesitation she pushed her way through the doorway, and I followed in her wake. There were four men huddled around one of the few tables. Three turned and looked at Ultimo with surprise written in their eyes. They had not expected her to come into this place of evil. The fourth one kept his back to us, but I saw his hunched shoulders tremble.

"I seek Tenorio!" Ultima announced. Her voice was strong and confident. She stood tall, with a nobleness to her stature that I had seen often when we walked on the llano. She was not afraid, and so I tried to stand like her and put my fears out of my heart.

"What do you want bruja!" the man who would not face us snarled.

"Give me your face," Ultima demanded. "Have you not the strength to face an old woman? Why do you keep your back to me?"

The thin, hunched body jumped up and spun around. I think I jumped at the sight of his face. It was thin and drawn, with tufts of beard growing on it. The eyes were dark and narrow. An evil glint emanated from them. The thin lips trembled when he snarled, "Because you are a bruja!" Spots of saliva curled at the edges of the mouth.

Ultimo laughed "Ay, Tenorio," she said, "you are as ugly as your dark soul." It was true, I had never seen an uglier man.

"¡Toma!" Tenorio shouted. He crossed his fingers and held the sign of the cross in front of Ultima's face. She did not budge. Tenorio gasped and drew back, and his three cronies pushed their chairs to the floor and backed away. They knew that the sign of the cross would work against any bruja, but it had not worked against Ultima. Either she was not a bruja, or to their way of thinking, she had powers that belonged to the Devil himself.

"I am a curandera," Ultima said softly, "and I have come to lift a curse. It is your daughters who do evil that are the brujas—"

"You lie, vieja!" he shouted. I thought he would attack Ultima, but his gnarled body only trembled with anger. He could not find the courage to touch her.

"Tenorio!" It was Ultima who now spoke sternly. "You are a fool if you do not heed my words. I did not need to come to you, but I did. Listen to my words of reason. Tell your daughters to lift the curse—"

"Lies!" he screamed as if in pain. He turned to the three men he had depended upon to act as witnesses, but they did not protest on his behalf. They nervously glanced at each other and then at Ultima.

"I know when and where the curse was laid," Ultima continued. "I know when Lucas came to your shop for a drink and to have his hair clipped by your evil shears. I know that your daughters gathered the cut hair, and with that they worked their evil work!"

It was more than the three men could stand. They were frightened. They lowered their eyes to avert Tenorio's gaze and scurried for the door. The door banged shut. A strange, dark whirlwind swept through the dusty street and cried mournfully around the corner of the saloon. The storm which had been around us broke, and the rising dust seemed to shut off the light of the sun. It grew dark in the room.

"¡Ay bruja!" Tenorio threatened with his fist, "for what you have said to shame my daughters and my good name in front of those men, I will see you dead!" His voice was harsh and ominous. His evil eyes glared at Ultima.

"I do not fear your threats, Tenorio," Ultima said calmly. "You well know, my powers were given to me by el hombre volador—"

At the mention of this great healer from Las Pasturas Tenorio drew back as if slapped in the face by an invisible power.

"I thought I could reason with you," Ultima continued, "I thought you would understand the powers at work and how they can wreck the destinies of many lives—but I see it is useless. Your daughters will not lift the curse, and so I must work the magic beyond evil, the magic that endures forever—"

"And my three daughters?" Tenorio cried.

"They chose to tamper with fate," Ultima answered. "Pity the consequence—" She took my hand and we walked out into the street. The choking dust was so thick that it shut out the sun. I was used to dust storms of early spring, but this one in the middle of summer was unnatural. The wind moaned and cried, and in the middle of the sky the sun was a blood-red dot. I put one hand to my eyes and with the other I gripped Ultima tightly as we struggled against the wind.

I was thinking about the evil Tenorio and how Ultima had made him cower when I heard the hoofbeats. If I had been alone I would have paid no heed to them, so concerned was I with finding some direction in the strange duststorm. But Ultima was more alert than I. With a nimble sidestep and a pull she jerked me from the path of the black horse and rider that went crashing by us. The rider that had almost run us down disappeared into the swirling dust.

"Tenorio!" Ultima shouted in my ear. "He is hurrying home to warn his daughters. Beware of his horse," she added, "he has trained it to trample and kill—" I realized how close I had been to injury or death.

As we approached my grandfather's house there was a lull in the storm. The sky remained dark around us, but the clouds of dust abated somewhat. The women who were already in mourning for my uncle Lucas took this opportunity to place their mantas over their faces and to scurry to their homes before the hellish storm raised its head again. It was very strange to see the women in black hurrying out of the house and into the howling storm. It was like seeing death leaving a body.

We hurried into the house. The door slammed behind us. In the dark my grandfather was waiting. "I grew worried," he said.

"Is everything ready?" Ultima asked.

"As you ordered," he said and led us through the dark, quiet rooms of the house. The flickering lantern he held cast our dancing shadows on the smooth, clean adobe walls. I had never seen the house quiet and empty like it was today.

Always there were my uncles and aunts and cousins to greet. Now it was like a quiet tomb.

Far in the deep recesses of the long house we came to a small room. My grandfather stood at the door and motioned. We entered the simple room. It had a dirt floor packed down from many water sprinklings, and its walls were smooth-plastered adobe. But the good clean earth of the room did not wash away or filter the strong smell of death in the room. The wooden bed in the room held the shrunken body of my dying uncle Lucas. He was sheathed in white and I thought he was already dead. He did not seem to breathe. His eyes were two dark pits, and the thin parchment of yellow skin clung to his bony face like dry paper.

Ultima went to him and touched his forehead. "Lucas," she whispered. There was no answer.

"He has been like this for weeks now," my grandfather said, "beyond hope." There were tears in his eyes.

"Life is never beyond hope," Ultima nodded.

"Ay," my grandfather agreed. He straightened his stooped shoulders. "I have brought everything you ordered," he nodded towards the small stove and pile of wood. There was clean linen on the chair next to the stove, and on the shelf there was water, atole meal, sugar, milk, kerosene, and other things. "The men have been instructed about the animals, the women in mourning have been sent away—I will wait outside the room, if you need anything I will be waiting—"

"There must be no interference," Ultima said. She was already removing her shawl and rolling up her sleeves.

"I understand," my grandfather said. "His life is in your hands." He turned and walked out, closing the door after him.

"Antonio, make a fire," Ultima commanded. She lit the kerosene lantern while I made the fire, then she burned some sweet incense. With the crackling warmth of the fire and the smell of purifying incense the room seemed less of a sepulchre. Outside the storm roared and dark night came.

We warmed water in a large basin, and Ultima bathed my uncle. He was like a rag doll in her hands. I felt great pity for my uncle. He was the youngest of my uncles, and I always remembered him full of life and bravado. Now his body was a thin skeleton held together by dry skin, and on his face was written the pain of the curse. At first the sight of him made me sick, but as I helped Ultima I forgot about that and I took courage.

"Will he live?" I asked her while she covered him with fresh sheets.

"They let him go too long," she said, "it will be a difficult battle—"

"But why didn't they call you sooner?" I asked.

"The church would not allow your grandfather to let me use my powers. The church was afraid that—" She did not finish, but I knew what she would have said. The priest at El Puerto did not want the people to place much faith in the powers of la curandera. He wanted the mercy and faith of the church to be the villagers' only guiding light.

Would the magic of Ultima be stronger than all the powers of the saints and the Holy Mother Church? I wondered.

Ultima prepared her first remedy. She mixed kerosene and water and carefully warmed the bowl on the stove. She took many herbs and roots from her black bag and mixed them into the warm oily water. She muttered as she stirred her mixture and I did not catch all of what she said, but I did hear her say, "the curse of the Trementinas shall bend and fly in their faces. We shall test the young blood of the Lunas against the old blood of the past—"

When she was done she cooled the remedy, then with my help we lifted my uncle and forced the mixture down his throat. He groaned in pain and convulsed as if he wanted to throw up the medicine. It was encouraging to see signs of life in him, but it was difficult to get him to keep the medicine down.

"Drink, Lucas," she coaxed him, and when he clamped his teeth shut she pried them open and made him drink. Howls of pain filled the small room. It was very frightening, but at length we got the medicine down. Then we covered him because he began sweating and shivering at the same time. His dark eyes looked at us like a captured animal. Then finally they closed and the fatigue made him sleep.

"Ay," Ultima said, "we have begun our cure." She turned

and looked at me and I could tell she was tired. "Are you hungry?" she smiled.

"No," I replied. I had not eaten since breakfast, but the things that had happened had made me forget my hunger.

"Still, we had better eat," she said, "it might be the last meal we will have for a few days. They had his fresh clipped hair to work with, the curse is very strong and his strength is gone. Lay your blankets there and make yourself a bed while I fix us some atole."

I spread the blankets close to the wall and near the stove while Ultima prepared the atole. My grandfather had brought sugar and cream and two loaves of fresh bread so we had a good meal.

"This is good," I said. I looked at my uncle. He was sleeping peacefully. The fever had not lasted long.

"There is much good in blue corn meal," she smiled. "The Indians hold it sacred, and why not, on the day that we can get Lucas to eat a bowl of atole then he shall be cured. Is that not sacred?"

I agreed. "How long will it take?" I asked.

"A day or two—"

"When we were in Tenorio's bar, you were not afraid of him. And here, you were not afraid to enter where death lurks—"

"Are you afraid?" she asked in turn. She put her bowl aside and stared into my eyes.

"No," I said.

"Why?"

"I don't know," I said.

"I will tell you why," she smiled. "It is because good is always stronger than evil. Always remember that, Antonio. The smallest bit of good can stand against all the powers of evil in the world and it will emerge triumphant. There is no need to fear men like Tenorio."

I nodded "And his daughters?"

"They are women who long ago turned away from God," she answered, "and so they spend their time reading in the Black Book and practicing their evil deeds on poor, unsuspecting people. Instead of working, they spend their nights holding their black masses and dancing for the devil in the darkness of the river. But they are amateurs, Antonio," Ultima shook her head slowly, "they have no power like the power of a good curandera. In a few days they will be wishing they had never sold their souls to the devil—"

The cry of hungry coyotes sounded outside. Their laughter-cry sounded directly outside the small window of the room. I shivered. Their claws scratched at the adobe walls of the house. I looked anxiously at Ultima, but she held her hand up in a sign for me to listen. We waited, listening to the howling wind and the cries of the pack scratching at our wall.

Then I heard it. It was the call of Ultima's owl. "O-oooo-ooo," it shrieked into the wind, dove and pounced on the coyotes. Her sharp claws found flesh because the evil laughter of the coyotes changed to cries of pain.

Ultima laughed. "Oh those Trementina girls will be cut and bruised tomorrow," she said. "But I have much work to do," she spoke to herself now. She tucked me into the blankets and then burned more incense in the room. I huddled against the wall so I could see everything she did. I was tired now, but I could not sleep.

The power of the doctors and the power of the church had failed to cure my uncle. Now everyone depended on Ultima's magic. Was it possible that there was more power in Ultima's magic than in the priest?

My eyelids grew very heavy, but they would not close completely. Instead of sleep I slipped into a deep stupor. My gaze fixed on my poor uncle and I could not tear my glance away. I was aware of what happened in the room, but my senses did not seem to respond to commands. Instead I remained in that waking dream.

I saw Ultima make some medicine for my uncle, and when she forced it down his throat and his face showed pain, my body too felt the pain. I could almost taste the oily hot liquid. I saw his convulsions and my body too was seized with aching cramps. I felt my body wet with sweat. I tried to call to Ultima but there was no voice; I tried to move but there was no movement. I suffered the spasms of pain my uncle suffered, and these alternated with feelings of elation and power. When the pain passed a wave of energy seemed to sweep through my body. Still, I could not move. And I could not take my eyes from my uncle. I felt that somehow we were going through the same cure, but I could not explain it. I tried to pray, but no words filled my mind, only the closeness I shared with my uncle remained. He was across the room from me, but our bodies did not seem separated by the distance. We dissolved into each other, and we shared a common struggle against the evil within, which fought to repulse Ultima's magic.

Time ceased to exist. Ultima came and went. The moaning of the wind and the cries of the animals outside mixed into the thin smoke of incense and the fragrance of piñón wood burning in the stove. At one time Ultima was gone a long time. She disappeared. I heard the owl singing outside, and I heard its whirling wings. I saw its wise face and fluttering wings at the window—then Ultima was by me. Her feet were wet with the clay-earth of the valley.

"The owl—" I managed to mutter.

"All is well," Ultima answered. She touched my forehead and the terrible strain I felt seemed lifted from my shoulders. "There is no fever," Ultima whispered to me, "you are strong. The blood of the Lunas is very thick in you—"

Her hand was cool, like the fresh air of a summer night.

My uncle groaned and thrashed about in his bed. "Good," Ultima said, "we have beaten the death spirit, now all that remains is to have him vomit the evil spirit."

She went to the stove and prepared a fresh remedy. This one did not smell like the first one, it was more pungent. I saw her use vials of oil she had not used before, and I saw that some of the roots she used were fresh with wet earth. And for the first time she seemed to sing her prayers instead of muttering them.

When she had finished mixing her herbs she let the small bowl simmer on the stove, then she took from her black bag a large lump of fresh, black clay. She turned off the kerosene lantern and lit a candle. Then she sat by the candlelight and sang as she worked the wet clay. She broke it in three pieces, and she worked each one carefully. For a long time she sat and molded the clay. When she was through I saw that she had molded three dolls. They were lifelike, but I did not recognize the likeness of the clay dolls as anyone I knew. Then she took the warm melted wax from the candle and covered the clay dolls with it so they took on the color of flesh. When they had cooled she dressed the three dolls with scraps of cloth which she took from her black bag.

When she was done she stood the three dolls around the light of the flickering candle, and I saw three women. Then Ultima spoke to the three women.

"You have done evil," she sang,
"But good is stronger than evil,
"And what you sought to do will undo you . . ."

• • •

She lifted the three dolls and held them to my sick uncle's mouth, and when he breathed on them they seemed to squirm in her hands.

I shuddered to see those clay dolls take life.

Then she took three pins, and after dipping them into the new remedy on the stove, she stuck a pin into each doll. Then she put them away. She took the remaining remedy and made my uncle drink it. It must have been very strong medicine because he screamed as she forced it down. The strong smell filled the room, and even I felt the searing liquid.

After that I could rest. My eyelids closed. My stiff muscles relaxed and I slid from my sitting position and snuggled down into my blankets. I felt Ultima's gentle hands covering me and that is all I remember. I slept, and no dreams came.

When I awoke I was very weak and hungry. "Ultima," I called. She came to my side and helped me sit up.

"Ay mi Antonito," she teased, "what a sleepy head you are. How do you feel?"

"Hungry," I said weakly.

"I have a bowl of fresh atole waiting for you," she grinned. She washed my hands and face with a damp cloth and then she brought the basin for me to pee in while she finished preparing the hot cereal. The acrid smell of the dark-yellow pee blended into the fragrance of the cereal. I felt better after I sat down again.

"How is my uncle Lucas?" I asked. He seemed to be sleeping peacefully. Before he did not seem to breathe, but now his chest heaved with the breath of life and the pallor was gone from his face.

"He will be well," Ultima said. She handed me the bowl of blue atole. I ate but I could not hold the food down at first. I gagged and Ultima held a cloth before me into which I vomited a poisonous green bile. My nose and eyes burned when I threw up but I felt better.

"Will I be all right?" I asked as she cleaned away the mess.

"Yes," she smiled. She threw the dirty rags in a gunny sack at the far end of the room. "Try again," she said. I did and this time I did not vomit. The atole and the bread were good. I ate and felt renewed.

"Is there anything you want me to do?" I asked after I had eaten.

"Just rest," she said, "our work here is almost done—"

It was at that moment that my uncle sat up in bed. It was a fearful sight and one I never want to see again. It was like seeing a dead person rise, for the white sheet was wet with sweat and it clung to his thin body. He screamed the tortured cry of an animal in pain.

"Ai-eeeeeeeeeee!" The cry tore through contorted lips that dripped with frothy saliva. His eyes opened wide in their dark pits, and his thin, skeletal arms flailed the air before him as if he were striking at the furies of hell.

"Au-gggggggggh! Ai-eeee!" He cried in pain. Ultima was immediately at his side, holding him so that he would not tumble from the bed. His body convulsed with the spasms of a madman, and his face contorted with pain.

"Let the evil come out!" Ultima cried in his ear.

"¡Dios mío!" were his first words, and with those words the evil was wrenched from his interior. Green bile poured from his mouth, and finally he vomited a huge ball of hair. It fell to the floor, hot and steaming and wiggling like live snakes.

It was his hair with which they had worked the evil!

"Ay!" Ultima cried triumphantly and with clean linen she swept up the evil, living ball of hair. "This will be burned, by the tree where the witches dance—" she sang and swiftly put the evil load into the sack. She tied the sack securely and then came back to my uncle. He was holding the side of the bed, his thin fingers clutching the wood tightly as if he were afraid to slip back into the evil spell. He was very weak and sweating, but he was well. I could see in his eyes that he knew he was a man again, a man returned from a living hell.

Ultima helped him lie down. She washed him and then fed him his first meal in weeks. He ate like a starved animal. He vomited once, but that was only because his stomach had been so empty and so sick. I could only watch from where I sat.

After that my uncle slept, and Ultima readied her things for departure. Our work was done. When she was ready she went to the door and called my grandfather.

"Your son lives, old man," she said. She undid her rolled sleeves and buttoned them.

My grandfather bowed his head. "May I send the word to those who wait?" he asked.

"Of course," Ultima nodded. "We are ready to leave."

"Pedro!" my grandfather called. Then my grandfather came into the room. He walked towards the bed cautiously, as if he were not sure what to expect.

Lucas moaned and opened his eyes. "Papá," he said. My grandfather gathered his son in his arms and cried. "Thanks be to God!"

Aunts and uncles and cousins began to fill the house, and there was a great deal of excitement. The story of the cure spread quickly through El Puerto. My uncles began to pour into the room to greet their brother. I looked at Ultima and knew that she wanted to get out of the commotion as quickly as possible.

"Do not tire him too much at first," Ultima said. She looked at Lucas, who gazed around with curious but happy eyes.

"Gracias por mi vida," he said to Ultima. Then all my uncles stood and said gracias. My grandfather stepped forward and handed Ultima the purse of silver which was required by custom.

"I can never repay you for returning my son from death," he said.

Ultima took the purse. "Perhaps someday the men of El Puerto will save my life—" she answered. "Come Antonio," she motioned. She clutched her black bag and the gunny sack that had to be burned. We pressed through the curious, anxious crowd and they parted to let us pass.

"¡La curandera!" someone exclaimed. Some women bowed their heads, others made the sign of the cross. "Es una mujer que no ha pecado," another whispered. "Hechicera." "Bruja—"

"No!" one of my aunts contested the last word. She knelt by Ultima's path and touched the hem of her dress as she passed by.

"Es sin pecado," was the last I heard, then we were outside. My uncle Pedro led us to his truck.

He held the door open for Ultima and said, "Gracias." She nodded and we got in. He started the truck and turned on the lights. The two headlights cut slices into the lonely night.

"Do you know the grove of trees where Lucas saw the brujas dance?" Ultima asked.

"Sí," my uncle said.

"Take us there," Ultima said.

My uncle Pedro sighed and shrugged. "You have performed a miracle," he said, "were it not for that I would not visit that cursed spot for all the money in the world—" The truck leaped forward. We crossed the ancient wooden bridge and turned right. The truck bounced along the cow path. On either side of us the dark brush of the bosque closed in.

Finally we came to the end of the rutty trail. My uncle stopped the truck. We seemed swamped by the thick brush of the river. Strange bird cries cut into the swampy night air. "We can go no farther," my uncle said. "The clearing of the witches is straight ahead."

"Wait here," Ultima said. She shouldered the sack that contained all the dirty linen and the evil ball of hair. She disappeared into the thick brush.

"Ay, what courage that old woman has!" my uncle exclaimed. I felt him shiver next to me, and I saw him make the sign of the cross to ward off the evil of this forsaken ground. Around us the trees rose like giant skeletons. They had no green on them, but were bare and white.

"Uncle," I asked, "how long were we in the room with my uncle Lucas?"

"Three days," he answered. "Do you feel well, Tony?" he rubbed my head. Next to Ultima it seemed the first human contact I had felt in a long time.

"Yes," I answered.

Up ahead we saw a fire burst out. It was Ultima burning the evil load of the sack exactly where the three witches had danced when my uncle saw them. A trace of the smell of sulfur touched the foul, damp air. Again my uncle crossed himself.

"We are indebted to her forever," he said, "for saving the

life of my brother. Ay, what courage to approach the evil place alone!" he added.

The burst of flames in the bush died down and smouldered to ashes. We waited for Ultima. It was very quiet in the cab of the truck. There was a knock and we were startled by Ultima's brown face at the window. She got in and said to my uncle, "Our work is done. Now take us home, for we are tired and must sleep."

from

_DRINKING: A
LOVE STORY_

CAROLINE KNAPP

_Caroline Knapp titled the memoir of her alcoholism "A
Love Story" because her relationship with alcohol
followed the same trajectory as an abusive relationship: painful, all-encompassing, and nearly
impossible to extricate oneself from. It took
strength—and support—to finally be free._

Between the day I knew I had to stop drinking and the day I finally did, I cried almost every night. I'd sit in a little room at Michael's house where he keeps his stereo and CD player, and I'd listen to the same sad Dwight Yoakam song over and over, "You're the One," and I'd weep. I felt like I was giving up the one link I had to peace and solace, my truest friend, my lover. I felt like I was trading in one form of misery for another, like I was about to leap into a void, like my life was ending.

The sense of panic and impending doom are familiar to anyone who's quit drinking. Wilfrid Sheed, author of *In Love with Daylight: A Memoir of Recovery,* writes that "giving up booze felt at first like nothing so much as sitting in a great art gallery and watching the paintings being removed one by one until there was nothing left up there but white walls." Norman Mailer put it a little more bluntly, stating darkly that sobriety kills off all the little "capillaries of bonhomie."

I spent weeks thinking in short, declarative sentences:

I'll never have fun at a party again.

I'll never have an intimate conversation again.

I'll never be able to get married. How can you get married without Champagne?

I drank every night, of course, and I drank every drink with the acute consciousness of an inmate on death row eating a final meal. My sister recommended a rehab center in New Hampshire called Beech Hill and I'd settled on February 20, so two months loomed ahead of me in chunks. My last month of drinking. My last week of drinking. My last Scotch at the Aku. My last beer in Michael's kitchen. My last glass of white wine.

I had my last drink in Michael's living room, a little before midnight. My friend Sandy, one of the few people I'd told, had come up for the weekend from Philadelphia and she and I went out to dinner together the night before I left. I had beer and wine before dinner and wine with dinner and Cognac at the bar after dinner, and when Sandy excused herself to go to the ladies' room, I stole a few slugs off her glass of brandy too. When we went back to Michael's, I opened another bottle of red. I don't remember this, but according to Michael, I stood up, announced, "I'm going to bed," then chugged a full glass of red wine and staggered out of the room.

I drove myself to the rehab: threw two suitcases in the back of my car and drove away from Michael's house. I was hungover. I smoked cigarettes the whole way and gagged a couple of times on the smoke: I was vaguely nauseated from the night before and jittery inside. I thought about one morning years earlier—I must have been in my early twenties—when my mother looked at me across the breakfast table and said,

"Honey, your *head* is shaking." It was true: sometimes when I was really hung-over my whole head would develop a slight but constant tremor, like my brains were shaking in a fry pan, and that was happening on the way to rehab. But aside from that I think I looked okay. And just in case, I stopped on the side of the road outside Dublin, New Hampshire, where Beech Hill was, and reapplied my lipstick. Appearances: I maintained them until the end. When I got there, the intake nurse took a Polaroid of me for my file. I look pale and thin and frightened, but my lipstick looks fabulous.

Beech Hill is located on top of a mountain, which sounds picturesque and serene but isn't, at least not in late February. Most of the time I was there the weather was frigid, the sky blank with fog, and when you looked out the picture windows in the cafeteria at the hills and countryside stretching out below, all you could see was a monochromatic winter blur: endless shades of brown and gray.

Inside, the building looked like a hospital, only slightly less obvious. A main entranceway led into a lounge, where people sat in chairs and watched TV or read or played board games; to the right of the entrance, through a set of double doors, was the cafeteria; to the left, past the lounge, two long corridors. Our rooms were in those corridors, simple, Motel 6–style rooms, with single beds and basic furniture: a desk, a dresser. I had two roommates, both in their midthirties, a large black woman from New Jersey with a crack problem whose name I forget, and a small blonde from Connecticut named Alison, an alcoholic like me, also in rehab for the first time.

Technically, this was my second visit to Beech Hill. I'd driven up there once before, in late January, for a "tour." This turned out to be unheard of, and would be a subject of great amusement among the people I met there, but it seemed perfectly appropriate to me: a visit, like touring a college campus before you decide to apply. I'd driven there during an ice storm, met with the director of admissions for about fifteen minutes, made sure the place didn't look like an insane asylum, then driven back, teary eyed the whole way. I'd told her I'd check in on the twentieth; she looked at me and said, "That gives you a lot of time to change your mind, you know," and I waved away the concern. I had no idea how many people decided to go to rehab then backed out at the last minute. Plenty, apparently.

Having made a *reservation*, as it were, I suppose I expected a welcoming committee when I finally arrived, some kindly nurse or receptionist to take my hand and lead me to my room and assure me that everything would be okay. *Oh! You're Miss Knapp! Welcome!*

That didn't happen. People arrive at rehab unannounced all the time, often dropped off roaring drunk by friends or relatives, and the staff takes you as you come. I checked in on a Sunday afternoon and that's how they took me. There was only a skeleton crew on hand, so I lingered for a while by the nurse's station, waiting for someone to deal with me.

A tall, thin man, a nurse's aide, finally led me to an intake area, took my vital signs, then helped me get my bags out of my car. They search your bags at rehab—standard practice, to make sure you haven't snuck in any drugs or alcohol—so he wandered off with my luggage. Someone else suggested I take a seat in the lounge or the smoking room and wait for a nurse who'd do a more complete intake exam.

The smoking room was built off the main entranceway, a dingy, glass-enclosed area equipped with what looked like retired lawn furniture, the glass stained yellow. They called it The Lung. I sat out there for half an hour, thinking: *What the fuck am I* doing *here?* An older man with a sad face named Ray sat at a nearby table, along with a slightly hysterical woman in her forties named Pat (inexplicably, she'd change her name to Penny halfway through my stay), and some wasted shell of a man whose name I forget, a heroin addict who'd also just arrived.

I never considered the possibility of quitting drinking without going to rehab, never considered just buckling down and joining AA at home. In fact, I never thought I'd end up in AA at all. I still associated AA with old men in smoke-filled rooms, images from that meeting I'd gone to five years earlier;

I'd also developed a semiconscious bias against the whole concept of twelve-step programs. They sounded New Age and cultlike, all that talk of a Higher Power, and every time I turned around some new, bizarre-sounding group seemed to have cropped up for another group of victims. Shoplifters Anonymous. Emotions Anonymous. Maxed-Out Visa Card–Holders Anonymous. Twelve-step programs seemed like a fad, and a mode of victimized self-definition, and I wanted no part of them. I suppose I figured I'd just go away for two weeks, dry out, then grit my teeth and get through.

But the rehab was a good place for me, providing equal doses of hope and fear.

The hope came that first afternoon, a sheer and simple feeling of surrender that came from telling the nurse who did my intake exam exactly how much I drank and not feeling I had to lie about it. The hope came from the sheer and simple act of seeing that I could get through twenty-four hours, and then seventy-two and then ninety-six hours, without a drink, something I hadn't done for more than five years. It came from one of the first sober conversations I had that first night, with a beautiful young woman named Elena, a speed freak from Manhattan who came up to me after dinner, saw how scared I was, and said "You look like you could use a cigarette."

We sat in a corner and talked for a little while and although I don't remember a word of the conversation I do remember the sense of relief: the feeling that my problems weren't nearly as unique as I'd thought they were; the sense that it might be possible to make connections without alcohol.

Some people in early sobriety experience the classic pink cloud, a euphoria that comes from feeling like you're *doing* something at last, taking charge of your life for the first time. I sailed along on that cloud for most of my time at Beech Hill, floated on a wave of relief. Finally, I'd identified the problem. Finally, I'd sought help.

The analogy is ridiculous, but rehab almost felt like camp to me, the way we were shuttled from activity to activity and meal to meal, the way we formed alliances, the sense of shared history and experience. Rehab sparked the good student in me, the good camper. During the day we went to lectures and therapy sessions; at night we went out to AA meetings in nearby towns in New Hampshire, or we sat around the cafeteria, or both. I listened intently to people— counselors, lecturers, other alcoholics. I surrendered easily to the routine, relieved to have nothing to do but focus on the problem at hand: why I drank, how I drank, how my experience compared to that of others. I felt like I'd made the right choice, at long last.

My third or fourth night there, I wrote a glowing note to my therapist, telling him I was fine, better than fine, telling him I'd never felt so much *love* from people in my life. I meant it. The place emanated a sense of survival, as though we'd all been through a horrible war and had landed, alive, in a safe place. Which, in many ways, was exactly right. I felt something I hadn't felt in many years: gratitude.

Small things reinforced that. I woke up without a hangover my first day, and then the next and the next. I didn't obsess about drinking—where, when, with whom, how much—because the possibility didn't exist, and that felt like liberation to me. I laughed. At night, shuttling off to an AA meeting on an old yellow school bus, we stopped at a traffic light and a young guy named Wayne leaned out the window. "Excuse me!" he yelled to the car stopped beside us. "Do you have any Grey Poupon?" I howled at that, a deep, genuine laughter that felt so much more real than drunken laughter, and I remember shaking my head, aware all of a sudden how rarely I'd really laughed in the last few years, and amazed, awed, that I could actually feel that good without a drink.

Rehab was by no means all fun and games. Beech Hill was a scary place, too, and the fear came from what I learned about the disease and what I saw. We'd hear horrible statistics at lectures: someone would stand in front of the room and say, "Look to the person on your right and the person on your left. Of the three of you, only one is going to make it." There are usually thirty or forty patients at the hospital at any given time and I had a hard time believing that only a handful of us were going to succeed. I'd figured everyone there would be more or less like me—young people who drank too much and came there, for the first and only time, to stop—but the client population was all over the map: young and old, male and female; people like me, facing their alcoholism for the first time; people with longtime sobriety who'd relapsed; people who'd been in and out of rehabs and detoxes for years—years and years.

Those were the ones who really scared me, the chronic relapsers. Tess, the woman who'd ended up that night in a hotel with some guy and miscarried the next morning, was one of them. She'd been in and out of rehab programs, in and out of AA for fourteen years and I couldn't understand how that happened, why she couldn't just stick with it. We became good friends, she and I and a group of four other people, and we'd spend our evenings together sneaking cigarettes in the cafeteria and drinking decaf and fruit juice from foam cups. One night my friend Chris tore the bottom off a paper cup, then jammed the paper circle onto a coffee stirrer and stuck it in my juice, an umbrella drink, Beech Hill–style.

Little things like that gave me hope for us: our humor was intact, at any rate, and I was sure the members of our clan would come through okay. We were all determined and motivated: Chris and Tess were heading back to the Boston area, as was George, the friend I'd spent that one evening with, talking about the business of hitting bottom. Sean, a tall, skinny marketing executive, was hoping to end up in a halfway house somewhere in eastern Massachusetts, and Tommy, a lovely, intelligent painter from a suburb of Hartford, Connecticut, promised he'd join us all in Boston for reunions. So we had plans to stay together, to go to meetings together, to support each other. I couldn't see how we wouldn't, we all had so much hope.

I felt that way in particular about Tess. "You're going to be a really important part of my sobriety," she'd say to me, and I'd say, "Oh, you too. I can't imagine doing this without you." She was so young and so pretty, so smart. If I could quit drinking, she could.

I saw Tess a handful of times after we both got back. She moved into a halfway house in Medford, Massachusetts, I was staying at Michael's, and we went to three or four meetings together. Then I heard from her less. I'd call her at the halfway house and she wouldn't call back, or she'd tell me she'd see me at a meeting and then she wouldn't show up.

I got a call from her about a month after we both left Beech Hill and she was back at the rehab, having slipped. Then I got another call, two months after that: back in again. Last I heard, she'd been kicked out of a sober house somewhere in Southern New Hampshire because she'd slipped again. She was going to meetings, but it didn't sound like she was doing too well. I don't know where she is now, or if she's sober.

George relapsed shortly after Tess did, checked himself

back into the rehab, then relapsed again. He called me from Beech Hill after the first relapse, promising he'd come to a meeting with me when he got back, but he never did. I haven't seen or heard from him since.

Sean relapsed next. He was one of my favorites, a whip-smart guy who'd been in and out of treatment for a long time. He'd stayed sober at one point for three years, but then decided to try an experiment in controlled drinking. He really wanted to prove to himself that he could find a way to drink, really believed he could do it this time if he just set the right limits. So he went out into the woods one day with a fifth of Scotch and a six-pack of beer and drank it all. One little spree; that would be it for a while. Then he drank on a Saturday, and the next few Saturdays after that. He'd buy a supply of liquor, an exact amount, and lock himself in his house, drink the liquor and blast old rock-and-roll music on his stereo. He truly believed he could continue to do this, but a few months later he was back to daily drinking, daily blackout drinking, and when he finally woke up one day and discovered that he'd gone to work in a complete blackout and wildly offended nearly every person in his company, he decided to check himself into rehab.

I saw Sean about a month later. He'd ended up in a halfway house in Connecticut, stayed for three weeks, then left and spent three weeks out drinking. He called me from New Hampshire, saying he wanted to check back into the halfway house and asking if he could come down to Cambridge and spend the night at my house before he went back. I called Chris and asked him to join us, thinking we'd have a nice rehab reunion.

Sean showed up reeking of booze, drunk and hostile. He sat at the kitchen table and lectured Chris and me, told us he drank because he loved to drink and because he needed to drink, told us we were fooling ourselves if we didn't think we loved and needed to drink too. He'd stashed beer outside, and when he went out to get it, I told Chris, "I can't deal with this."

In the end, after a long altercation, we finally drove him out to the halfway house he planned to check back into and left him there, under a tree with his bag of beer, at eleven-thirty at night.

I heard from Sean one more time, about six months later. He was sober again, living in another halfway house outside of Boston, but I've been wary about seeing him. Watching someone up close like that in the middle of a relapse scared me too much, so I've kept my distance.

Finally, there was Tommy, the painter, whose alcoholism seemed as improbable as mine. I saw him once, about five months after we'd both left New Hampshire. He'd relapsed twice since then, and he stopped through Boston on his way back from a bender in Provincetown. He said he really wanted to get sober this time, really wanted to start going to more meetings, but he sounded halfhearted about it.

We went out to dinner that night, and he told me a story about getting incredibly drunk a week or two earlier and throwing a pot of broccoli soup out the window, straight off the deck of his second-floor condo. He laughed at that, as though it had been a truly hilarious episode, just one of those silly things you do when you drink too much. I had a hard time laughing back.

When Tommy left that night, he said, "It gives me hope to see you. You look so healthy," but something about the words sounded empty, something about his expression looked blank, and I had the feeling I'd never see him again. I haven't yet.

Tess, George, Sean, Tommy: watching them was like seeing dominoes fall, one after the other. Only two of us, me and Chris, have stayed sober continuously since leaving New Hampshire and every time I think about the others, I get a shiver of nerves, a reminder of exactly how precarious sobriety can be.

The rehab was like an AA boot camp: the people who ran it and worked there as doctors and nurses and counselors pushed AA and used AA language and communicated, directly and indirectly, their belief that joining AA was the single most reliable way to stay sober, if not the only way.

Some people find the absolutism of this approach oppressive at best. Wilfrid Sheed describes his own thirty-day stay at a rehab as damn tedious, a full month of AA brow-beating and brainwashing and dogma, and although he sub-sequently came to appreciate AA meetings—the drama, the camaraderie—he initially felt, he writes, "like a recruit who's been stuffed into the same-size uniform as all the other recruits, because it's the only size they have. 'One dis-ease fits all.'"

I can see his point—the language of twelve-step pro-grams is nothing if not repetitive, and right from the start you hear the same clichés and catchphrases and slogans over and over and over. *Don't drink, go to meetings, ask for help*: the AA mantras. *Keep it simple. One day at a time. Let go and let God.* But I welcomed the sense of brainwashing. I felt like my brain could use a good scouring out by then and I was both frightened and desperate enough to set aside whatever biases I'd brought and just listen, to absorb. I believed what I was told and I believed I belonged there, and every time I heard someone tell his or her story at an AA meeting, I connected with some part of it, saw a piece of myself. The people I heard at meetings also had a confidence, a calm self-accep-tance, I'd coveted all my life, and I wanted what they had: serenity.

Rehab, in the form of AA's twelve steps, also seemed to provide a blueprint for living, something I'd always felt I needed and lacked, as though I'd missed some crucial handout years ago in personal-conduct class. If you'd asked me, prerehab, what the twelve steps were, I'd have shrugged: something about powerlessness; something else about finding a power greater than yourself. I was astonished to discover that only one of the twelve steps, the first one, mentions the word *alcohol* (specifically, the admission of powerlessness over drink). The other eleven all have to do with getting by, with learning to be honest and responsible and humble, to own up to your mistakes when you make them, to ask for help when you need it. I remember sitting in on one of many lectures that described the twelve steps and thinking, *Oh! So* that's *how you're supposed to live.* The serenity I heard at meetings seemed not only available at that moment, but attainable.

When I got home two weeks later, I did everything I'd been told, followed every last suggestion. I went to ninety meetings in ninety days, one each night. I forced myself to raise my hand during meetings and tell people I was new. I asked people for their phone numbers and I called them up, feeling as timid and self-conscious as a teenage boy calling up a girl for a date. I felt like an alien in my own life and I don't think I've ever been so scared.

My first day home, at Michael's house, I opened up the refrigerator and froze, unable to quite believe there was no beer in there, nothing substantial to reach for. That night we sat on his sofa and watched a movie. It was the first time since I'd known him, the first time ever, that we'd passed an evening together without a drink and I felt exactly like Michael Keaton in *Clean and Sober*, anxious and restless and disoriented, as though I was trying to adjust to an amputation.

Which, of course, I was. You take away the drink and you take away the single most important method of coping you have. How to talk to people without a drink. How to sit on the sofa and watch TV and not crawl right out of your own skin. How to experience a real emotion—pain or anxiety or sadness—without an escape route, a quick way to anesthetize it. How to sleep at night.

The answer in AA is both simple and complex: you just do it, a day at a time. You practice. You ask for help. For a long time you panic and squirm and you live through the discomfort until it eases. And it does ease.

I got back from rehab on a Saturday and went back to work two days later. That first day I asked my friend Beth, the only person in my office who knew I'd quit drinking, to go out for coffee with me after work. I was so accustomed to going out for drinks with her, to sipping that first glass and sliding gently into that more relaxed and sociable version of myself, I thought I might wither away, right there at the coffee shop. We went to a café in Harvard Square, and I remember feeling acutely self-conscious, groping for things to talk about, verbally clumsy, *stupid*.

You do everything for the first time. Here I am, going to a restaurant for the first time and not drinking. Here I am, at a work-related function, not drinking. Here I am, celebrating my birthday without a drink. Liquor stores loom out at you on every street corner, people holding glasses of wine or tumblers of Scotch jump out at you from TV and movie screens, and you realize how pervasive alcohol is in our culture, how it's absolutely *everywhere*, how completely foreign it is to abstain.

Can I get you something from the bar? Here's the wine list. Anything to drink?

You can't go a week without hearing phrases like that, and sometimes, especially early on, they infuriate you, constant reminders that everyone in the world can have a drink, a single simple drink at the end of the day to take off the edge, and you can't. One drink. Just one drink.

A few weeks after I quit drinking, I walked into Michael's house at the end of the day and sat down on the sofa. I wanted a drink, a single glass of white wine, so badly I thought I'd cry. I just sat there with my teeth clenched. I thought about pouring the wine into the glass, walking with the glass from the kitchen to the living room, curling up on the sofa and taking the first sip. I wanted that wine so badly I could taste it, and the only thing that kept me from rushing out to the liquor store to buy a bottle was the understanding that as soon as I drank the first glass, I'd be obsessing about the next one, and the next and the next and the next. I would not drink one glass; I would drink—and obsess about—one bottle, possibly more. That's the only option at times like that, to think past the first glass, to think it through. You've never had "just one drink" in your life.

I held on to the things people in meetings told me. *One day at a time. You don't have to tell yourself you're never going to drink again. Just today. Just do it today.* I clung to stories about people whose lives got better. I heard the phrase, "If you're new, keep coming," and I kept coming. Just as when I drank, I didn't know what else to do.

People do get and stay sober without AA. Pete Hamill did, and hasn't had a drink for more than twenty years. Wilfrid Sheed went to meetings for a few years, stopped when he realized he was going for the entertainment alone, and has stayed sober without them. But I'm sure I couldn't stay away from alcohol without AA, without the support and the sense of camaraderie and the knowledge that it's out there, a place where you can constantly be reminded of what you are, where you came from, what you need to do in order to change.

After a month or so I began to realize that the meeting at the end of the day provided relief the same way the drink used to, that it gave me the same sense of easing into a kind of comfort. AA is like a daily shot of hope: you see people around you grow and change and flower. You hear people struggling, out loud, to get through the days. Meetings keep things in perspective.

from DRINKING: A LOVE STORY

During my first year a woman at a meeting raised her hand and said that her brother had died very suddenly of a brain aneurysm several days earlier. The woman was still shell-shocked and disbelieving but she talked for about five minutes about what it was like to get through this experience without a drink, about how painful it was but also how grateful she felt to be *present*, available to her family, capable of feeling the full range of emotions that accompany such experiences.

When people talk like that about their deepest pain, a stillness often falls over the room, a hush that's so deep and so deeply shared it feels like reverence. That stillness keeps me coming, and it helps keep me sober, reminding me what it means to be alive to emotion, what it means to be human.

from

THE PATIENT WHO CURED HIS THERAPIST

STANLEY SIEGEL
with ED LOWE

*As this true story from veteran psychotherapist Stanley
Siegel shows us, the power of the cure can affect the
healer as much as the healed—especially surprising in
this case, since the therapist in question felt the
treatment had been a complete failure for
all involved.*

Starting with the premise that failures often are quite functional, we can see that an apparent impasse in any kind of relationship often can be found to be accomplishing some yet undefined, undetermined purpose. When called upon by a colleague therapist, for instance, to help with a therapeutic relationship that she considered a failure, I was inclined to try to discover what such a failure could be accomplishing. As always, the discovery wrought surprises.

Buffalo, New York, Winter 1986

Judy Reed had been seeing Tom Martin on and off for two or three years. She told me that she had been stymied by what she saw as his steadfast refusal to reveal himself to her, to trust her, to open up and communicate with her. She had tried everything, she said, and she predicted that within minutes I would see what she meant. I would be confronted with an obviously intelligent, articulate, and fairly well-educated man who would converse in monotonic monosyllables, and at a pace that would have me squirming. Dark-eyed and slender, Judy was intense, articulate, and eager. Initially I was excited by her enthusiasm for the work. She did not appear to be offering me her most frustrating case to test me; she seemed truly desperate to help her client. "He is simply the most withdrawn person I have ever encountered," she said. "No man is an island? This man is an island!"

Because she was so graphically convincing in her description, I had to step away for a few moments before the session began. I felt I had to erase some of the strength of her impressions from my mind. Later, I attempted to explain that seemingly odd, meditative departure to some assembled student therapists, wondering all the while if they considered me crazy.

I told them that once, while I was seated in the living room of an apartment, waiting for a friend to shower and dress, I had amused myself by staring at a crimson Christmas stocking hanging from his mantel. Emblazoned in neat script at the top of the stocking was his son's first name, Paul, written in sprinkles of silvery confetti. I noticed that I could not look at the script without my mind forming the imaginary "sound" of the word *Paul*. I tried to force myself to see the symbols otherwise. What would "Paul" look like to me if I had just landed from another planet with another kind of written language, and I had never seen such symbols before?

The first symbol was like a tree leaning to the right, its boughs and branches growing only on its right side. The tree's root proceeded in that direction, too, from ground level and then upward to the top of an adjacent short, round bush. It also leaned to the right, as did every symbol following. Connected from the second symbol's bottom were two similarly short, vertical symbols of growth, as I tried to view them. They were connected from their bases to each other, and finally to another right-leaning tree that bore no branches or boughs.

The exercise was nearly impossible, because my knowledge and memory of the word *Paul* kept getting in my way. I knew that the symbols existed apart from my knowledge and assumptions, but it seemed that I could not make myself see them without associating them with the sound Paul. Eventually I did it, but only for a fraction of a second. I saw "Paul" as an interesting scribble, unhampered by prior knowledge or prior impressions. I saw the symmetry of the symbols, their directional preference, their liquidity, their individuality, and their interdependence. They seemed like a scouting party of hieroglyphics, headed eastward under the leadership of their stoutest member. Then *Paul* jumped back into my head, and it was over. I could not retrieve it again.

I said I found it to be an exciting exercise and recommended that they try it some time, with numbers, with symbols, with people. An exercise in erasing crippling assumptions, it would both force and allow them to view a problem entirely differently, and I was about to do exactly that.

In preparation for my visit, and as standard protocol for visiting clinical lecturers, Judy Reed had suggested to her patient that their protracted impasse might best be served by a second opinion. She had asked if he would be willing to participate in a consultation with a therapist from New York City who would be visiting as part of a clinical-teaching seminar. After asking for details about what exactly would take place and hearing her explanation that it would be a session observed by her and her colleagues and would possibly be of benefit to him and everyone else, Tom Martin consented.

He entered the room. I sat opposite him, my back to the two-way glass. I told him we would be videotaped if he didn't mind. He nodded his head toward the left very slightly, and raised one eyebrow almost imperceptibly in a gesture that I took to mean a contraction of a shrug, which in turn meant either "No problem" or "If it's my permission you want, you've got it." Dark-eyed, he had a receding hairline that emphasized a pleasant, roundish face, one you might expect to see on a priest or a pharmacist.

He sat down, crossed his legs, placed his hands in his lap, and seemed for all the world to be comfortable. I asked him how he felt. He shrugged and said, "Fine," and then after a pause, added, "Thank you." We laughed together at his belated politeness. I asked how long he had been coming to the center for sessions; he answered, "Several years, on and off. Two years." I asked how he had started, what had prompted his coming in the first place.

"My girlfriend brought me here," he said.

Right away I had a therapist experiencing difficulty communicating with a patient who had not come to her with any problem of his own. The patient's girlfriend had brought him to the center. What was her problem?

"Why? Why do you think she brought you?" I asked.

"She doesn't feel that I communicate well. I guess I don't talk to her enough about how I feel."

So far he was merely telling me what he thought he ought to be telling me. The easy trap would have been for me to then ask how he felt. If he didn't tell me, his girlfriend and his therapist and I would all be in the same predicament. But instead I asked, "What happens when you don't express yourself?"

"She gets angry with me," he said. "She tries harder."

"Well, then what happens? What do you do next?"

He paused for a long time. As it turned out, this was the answer to my question. She tried to get him to express himself, and he paused. She tried harder; he paused longer. That frustrated her, and not only her.

"I don't know what to do," he said finally. "She's angry, and I'm the cause."

"Do you get angry in response?"

"No," he said calmly. "But I feel bad."

"You feel that you're disappointing her," I declared.

He paused again, but contemplatively, not artificially, not frozen with dread or muted by shame or confusion. He was taking his time, thinking about the suggestion. I waited. The silence in the room seemed long but not threatening. Most patients would have felt obligated to break it. Tom did not. He was content to think, and I was curious enough not to interrupt him. He seemed serene. He *was* serene.

After ten seconds or so, he said, "Yeah."

Now *I* let some time pass. I would share in his tempo, his pace. I found it increasingly remarkable that this man felt no uneasiness during any of the vast lulls in our talk. He wasn't trying to impress anyone. He wasn't trying to convince anyone. He seemed to feel no social needs, to harbor no anxieties about what I might have been thinking. It was not as uncomfortable as I might have thought it would be, either, although I am certain that it presented a problem to the observers, especially Judy, Tom's therapist. If his serenity bothered his girlfriend, and possibly Judy, as well, now here, were *two* serene men. One was believed to have a problem that required fixing; the other was the expert called in to fix it.

The therapist who had framed Tom as withdrawn now had a dilemma. In deciding to meet Tom on his own wavelength, I also was deciding—and, in fact, declaring—that it was not bad to be this kind of man. I was conscious of it at the moment I entered his universe. It became very clear to me that I was not going the active route that his therapist had taken; she had focused on qualities she saw as opposite hers. I was finding sameness, respecting Tom's absolute calm. I didn't know what I was going to do yet, but I could see what was going on, and I could actually experience the depth of his serenity. Then, of course, I began wondering why a therapist in the face of such a peaceful man would want him to be otherwise. Maybe *she* had a problem.

Tom's universe, by the way, was much less pressured than ours. I enjoyed my time in it. If he felt no obligation to fill the temporal spaces between questions and answers, there was no need to me to feel any. It became fairly relaxing, in a way, and peaceful.

"Are you disappointing her?" I asked after some time.

Another long pause before he said, "I don't know."

"Could it be that she doesn't appreciate you?"

He looked down and to the right, in further contemplation, almost as if he were puzzled by this "new" notion: that his girlfriend's problem with him could be hers and not his, that his therapist's problem could be her own, too. I let another five seconds go by without a response and then said, "You seem quite serene to me."

Long pause. "I do?"

Short pause (I wasn't quite as serene). "You do."

The pace must have been driving the observers nutty.

He paused again, then said, "I've had a lot of practice"—a remark whose significance absolutely slipped by me until much later.

"It's puzzling to me," I said, "because I don't know why you would want to change that. I don't know why anybody would want to be less comfortable or less serene."

Gigantic pause.

"So, how is it that people, or at least women, don't understand what kind of man you are?" I asked. "You're extremely sensitive to what other people think?"

"Quite a bit, yeah."

"Well, that clarifies something for me."

"What does it clarify?" He was suddenly curious.

"Well, my experience with you, which has been brief, is that you are a man endowed with some wonderful qualities. You are content, serene. You are generous, to the degree that you care so much about how your behavior disturbs your girlfriend, you have come to therapy sessions for two years. Yet the woman you live with does not appreciate those things about you. And somehow you have accepted that their view of you is better than your own view of you."

I stopped. He pondered. Another ten or fifteen seconds passed. He rubbed his forefinger under his nose. He stared down and to the right. At length he said:

"Could be."

"What is your view of the therapy that has happened so far?" I asked. "It's been a long time. Two years."

Huge pause. He did not want to say to a therapist that therapy was a waste of time, though I suspect he felt it was.

"Are you addicted to it?" I asked.

"To the weekly counseling sessions? I don't know," he said, lapsing into more deliberation. "It's an interesting question. I never thought of it. I haven't thought of myself as addicted to it. I don't know."

"Is Judy Reed addicted to you? You know, your therapist?"

"I don't know. Maybe she is."

"You have some suspicion to that effect."

"Possibly. Yeah."

"What would make you think that?"

"Maybe because she sought me to participate in this consultation. Maybe she wants . . . maybe she's addicted to her desire to see a change in me."

Another long pause. I knew what I was going to do now. I thought of Judy's description of him, one of frustration, not one of respect. Neither his girlfriend nor his therapist respected or appreciated this man. They had failed him and had then accused him of failing them; and convincingly, too, evidently. The therapist's failure was simple: she merely took over the job of the girlfriend in not respecting Tom Martin and in insisting that he behave differently. In effect, the girlfriend had said, "You need help in being the person I want you to be. I will introduce you to a professional person who agrees with me, and she will help you fix yourself so that you can more closely resemble my idea of you."

A popular psychological myth declares that it is always better to be an expressive person, not to be withdrawn or retiring. In many cases, this is how women want men to be, and how therapists want patients to be. And in many cases, I'm sure it *is* better to be expressive. For Tom Martin, however, that would have been alien. It simply was not him.

"It's sad, isn't it?" I said, referring to Judy's addiction.

"If it were true, it might be. I don't know if it's true."

"Well," I ventured, "how are you going to cure your therapist?" I wanted to tell him that not only was he all right, but in his serene kindness he was serving needs in both his girlfriend and his therapist.

He grinned, but he thought about the question. "Cure her from what?" he asked. "Trying to change me?"

"Precisely."

"I don't know," he said, grinning again.

"Can *you* be *her* therapist?" I asked him.

"I don't think so."

"I think she needs to be cured by you."

"If and when I cure her, then what?"

"Then she won't need you anymore. Then perhaps she'll understand what a lovely man you are."

"How do I cure her?"

"Well, suppose I bring her in, and you give it a try." I waited, and then added, "You're a very competent man. You can rely on your creativity and your competence. I think that you can find ways in which to let those important people in your life know what kind of man you are, what fine qualities you are endowed with."

"What would that do for me?" he asked. "How will that make me feel better?"

"Don't you want to be appreciated?"

He did not answer. I decided it was time to do something, and I rose and announced that I would go outside to the observers' room and invite Judy Reed in. I said that he would be her therapist instead of the other way around. She seemed nervously amused at the idea. In fact, everybody in the observers' room seemed nervous. The tables had turned. It was clear that Tom had become a stand-in for a character in his therapist's life.

We watched as Judy sat in my chair and waited for Tom to speak.

"I'm supposed to cure you," he said, eliciting a burst of laughter from two people in the room with me. Tom laughed, too. "How long have you been having these problems?" he joked, to more laughter.

"Mr. Siegel says that you have an addiction to me, that you don't appreciate me. You don't appreciate my fine qualities: I'm serene and I'm comfortable, and you must not appreciate that, because you're trying to change that, to change me. And there is another person who tried, who also does not appreciate me: my girlfriend."

Tom put his hands together, fingertips to fingertips, as if in prayer.

His analysis was perfect, as far as I was concerned: the

perfect dilemma presented by the idea of change. He was content with himself; they were not. If he were to make them happy, he would have to change. If he changed, he might not be content anymore.

"So, I'm going to cure you," he continued. "I don't know how. You know, a lot of people would love to be as comfortable as I am, or at least as comfortable as I sometimes appear to be—"

She nodded in agreement. "I think I'm becoming aware of that," she said, "aware that you're a lot more comfortable. I think that I probably misjudged you, or didn't see it."

Long pause. Tom was openly communicating with one of the women who had been trying unsuccessfully to get him to do just that. Paradoxically, in explaining the potential perils of change, he was changing.

"You don't appreciate me," he said.

"Why not?" she asked, trying to regain her former role.

"Why do you not appreciate me?" he said, suggesting by his tone that only she could answer the question. I thought, "Nice move, Tom." In the room where I sat, there were many stunned faces. Not only was Tom expressing himself, he was openly challenging his therapist's persistent negative view of him.

"I guess because I thought you should be different," she said. "Maybe in some ways, not be so serene."

"The whole Alcoholics Anonymous prayer is based on serenity," he said, startling me.

"Alcoholics Anonymous!" I said, out of earshot. I turned to one of the observers familiar with the case history, Linda Duly, a colleague in Judy's study group.

"Tom Martin is in AA?" I asked.

"Yes, for some years," she said. "This is pretty remarkable what's happening here. You probably also ought to know, given the circumstances, that Judy's husband doesn't talk to her very much and that it troubles her deeply. In fact, her marriage is pretty tense right now. In fact—God, it's all shaping up—according to Judy, her father is as withdrawn and distant as Tom Martin appears to be. That distance always has been a problem in Judy's family. In our study group—where we examine each other's family dynamics— Judy revealed that at an early age she became her mother's ally in trying to get the father more involved with the family. What's becoming clear to me is that Judy appears to have recreated the same relationship with her husband as her mother had with her father, and then recreated it again here with this patient. It's really amazing."

"She's very consistent, isn't she?" I said.

Linda looked at me quizzically but fondly as well. "Your cup is always half full, isn't it?" she said.

I said I viewed Judy as someone who was constantly trying to repair a ruptured relationship from her past, someone who was therefore always hopeful, always patient, because she was still trying to repair an old relationship. "If she's still trying," I said, "then somehow she must still believe that it can be repaired and that it is worth the effort. I'm not reading that positiveness into the situation, either. I'm quite convinced that it's there. I'm convinced that we are better than conventional psychology has made us out to be."

Tom, meanwhile, was still acting as his therapist's therapist. "The prayer is *based* on serenity," he said. "The first half of it says to grant me the serenity to accept what I can't change. But then they throw in, 'Give me the courage to change what I can.' And then they add, '. . . and the wisdom to know the difference.'"

Judy was weeping softly. "I think that I didn't know the difference," she said, her fingertips massaging her forehead.

"Is there something wrong with being comfortable?" he asked.

"I guess not. Maybe I was trying to change *my* discomfort, thinking that I knew what was better for you."

"If I change my comfortableness and my serenity, that would mean being uncomfortable. I don't want to do that. When people become uncomfortable . . . bad things could happen. What could happen?" he asked. "What could happen if I was not serene, not comfortable?"

"I don't know, but I should have asked a long time ago."

Exactly, I thought. I decided to interrupt. The paradox already had occurred. By entering his universe, I had disrupted the pattern, gotten Tom to tell me who he was rather than how he thought he should change. Paradoxically, he *had* changed. He had changed his perception of himself. Now I wanted him to take advantage of the opportunity to express to one of these pursuing women who he was and how he was *not* going to change, and maybe why. If he expressed it to Judy, I thought, it might serve as a model for how he might later express himself to his girlfriend.

Outside, I told Tom that I wanted him to cure her by teaching her to be serene. I told him that he was the expert, she his student. He returned to the chair and tried more or less unsuccessfully to continue. I interrupted him again and asked him to stand up and tell her why he deserved her appreciation.

Standing, he folded his arms and said, "How can I teach you to be serene? Don't take risks. If you never risk anything, you'll never be uncomfortable. Don't change anything. If you try to change things, that, too, can lead to discomfort. Don't try to change other people. Appreciate them as they are. Appreciate their qualities, and don't try to change them. If you try to change them—"

"I lose out," she said.

"You can lose out. You can lose serenity that way, by trying to change other people, by trying to control them. All role-playing aside, that I know to be true. Because I've tried to control and change people a lot in the past. And it gives me a lot of discomfort, a lot of—whatever the opposite was of serenity—whenever I tried to do that. But the key to that is knowing the difference. Knowing what you can change and what you can't."

"I believe it," she said.

"Good." He paused, then smiled. "Is it because I'm standing up?" he asked gently.

"No," she said, looking up at him and smiling slightly herself.

I knocked again. "I think you've done well," I told Tom. "You can sit down." I walked to his chair and placed my right hand on his shoulder. "I think that she probably needs another session with you. Probably one more. Would you agree?"

"I agree," he said.

"So, we'll stop for now. But you can see if you can fit her in your appointment book."

"I'll have to see my secretary," he said.

We laughed, all three of us.

Judy later told me that she subsequently met several times with members of her family, particularly her father, and discussed his isolation and his withdrawal. He told her that he always had felt excluded by his wife and her family, with whom Judy had become very involved as daughter and granddaughter, and that after a while he had stopped risking feeling their rejection by just keeping to himself, especially around them. Following those conversations, Judy said, she eventually forgave her father.

Judy also told me that Tom had seen her for one more session, and that he and his girlfriend eventually had separated. I don't know what happened after that. But I thought about him often, and I incorporated that case into lectures about achieving failure.

Tom Martin had refashioned himself into a serene man in a heroic effort to change from alcohol-dependent to alcohol-independent. Was he to change again and become expressive in order to satisfy the needs of the women in his life? He was afraid to, but he felt obligated to, because he had accepted their perception of him as a withdrawn, noncommunicative, and therefore a failing personality. Once his perception changed, he first began to appreciate himself better, then became expressive enough to say that he wanted their appreciation but was not going to change to get it. That in itself represented a profound change, so Tom moved on and evidently left the others behind.

His "failure" in therapy with Judy Reed had protected his serenity. Judy's failure, meanwhile, gave her an opportunity to continue to attempt to repair her relationships with men in general, with her father and her husband specifically. Her stubborn persistence stemmed from an indefatigable optimism about fixing those old relationships, just as heroic, in a way, as Tom's steadfast refusal to yield to her notion of what should have been his behavior. In the wrong place, Judy's optimism served her purpose rather than Tom's therapy. In turning the tables, we provided the opportunity for the failure between them to become success. Tom articulated his serenity, ending Judy's failure, and then he rid himself of both women who refused to respect his success at achieving serenity. And Judy recognized and repaired her relationships with her men, so that she no longer needed to fail as Tom's therapist.

from

THE MEASURE
OF OUR DAYS

JEROME GROOPMAN

*Dr. Groopman, one of the world's leading researchers
on cancer and AIDS, has compiled a collection of the
histories of eight patients confronting—and sometimes defying—serious illnesses. This is the story
of Groopman's dearest friend, Elliott, his
inspired battle against leukemia, and
the many ways it affects both men.*

Jerry, it's Elliott. In Jerusalem. I know it's early, but it's an emergency."

Emergency. I felt a burst of adrenaline race through my body.

It was still dark in the bedroom. The glowing red digits of the night-table clock read 5:03 a.m., making it just after noon in Jerusalem.

"What is it, Ell? How I can help?"

I imagined the worst—Elliott's wife, Susan, or son, Benjamin, injured by a terrorist bomb or a car accident.

"I have a growth of lymph nodes in my chest. It's interfering with my breathing. A few hours ago, my doctor told me I need surgery. What do I do?"

Elliott was transformed in my mind from one of my closest and oldest friends into a "patient." I mentally organized his particulars into the format of a clinical case: a forty-three-year-old previously healthy Caucasian male, non-smoker, working as a journalist in the Middle East, with enlarged lymph nodes in his chest, considered for surgery.

"Ell, tell me first what happened, from the beginning," I evenly replied, following the principle that the best history of an illness is elicited in the patient's own words. That way, the physician does not prejudice the recounting and keeps an open mind to the full breadth of possible diagnoses.

He had first become aware of something wrong eight weeks before, during his regular early morning jog on the hills between West and East Jerusalem. It was a temperate spring day, the sun hardly over the horizon, the cool night-time air from the Judean desert still lingering over the city. Elliott started at his house in the German Colony, at his usual pace, aiming to complete his regular four-mile course. But at the very first ascent, at the Bethlehem Road, he had been forced to stop.

"My chest felt tight, heavy, like there was a weight pressing on it. I couldn't get enough air to make it up the hill. I figured I was coming down with a cold, and walked back home."

I asked Elliott if he had had any fever or chills. None whatsoever; he had checked his temperature when he returned from the aborted run, and several times since. Cough or sputum? He had recently developed a dry cough, but without phlegm.

As I listened, I was creating a list of diagnoses in my mind. By my own convention, I always started with the worst category. In the case of a mass of lymph nodes in the chest, it would be cancer.

I considered the different types. First, cancer of the lung: Elliott had never smoked cigarettes that I could recall. But lung cancer also occurred from exposure to environ-mental toxins like asbestos, once commonly used in house insulation. I recalled that Elliott and Susan had renovated their house in Jerusalem three years before. Elliott could have been exposed to the material then, but the incubation period from exposure to lung cancer was usually much longer, a decade or more. Next was malignant lymphoma: very possible, and often involving the chest. Lymphoma was classified as Hodgkin's or non-Hodgkin's, and either type generally occurred in teenagers and young adults when centered in the chest. I moved down the list to the less common cancers. Thymoma, or cancer of the thymus gland: often associated with a disease called myasthenia gravis, which impairs muscle function. Elliott would not be regularly running four miles if he had myasthenia. Thyroid cancer: more frequent in women, and related to radiation exposure. Such exposure was remote for Elliott in his occupation as a writer. Testicular cancer: often overlooked and important to consider, since the embryonic testes originate in the upper chest and migrate during fetal development into the pelvis; vestigial deposits in the thorax can become cancerous in adulthood.

"Ell, you never smoked, correct? And you weren't in contact with asbestos during the house renovation?"

"Never smoked, except grass of course. A contractor did the renovation, and we were assured for Benjamin's sake that all precautions were taken when they stripped the old pipes."

I continued down my mental list to the second category—

infection. Tuberculosis: quite possible in a world traveler now residing in the Middle East. Fungal diseases like coccidioidomycosis: prevalent in the Sacramento Valley of California, where Susan's parents lived and Elliott often visited. Toxoplasmosis: a parasitic infestation from cats, ubiquitous animals, but generally causing a self-limited flu-like illness. All three—TB, fungus, and toxoplasmosis—would have fever as a prominent manifestation, and Elliott had affirmed he had had a normal temperature throughout.

I ended my list with the category "miscellaneous," considering rare disorders like sarcoidosis. Sarcoidosis is a condition where the body becomes allergic to its own tissues, resulting in inflamed masses of lymph nodes in the chest. It is most common in African-Americans. There is scarring of the lung tissue, which would be evident on chest X rays in addition to the nodes. Sarcoidosis often caused red nodules in the skin and inflammation of the eyes.

"Any rashes or skin bumps? Do you have conjunctivitis or a gritty feeling in your eyes?"

"None of that, Jerry. I'm just totally winded. And not only when I try to run. Even walking fast, I feel the tightness."

Elliott had begun to worry when the chest tightness persisted through the week. He called his general practitioner, Jeremy Levy. But the doctor, also an American who had emigrated to Israel, was on military reserve duty out of the city. The covering physician had Elliott come to the office, but there he was not examined, not even his chest, just handed a prescription for erythromycin for a presumed bronchitis.

"Even though you had no fever or sputum?"

"Correct."

After two weeks on the antibiotic, there was no change in his symptoms. His regular doctor was still away. This time, the covering physician listened to his lungs and heard some wheezing. Elliott was told he might have asthma and was prescribed an inhaler. This afforded some relief, but he still couldn't make it up the hill when he tried to jog again.

"Finally Dr. Levy returned from the army. He ordered a chest X ray. After two months of this growing inside me."

I maintained my calm and even voice, even though I felt angry and anxious. My friend, a reliable person complaining for two months of a disabling symptom, had been incompetently evaluated. Critical time may have been wasted. For a fleeting moment I saw my father, gasping in the throes of heart failure, a general practitioner standing confused at his bedside. My father's life was lost because of medical mistakes. This memory painfully gripped me, and I forced myself to disengage from it and return my focus to Elliott.

"Did you have any blood tests? Did Dr. Levy describe what was seen on the chest X ray?"

"I'm not anemic and my white count is O.K. Susan had me get a copy of the X-ray report. It says, and I'm translating from Hebrew, so give me a minute: 'Enlarged mediastinal lymph nodes—' What's mediastinal?"

"Just medical jargon for the central area of the chest under the sternum, the breastbone."

"Right. 'Enlarged mediastinal lymph nodes measuring eight centimeters in maximum diameter and surrounding'— better English would be "encasing"—'the trachea and extending to the aorta. Compression of the right bronchus. Lung fields otherwise clear.'"

I paused to assess the information. The dimensions of the mass, the compression of his airway, and the adjacent surrounding unscarred lung, taken with the absence of fever or sputum, made cancer overwhelmingly likely.

I began to review my diagnostic list of cancers, but felt my concentration slipping. It was not the early hour and interrupted sleep. Rather, my focus was clouded by a collage of intersecting memories—Elliott and I lingering over coffee in his Manhattan apartment, talking about his aspirations as a writer at *Time* and mine as a future doctor; Pam in her bridal gown and me in a tuxedo joined with Elliott in a triangular embrace at our wedding; Elliott gently dabbing drops of sweet red wine in my firstborn son Steven's mouth to "anesthetize" him before his ritual circumcision.

The collage was erased by the sound of Elliot's quivering, plaintive voice.

"Jerry—what do I do?"

I paused a moment, then said: "Put Susan on the phone."

Susan, an émigrée from California, worked as a political and business consultant and was a coolheaded master of logistics. Her native American optimism had been mixed with an acquired Israeli toughness, so in a notoriously bureaucratic country like Israel she was able to make things happen quickly and efficiently.

"Hi, Jerry," Susan began. "We really don't know where we are yet. I checked out the surgeon Dr. Levy recommended at Hadassah Hospital. He's said to be good. And I know enough powerful people there to make sure Elliott gets special attention. But we want the best, the *very best*, so maybe it makes sense to come back to the States."

The "very best" in clinical medicine was not only expert physicians and technologically advanced hospitals. There were many of those to choose from, throughout the world. Serious illness demanded more. It was like a wild rodeo bronco, often exploding in unanticipated directions, stubbornly bucking to throw you off its back. The "very best" required tight and determined hands on the reins. There needed to be attention to every detail and nuance of diagnosis and treatment. Even seemingly minor errors—a misread CAT scan or a too rapidly administered medicine or the lack of an available catheter—could allow the situation to spiral out of control and be catastrophic. Who would exert such control in Elliott's case?

"I can't make the decision for Elliott and you. Medicine is quite good in Israel, although many new drugs are not yet available there. You need to be sure that the specialist in charge will be totally focused on Elliott's case, covering every aspect of the situation. You also have to consider the practical dimensions—your jobs, your insurance, Benjamin's school, and a host of other things holding you there."

Susan paused but a moment.

"But we don't have you, Jerry. We're coming to Boston. Expect us the day after tomorrow. I'll arrange to get seats on the next El Al flight."

It all happened in rapid succession. They arrived early Tuesday morning, just after my sons, Steven and Michael, left for school. Elliott was anxious and pensive, an ashen shell of his ebullient self. I embraced him forcefully, and could feel a weak shiver pass through his body as he tried to return my hug.

Susan quickly occupied herself with organizing their luggage in the upstairs playroom where Pam had opened the couch into a sofa bed. Benjamin, a cute three-year-old with jet black hair and almond brown eyes like his mother, immediately fell asleep after the fifteen-hour plane trip.

Elliott and I sat in tense silence during the car ride to my office, each absorbed with his own thoughts of what the day would hold. I had designated myself as his physician of record and arranged for blood tests, a CAT scan of the chest, and appointments with Peter Draper, a thoracic surgeon, and Tom Cramer, an anesthesiologist, in anticipation of surgery the following day. Before sending Elliott off on this schedule, I thoroughly examined him.

I moved Elliott's long auburn hair off his neck so I could palpate for lymph nodes. He still affected a bohemian look, the same look he had when we first met two decades before. We had been introduced by a mutual friend, Anne Albright, who brought us together because she was struck by how similar we were.

"You could be brothers, so tall, with those deep-set, soulful eyes," Anne had teased us over mugs of French roast coffee one Sunday morning in her Riverside Drive apartment.

But it was not just our physical resemblance that had struck Anne. She said it was how much we shared in spirit— our appetite for information, our sense of humor, our loquaciousness. Elliott and I had blushed at her bold praise.

"You look worried," Elliott stated as I removed my hand from his neck.

Just above his collarbone was a matted hard tongue of tissue. It resisted the compressive force of my fingertips. The mass was growing up now, from the mediastinum to the apex of his thorax. I had noted a subtle bulge in the veins in his neck, and a slowing of their rhythmic flow.

I hesitated in responding, not wanting to tell him what I

observed. But I knew I should not deviate from my policy of honesty with a patient, even a patient who was like a brother to me and whose condition caused me deep anguish. If I did not tell the truth always, I would not be trusted when I had a truth to tell.

I explained that the veins in his neck were dilated, and this indicated "superior vena caval syndrome." The vena cava, the large vein that drains the blood from the upper body, was being compressed by the mass of nodes in his chest before it emptied into the right atrium of his heart. That backed up circulation in the brain and could cause increased intracranial pressure, manifest first as a headache.

"I've had a constant headache over the last few days, but figured it was stress."

I agreed that his headache could be due to stress, but the compression of the vena cava was contributing as well. By tomorrow we would diagnose the nature of the mass, and begin to treat it. That would decompress the vena cava.

Elliott looked knowingly into my eyes, and then returned my honesty with his own.

"Jerry, don't let me die."

I shuddered at his words.

I had cared for many patients who had intuited their own deaths. Sometimes it was obvious to all, to patient, physician, family. Then the disease was widespread, the treatment failing. But occasionally there was no clinical sign that pointed in that final direction. I had come to believe strongly in how a patient feels and reads his body. Beyond any objective tests, blood chemistries, cardiograms, or CAT scans, a patient's sense of impending death often proved true.

I gripped Elliott's exposed shoulder tightly, holding fast as I offered words of comfort. He was exhausted from the trip and from worry, I said, and should not rely on grim feelings in such a state. We did not yet know the cause of the enlarged lymph nodes. Once we made the diagnosis, we would embark on our course of action.

But as I continued with my reassurances, I studied the distant look in his eyes, and wondered whether he had indeed seen the arrival of life's last visitor.

"Scalpel"—"Scalpel"; "Clamp"—"Clamp"; "Suture"—"Suture."

We were well into the second hour of the operation. Peter Draper, the thoracic surgeon, had finished dissecting between the vital structures of the mediastinum—heart, aorta, lungs—and had just reached a dense band of inflamed fibrous tissue overlying the mass of nodes.

I stood slightly away. It was too distressing to watch a person whom I understood as I understood myself—as thoughts and feelings projected in the external form of the body—exposed as a conglomeration of tissues and vessels seeping blood and lymph.

I looked upward from the operative field. Elliott's lids

were closed over his china blue eyes and his face rested in a motionless mask. He had been transformed by the anesthetic into that intermediate state between what we know as life and what we imagine as death, where consciousness and feeling are suspended. In this state, I pictured his soul waiting in the anteroom of time, ready to pass back into life should the surgery succeed, or exit on its voyage with death. As I gazed at Elliott's immobile form, I silently prayed for his return to life.

Elliott's life. I knew its intimate details, learned during twenty years of friendship.

He had been a child prodigy from an Orthodox Jewish family in Brooklyn, excelling in languages, mathematics, music. His father, whom I still deferentially referred to as "Professor Ehrlich," was a renowned scholar of medieval Jewish history; his mother was the principal of a Hebrew high school.

Elliott was one of the first students from his yeshiva to go to Harvard, where he graduated magna cum laude in American studies. Following in his family's professorial tradition, he began a doctoral program in Colonial history at Yale. But he found the academic life too quiet and staid, the dimensions of the ivory tower too small.

So he left Yale for a job at *Time* in New York. For a while Elliott had found it exciting. It wasn't the New York he had known—Brooklyn with its sedate, tree-lined streets with two-family houses and elderly denizens chatting on the sidewalks. It was Manhattan, with all its intensity, grit, and ambition. At *Time* he found many like himself, educated at Ivy League colleges, poised to conquer the larger world. It was when Elliott was at *Time* and I was a medical student at Columbia that Anne Albright introduced us.

Although Elliott had made a living at *Time*, what his parents called a "decent" living for a single person in Manhattan, after three years he felt unsatisfied. The thrill of seeing his name among several on a joint byline waned, and he did not advance to a regular national column or produce an article that was considered for a national prize.

In June 1976, as I was leaving New York for my internship in Boston, Elliott quit the magazine and set out for L.A. He hoped Hollywood would provide what Harvard and Yale and *Time* had not.

"You bring yourself wherever you go," his father reminded him. I recalled remarking to Elliott at the time that it was the kind of advice my father, had he been alive, would have offered.

I heard Peter Draper sharply announce that he had snared the upper lip of the mass and that the attending pathologist, Ned Waterman, should enter the operating theater. I watched Peter deliver a glistening cube of tissue from the deep cavity of Elliott's open chest. He placed it on a sterile gauze sponge and then cut it into three equal pieces. Ned Waterman quickly moved his pathologist's forceps onto

the field and distributed each piece into a different recep-
tacle: one flash-frozen in liquid nitrogen; one placed in a
plastic container with fixative; the last dispersed into a cell
suspension in a saline-filled tube.

Peter Draper looked up and nodded to me. It was a signal
that all was proceeding smoothly. I relaxed a bit, feeling the
tension in my legs ease, and returned to my thoughts of Elliott.

Perhaps he occupied such a special place in my life
because, among all my friends, he was my alter ego. Through
his odyssey I acknowledged my own restlessness, my own
fantasies of taking risks in life, of deviating from the path of
the "good Jewish boy."

When I left Harvard for my training in hematology and
oncology at UCLA, Elliott was working as a script writer in
Hollywood. He lived in a rundown cottage on a hill in
Malibu, overlooking the churning Pacific Ocean. There,
Elliott entertained glamorous women he met at the studios,
charming them with his humor and warmth.

His quest was to write a film about the formation of the
first-generation American identity. He searched for cinematic
venues not only in urban centers but in the far reaches of the
country, traveling to the remote Arizona desert, small towns
of east Texas, the wild chaparral of Montana. As he reached
more deeply into the diversity of American culture, he
became ambivalent about his parochial background. Still
profoundly bound up with the Jewish people, their triumphs

and neuroses, he was nonetheless eager to stretch his roots—suspending his celebration of religious holidays, no longer keeping kosher, preferring the company of non-Jewish women.

Elliott was financially successful in L.A., earning a hundred thousand dollars or more a year on options and commissions for scripts. A few of his works became TV movies, and one was almost made into a motion picture, but was killed at the last minute by the studio that bought it. But the major project on the American experience—his serious work of cinematic art—never came to be.

The surgical team was closing now. The ribs were realigned and the final sutures placed in the overlying skin. Elliott soon would be re-formed as he had always appeared to me.

In the adjacent room, Ned Waterman, the pathologist, was already studying the slices of snap-frozen tissue to obtain an initial diagnosis. I exited the operating room to join him. As I sat at the two-headed microscope with him, I began to review in my mind the diagnostic list I had formulated, but my thinking stalled. I felt my deeper mind repelling my conscious aim, as when two magnets are brought together at the same poles.

I suspended my effort to review the diagnostic list and momentarily retreated into recollections of the past, before the emergency phone call some four long days before.

Elliott stayed in L.A. after I came back to Boston. We spoke often, and I heard the disappointment in his voice as he described deal after deal that did not come to fruition. Three years after I left UCLA, in the summer of 1986, Elliott decided he needed a break from Hollywood. He traveled through Europe and then to Israel, where his parents had retired. At a garden party in Jerusalem he met Susan. They fell in love, married, and Elliott started yet another life, in Israel.

Elliott told me how he looked forward to living in Jerusalem, how he imagined the city would be his "teacher." He believed that the radical change in culture from the superficial, narcissistic world of Hollywood to the ancient holy city would nourish his creative powers and facilitate his writing of a major work. To support himself he took a job as a columnist for a new English-language periodical, *The Israel Bulletin*, and a position teaching film criticism at Hebrew University.

"Look at those cells," Ned Waterman said.

Gazing into the aperture, I found it hard to comprehend that the tissue I was studying under the microscope was a part of Elliott. The magnified field should have been recognizable but was confusing, almost surreal. Large cells swirled and danced like the intoxicated moon and stars in the frenzied paintings of the mad Van Gogh.

"It's a T-cell lymphoma," Ned Waterman tersely concluded.

My heart sank.

I tried to sustain my emotional equilibrium and think about Elliott's situation in a considered, clinical way. I recited to myself the details of T-cell lymphoma, as if I were teaching on rounds with a group of medical students and interns:

T-cell lymphoma represents some 2 percent of adult lymphomas. It is aggressive, marked by invasion of vital organs, particularly liver, bone, and brain. It is generally of unknown etiology, as it likely would be in this case. Recently, a mutation in a tumor suppressor gene called p16 was found in T-cell lymphoma. The pl6 gene normally puts a brake on cell division in the T cell, but when mutated, the genetic brake loses its traction and the cells are released in a headlong rush of growth. There is a rare form of T-cell lymphoma endemic in southern Japan and the Caribbean. It arises not from a mutation in the pl6 gene but from infection with a virus called HTLV, an acronym for human T-cell lymphoma/leukemia virus.

I halted my didactic mental exercise, recalling that I had studied HTLV at UCLA in the late 1970s, while Elliott lived on the hill in Malibu. Could he have contracted this rare virus from one of his romantic liaisons? We would test him, but it would almost certainly be negative.

I paused, my mouth dry, feeling slightly nauseated. I

envisioned the next steps. We would clinically "stage" his lymphoma, assessing by CAT scan and tissue biopsy where, beyond his chest, the cancer cells might be growing. Although it might be confined to the mediastinum, given the size of the nodes and the two-month delay in diagnosis, I suspected we would find it elsewhere.

Elliott then would require very intensive treatment. At least five different chemotherapy drugs administered together for nine months, followed by two years of so-called maintenance therapy with three more agents. The aim was to destroy every last lymphoma cell. The treatment would bring him to the cusp of death, damaging much healthy tissue—in bone marrow, liver, skin, mouth, and bowel—in order to purge the cancer completely.

My mind stumbled in its clinical mode as I considered the prognosis of a "forty-three-year-old Caucasian male, previously healthy, with T-cell lymphoma presenting as an 8-centimeter chest mass." The numbers would not hold together. Each time I approached the statistics on long-term survival, less than 50/50, my heart sank again.

I knew at that moment that I could not be Elliott's doctor. For the first time in my career I had reached my limits as a treating physician. I was unable to function with the clinician's necessary analytical detachment. I realized that my inability was not just because of our closeness. It was also because Elliott was too much a mirror of myself.

His situation had sparked memories of my father's death, of my youth as a student, and of my dreams as a physician-in-training. The arrival of Benjamin and Susan had made me consider how Pam would manage with our children if I were the one suddenly stricken with a life-threatening disease. In the operating room I had averted my eyes because I feared seeing myself as he was then, exposed for what we all are: vulnerable flesh and blood. Later, during his therapy, I would wonder how the poisonous drugs flowing into his veins would feel flowing into mine. And—I shuddered at the thought—I knew I would perceive the final throes of his death as a vision of my own.

I realized I could not trust myself to be his primary care provider, to walk each morning into his hospital room and see the suffering that had to be if he had any chance of surviving—the vomiting and diarrhea and hair loss and bleeding and fevers and infections and mouth blisters and skin sloughing and a host of other side effects from the treatment. I feared that his physical suffering and psychological anguish would color my judgments and cause me to make a mistake— a mistake that could cost him his life.

I would never forgive myself for that, as I never forgave the physician who failed my father. That physician did not know his limits. I knew that my father might have died even in the most competent hands and the most modern hospital. But then I and my family would have known that all had been done that could have been done, and we would live without added anguish or regret.

I could think more clearly now that I understood the basis for my inner conflict.

I decided I could not, would not, remove myself entirely from Elliott's case and medically abandon him. I desperately wanted to help.

I arrived at a solution. I would offer myself as "a physician once removed." My scientific knowledge and technical expertise would be brought to bear at each step of Elliott's illness as they might be useful. After the clinical staging of the lymphoma, I would identify a competent and committed oncologist. With this specialist, I would help set the treatment strategy and advise on the medical response to problems and complications—as they undoubtedly would occur.

I stood in the surgical recovery room, grasping Elliott's pale hand. Susan leaned over, wiping beads of perspiration from his forehead with a damp cool cloth. She took the news of his cancer without flinching. I sensed she had expected it from the start.

"Elliott will defeat it," Susan forcefully asserted. "I know him, how tough and determined he can be."

Elliott looked at her with measured appreciation. He whispered, his voice still heavy from the anesthesia, an echo of her sentiments: "I'm ready to fight. I want to live. Above all, for you and Benjamin. And my daughter-to-be."

I looked at her with surprise, and then understood. Susan had seemed heavier, her taut facial features subtly expanded, her waist wide. I thought it was the first changes of middle age, she being in her early forties.

Susan smiled softly at me.

"I'm just in the first trimester."

"Mazel tov," I congratulated them, wishing literally "good luck." The traditional phrase hung heavily between us. We would need all the luck possible for their unborn daughter to know her father.

Later that evening in his hospital room, after Elliott had taken his first nourishment and the effects of the anesthetic waned, we began to discuss the logistics of his care. I began by outlining the further staging that needed to be done, two separate biopsies of his bone marrow and an MRI scan of his brain followed by a spinal tap. We would begin a short course of radiation to the mass tomorrow to free the vena cava and restore the free flow of blood from his head.

I hesitated and then, in faltering speech, began to discuss the question of where he should receive his nine months of chemotherapy.

Elliott looked knowingly at me. Before I could broach the issue of my being his primary physician, Elliott asserted that it didn't make sense to be treated in Boston.

Now that the situation was under control, we could think more pragmatically.

He reached for my hand, gripping it with considerable force. He said he knew I would be there for him every step of the way, and my presence meant a great deal, more than he could express. But someone else, whom I knew and trusted, should take over his case.

I rallied, feeling grateful he had read my feelings and relieved me of my conflict.

We analyzed the options of which location and hospital and medical team would be the "very best," and concluded Elliott should go to Alta Bates Hospital in Berkeley, California. A warm-hearted and skilled colleague, Dr. Jim Fox, directed its outstanding program in blood diseases and cancer. Jim, I knew, would make the personal commitment to Elliott's care. A key factor in this choice was Susan's family. Her parents lived in Sacramento and owned a condominium in San Francisco. Susan and Benjamin would stay there while Elliott was receiving treatment. When the new baby arrived, there would be the support and resources of nearby grandparents.

Before Elliott left, we administered two short pulses of radiation to the mass. Within forty-eight hours the veins of his neck had flattened, and his headache disappeared. It would buy enough time for him to make it to the West Coast and begin definitive treatment.

I contacted Jim Fox, reviewing Elliott's case in detail, and then sent him by overnight mail the pathology slides, copies of X rays, and the operative report. The lymphoma, as I had feared, had spread to the bone marrow, but mercifully it had spared his liver and brain.

Elliott began the chemotherapy regimen four days after leaving Boston. He developed the expected side effects from the treatment: nausea, vomiting, hair loss, mouth blisters, diarrhea, and then less common complications. First was chemical pancreatitis, an inflammation of the pancreas from the drug L-asparaginase. He suffered weeks of severe abdominal pain that bored into his midback, and wild fluctuations in his blood sugar as insulin production fell. The high doses of chemotherapeutic drugs also injured the small vessels of his circulation. Fluid transited from his capillaries and swelled the soft tissues of his arms, legs, and face. This was eventually brought under control by aggressive administration of diuretics and restriction of his fluid intake.

The repeated courses of steroids resulted in painful necrosis of the bone of his right hip. It was decided that Elliott ultimately would need surgery and an artificial joint. The steroids also made his lungs a breeding ground for a fungus called *Aspergillus*. This fungal infestation triggered spasm of his airways and severe air hunger. He needed oxygen, antibiotics, and bronchodilators.

Elliott stoically absorbed each awful side effect, and

looked to his humor to diffuse his pain and fear. "I'm the Pillsbury Doughboy," he said when his body ballooned from the edema. "They say mature women like Susan love bald men," he quipped when his distinctive auburn hair was completely gone. With a raging fever and harsh cough from the fungal infection, his mouth ulcerated and his intestines unable to hold the little he took in, Elliott hoarsely concluded, "I think I finally outdid Job."

I stayed in close contact with Jim Fox by phone, fax, and e-mail. After receiving the clinical update, I would speak with Elliott. Our conversation developed a regular pattern, first mulling over the medical issues and then discussing his emotional state and the state of his family. I also visited him, using my frequent trips to scientific meetings in California as opportunities to see him in San Francisco or Sacramento.

Beyond clinical assistance, Elliott looked to me for hope. I told him all these complications were reversible, and we were very much on track with the lymphoma regimen. He began to ascribe to such words of support and reassurance a deeper significance, as if I were privy to a world of certainty beyond that of our senses. Susan, the hard-driving political operative, surprised me by also taking up this line. She regularly ended our joint discussions of his condition with the assertion "If Jerry says it will be O.K., then it will O.K., Elliott."

I felt deeply uncomfortable in such a role. I knew all too

well how desperate we become facing life-threatening illness and its toxic treatments, and understood how we grasp at straws, wanting to believe that the doctor, with credentials and experience, can see the future clearly.

I tried to defuse their statements while still being encouraging, to gently restate the truth as I knew it, in scientific terms. I reiterated that the sum of the clinical data so far indicated that Elliott's chances were increasingly good that he would survive, but there were still major hurdles to overcome.

After his third course of the five-drug chemotherapy regimen, the mass of lymph nodes disappeared in his chest. After the fifth course, no lymphoma cells were seen on his repeat bone marrow biopsy.

With each positive advance, Susan and Elliott reaffirmed that I, like an oracle, had predicted everything would turn out fine, and my words were being proven true.

Elliott completed his eighteen months of intensive therapy. He then underwent complete restaging, with CAT scans of his chest and abdomen, bilateral bone marrow biopsies, and a spinal tap. There was no evidence of lymphoma. After so many invasive examinations, Elliott offered: "I always tested well, and this one was open-book."

Elliott was declared to be in complete remission. It would take five years of follow-up before it was safe to state he was cured—after that time, relapse was very rare.

"I will live with that uncertainty," Elliott asserted. "If I've learned anything from developing this disease, it is the fundamental uncertainty of all of life."

Two years later, in early June 1994, Elliott and his family visited Cambridge for his twenty-fifth Harvard reunion. I had never met his daughter, Tikva, now three years old. A petite and outgoing girl, she greeted me with a clever smile. Born after the fifth cycle of Elliott's therapy, when the lymphoma disappeared from his bone marrow, she was given her name as an expression of thanks. In Hebrew, *tikva* means "hope." Susan said the name embodied their tenacious optimism.

Elliott walked briskly with his family and me through Harvard Yard. Despite his artificial hip, he only occasionally depended on his cane to negotiate the inclines in our path. He was wearing sharply cut clothes he had purchased at Banana Republic in Berkeley to celebrate his complete remission: a white collarless shirt, beige linen pants, and a matching vest. His hair was thick and long, tied artfully in a pony tail. Susan remarked with a loving grin he was "Samson with his strength back."

Susan took Tikva and Benjamin for an early lunch while Elliott and I rested on the steps of Widener Library. We watched the preparations for commencement to be held the next day in the Yard, the stage arranged before Memorial Church, where the president, deans, and tenured faculty would be seated facing the graduates.

Elliott was in a reflective mood, moved by his return to a place he cherished, where every student was told he was one of the chosen, graced to attend America's most prestigious university.

He candidly shared his recent thoughts with me. He allowed that for the first few months after returning to Israel he was thankful just to be alive, taking each day as a gift. To eat without mouth ulcers and diarrhea, to breathe without oxygen pumped from a mask, to move his limbs without intravenous lines restraining them, this was enough to greet each morning with joy.

But now that he had fully resumed his former routine, writing at *The Israel Bulletin* and teaching film to undergraduates at the university, he was feeling deeply unsettled. During this reunion, he was realizing more forcefully than ever what had eluded him since leaving his alma mater. He wanted, finally, real success. Returned now to health, he was determined to obtain it.

I was aware we were moving into charged territory. We all want to succeed, and we usually define it in comparison to others, a problematic exercise. I feared that I might sound condescending or patronizing by saying this. Not knowing quite what to say, I remained silent.

"What have I accomplished?" Elliott continued as he gazed at the workmen hanging the rich crimson banners of each of Harvard's schools—law, medicine, business, divinity—from the poles of the stage. "This is what I have: a monthly column in a struggling Jewish magazine; two TV movies and countless unmade scripts; a part-time teaching job in cinema at Hebrew University.

"I know I almost died. It's not that I'm ungrateful for life. It's that I can't live on the edge every day, just thanking God and my doctors for my life. No one can live that way—it's a state of paralysis, a suspension of life. I have to deal with living again, in all its petty details—getting the kids to school and the car fixed and the taxes paid and the laundry done. And I have to deal with my larger issue—my desire to do something truly major.

"It was good to come back to Harvard, now, at this juncture in my life, after facing death. It energizes me to do what was always expected of me. And what I expected for myself."

He was thinking about finally writing a book. It was envisioned as a major work about the transformation of American culture. It would draw on the experiences he had had in a series of portraits of places in time: Brooklyn in the 1950s when the American dream was like a collective unconscious; Harvard in the '60s, the relinquishing of WASP hegemony, of New England gentlemanliness as authority was being challenges by the upheaval of Vietnam protests and experimentation with drugs; then the New York scene in the '70s, the rebirth of careerism, the social climbing, the attempt to find an anchor and direction; L.A., meaning Hollywood, the wanna-bes, the groveling, the raw crassness of money and fame. And finally the West Coast in the '90s, with the ascendancy of the wonks, computer nerds and their venture people, who have changed the way knowledge is received and processed by society.

"The experience of my cancer hasn't only made me want to do what I've always aimed to do—produce something substantial and important, a book that will be respected by the people whom I respect. I think I may have broken down the block to doing it. My illness has given me insights into myself that weren't apparent before."

Susan returned from lunch with Tikva and Benjamin, and we continued our stroll with them through the campus. We moved on to other subjects, the political situation, how the peace process was slowly but surely moving forward after the historic meeting between Rabin and Arafat. It was a time of hope and opportunity in Israel, and Elliott commented that, despite prior frustrations and failures, it was never too late for new beginnings.

One year after his Harvard reunion, Elliott had another opportunity to visit Boston. In addition to writing his biweekly column, he was now engaged in frequent travel as a public speaker. He had developed a reputation as a fresh voice in the Jewish intellectual scene. His commentaries drew on his considerable knowledge of Jewish history and tradition but added a modern secular slant. His subjects ranged from politics to cinema to books to religion. His readership in *The Israel Bulletin*, although select, was widely distributed throughout the Jewish world. He had addressed communities in Australia, Canada, and England already this year, and was now invited to New York to address a large rabbinical gathering. It was a special challenge, Elliott remarked, to "sermonize to the pros." He would come up to Boston midweek after his speech. Almost as an aside, he asked me to recheck his blood counts. On a routine visit last week with Dr. Levy, his general practitioner, his white blood cell count was noted to be just below normal.

"I'm at the tail end of a cold which I picked up from Tikva. Jeremy Levy thought this might have slightly depressed the number. You think it has anything to do with the lymphoma?"

I said I didn't. I agreed with Dr. Levy. Respiratory viruses often caused a minor diminution in the leukocyte count.

Elliott arrived looking strong and energized. There was a bronze color to his face from the Middle Eastern sun. His chest and shoulders were broad from his new passion, swimming. He no longer limped, having adapted to the artificial hip. We embraced forcefully, feeling the triumph that marked his survival. Pam and the kids welcomed him, as usual, with warm kisses.

Elliott did justice to a hearty homemade dinner, and rose

early to read *The New York Times*. We spoke of the continuing move toward peace, how the redeployment in the West Bank was proceeding, and the chances that Rabin's Labor Party would triumph in next year's elections.

When we arrived at my office, Youngsun greeted Elliott with great excitement, and spent much time inspecting his photographs of Benjamin and Tikva.

Two hours later, I sat with Ned Waterman, the same pathologist who had reviewed the biopsy of Elliott's lymphoma. We systematically scanned the slide made from a single drop of Elliott's blood, which held thousands of white cells. Swimming among the normal white cells were several large ragged forms. These unkempt cells had bloated nuclei and bright pink splinters littering their cytoplasm. I looked at the face of my colleague across the microscope, how his brow arched and the muscles of his cheeks tightened. The diagnosis could be made by a first-year medical student, the morphology of the large, distorted cells was so distinctive. Elliott had acute leukemia.

I closed my eyes, the residual image of the leukemic cells lingering on my retinae. Then all I saw was deep blackness. I felt hollow, as if the darkness before my eyes had coursed down into the core of my being and emptied me of feeling. There was no anger, no pain, just a cold numbness, like the unfeeling shock of a person swiftly cut by a sharp knife who has no sensation of the wound.

Despite my emotional void, I immediately understood on a rational plane what had happened.

"Treatment-related leukemia" was the term applied to Elliott's condition, the cruel outcome of modern chemotherapy, which provided a lifesaving result at first only to trigger, years later, a second potentially fatal disease in an unlucky few. The drugs that Elliott was given to destroy the lymphoma had damaged the DNA of his normal bone marrow cells. Most of these cells had died from the trauma, unable to survive with an impaired genetic program; a few had accumulated, by chance, the necessary mutations to lead to the opposite of cell death—the unrestricted growth of cancer.

I returned to my office, where Elliott was waiting for me. We had planned to go to lunch at Rebecca's Café, the gourmet fast-food place near the medical school. He had spent the morning at the Harvard Coop buying T-shirts for his kids and wandering around his beloved campus.

"It's incredible how fast they grow," Elliott remarked as I entered the office. "Last year at the reunion, we bought them all sorts of Harvard outfits, and they've outgrown everything."

I agreed, saying kids grew like happy weeds, and then sat down. I looked into his soft blue eyes, knowing what they would soon see.

"Ell, I just returned from reviewing the slide of your blood test."

I paused. The cold emptiness that I had felt was now quickly replaced by searing pain.

I was tempted to hide behind euphemisms, to say there were some "abnormalities" noted and "further tests" would be needed. I had thought that might ease him into the news, the awful crushing news, that after all he had endured, he now faced more, much more—a treatment as intensive and battering as any that existed in clinical medicine. To definitively eradicate the leukemia and cure him, chemotherapy would not be enough. He now required a bone marrow transplant.

But I knew, as before when I had informed him of this T-cell lymphoma, that it was best for him to know everything, as soon as possible, in honest detail.

"Elliott, it appears your white count is low because you've developed leukemia."

Elliott paused after my words and then nodded knowingly, as if he recognized a familiar face. I had expected him to flinch from the harsh blow just delivered, to break down in tears. I was fighting to prevent myself from doing so. But he sat still and silent.

I took his silence as assent to inform him of what was needed to cure him, a bone marrow transplant, and what that meant, since it was often misunderstood by many laypeople. All the blood cells in his body would have to be destroyed. This would be accomplished by administering radiation, the kind of radiation that was called "total body" because it penetrated every millimeter of tissue, like the radiation from a nuclear bomb.

Once all his blood cells were destroyed, he would be given the most primitive marrow cells of a compatible donor. These primitive cells were called "stem cells," because they grew into all the mature blood components—white cells, red cells, platelets—and could reconstitute his entire hematological system.

I waited for questions, but his silence continued, and I wondered if Elliott was really processing the information, whether it was all too much and he was overwhelmed.

"Am I clear, Ell? I know it's a lot, coming fast and furious."

He finally spoke.

"What if there is no match for me, no one compatible to provide the needed stem cells?"

It was clear that he did understand, all too well, because this was the key issue. Even if he passed through the treatment for the leukemia and entered remission, he could be left in a netherworld of waiting, unable to proceed to the transplant. Desperate options were then considered.

"If, God forbid, there is no match, from your family or the worldwide registry of marrow donors, then there are two options. One is conservative—to live in remission from your leukemia, knowing it will come back in months to years. You are healthy and functioning during that time, and, we hope, research advances give us a second curative path before the leukemia returns. The second option is fraught with risk—an unmatched transplant. With an unmatched transplant, the stem cells grow into blood cells that will recognize the tissues of your body as foreign, and attack. This is 'graft-versus-host' disease—the unmatched transplanted blood cells are the 'graft,' and they charge against your liver and skin and bowel, as the 'host.'"

"And the outcome of the battle?"

"Not usually in favor of the host."

I retreated from this discussion to focus on the most immediate step, treating his acute leukemia. I said we should operate under the assumption that he would have a compatible donor—Michael or Simon, his brothers, whose genetically related cells would be unlikely to cause a severe graft-versus-host reaction. I reviewed the logistics and latest statistics on matched transplants; at each point emphasizing the positive edge he might have: his general robust health, his relatively young age, the diagnosis of the leukemia early in its evolution. I was functioning as I usually functioned, as a clinician, with calm and expertise and honest optimism in the face of a complex and frightening disease. I thought I was transmitting to Elliott a sense of determination and authentic hope.

But Elliott seemed to move all the clinical science to the side, and surprised me with his response.

"What is your *choosh*, your sense, Jerry? Am I going to live?"

Choosh is a biblical Hebrew word, meaning "sense" or "feeling." It is onomatopoeic, capturing the sound of a rush of breath that emanates from the deep reaches of the spirit. It is a word that speaks not of rational deliberation and assessment, but of inner vision.

I paused, not expecting to have a *choosh* but an *opinion* as a sober clinician, one drawn from weighing the factors that went in his favor and those that did not.

But within me I had *felt*, not calculated, a reply.

"My *choosh* is good. I believe you will make it, that you're going to live."

I stood from my chair and hugged him tightly, tears now streaming down both our cheeks.

I wondered if I had gone mad, whether the anticipated pain and loss from imagining his death was so great that, after I rebounded from the numbing shock of the news, my rationality had collapsed and I was retreating into delusion. Who was I to pretend to be a prophet, to have extrasensory perception? What did my *choosh* mean in clinical reality? Was I indulging myself and my closest friend in a convenient lie?

But it was not a lie. I had felt it, clearly and strongly. Deep inside me was a prevailing calm. I clearly realized all the obstacles and uncertainties that lay ahead—the induction chemotherapy for the acute leukemia, the identification of a compatible match, the preparation with total body radiation for the transplant, the tense waiting to see if the graft of stem cells would "take" in his marrow space and grow to repopu-late his blood, then the risk of graft-versus-host disease. All the while, Elliott would be in a tenuous state—without an immune system—vulnerable to overwhelming and often deadly infections. He would be placed in an isolation room with special purified air and food, rare visitors allowed for short times and only under mask and gloves and gown, secluded as completely as possible from our world of ambient microbes while he lived without any bodily defenses.

But all these clinical realities faded under the powerful feeling that he would survive. I did not see light or hear words or otherwise hallucinate. And when I first heard his question, I assumed I would evade addressing it because in medical science *choosh* was meaningless.

But I had sensed that he would live, and it would have been a lie not to tell him.

"Let's call Susan," I said, anxious to move away from the moment of mystical feeling and focus on logistics. "We should figure out the next steps with her."

"She's probably back from work by now," Elliott replied, looking at his watch.

I dialed their number in Jerusalem, which I knew by heart, and as I listened to the flat ringing of the phone, won-dered again if my experience of Elliott's illness was teaching me my limits.

• • •

Elliott decided to return to Jim Fox at Alta Bates Hospital in Berkeley for the leukemia therapy and the marrow transplant. Its clinical unit was state of the art, there was added comfort in knowing the nurses and the hospital routine, and the close-by resources of Susan's parents would again be of great help. Moreover, Jim had become not just his physician but his friend.

Susan flew to join Elliott in California, leaving Benjamin and Tikva in Jerusalem with Elliott's mother. The kids were in the middle of the school year, and it would have been disruptive to take them out of class. They were informed that Daddy had to go into the hospital again. They reacted appropriately, disappointed but with understanding, since Daddy had spent so much time in and out of hospitals during their young lives.

Elliott received high doses of Ara-C, a chemotherapy drug very effective against treatment-related leukemia but with terrible neurological side effects. He vomited for days despite powerful supportive antinausea medications, and then went into a swirl of vertigo as the Ara-C temporarily shocked his cerebellum, the balance center of the brain. He could hardly speak, lying with his eyes closed and his head immobile. These side effects slowly passed over the course of two weeks. Then his hair fell out, his mouth blistered, his bowels ulcerated, and his blood counts fell. He developed streptococcal pneumonia and required oxygen and high doses of antibiotics. It was all too familiar.

Through each blow Susan clung to my words like a sure

lifeline, repeating as a mantra: "Jerry's *choosh* is that Elliott is going to live."

After six weeks Elliott passed the first critical hurdle— the leukemia went into remission. He was discharged from the hospital. A week later I was called by Elliott and Susan from her parents' apartment in San Francisco. Susan was the one to break the great news: Elliott's older brother, Michael, was an excellent match to be the marrow donor. She exuded determination, like a tank commander leading a charge.

"On to the radiation. Then the transplant. Michael's cells are perfect! Just a few more steps forward. Everything will turn out fine, just as you predicted, Jerry. Right, Elliott?"

Elliott had not spoken yet. There was a long pause before he affirmed Susan's words. Then in a flat voice, he simply said: "Right. Everything will be fine."

Later that night the phone rang. I was in the kitchen, unloading the dinner dishes from the washer. It was well past ten, the kids asleep in bed, Pam reading in the den before we would retire for the night.

"Jerry, it's Elliott." His voice was hushed.

"You O.K.? Why are you whispering?"

"I don't want Susan to hear me. She's watching TV in the other room."

He paused and drew a deep breath. "I don't know if I can continue. I don't know if I can go ahead with the transplant."

I could hear him trying to control the quavering of his voice.

"Why not? You've done great so far. You've come through the leukemia treatment beautifully. Michael is a perfect match. We're almost there."

"I'm not sure why . . ." He began to sob. "I just don't know . . . if I can . . ."

He paused to collect himself, and then continued, his voice still shaking.

"Susan and you and my parents and Michael and Jim Fox—everyone just expects me to do it. But I don't know . . . if I can fulfill your expectations."

I felt the distance of thousands of miles, the difficulty of finding the right words to reply without the benefit of seeing his face, touching his hand, following his eyes.

"Jerry, the transplant has become in my mind like writing my great novel or my major film script. The expectations that surround me—that have surrounded me all my life— everyone believing I could accomplish great things—it's all now focused on this. I just don't know if I can do it."

I paused to collect my thoughts. It was not my place to explore the degree of success or lack thereof in Elliott's life. That was not the critical issue now. What was critical was having him move ahead with the transplant, his only chance to be cured. I first tried an analytical approach, explaining to Elliott what I thought was happening to him psychologically, hoping the insight would comfort him and bolster his courage.

"Ell, it's normal to be frightened. Especially on the second go. It's like a soldier sent back to the front after surviving a first bombardment. You're still shell-shocked. You lose your nerve. That's natural, normal. I've seen this countless times with other people—a flood of self-doubt, all the secret insecurities rising threatening to drown you,

"But you won't drown. We're all there supporting you, not with expectations but with love. I know Susan can be tough and drives you forward. It's her way of coping, her way of trying to keep herself, as well as you, intact."

"You don't understand, Jerry."

I heard him sigh, a desperate frustrated sigh.

"All my life I was expected to hit home runs, to slug it out of the park. Harvard. Yale. *Time.* Hollywood. But I'm not a home-run hitter. I hit singles—short grounders in the infield and pop flies. This time my life depends on a home run, and there isn't another chance at bat."

I continued to reassure him, that he was battle-fatigued, that Susan and I and Jim Fox and his parents were only trying to reinforce his will and confidence, not pressure him with expectations. But my words seemed hollow and I feared would be ineffective.

I paused to regroup my thoughts, and could hear Elliott begin to sob again.

I tried to see the impending transplant from Elliott's perspective and then modify that perception to make it more manageable.

"My words are just words, Ell. I've only seen it from the other side of the bed, the doctor's side. But I don't think it has to be a home run to score. It can be a series of base hits, one single after another. It may sound like a silly metaphor, but think of it that way. Break it down into a series of manageable pieces, instead of seeing it as a daunting whole. You've already proven with the lymphoma and the leukemia that you have the strength to swing the bat. You don't have to prove anything more, to yourself, to Susan or to—"

"Tell me your *choosh* about the transplant, Jerry," Elliott interrupted, his voice now more even and calm.

I sat silently, calling on my deepest feelings, seeking my inner sense of harmony or disharmony. It was again strange, because I did not resist his request. On a conscious level I wondered again whether this was all a game, my lack of resistance a way to extricate myself from a situation which had no ready solution. It was like a child's belief in the truth of fairy tales and the power of magic. I thought of the stories I had heard from my Hasidic relatives while growing up, of wonder rabbis, seers, diviners to whom the secret workings of time and space were revealed through angelic visitations and the study of mystical texts, *kabbalah*. I had been instructed by my parents to discount such tales as primitive and nonsensical. Was I assuming such a role for Elliott, or for me, or both?

But deep inside I had *felt* an answer, and offered what I sensed, not what I knew.

"I feel you're going to make it, Elliott. I really do."

Elliott returned to Jerusalem after the required one hundred days under observation in Berkeley. The marrow transplant had followed a remarkably smooth and uncomplicated course. His brother Michael's stem cells had found their niches in Elliott's emptied marrow space, and over six weeks began to spawn all the cells of Elliott's blood system. The growth factor G-CSF was given to expedite the maturation of the transplanted white cells, which reached normal numbers by week 10. There was no sign of graft-versus-host disease, and the medications that were used to prevent this complication were soon to be tapered off.

We had spoken several times each week during these critical one hundred days. After assessing the progress of the transplant, we discussed the biology and medical science that gave rise to the procedure. Elliott had brought a laptop computer into his isolation room, and in addition to e-mail and writing, had researched the history of the technique on the Web.

The Nobel Prize was awarded in 1990 to E. Donnall

Thomas, now at the Fred Hutchinson Cancer Research Center, for developing marrow transplantation. It was the culmination of a remarkable story. The first eleven patients treated by Dr. Thomas had died within a few weeks. It was an extraordinary act of determination to persevere, to believe that the barriers to transplantation of human bone marrow could be surmounted.

The biology of the process is similarly remarkable. The rare stem cells, present only at a frequency of one in 10,000 donated marrow cells, could be infused into a recipient's vein, circulate through the body, home specifically to the emptied marrow space, and then grow to fully reconstitute our entire blood system—its billions and billions of cells that make up our immune defenses, oxygen-carrying capacity, clotting functions. It is a testimony to nature's astounding regenerative powers.

Elliott commented that beyond the exceptional history and biology was another dramatic dimension to marrow transplantation, one likely to be experienced only by the fortunate recipient. It was expressed by a verse from Leviticus: "The life of the flesh is in the blood." Within him, flowing in every tissue space—heart and brain and muscle and gut— were the life-giving blood cells of his brother Michael.

"I feel as if I've been reborn, like I participated in a new form of creation, joining the hand of God with the hand of man."

While I rejoiced in Elliott's metaphor, I somberly remembered what it had taken to bring bone marrow transplantation to the sophisticated state it now enjoyed. Some two decades earlier, when I was a hematology fellow at UCLA, bone marrow transplant was still in its infancy. Dr. Thomas had just passed the first hurdles and achieved sustained grafts. A transplant unit was established in our department. There were many, many failures which now would have been successes. Little was known about how to optimally administer total body irradiation and the adjunctive support to carry a patient through the procedure. There were no available growth factors like G-CSF to stimulate white blood cell production from stem cells and accelerate the return of the body's defenses. As a fellow on the transplant ward, I watched impotently as patient after patient developed overwhelming infections and died. The medication Elliott was taking— cyclosporine, to modulate the "education" of the grafted cells, so they gradually "learned" to tolerate their new home and not rebel in a tantrum of graft-versus-host disease—this too did not exist when I was in training. The ravages of this awful graft-versus-host reaction, with liver damage, diarrhea, and skin sloughing, were all too frequent then. If a patient survived, he was generally left incapacitated.

Elliott, my beloved friend, husband of Susan, father of Benjamin and Tikva, had been given back his life because of the stubborn commitment to research of physicians like Donnall Thomas. Science did change the world, fundamentally and for the better.

Elliott called me from Jerusalem three weeks after his return to tell me that Susan and his parents were planning "a survival party." Pam and I were invited, although they doubted we could come.

I told him we would celebrate in spirit from Boston, and toast the miracle of science that had returned him to family and friends.

"You saw it all along, Jerry. Your *choosh* was that I would make it."

I felt uncomfortable. I wanted to celebrate the triumph of medical research, not vague mystical intuitions.

"I don't know what my *choosh* meant, Ell. I did feel it, but perhaps it was just a delusion, a psychological mechanism to help me cope with the nightmare you were in."

Elliott paused and then replied thoughtfully.

"I've come to believe more in that mystical dimension, Jerry. Isolated all those days, my own cells forever gone, the stem cells of Michael growing into my new blood, I had a strange *choosh* of my own.

"I sensed it wasn't only coincidence that Anne Albright brought us together, but that she envisioned you as my brother, and then my two 'brothers'—you in spirit and Michael in flesh—saved my life. I felt a visceral connection to you, to Anne, to all the people who have loved and cared for me during my life. I felt this at the moment of the transplant. I felt as if all your spirits were being infused into me along with the marrow. As much as Michael's stem cells revitalized my body, your spirits breathed life again into my soul."

We left it at that, making these mystical experiences a part of the history between us, and moved on to talk about work-related things.

"I haven't figured out what I want to do yet," Elliott confided. "Whether it makes sense to continue at the *Bulletin* and on the lecture circuit, or do something different.

"I'm trying to understand what 'success' means in my life. That's not easy. It's a struggle. I've been thinking about how I measure success in light of what I've been through.

"When I couldn't hold a pen to write, focus my eyes to see, or even lift my head to speak, I realized that performing such simple acts then would have been a 'great' success. It's a cliché but true, that you don't appreciate what you have until it's gone.

"I learned in yeshiva years ago the question posed by the Talmud: *Eizehoo ashir?*—Who is wealthy? And the rabbi's response: *Ha sameach b'chelko*—He who rejoices in his portion.

"It wasn't always easy in the past for me to rejoice in my portion. But in my isolation room, as my new blood was being created, I was able to write my column again. And I *rejoiced* in doing it.

"You know my first article was about my leukemia and the transplant. After it appeared in the *Bulletin*, I was deluged with mail. So many readers wrote, not only wishing me a speedy recovery and sending words of support, but affirming how powerfully my ideas affected them, I realized that sometimes they do cheer you when you get on first base, that singles do count in the game.

"I have hardly lost my ambition. I still want to write a book of substance, of significance. But I see the reason for my ambition differently this second time. Above all, I have to find it satisfying, I should rejoice in it. I want to look inward, not outside myself, for a measure of its success."

I understood Elliott's struggle. The desire for greatness, to be recognized for your achievements, was an insatiable worm that gnawed at your consciousness, invaded your dreams. Who didn't suffer its effects? Driven to do more, make more, rise higher. But it was a fruitless climb because there was no real summit.

I knew this from my perch as a physician, witnessing the moment when the seemingly endless climb is abruptly, unexpectedly, irreversibly halted by the advent of life's end. As death looms, so much of the "success" that we have lusted for appears useless and vain.

There are, of course, lasting achievements in life. I thought of the success of Donnall Thomas. He was certainly driven by ambition, pushed forward by the desire to conquer nature's barriers and do what had not before been possible. And he had been awarded the Nobel Prize, science's highest honor. But that wordly acclaim paled before a greater honor—the legacy that he had created for Elliott and others like him who now could live.

"It's very hard to live by one's own inner standards, Ell."

"Probably impossible. But I'll try. And when I feel myself slipping back, I'll tell myself to reflect on how I felt during the transplant, how my life was so brutally constrained, how my days were literally numbered."

"Literally numbered?" I wasn't sure what Elliott meant.

"Yes. Each day on rounds, Jim and the nurses would number the days: day zero was the day my blood was destroyed by the total body irradiation. Then day one was the infusion of Michael's stem cells. Each subsequent day was numbered. It was a weird experience, to listen to Jim Fox count at my bedside and declare to the medical team: 'Today is day fourteen post-transplant, vital signs stable, no sign yet of recovery of the graft.'

"I was both terrified and hopeful—terrified because I knew Jim could be counting the last days of my life, but hopeful because it felt like he might be numbering the days of my second creation. And if I survived, I knew I would be reborn in a unique way, not like the infant with a blank slate, but with memory and insight from all that I experienced."

Elliott's words brought to my mind the verses from Psalm 90, a psalm of life and death. It is recited in my synagogue to begin the mournful service of *yizkor*, the service of rememberance of those loved ones who are gone. I saw myself then, standing deep in prayer, my eyes closed, seeking insight from memory. This time the words spoke to me not of loss but of gain:

> *The stream of human life is like a dream;*
> *In the morning, it is as grass, sprouting, fresh;*
> *In the morning, it blossoms and flourishes;*
> *but by evening, it is cut down and withers. . . .*
> *Our years come to an end like a fleeting whisper.*
> *The days of our years may total seventy;*
> *if we are exceptionally strong, perhaps eighty;*
> *but all their pride and glory is toil and falsehood,*
> *and, severed quickly, we fly away. . . .*
> *So teach us to number our days that*
> *we may attain a heart of wisdom.*

from

AN
ANTHROPOLOGIST
ON MARS

OLIVER SACKS

*In the course of her extraordinary life, Dr. Temple
Grandin, a biologist and engineer in the animal
sciences department at Colorado State University, has
largely broken free of the circumscribed world imposed
on those labeled as autistic. Neurologist Oliver Sacks
shows some of the ingenious strategies
Dr. Grandin has improvised to help her
get through each day.*

I had, of course, heard of Temple Grandin—everyone interested in autism has heard of her—and had read her autobiography, *Emergence: Labeled Autistic,* when it came out, in 1986. When I first read the book, I could not help being suspicious of it: the autistic mind, it was supposed at that time, was incapable of self-understanding and understanding others and therefore of authentic introspection and retrospection. How *could* an autistic person write an autobiography? It seemed a contradiction in terms. When I observed that the book had been written in collaboration with a journalist, I wondered whether some of its fine and unexpected qualities—its coherence, its poignancy, its often "normal" tone—might in fact be due to her. Such suspicions have continued to be voiced, in regard to Grandin's book and to autistic autobiographies in general, but as I read Temple's papers (and her many autobiographical articles) I found a detail and consistency, a directness, that changed my mind.[1]

Reading her autobiography and her articles, one gets a

[1]What one does see in Temple's writings (and in the writings of other very able autistic adults, not excluding some with marked literary gifts) are peculiar narrational gaps and discontinuities, sudden, perplexing changes of topic, brought about (so Francesca Happé suggests in a recent essay on the subject) by Temple's failure "to appreciate that her reader does not share the important background information that she possesses." In more general terms, autistic writers seem to get "out of tune" with their readers, fail to realize their own or their readers' states of mind.

feeling of how strange, how different, she was as a child, how far removed from normal.[2] At six months, she started to stiffen in her mother's arms, at ten months to claw her "like a trapped animal." Normal contact was almost impossible in these circumstances. Temple describes her world as one of sensations heightened, sometimes to an excruciating degree (and inhibited, sometimes to annihilation): she speaks of her ears, at the age of two or three, as helpless microphones, transmitting everything, irrespective of relevance, at full, overwhelming volume—and there was an equal lack of modulation in all her senses. She showed an intense interest in odors and a remarkable sense of smell. She was subject to sudden impulses and, when these were frustrated, violent rage. She perceived none of the usual rules and codes of human relationship. She lived, sometimes raged, inconceivably disorganized, in a world of unbridled chaos. In her third year, she became destructive and violent:

> Normal children use clay for modelling; I used
> my feces and then spread my creations all over
> the room. I chewed up puzzles and spit the card-

[2] Authentic memories from the second (perhaps even the first) year of life, though not available to "normals," may be recalled, with veridical detail, by autistic people. Thus, Lucci et al. write of one such boy, "He seems to recall, in exquisite detail, events from when he was two or three years old." Coenesthetic memories of infancy are also reported by Luria of S., the mnemonist he studied.

board mush out on the floor. I had a violent
temper, and when thwarted, I'd throw anything
handy—a museum quality vase or leftover feces. I
screamed continually . . .

And yet, like many autistic children, she soon developed an
immense power of concentration, a selectivity of attention
so intense that it could create a world of its own, a place of
calm and order in the chaos and tumult: "I could sit on the
beach for hours dribbling sand through my fingers and fash-
ioning miniature mountains," she writes. "Each particle of
sand intrigued me as though I were a scientist looking
through a microscope. Other times I scrutinized each line in
my finger, following one as if it were a road on a map." Or
she would spin, or spin a coin, so raptly that she saw and
heard nothing else. "People around me were transparent. . . .
Even a sudden loud noise didn't startle me from my world." (It
is not clear whether this hyperfocus of attention—an attention
as narrow as it is intense—is a primary phenomenon in autism
or a reaction or adaptation to an overwhelming, uninhibited
barrage of sensation. A similar hyperfocus is sometimes seen
in Tourette's syndrome.)

At three, Temple was taken to a neurologist, and the
diagnosis of autism was made; it was hinted that lifelong
institutionalization would probably be necessary. The total
absence of speech at this age seemed especially ominous.

How, I had to wonder, had she ever moved from this almost unintelligible childhood, with its chaos, its fixations, its inaccessibility, its violence—this fierce and desperate state, which had almost led to her institutionalization at the age of three—to the successful biologist and engineer I was going to see?

I phoned Temple from the Denver airport to reconfirm our meeting—it was conceivable, I thought, that she might be somewhat inflexible about arrangements, so time and place should be set as definitely as possible. It was an hour-and-a-quarter drive to Fort Collins, Temple said, and she provided minute directions for finding her office at Colorado State University, where she is an assistant professor in the Animal Sciences Department. At one point, I missed a detail, and asked Temple to repeat it, and was startled when she repeated the entire directional litany—several minutes' worth—in virtually the same words. It seemed as if the directions had to be given as they were held in Temple's mind, entire—that they had fused into a fixed association or program and could no longer be separated into their components. One instruction, however, had to be modified. She had told me at first that I should turn right onto College Street at a particular intersection marked by a Taco Bell restaurant. In her second set of directions, Temple added an aside here, said the Taco Bell had recently had a face-lift and been housed in a fake cottage, and no longer looked in the least "bellish." I was struck by the charming, whimsical adjective "bellish"—autistic people are often called humorless, unimaginative, and "bellish" was surely an original concoction, a spontaneous and delightful image.

I made my way to the university campus and located the Animal Sciences Building, where Temple was waiting to greet me. She is a tall, strongly built woman in her midforties; she was wearing jeans, a knit shirt, western boots, her habitual dress. Her clothing, her appearance, her manner, were plain, frank, and forthright; I had the impression of a sturdy, no-nonsense cattlewoman, with an indifference to social conventions, appearance, or ornament, an absence of frills, an absolute directness of manner and mind. When she raised her arm in greeting, the arm went too high, seemed to get caught for a moment in a sort of spasm or fixed posture— a hint, an echo, of the stereotypies she once had. Then she gave me a strong handshake and led the way down to her office. (Her gait seemed to me slightly clumsy or uncouth, as is often the case with autistic adults. Temple attributes this to a simple ataxia associated with impaired development of the vestibular system and part of the cerebellum. Later I did a brief neurological exam, focusing on her cerebellar function and balance; I did indeed find a little ataxia, but insufficient, I thought, to explain her odd gait.)

She sat me down with little ceremony, no preliminaries, no social niceties, no small talk about my trip or how I liked Colorado. Her office, crow led with papers, with work done and to do, could have been that of any academic, with photographs of her projects on the wall and animal knickknacks she had picked up on her travels. She plunged straight into talking of her work, speaking of her early interests in psychology and animal behavior, how they were connected with self-observation and a sense of her own needs as an autistic person, and how this had joined with the visualizing and engineering part of her mind to point her toward the special field she had made her own: the design of farms, feedlots, corrals, slaughterhouses—systems of many sorts for animal management.

She handed me a book containing some of the layouts she had developed over the years—the book was titled *Beef Cattle Behaviors, Handling, and Facilities Design*—and I admired the complex and beautiful designs inside, and the logical presentation of the book, starting with diagrams of cattle and sheep and hog behavior and moving through designs of corrals to ever more complex ranch and feedlot facilities.

She spoke well and clearly, but with a certain unstoppable impetus and fixity. A sentence, a paragraph, once started, had to be completed; nothing was left implicit, hanging in the air.

I was feeling somewhat exhausted, hungry, and thirsty—
I had been traveling all day and had missed lunch—and I
kept hoping Temple would notice and offer me some coffee.
She did not; so, after an hour, almost fainting under the barrage of her overexplicit and relentless sentences, and the
need to attend to several things at once (not only what she
was saying, which was often complex and unfamiliar, but also
her mental processes, the sort of person she was), I finally
asked for some coffee. There was no "I'm sorry, I should have
offered you some before," no intermediacy, no social junc-
tion. Instead, she immediately took me to a coffeepot that was
kept brewing in the secretaries' office upstairs. She introduced me to the secretaries in a somewhat brusque manner,
giving me the feeling, once again, of someone who had
learned, roughly, "how to behave" in such situations without
having much personal perception of how other people felt—
the nuances, the social subtleties, involved.

"Time to get some dinner," Temple suddenly announced
after we had spent another hour in her office. "We eat early
in the West." We went to a nearby western restaurant, one
with swinging doors and with guns and cattle horns on the
walls—it was already crowded, as Temple had said it would
be, at five in the afternoon—and we ordered a classic
western meal of ribs and beer. We ate heartily and talked
throughout the meal about the technical aspects of

Temple's work and the ways in which she sets out every design, every problem, visually, in her mind. As we left the restaurant, I suggested we go for a walk, and Temple took me out to a meadow along an old railway line. The day was cooling rapidly—we were at five thousand feet—and in the long evening light gnats darned the air and crickets were stridulating all around us. I found some horsetails (one of my favorite plants) in a muddy patch below the tracks and became excited about them. Temple glanced at them, said "Equisetum," but did not seem stirred by them, as I was.

On the plane to Denver, I had been reading a remarkable piece of writing by a highly gifted, normal nine-year-old—a fairy story she had created, with a wonderful sense of myth, a whole world of magic, animism, and cosmogonies. What, I wondered as we walked through the horsetails, of Temple's cosmogony? How did she respond to myths, or to dramas? How much did they carry meaning for her? I asked her about the Greek myths. She said that she had read many of them as a child, and that she thought of Icarus in particular—how he had flown too near the sun and his wings had melted and he had plummeted to his death. "I understand Nemesis and Hubris," she said. But the loves of the gods, I ascertained, left her unmoved—and puzzled. It was similar with Shake-speare's plays. She was bewildered, she said, by Romeo and Juliet ("I never knew what they were up to"), and with *Hamlet* she got lost with the back-and-forth of the play.

Though she ascribed these problems to "sequencing diffi-culties," they seemed to arise from her failure to empathize with the characters, to follow the intricate play of motive and intention. She said that she could understand "simple, strong, universal" emotions but was stumped by more com-plex emotions and the games people play. "Much of the time," she said, "I feel like an anthropologist on Mars."

She was at pains to keep her own life simple, she said, and to make everything very clear and explicit. She had built up a vast library of experiences over the years, she went on. They were like a library of videotapes, which she could play in her mind and inspect at any time—"videos" of how people behaved in different circumstances. She would play these over and over again and learn, by degrees, to correlate what she saw, so that she could then predict how people in similar circumstances might act. She had complemented her experi-ence by constant reading, including reading of trade journals and the *Wall Street Journal*—all of which enlarged her knowledge of the species. "It is strictly a logical process," she explained.

In one plant she had designed, she said, there had been repeated breakdowns of the machinery, but these occurred only when a particular man, John, was in the room. She "cor-related" these incidents and inferred at last that John must be sabotaging the equipment. "I had to learn to be suspicious, I had to learn it cognitively. I could put two and two together, but I couldn't see the jealous look on his face." Such incidents have not been uncommon in her life: "It bends some people out of shape that this autistic weirdo can come in and design all the equipment. They want the equipment, but it galls them that they can't do it themselves, but that Tom"—an engineering colleague—"and I can, that we've got hundred-thousand-dollar Sun workstations in our heads." In her ingenuousness and gullibility, Temple was at first a target for all sorts of tricks and exploitations; this sort of innocence or guilelessness, arising not from moral virtue but from failure to understand dissembling and pretense ("the dirty devices of the world," in Traherne's phrase), is almost universal among the autistic. But over the years Temple has learned, in her indirect way, by inspecting her "library," some of the ways of the world. She has, in fact, been able to found her own company and to work as a freelance consultant to and designer of animal facilities all over the world. By professional standards, she is extraordinarily successful, but other human interactions—social, sexual—she cannot "get." "My work is my life," she told me several times. "There is not that much else."

There seemed to me pain, renunciation, resolution, and acceptance all mixed together in her voice, and these are the feelings that sound through her writings. In one article she writes:

• • •

I do not fit in with the social life of my town or university. Almost all of my social contacts are with livestock people or people interested in autism. Most of my Friday and Saturday nights are spent writing papers and drawing. My interests are factual and my recreational reading consists mostly of science and livestock publications. I have little interest in novels with complicated interpersonal relationships, because I am unable to remember the sequence of events. Detailed descriptions of new technologies in science fiction or descriptions of exotic places are much more interesting. My life would be horrible if I did not have my challenging career.

Early the next morning, a Saturday, Temple picked me up in her four-wheel-drive, a rugged vehicle she drives all over the West to visit farms, ranches, corrals, and meat plants. As we headed for her house, I quizzed her about the work she had done for her Ph.D.; her thesis was on the effects of enriched and impoverished environments on the development of pigs' brains. She told me about the great differences that developed between the two groups—how sociable and delightful the "enriched" pigs became, how hyperexcitable and aggressive (and almost "autistic") the "impoverished" ones were by contrast. (She wondered whether impoverishment of experience was not a contributing factor in human autism.) "I got to love my enriched pigs," she said. "I was very attached. I was so attached I couldn't kill them." The animals had to be sacrificed at the end of the experiment so their brains could be examined. She described how the pigs, at the end, trusting her, let her lead them on their last walk, and how she had calmed them, by stroking them and talking to them, while they were killed. She was very distressed at their deaths—"I wept and wept."

She had just finished the story when we arrived at her home—a small two-story town house, some distance from the campus. Downstairs was comfortable, with the usual amenities—a sofa, armchairs, a television, pictures on the wall—but I had the sense that it was rarely used. There was an immense sepia print of her grandfather's farm in Grandin, North Dakota, in 1880; her other grandfather, she told me, had invented the automatic pilot for planes. These two were the progenitors, she feels, of her agricultural and engineering talents. Upstairs was her study, with her typewriter (but no word processor), absolutely bursting with manuscripts and books—books everywhere, spilling out of the study into every room in the house. (My own little house was once described as "a machine for working," and I had a somewhat similar impression of Temple's.) On one wall was a large cowhide with a huge collection of identity badges and caps, from the hundreds of conferences she has lectured at. I was amused to see, side by side, an I.D. from the American Meat Institute and one from the American Psychiatric Association. Temple has published more than a hundred papers, divided between those on animal behavior and facilities management and those on autism. The intimate blending of the two was epitomized by the medley of badges side by side.

Finally, without diffidence or embarrassment (emotions unknown to her), Temple showed me her bedroom, an austere room with whitewashed walls and a single bed and, next to the bed, a very large, strange-looking object. "What is that?" I asked.

"That's my squeeze machine," Temple replied. "Some people call it my hug machine."

The device had two heavy, slanting wooden sides, perhaps four by three feet each, pleasantly upholstered with a thick, soft padding. They were joined by hinges to a long, narrow bottom board to create a V-shaped, body-sized trough. There was a complex control box at one end, with heavy-duty tubes leading off to another device, in a closet. Temple showed me this as well. "It's an industrial compressor," she said, "the kind they use for filling tires."

"And what does this do?"

"It exerts a firm but comfortable pressure on the body, from the shoulders to the knees," Temple said. "Either a steady pressure or a variable one or a pulsating one, as you wish," she added. "You crawl into it—I'll show you—and turn the compressor on, and you have all the controls in your hand, here, right in front of you."

When I asked her why one should seek to submit one-self to such pressure, she told me. When she was a little girl, she said, she had longed to be hugged but had at the same time been terrified of all contact. When she was hugged, especially by a favorite (but vast) aunt, she felt overwhelmed, overcome by sensation; she had a sense of peacefulness and pleasure, but also of terror and engulfment. She started to have daydreams—she was just five at the time—of a magic machine that could squeeze her powerfully but gently, in a huglike way, and in a way entirely commanded and con-trolled by her. Years later, as an adolescent, she had seen a picture of a squeeze chute designed to hold or restrain calves and realized that that was it: a little modification to make it suitable for human use, and it could be her magic machine. She had considered other devices—inflatable suits, which could exert an even pressure all over the body—but the squeeze chute, in its simplicity, was quite irresistible.

Being of a practical turn of mind, she soon made her fan-tasy come true. The early models were crude, with some snags and glitches, but she eventually evolved a totally com-fortable, predictable system, capable of administering a "hug" with whatever parameters she desired. Her squeeze machine had worked exactly as she hoped, yielding the very sense of calmness and pleasure she had dreamed of since childhood. She could not have gone through the stormy days of college without her squeeze machine, she said. She could not turn to human beings for solace and comfort, but she could always turn to it. The machine, which she neither exhibited nor concealed but kept openly in her room at college, excited derision and suspicion and was seen by psychiatrists as a "regression" or "fixation"—something that needed to be psychoanalyzed and resolved. With her characteristic stubbornness, tenacity, single-mindedness, and bravery—along with a complete absence of inhibition or hesitation—Temple ignored all these comments and reactions and determined to find a scientific "validation" of her feelings.

Both before and after writing her doctoral thesis, she made a systematic investigation of the effects of deep pressure in autistic people, college students, and animals, and recently a paper of hers on this was published in the *Journal of Child and Adolescent Psychopharmacology*. Today, her squeeze machine, variously modified, is receiving extensive clinical trials. She has also become the world's foremost designer of squeeze chutes for cattle and has published, in the meat-industry and veterinary literature, many articles on the theory and practice of humane restraint and gentle holding.

While telling me this, Temple knelt down, then eased herself, facedown and at full length, into the "V," turned on the compressor (it took a minute for the master cylinder to fill), and twisted the controls. The sides converged, clasping her firmly, and then, as she made a small adjustment, relaxed their grip slightly. It was the most bizarre thing I had ever seen, and yet, for all its oddness, it was moving and simple. Certainly there was no doubt of its effect. Temple's voice, often loud and hard, became softer and gentler as she lay in her machine. "I concentrate on how gently I can do it," she said, and then spoke of the necessity of "totally giving in to it. . . . I'm getting real relaxed now," she added quietly. "I guess others get this through relation with other people."

It is not just pleasure or relaxation that Temple gets from the machine but, she maintains, a feeling for others. As she lies in her machine, she says, her thoughts often turn to her mother, her favorite aunt, her teachers. She feels their love for her, and hers for them. She feels that the machine opens a door into an otherwise closed emotional world and allows her, almost teaches her, to feel empathy for others.

After twenty minutes or so, she emerged, visibly calmer, emotionally less rigid (she says that a cat can easily sense the difference in her at these times), and asked me if I would care to try the machine.

Indeed, I was curious and scrambled into it, feeling a little foolish and self-conscious—but less so than I might have been, because Temple herself was so wholly lacking in self-consciousness. She turned the compressor on again and filled the master cylinder, and I experimented gingerly with the controls. It was indeed a sweet, calming feeling—one that reminded me of my deep-diving days long ago, when I felt the pressure of the water on my diving suit as a whole-body embrace.

from

THE STORY OF MY LIFE

HELEN KELLER

This is not a traditional story of healing. Helen Keller's disabilities—her blindness and deafness—were not illnesses that could be cured. Instead, it was her spirit that needed nurturing and healing. Before Anne Sullivan came into her life, Helen Keller was an angry child who would not accept help. But with love and patience, she was able to excel beyond anyone's expectations.

The most important day I remember in all my life is the one on which my teacher, Anne Mansfield Sullivan, came to me. I am filled with wonder when I consider the immeasurable contrasts between the two lives which it connects. It was the third of March, 1887, three months before I was seven years old.

On the afternoon of that eventful day I stood on the porch, dumb, expectant. I guessed vaguely from my mother's signs and from the hurrying to and fro in the house that something unusual was about to happen, so I went to the door and waited on the steps. The afternoon sun penetrated the mass of honeysuckle that covered the porch, and fell on my upturned face. My fingers lingered almost unconsciously on the familiar leaves and blossoms which had just come forth to greet the sweet southern spring. I did not know what the future held of marvel or surprise for me. Anger and bitterness had preyed upon me continually for weeks and a deep languor had succeeded this passionate struggle.

Have you ever been at sea in a dense fog, when it seemed as if a tangible white darkness shut you in, and the great ship, tense and anxious, groped her way toward the shore with plummet and sounding-line, and you waited with beating heart for something to happen? I was like that ship before my education began, only I was without compass or sounding-line, and had no way of knowing how near the harbour was. "Light! give me light!" was the wordless cry of my soul, and the light of love shone on me in that very hour.

I felt approaching footsteps. I stretched out my hand as I supposed to my mother. Some one took it, and I was caught up and held close in the arms of her who had come to reveal all things to me, and, more than all things else, to love me.

The morning after my teacher came she led me into her room and gave me a doll. The little blind children at the Perkins Institution had sent it and Laura Bridgman had dressed it; but I did not know this until afterward. When I had played with it a little while, Miss Sullivan slowly spelled into my hand the word "d-o-l-l." I was at once interested in this finger play and tried to imitate it. When I finally succeeded in making the letters correctly I was flushed with childish pleasure and pride. Running downstairs to my mother I held up my hand and made the letters for doll. I did not know that I was spelling a word or even that words existed; I was simply making my fingers go in monkey-like imitation. In the days that followed I learned to spell in this uncomprehending way a great many words, among them *pin, hat, cup* and a few verbs like *sit, stand* and *walk*. But my teacher had been with me several weeks before I understood that everything has a name.

One day, while I was playing with my new doll, Miss Sullivan put my big rag doll into my lap also, spelled, "d-o-l-l" and tried to make me understand that "d-o-l-l" applied to both. Earlier in the day we had had a tussle over the words "m-u-g" and "w-a-t-e-r." Miss Sullivan had tried to impress upon me that "m-u-g" is *mug* and that "w-a-t-e-r" is *water*, but I persisted in confounding the two. In despair she had dropped the subject for the time, only to renew it at the first opportunity. I became impatient at her repeated attempts and, seizing the new doll, I dashed it upon the floor. I was keenly delighted when I felt the fragments of the broken doll at my feet. Neither sorrow nor regret followed my passionate outburst. I had not loved the doll. In the still, dark world in which I lived there was no strong sentiment or tenderness. I felt my teacher sweep the fragments to one side of the hearth and I had a sense of satisfaction that the cause of my discomfort was removed. She brought me my hat, and I knew I was going out into the warm sunshine. This thought, if a wordless sensation may be called a thought, made me hop and skip with pleasure.

We walked down the path to the well-house, attracted by the fragrance of the honeysuckle with which it was covered. Someone was drawing water and my teacher placed my hand under the spout. As the cool stream gushed over one hand she spelled into the other the word *water*, first slowly, then rapidly. I stood still, my whole attention fixed upon the motions of her fingers. Suddenly I felt a misty consciousness as of something forgotten—a thrill of returning thought; and somehow the mystery of language was revealed to me. I knew then that "w-a-t-e-r" meant the wonderful cool something that was flowing over my hand. That living word awakened my soul, gave it light, hope, joy, set it free! There were barriers still, it is true, but barriers that could in time be swept away.

I left the well-house eager to learn. Everything had a name, and each name gave birth to a new thought. As we returned to the house every object which I touched seemed to quiver with life. That was because I saw everything with the strange, new sight that had come to me. On entering the door I remembered the doll I had broken. I felt my way to the hearth and picked up the pieces. I tried vainly to put them together. Then my eyes filled with tears; for I realized what I had done, and for the first time I felt repentance and sorrow.

I learned a great many new words that day. I do not remember what they all were; but I do know that *mother, father, sister, teacher* were among them—words that were to make the world blossom for me, "like Aaron's rod, with flowers." It would have been difficult to find a happier child than I was as I lay in my crib at the close of that eventful day and lived over the joys it had brought me, and for the first time longed for a new day to come.

I recall many incidents of the summer of 1887 that followed my soul's sudden awakening. I did nothing but explore with my hands and learn the name of every object that I touched; and the more I handled things and learned their names and uses, the more joyous and confident grew my sense of kinship with the rest of the world.

When the time of daisies and buttercups came Miss Sullivan took me by the hand across the fields, where men were preparing the earth for the seed, to the banks of the Tennessee River, and there, sitting on the warm grass. I had my first lesson in the beneficence of nature. I learned how the sun and the rain make to grow out of the ground every tree that is pleasant to the sight and good for food, how birds build their nests and live and thrive from land to land, how the squirrel, the deer, the lion and every other creature finds food and shelter. As my knowledge of things grew I felt more and more the delight of the world I was in. Long before I learned to do a sum in arithmetic or describe the shape of the earth, Miss Sullivan had taught me to find beauty in the fragrant woods, in every blade of grass, and in the curves and dimples of my baby sister's hand. She linked my earliest thoughts with nature, and made me feel that "birds and flowers and I were happy peers."

But about this time I had an experience which taught me that nature is not always kind. One day my teacher and I were returning from a long ramble. The morning had been fine, but it was growing warm and sultry when at last we turned our faces homeward. Two or three times we stopped to rest under a tree by the wayside. Our last halt was under a wild cherry tree a short distance from the house. The shade was grateful, and the tree was so easy to climb that with my teacher's assistance I was able to scramble to a seat in the branches. It was so cool up in the tree that Miss Sullivan proposed that we have our luncheon there. I promised to keep still while she went to the house to fetch it.

Suddenly a change passed over the tree. All the sun's warmth left the air. I knew the sky was black, because all the heat, which meant light to me, had died out of the atmosphere. A strange odour came up from the earth. I knew it, it was the odour that always precedes a thunderstorm, and a nameless fear clutched at my heart. I felt absolutely alone, cut off from my friends and the firm earth. The immense, the unknown, enfolded me. I remained still and expectant; a chilling terror crept over me. I longed for my teacher's return; but above all things I wanted to get down from that tree.

There was a moment of sinister silence, then a multitudinous stirring of the leaves. A shiver ran through the tree, and the wind sent forth a blast that would have knocked me off had I not clung to the branch with might and main. The tree swayed and strained. The small twigs snapped and fell about me in showers. A wild impulse to jump seized me, but terror held me fast. I crouched down in the fork of the tree. The branches lashed about me. I felt the intermittent jarring that came now and then, as if something heavy had fallen and the shock had traveled up till it reached the limb I sat on. It worked my suspense up to the highest point, and just as I was thinking the tree and I should fall together, my teacher seized my hand and helped me down. I clung to her, trembling with joy to feel the earth under my feet once more. I had learned a new lesson—that nature "wages open war against her children, and under softest touch hides treacherous claws."

After this experience it was a long time before I climbed another tree. The mere thought filled me with terror. It was the sweet allurement of the mimosa tree in full bloom that finally overcame my fears. One beautiful spring morning when I was alone in the summer-house, reading, I became aware of a wonderful subtle fragrance in the air. I started up and instinctively stretched out my hands. It seemed as if the spirit of spring had passed through the summerhouse. "What is it?" I asked, and the next minute I recognized the odour of the mimosa blossoms. I felt my way to the end of the garden, knowing that the mimosa tree was near the fence, at the turn of the path. Yes, there it was, all quivering in the warm sunshine, its blossom-laden branches almost touching the long grass. Was there ever anything so exquisitely beautiful in the world before! Its delicate blossoms shrank from the slightest earthly touch; it seemed as if a tree of paradise had been transplanted to earth. I made my way through a shower of petals to the great trunk and for one minute stood irresolute; then, putting my foot in the broad space between the forked branches, I pulled myself up into the tree. I had some difficulty in holding on, for the branches were very large and the bark hurt my hands. But I had a delicious sense that I was doing something unusual and wonderful, so I kept on climbing higher and higher, until I reached a little seat which somebody had built there so long ago that it had grown part of the tree itself. I sat there for a long, long time, feeling like a fairy on a rosy cloud. After that I spent many happy hours in my tree of paradise, thinking fair thoughts and dreaming bright dreams.

I had now the key to all language, and I was eager to learn to use it. Children who hear acquire language without any particular effort; the words that fall from others' lips they catch on the wing, as it were, delightedly, while the little deaf child must trap them by a slow and often painful process. But whatever the process, the result is wonderful. Gradually from naming an object we advance step by step until we have traversed the vast distance between our first stammered syllable and the sweep of thought in a line of Shakespeare.

At first, when my teacher told me about a new thing I asked very few questions. My ideas were vague, and my vocabulary was inadequate; but as my knowledge of things grew, and I learned more and more words, my field of inquiry broadened, and I would return again and again to the same subject, eager for further information. Sometimes a new word revived an image that some earlier experience had engraved on my brain.

I remember the morning that I first asked the meaning of the word, "love." This was before I knew many words. I had found a few early violets in the garden and brought them to my teacher. She tried to kiss me; but at that time I did not like to have any one kiss me except my mother. Miss Sullivan put her arm gently round me and spelled into my hand, "I love Helen."

"What is love?" I asked.

She drew me closer to her and said, "It is here," pointing to my heart, whose beats I was conscious of for the first time. Her words puzzled me very much because I did not then understand anything unless I touched it.

I smelt the violets in her hand and asked, half in words, half in signs, a question which meant, "Is love the sweetness of flowers?"

"No," said my teacher.

Again I thought. The warm sun was shining on us.

"Is this not love?" I asked, pointing in the direction from which the heat came, "Is this not love?"

It seemed to me that there could be nothing more beautiful than the sun, whose warmth makes all things grow. But Miss Sullivan shook her head, and I was greatly puzzled and disappointed. I thought it strange that my teacher could not show me love.

A day or two afterward I was stringing beads of different sizes in symmetrical groups—two large beads, three small ones, and so on. I had made many mistakes, and Miss Sullivan had pointed them out again and again with gentle patience. Finally I noticed a very obvious error in the sequence and for an instant I concentrated my attention on the lesson and tried to think how I should have arranged the beads. Miss Sullivan touched my forehead and spelled with decided emphasis, "Think."

In a flash I knew that the word was the name of the process that was going on in my head. This was my first conscious perception of an abstract idea.

For a long time I was still—I was not thinking of the beads in my lap, but trying to find a meaning for "love" in the light of this new idea. The sun had been under a cloud all day, and there had been brief showers; but suddenly the sun broke forth in all its southern splendour.

Again I asked my teacher, "Is this not love?"

"Love is something like the clouds that were in the sky before the sun came out," she replied. Then in simpler words than these, which at that time I could not have understood, she explained: "You cannot touch the clouds, you know; but you feel the rain and know how glad the flowers and the thirsty earth are to have it after a hot day. You cannot touch

278

love either; but you feel the sweetness that it pours into everything. Without love you would not be happy or want to play."

The beautiful truth burst upon my mind—I felt that there were invisible lines stretched between my spirit and the spirits of others.

From the beginning of my education Miss Sullivan made it a practice to speak to me as she would speak to any hearing child; the only difference was that she spelled the sentences into my hand instead of speaking them. If I did not know the words and idioms necessary to express my thoughts she supplied them, even suggesting conversation when I was unable to keep up my end of the dialogue.

This process was continued for several years; for the deaf child does not learn in a month, or even in two or three years, the numberless idioms and expressions used in the simplest daily intercourse. The little hearing child learns these from constant repetition and imitation. The conversation he hears in his home stimulates his mind and suggests topics and calls forth the spontaneous expression of his own thoughts. This natural exchange of ideas is denied to the deaf child. My teacher, realizing this, determined to supply the kinds of stimuli I lacked. This she did by repeating to me as far as possible, verbatim, what she heard, and by showing me how I could take part in the conversation. But it was a long time before I ventured to take the initiative, and still longer before I could find something appropriate to say at the right time.

The deaf and the blind find it very difficult to acquire the amenities of conversation. How much more this difficulty must be augmented in the case of those who are both deaf and blind! They cannot distinguish the tone of the voice or, without assistance, go up and down the gamut of tones that give significance to words; nor can they watch the expression of the speaker's face, and a look is often the very soul of what one says.

The next important step in my education was learning to read.

As soon as I could spell a few words my teacher gave me slips of cardboard on which were printed words in raised letters. I quickly learned that each printed word stood for an object, an act, or a quality. I had a frame in which I could arrange the words in little sentences; but before I ever put sentences in the frame I used to make them in objects. I found the slips of paper which represented, for example, "doll," "is," "on," "bed" and placed each name on its object; then I put my doll on the bed with the words *is, on, bed* arranged beside the doll, thus making a sentence of the words, and at the same time carrying out the idea of the sentence with the things themselves.

One day, Miss Sullivan tells me, I pinned the word *girl*

on my pinafore and stood in the wardrobe. On the shelf I arranged the words, *is, in, wardrobe.* Nothing delighted me so much as this game. My teacher and I played it for hours at a time. Often everything in the room was arranged in object sentences.

From the printed slip it was but a step to the printed book. I took my "Reader for Beginners" and hunted for the words I knew; when I found them my joy was like that of a game of hide-and-seek. Thus I began to read. Of the time when I began to read connected stories I shall speak later.

For a long time I had no regular lessons. Even when I studied most earnestly it seemed more like play than work. Everything Miss Sullivan taught me she illustrated by a beautiful story or a poem. Whenever anything delighted or interested me she talked it over with me just as if she were a little girl herself. What many children think of with dread, as a painful plodding through grammar, hard sums and harder definitions, is to-day one of my most precious memories.

I cannot explain the peculiar sympathy Miss Sullivan had with my pleasures and desires. Perhaps it was the result of long association with the blind. Added to this she had a wonderful faculty for description. She went quickly over uninteresting details, and never nagged me with questions to see if I remembered the day-before-yesterday's lesson. She introduced dry technicalities of science little by little, making every subject so real that I could not help remembering what she taught.

We read and studied out of doors, preferring the sunlit woods to the house. All my early lessons have in them the breath of the woods—the fine, resinous odour of pine needles, blended with the perfume of wild grapes. Seated in the gracious shade of a wild tulip tree, I learned to think that everything has a lesson and a suggestion. "The loveliness of things taught me all their use." Indeed, everything that could hum, or buzz, or sing, or bloom, had a part in my education— noisy-throated frogs, katydids and crickets held in my hand until, forgetting their embarrassment, they trilled their reedy note, little downy chickens and wildflowers, the dogwood blossoms, meadow-violets and budding fruit trees. I felt the bursting cotton-bolls and fingered their soft fiber and fuzzy seeds; I felt the low soughing of the wind through the cornstalks, the silky rustling of the long leaves, and the indignant snort of my pony, as we caught him in the pasture and put the bit in his mouth—ah me! how well I remember the spicy, clovery smell of his breath!

Sometimes I rose at dawn and stole into the garden while the heavy dew lay on the grass and flowers. Few know what joy it is to feel the roses pressing softly into the hand, or the beautiful motion of the lilies as they sway in the morning breeze. Sometimes I caught an insect in the flower I was plucking, and I felt the faint noise of a pair of wings rubbed together in a sudden terror, as the little creature became aware of a pressure from without.

Another favourite haunt of mine was the orchard, where the fruit ripened early in July. The large, downy peaches would reach themselves into my hand, and as the joyous breezes flew about the trees the apples tumbled at my feet. Oh, the delight with which I gathered up the fruit in my pinafore, pressed my face against the smooth cheeks of the apples, still warm from the sun, and skipped back to the house!

Our favourite walk was to Keller's Landing, an old tumble-down lumber-wharf on the Tennessee River, used during the Civil War to land soldiers. There we spent many happy hours and played at learning geography. I built dams of pebbles, made islands and lakes, and dug river-beds, all for fun, and never dreamed that I was learning a lesson. I listened with increasing wonder to Miss Sullivan's descriptions of the great round world with its burning mountains, buried cities, moving rivers of ice, and many other things as strange. She made raised maps in clay, so that I could feel the mountain ridges and valleys, and follow with my fingers the devious course of rivers. I liked this, too; but the division of the earth into zones and poles confused and teased my mind. The illustrative strings and the orange sticks representing the poles seemed so real that even to this day the mere mention of temperature zone suggests a series of twine circles; and I believe that if any one should set about it he could convince me that white bears actually climb the North Pole.

Arithmetic seems to have been the only study I did not

like. From the first I was not interested in the science of numbers. Miss Sullivan tried to teach me to count by stringing beads in groups, and by arranging kindergarten straws I learned to add and subtract. I never had patience to arrange more than five or six groups at a time. When I had accomplished this my conscience was at rest for the day, and I went out quickly to find my playmates.

In the same leisurely manner I studied zoölogy and botany.

Once a gentleman, whose name I have forgotten, sent me a collection of fossils—tiny mollusk shells beautifully marked, and bits of sandstone with the print of birds' claws, and a lovely fern in bas-relief. These were the keys which unlocked the treasures of the antediluvian world for me. With trembling fingers I listened to Miss Sullivan's descriptions of the terrible beasts with uncouth, unpronounceable names, which once went tramping through the primeval forests, tearing down the branches of gigantic trees for food, and died in the dismal swamps of an unknown age. For a long time these strange creatures haunted my dreams, and this gloomy period formed a somber background to the joyous Now, filled with sunshine and roses and echoing with the gentle beat of my pony's hoof.

Another time a beautiful shell was given me, and with a child's surprise and delight I learned how a tiny mollusk had built the lustrous coil for his dwelling place, and how on still nights, when there is no breeze stirring the waves, the Nautilus sails on the blue waters of the Indian Ocean in his "ship of pearl." After I had learned a great many interesting things about the life and habits of the children of the sea—how in the midst of dashing waves the little polyps build the beautiful coral isles of the Pacific, and the foraminifera have made the chalkhills of many a land—my teacher read me "The Chambered Nautilus," and showed me that the shell-building process of the mollusks is symbolical of the development of the mind. Just as the wonder-working mantle of the Nautilus changes the material it absorbs from the water and makes it a part of itself, so the bits of knowledge one gathers undergo a similar change and become pearls of thought.

Again, it was the growth of a plant that furnished the text for a lesson. We bought a lily and set it in a sunny window. Very soon the green, pointed buds showed signs of opening. The slender, fingerlike leaves on the outside opened slowly, reluctant, I thought, to reveal the loveliness they hid; once having made a start, however, the opening process went on rapidly, but in order and systematically. There was always one bud larger and more beautiful than the rest, which pushed her outer covering back with more pomp, as if the beauty in soft, silky robes knew that she was the lily-queen by right divine, while her more timid sisters doffed their green hoods shyly, until the whole plant was one nodding bough of loveliness and fragrance.

Once there were eleven tadpoles in a glass globe set in a window full of plants. I remember the eagerness with which I made discoveries about them. It was great fun to plunge my hand into the bowl and feel the tadpoles frisk about, and to let them slip and slide between my fingers. One day a more ambitious fellow leaped beyond the edge of the bowl and fell on the floor, where I found him to all appearance more dead than alive. The only sign of life was a slight wriggling of his tail. But no sooner had he returned to his element than he darted to the bottom, swimming round and round in joyous activity. He had made his leap, he had seen the great world, and was content to stay in his pretty glass house under the big fuchsia tree until he attained the dignity of froghood. Then he went to live in the leafy pool at the end of the garden, where he made the summer nights musical with his quaint love-song.

Thus I learned from life itself. At the beginning I was only a little mass of possibilities. It was my teacher who unfolded and developed them. When she came, everything about me breathed of love and joy and was full of meaning. She has never since let pass an opportunity to point out the beauty that is in everything, nor has she ceased trying in thought and action and example to make my life sweet and useful.

It was my teacher's genius, her quick sympathy, her loving tact which made the first years of my education so beautiful. It was because she seized the right moment to impart knowledge that made it so pleasant and acceptable to me. She realized that a child's mind is like a shallow brook which ripples and dances merrily over the stony course of its education and reflects here a flower, there a bush, yonder a fleecy cloud; and she attempted to guide my mind on its way, knowing that like a brook it should be fed by mountain streams and hidden springs, until it broadened out into a deep river, capable of reflecting in its placid surface, billowy hills, the luminous shadows of trees and the blue heavens, as well as the sweet face of a little flower.

Any teacher can take a child to the classroom, but not every teacher can make him learn. He will not work joyously unless he feels that liberty is his, whether he is busy or at rest; he must feel the flush of victory and the heart-sinking of disappointment before he takes with a will the tasks distasteful to him and resolves to dance his way bravely through a dull routine of textbooks.

My teacher is so near to me that I scarcely think of myself apart from her. How much of my delight in all beautiful things is innate, and how much is due to her influence, I can never tell. I feel that her being is inseparable from my own, and that the footsteps of my life are in hers. All the best of me belongs to her—there is not a talent, or an inspiration or a joy in me that has not awakened by her loving touch.

from

INSIDE THE HALO AND BEYOND

MAXINE KUMIN

*Pulitzer Prize–winning poet Maxine Kumin suffered
an injury to her spinal cord during a fall from her
horse that should have killed her or left her paralyzed.
However, less than a year later, she was walking—
and even riding her horse again. It may have not
only been luck, strength of character, and
family which helped her through—but
the cathartic power of putting
her struggle into words.*

. . . Imagine a bird cage big enough for a large squawking parrot. Nothing fancy; no rococo bars with curlicues at the top, just a sturdy cage fashioned from titanium and graphite, but missing a few bars front and back. Imagine a human head inside the cage fastened by four titanium pins that dig into the skull. The pins are as sharp as ice picks. I wake up in this cage, disoriented, desperate, sicker than I have ever been. No feeling in my arms or legs, but a vague sense that my head is entrapped forever. No movement left or right, up or down. I am a stationary parrot inside my strict cage.

Some orthopedic wag dubbed this form of axial traction a halo. First applied in 1959, it was attached to a rigid full-body cast and was used to immobilize paralyzed polio patients whose airways were in danger because they could not hold their heads upright. Later, its usage extended to postop patients with cervical spine injuries, tumor removals, and congenital spinal malformations. The early halos, weighing upwards of ten pounds, were made of metal, which was opaque to X ray and was not MRI or CT scan compatible. Modern halos are made of lightweight composites. The full-body cast has given way to an adjustable plastic vest and the metal uprights of the cage are made of anodized metals so that they don't "seize" during tightening. Knurled bars are designed to prevent slipping; the entire halo must remain structurally intact. . . .

Thousands of people are confined in halo restraints in the United States and Europe every year. At least ten companies are manufacturing these devices in the U.S. alone. Gradually I meet others of my kind, doggedly slogging around under the burden of our equipment, some tipped slightly forward, some tipped slightly back, to compensate for the neck fractures that landed us in this predicament in the first place.

I don't remember, or choose to remember, much about how I got here. It was Kathy who stabilized my head for almost an hour as I lay paralyzed on the field, Kathy who sent someone to call the rescue squad and who lobbied, once they arrived, for them to call in the Medivac team. Getting a helicopter takes protocol in this rural area, but once it was on the ground beside me, only six or eight minutes elapsed before I was airlifted to a local major medical center. I remember coming to and begging for painkillers en route, which the team is not permitted to administer. I remember kind strangers calling me "honey" and "sweetheart" and how this intimacy surprised me. I did not know then that they were afraid I would not survive the trip.

The vertebrae I broke are at the very top of the spinal column: C1, which is ring-shaped and fits around the odontoid, C2, which looks rather like a thumb. In the trade, one form of C2 break is known as the hangman's fracture, because the same vertebra is snapped when the trapdoor opens under the gallows. Mine, I learn long after the fact, is a Type II fracture, located in the narrowest region of the odontoid, the "waist" of the thumb.

Things are coming back to me little by little, but I am stuffing them down in a dirty laundry bag to be reviewed and shaken out later, when I get my courage back. I realize from the outset, though, that I've lost all feeling in all four limbs, and I think at that moment I'd rather be dead. In fact, thinking about being dead absorbs a lot of my energy these first days. While I am pinioned flat on my back, I am almost as black and blue with grief and guilt for causing anguish to my family as is my torn body. I have two black eyes and a large contusion on my right cheekbone. My whole right side is purple, shoulder and arm especially brilliant. Apparently I have also punctured a lung, broken eleven ribs, bruised a kidney and my liver, and suffered considerable internal bleeding. I've been given two units of packed red blood cells. There's an IV line in the vein below my right shoulder supplying me with morphine and glucose and an oxygen tank feeds the tubes in my nostrils. These accompany me as I am wheeled from CT scan to angiogram to MRI.

(Later, I learn from my medical records, which I devour with hungry voyeurism, that I occasionally came to and spoke clearly while the paramedics applied a cervical spine board and turned me over, like an immense beetle specimen, for transport. From my husband Victor's E-mails to family and friends, I further learn how many people were pulling for me from the outset. His communiqués are detailed and invariably upbeat, even in the first worst days: "Max's eye blink responses have indicated alertness and she has begun to whisper-talk with the breathing tube out. Breathing gets better by the hour. Hematomas are receding. She's a REAL fighter which is of course why I wanted to marry her!") . . .

July 23

The family assembles. Our son Danny, who lives about thirty miles from our farm, raced up the highway from the southern part of the state where he had been blissfully reading the *New York Times*, a luxury in rural New Hampshire, while his Saab was being lubricated.

"You never saw a car come off a lift so fast," he tells me long after the fact. Notorious for crowding the speed limit as a matter of course, he says, "I more than exceeded it; I abolished it."

Daughter Judith, press officer for the United Nations High Commission for Refugees in Geneva, Switzerland, took the first available flight, arrived in Boston within thirty-six hours of my debacle, rented a car, and hurried north. Our older daughter, Jane, in close touch by phone, came a few days later from San Francisco. Dan's' wife Libby came evenings; after some discussion, she brought their eight-year-old son with her.

"I wasn't exactly scared," Noah told me months later. "I mean, I didn't know who you were, you looked so awful on the bed. But I asked Mom when you would be Ga [the name he calls me] again and she said it would take a while but it would happen.". . .

July 27

Neurological response has returned to my arms. A volleyball team of orthopedists and orthopedic residents assembles at my bedside. Even in my morphine-induced haze, I resent the fact that they poke, prod, and squeeze, and speak to each other but never directly to me. When they leave, my nurse has a few things to say on the subject of orthopedists. I treasure this one: "Orthopedic surgeons are like little boys with Meccano toys [the British equivalent of our Erector sets]. They like to take things apart and put them together again. they never have to look people in the eye."

Today I am released from traction, and the halo vest (which together with the bird cage contraption immobilizes my head, neck and shoulders) is put on. I am moved onto a regular hospital bed. The various IV lines are removed. A nurse cranks the back of the bed up a little, and for the first time in a week I see something other than the ceiling. Danny sits beside me feeding me ice chips one at a time. He is very tactful with the chips; I can't tolerate having anything held up to my face without my express consent. Even this hand that I know and love is a menace. He waits until I signal with a small nod, then offers me another sliver of ice from the plastic spoon. . . .

August 11

Three weeks have gone by since the accident. This is my first full day in the rehab hospital. A procession of nurses and aides and social workers files in and out to introduce themselves. Everybody wants to know how I broke my neck. I say merely that I had a carriage-driving accident. The social worker questions me further: "But how do you feel about your accident?" Although shaken, my tactic with her is not to reply. (In the subsequent medical report I am said to be "slightly confused, unable to relate history well.")

When I retell this incident to Judith she says it reminds her of an interview she saw recently with an Iraqi Kurdish refugee who had arrived, via Turkey, by small boat on a Greek island. His wife and baby had drowned during the voyage. The television reporter shoved a microphone into his face and asked him: "How do you feel about your decision to flee Iraq, now that your wife and child have died?"

How I feel about my accident defies description. I don't let myself come close to reviewing the actual event, except to think over and over that it would have been better to have been killed outright. Yes, my wonderful family would have grieved, but eventually they would have gotten on with their lives. Yes, Victor, above all others, would have been terribly bereft, but with his proactive and optimistic nature, he too would have picked up the pieces of his life and gotten on with it. Perhaps he would sell the farm, move to the seacoast which he loves, and resume sailing. Possibly he would go back to the city with its subways and skyscrapers and museums and theaters—for aren't these the things I lured him away from? How I feel about my accident is quite simply that I screwed up everybody's life by living through it. . . .

August 15

My first trip down to the gym, via wheelchair. It's a great open space with windows on two sides beckoning the viewer to shrubbery, flowers, grass, and a grid of surfaces designed to test the balance skills of the newly walking—bricks, a boardwalk, gravelly asphalt, ramps, and sturdy stairs with double banisters. I think to myself that I'll never be up to these challenges.

"You'll walk," the therapists tell me. "You will positively absolutely learn to walk and we're here to teach you." My initial chore is to learn to rise from the wheelchair and grab onto Eva. It's all so hard and so tiring. I wish everyone would go away and leave me alone.

I am to have at least two sessions each day of physical

and occupational therapy. The PTs work with legs, endurance, and balance. The OTs work on arms, hands, and fingers. My range of motion is almost nonexistent and I can hold neither a cup nor a spoon. In addition, I am assigned a speech therapist to assess my mild aphasia, which, along with some retrograde amnesia, is thought to be a residual of the concussion.

The two PTs who work with me are kind but demanding. Sue is tall and slim, somewhat reserved, very well spoken. She started in medical school and then changed direction. Wendy, a high school dropout, is stocky, blond, and tough. Her attitude is no-nonsense, let's get it done, and I will never lie to you. Both of them seem to think I can perform what are to me impossible feats of endurance. They chivvy and push me; I must. To walk forty steps with one of them holding me up by my voyaging belt—a broad woven band worn around the waist—and the other on the alert to catch me if I stumble becomes a heroic journey. My halo is no excuse; they've dealt with dozens of spinal cord patients in halos who have learned to stand up straight, keep their balance, and swing their arms as they walk. "Come on, let's go!" they say. And go again. After every session I am wheeled back upstairs, collapse on my bed, and drift into uneasy sleep, only to be fetched awake by an aide for the next session.

Transferred from wheelchair to bed, I have just dozed off

when the speech therapist arrives to investigate my deficiencies. My speech appears haltingly slow to me; some of my words feel slurred. These problems, she assures me, will pass. She hazards the opinion that I am only conscious of these marginal changes because of my past history of speaking in public. More troubling are the gaps—words I cannot find. "Give me an example," she says.

"The word for the thing you turn eggs over with. Or pancakes."

"Think of another way to describe it," she urges. "What is it made of? Is it thin or thick?"

"It's made of metal," I say petulantly, "it's broad, with cutouts. And it flexes." We wallow around in this conundrum for a few minutes until suddenly the word appears. "Spatula!" I say.

Equally troubling to me is the way my voice sounds. I think I am slurring my words, as if I have had too much to drink. I enunciate elaborately, but when I do this, I feel I am talking too slowly, like a recent stroke victim. My therapist explains that I lost consciousness for several minutes following the accident and the concussion I sustained may be responsible for these side effects. She finds them barely perceptible. Much as I want to be reassured, I don't quite trust this assessment.

As we get to know each other, I begin to look forward to her comforting presence each day, even if our session only lasts twenty minutes or so. She is reading my essays and stories in *Women, Animals, and Vegetables*, having found a copy in her local library. Our conversations are inconsequential but they help to restore my self esteem; I begin to reabsorb the being I was before the accident. Even in my reduced, supine position, I am not quite a total prisoner. I am capable of sustained thought. I can communicate that thought. . . .

August 17

Judith arrives today with her laptop computer. Actually, she's brought it along a few times before this and used it to catch up on UN business while I attend PT or doze, exhausted, after a learning-to-walk session. But today she announces her intent.

"Mom, you're always saying that if you're a writer nothing is ever all for nothing. I'm going to take dictation, starting now. Let's write about this." She gestures around the room. "I know you can do it. We'll get an article out of it! You talk and I'll type."

And so it begins. From this day on we find some place to hide for forty-five minutes or an hour, or even a little longer. I do indeed talk. Everything comes pouring out: the grief, anger, frustration, fear—not in these abstract words, but in the feelings they evoke. I particularize as best I can.

We try to keep this activity secret. I don't want to trade on my status as a writer and I especially don't want any prying eyes to see what we're doing. Judith is very discreet.

She prints out pages at home and brings them to me to read the next day. I can't even separate the pages myself with my numb fingers; she turns them for me one at a time. . . .

September 4

. . . I am trundled down the hall to the dead end—the opposite end from my old room, where I could overhear every conversation, mostly concerning boyfriends or husbands, that took place at the noisy nurses' station. My new roommate, Nicole, is a very attractive twenty-one-year-old woman who has lost the use of her legs. The prospects for her regaining any feeling at all in them are dim. She is clamped into a hard plastic clamshell brace that covers her entire torso; it must stay in place for three months until her back heals from the very extensive surgery. (Later, she makes a bracelet of the fifty-four staples removed from her incision.) Even though her accident—she fell off a second-story ladder—occurred just four weeks ago, she is agile in her wheelchair. In spite of the ever-present pain she feels, in spite of the grim prognosis she faces, Nicole exudes optimism. That very afternoon she leaves to attend a meeting on kayaking saying, "Now this is a sport I can do."

Judith tells me she learned from the case manager that there had been a heated staff meeting to discuss whether Nicole and I should room together, since although we are both spinal cord injuries, fifty-two years separate us.

September 5

Nicole is spending the night with her husband in the hospital's guest suite; family visits are encouraged. The new night nurse helps me to get ready for bed. Leaving, she closes the door firmly. I hear the latch click shut and am seized with an irrational panic. My ears fill with roaring and shrieking. My side rails are up, I am not strong enough yet to extricate myself from the bed without assistance. Delirious with fear, unable even to breathe, I am trapped. I pound and pound on my call button.

Where did this terror come from? In kindergarten at the Convent of the Sisters of St. Joseph, conveniently next door to the house I grew up in, I was told stories of the martyrdom of nuns. They died in a bizarre array of circumstances, but the story I could never let go of was the tale of the nun who was pressed slowly to death. Faithful to the end, she welcomed it. Nothing seemed more terrible to my five-year-old imagination. Now, death by suffocation, death by squeezing the air out of your lungs, the death I came so close to on July 21 reasserts itself in every even mildly claustrophobic situation I encounter—in the elevator, on an examining table, in a room with the door closed.

Martyrdom, penitence, submission were the lessons I absorbed in parochial school. The public school was a mile away; there was no bussing. Moreover, I could come home for lunch. My parents—minimally observant Jews—thought that I was too young to absorb the tenets of Catholicism. They didn't understand how impressionable I was. A life-size crucifix hung at the end of the classrooms hallway; if I squinted at it hard enough, I could make Jesus writhe, dying for all of us over and over. The lives of the saints also reinforced what I already knew from observing my father's dedication to work: one must be prepared to endure every hardship to be saved. In suffering seek salvation, was the message.

Now, I am a penitent like my darling nun, forced to submit not to death by squeezing, but to carrying my halo on my shoulders, my head cantilevered in a forward position, eye level with everyone's navel. I have no peripheral vision and must turn my entire body to see to the left or the right. Every bodily activity I once took for granted is a difficult hurdle. The so-called shower from the waist down as I perch on the shower bench requires the help of an aide to support the shower wand. Trammelled by the shoulder pieces that hold the halo in place, I cannot reach my own feet. It is exquisite torture to have foreign hands washing between my toes and then invading them further to dry them. An aide also must help me dress and undress. In addition to the size 22 V necks, Judith has sacrificed three of my T-shirts by slitting the shoulder seams wide enough to accommodate the halo frame. Squirming into and out of them, even with assistance, is an ordeal. . . .

September 10

One of my physical therapists is practicing a form of relaxation known as Reiki in hopes of achieving some pain relief for me. She puts her hands gently on my face. I flail out in all directions and somehow am able to get upright in my terror. Tears stream down my cheeks. This is not the only time I react to what I perceive as entrapment like a helpless child battling nighttime demons.

My old friend Tim O'Brien, who once wrestled fallen trees out of our pastures in New Hampshire, confessed recently in an interview with the *New York Times* that in his recurring nightmare the Vietnam War is still going on. Night after night he is drafted again. My own terror began with that first terrible moment when I hit the ground, lost all feeling in arms and legs, and found I could not breathe.

Now seven weeks have elapsed and I am up to learning the details of the first days after my accident. I ask for and receive the discharge summary from the critical care hospital. Reading it, I begin to understand my claustrophobia: "The patient unfortunately had to be intubated in the emergency room because of the development of stridor and the need to protect her airway." Translation: Like my martyred nun, I was suffocating.

I am told the terrors will diminish. I am told to practice deep breathing. But after sunset is still the worst time. Every night I am confronted anew by a mounting sense of dread. I cannot tolerate having the door closed, and cannot sleep with it open. Even with medication, there are nights when sleep evades me. If only, like Ra, I could drop down under the world and begin the slow journey back to sunrise. . . .

September 24

Homecoming day! Victor comes to collect me. The PTs and OTs see us out, along with my case manager and assorted well-wishers, even knowing I will be back in five days to begin outpatient therapy. I try to keep up a good front; I am supposed to be overjoyed, elated, at returning to my native heath, but in truth I am full of foreboding. They are kicking me out of the nest. Now I must go back into the world, still trammelled by this ever more oppressive halo, and try to resume my old life.

Judith has left a variety of prepared meals that need only to be moved from freezer to microwave, and in short order Victor serves up a sumptuous meal. I am unable to eat most of it but I try to share his enthusiasm. My fatigue is overwhelming. (Fatigue, in fact, is my chief complaint for the next several weeks. I am so consistently tired that I begin to fantasize other ailments—leukemia, an undiscovered cancer, a blocked artery.) It seems that I am always in the process of lying down or struggling up to find some more comfortable place to stretch out in—a sofa, a studio couch, the double bed in the little back bedroom. I am grateful for the prescriptions for Restoril and Xanax that came home with me. These have been my nightly mainstays for the last two months, easing me to sleep inside my cage in a fixed position on my back. Even so, I rarely manage more than five hours of unconsciousness on any given night . . .

October 10
I tie my own shoes for the first time. The average four-year-old has somewhat more dexterity than I. Still, I've made the loop with my right hand and poked the other loop through with my left and finally, after several tries, caught it with my sensationless thumb and forefinger and achieved a lopsided bow. "No cheerleading, please," I say to Victor, who oversees this project. He understands the mixture of triumph and shame I feel . . .

October 21
This is a tense day. I don't know what to expect. Danny comes to drive me to the hospital. Once again I am subjected in my halo to the savageries of the rutted dirt roads.

It is always comforting to travel with Danny. Even if he isn't relaxed he puts up a good front and we manage light-hearted chat during the hour-long trip. He too is a freelance writer, but in the electronic and acoustical fields. A regular contributing editor for several audio-video magazines, he has deadlines to meet. Often he'll call me in a mock-distraught tone to ask if I can hunt up the source of a quote he wants to use. If neither of us can find it, he falls back on "As one nineteenth-century pundit said . . ." Frequently we exchange confidences about writer's block, disagree about a book we have both read, or commiserate about editors who always want a project completed the day after they invented it.

Danny calls me Ma, as opposed to Mom. I think he took this up in his early teens as a gibe directed at the sanctity of motherhood. He was, after all, a child of the sixties. Gradually it evolved into an affectionate term. I've come to depend on him mightily these last six or seven years as I made the transition from typewriter to word processor and from that capability to E-mail. Because his office is in his house, I can almost always consult him when I hit a snag. He tries to be patient with my lack of comprehension; even *Macs for Dummies* is often beyond my intelligence quotient.

Happiest picking away at ideas and concepts on his own, in another era Danny might have been a Talmudic scholar. His work hours may stretch well past midnight, absorb a Sunday, or go by the board for two or three days in a row. Once a week he plays electric guitar in a group; although some are paying gigs, he considers them recreation. In adolescence he studied clarinet, saxophone and bassoon and achieved reasonable proficiency on all. While a student at Bennington College, he played bassoon with the Vermont Symphony, driving to the forty-dollar-a-night rehearsals at opposite ends of the state in his VW Bug. He can fake it, as he likes to say, on the double bass and piano, and once taxed me with the question, "Why didn't you make me take piano lessons?"

"Piano lessons? I couldn't even get you to pick up your underwear," I remember saying.

A music major, he started composing while at Bennington. When Anne Sexton formed her poetry/rock group, "Anne Sexton and Her Kind," Danny provided original music for the background to her poem "The Little Peasant." Still writing music at intervals, he said to me once that what he'd really like to be doing is composing string quartets instead of making a living.

"A couple of centuries ago," he said, "I could have had a patron."

Now he has fruit trees, a few raised vegetable beds aesthetically placed to enhance the greensward he cultivates, and this coming summer he plans to add an asparagus trench I've promised to supply with three-year-old roots. Baltimore orioles grace his trees. He's quite likely to call me at an odd hour to report on a kingfisher, a saw-whet owl, a scarlet tanager. Wild turkeys are a commonplace now on both our properties, but sighting a fox is rare enough to comment on. Danny is absolutely sure that what woke him two nights in a row last May whiffling around under the bird feeder was a black bear. I am willing to cede him that.

Today I have packed a book bag with pillow, pain pills,

and two magazines; this was a good idea because we are put on hold in the waiting room for an hour and a half after we arrive. There is no appropriate chair for a halo-wearer. My discomfort level escalates minute by minute.

First there is a routine standing X ray. Then, the CT scan. My head in a large white doughnut affair, I lie still while the machine takes dozens of cross-sectional pictures of my neck. Then another lengthy wait, as there is "some problem" with the fluoroscope. It requires conscripting every reserve not to panic while I wait to find out whether I am healing or heading for surgery.

Danny is permitted to stay for the fluoroscopy. They give him a lead apron to put on and he stands on the sidelines, a reassuring presence. The orthopedic surgeon unscrews the bars that run from the halo to the vest, thus liberating my head for the first time in three months. I am then instructed to lean my head back as far as possible, which turns out not to be very far at all. Danny says: "That's about as far back as she was ever able to reach." That seems to satisfy the doctor. Next I am asked to flex the other way. My neck, unused to any movement at all, seems to jitter and wobble the few inches I am able to move it. But before I even try to lower my head, I ask the surgeon, "Can you guarantee my head won't fall off in this maneuver?" Either in humor or as protection against a lawsuit, he responds: "No, I can't guarantee it. But I don't think it will."

Pictures are taken but they are deemed insufficient evidence and the whole procedure has to be repeated. This time I dare to try harder and am able to bend my chin a bit lower. The surgeon overlays the extension and flexion prints and studies them. The bones have not moved. He says that the neck appears stable but he can't figure out why, as there is no physical evidence of fusion. He has never seen this before. He is mystified.

He replaces the bars on the left side of my halo to provide stability, and sends me back for a second CT scan. Danny is not certain that I can lie down on the gurney with only one side of the halo attached, and the technician shares his concern. There is a hasty telephone conference. Then we proceed with the halo still unattached on one side.

Back to the surgeon's office, another lengthy walk from one wing to the next. Danny and I wait for him to study all the films on his light box. Something strange begins to happen to my vision. Lightning jags appear all around the periphery and I recognize I am experiencing the aura that precedes a migraine. This has occurred possibly four times in my life, always triggered by bright sunlight, particularly on snow. But luckily I have never gotten the headache that usually follows an aura.

The surgeon comes back in and announces he is removing the halo. While he is undoing one of the back pins I tell him about the aura, and then, as he moves to the remaining front pin, the whole apparatus releases as if it had been clamped to my skull on springs. The aura vanishes just as suddenly as it appeared. He has no explanation for this phenomenon. In fact, he seems totally uninterested in it. The forehead pin sites are bloody. The surgeon dabs at them with sterile gauze and provides further gauze packs just in case. Then he fits me with a tall rigid foam neck collar, admonishing me that it must never be removed, except for my daily shower, and then only under supervision. He will see me, he says, in a week's time.

I am dumbfounded by my good fortune. Even though surgery has merely been postponed, not positively cancelled, I am out of the halo. I hardly dare move my head the few inches of freedom the collar allows.

"It's like a kid learning to ride a bicycle," he says. "Joyous and scared at the same time."

This is the first empathetic remark he has made. I am touched by it.

It's already two o'clock. We have fifteen minutes before my appointment for an ultrasound of my uterus. It was only when I asked for and received a copy of my medical records, while in the rehab hospital, that I discovered that my family had been worrying about yet another problem. The MRI done shortly after my accident had shown a large mass outside the uterus. My gynecologist was consulted but there was a conspiracy not to tell me about this. It was felt I had enough on my plate.

Today the ultrasound shows no mass, but it does reveal

a not very significant fibroid in the upper reaches of the uterus. It is hypothesized that the mass was merely coagulated blood from my rather extensive internal bleeding, and that after thirteen weeks it has been reabsorbed. The radiologist who comes in to give me this news is a rather starchy gentleman with upright bearing and a slight paunch. He wants to know about my accident, how it happened and where. And rather reluctantly, I give him a brief account. I tell him about my friend Kathy, an emergency room nurse in this facility, who saved my life.

"Most people's accidents are quite boring, you know," he says, "but yours is really very interesting. Very interesting! You shouldn't have lived through it and yet here you are."

I murmur some appropriate response.

"As far as I'm concerned," he says, "the only fit place for horses is in an Alpo can."

I am still lying on the examining table and am perfectly positioned to kick this man in the groin. The intravaginal probe still in place restrains me from yielding to the impulse. Meanwhile, Danny has gone to the phone to deliver the good news of postponed surgery and halo removal to Victor, who doesn't answer. He leaves a message on the machine.

It is a little past 4 p.m. when we return home. Judith has just preceded us, having rented a car at the airport after her flight from Geneva. From the expression on her face I can tell that the phone message never got through. We have a giddy reunion, much as if I had just been released from the penitentiary.

That night, lying restlessly awake in this new, stiff restraint, I mull over the surgeon's remark: "I am mystified."

"Je suis mystifié," is what the Swiss obstetrician said when Judith began hemorrhaging three days postpartum. I had flown to Geneva to be her birth partner. Everything seemed to be in order until that third afternoon. Her blood pressure dropped dramatically. As she lay on the gurney preparing for surgery, she made me promise to raise her baby if she didn't survive. Tonight, seventeen years later, I give in to a torrent of tears. That baby is now a junior in high school and Judith has taken a second leave from her UN post to be with me for the spinal fusion surgery that was "pencilled in" and has now been deferred, if not quite cancelled.

Family glue, Victor likes to call it. Judith's son Yann came to stay with us on the farm every summer from the time he was six years old until, at fourteen, he opted for tennis camp. Every June we signed for him at the airport, like a FedEx package, as he came through customs, arriving from Thailand or Yugoslavia or Germany, wearing the UM (Unaccompanied Minor) tag around his neck.

October 22
Tonight, in my Philadelphia Tracheotomy Collar—this is its official name, we learn from the enclosed instruction sheet—

I prepare to take the first standing-up shower I've had since July 21. Freed of the halo and vest, I feel resplendently naked; with hot water streaming down my back I moan in ecstasy. Judith is monitoring me from her perch on the laundry hamper.

"Do you think this thing [meaning the accident] has improved me morally?" I call out to her.

"What?"

"Morally," I shout over the running water. "You know. Has it made me more patient, kinder, more compassionate?"

"Probably not."

Once I've dried off, she helps me replace the wet collar with the dry one. It is relatively easy to position, we need only center the hole for a tracheotomy over my Adam's apple.

"Now I could go into anaphylactic shock, I suppose," I say. "In case I get stung by a swarm of hornets. They wouldn't even have to take the collar off to save my life."

Judith, ever practical, points out that since we've already had a hard frost, the arrival of hornets is highly unlikely. . . .

November 10

The closer I get to November 12, the more my anxiety builds. This will be my third evaluation by X ray and fluoroscopy and I think I am more terrified than ever. What if, my brain plays over and over. What if the bones have shifted after all and I must undergo surgery to fuse C1 and C2? Why didn't we get this over with on October 26 as planned? If we had, I would now be three weeks down the road to recovery. I've read about this surgery in Christopher Reeve's book, *I'm Still Me*; at least I tried to read his detailed description but turned away in fear. It was too graphic.

When my surgeon was first mulling over the mystery of my seemingly stable neck, he said, "It would be a shame to open you up and find the bones had fused on their own."

He didn't expatiate on this thought; he didn't have to. Knowing that this operation begins with a deep incision in the hip to access necessary live bone for the repair, I am horrified by the possible scenario. Having come this far, I ought to be thinking positively. I ought to believe in my body's ability to heal itself. Even if C1-C2 have grown together in a funny offset arthritic way, I have outfoxed the fates who so cruelly severed Reeve's spinal cord but were content merely to bruise mine.

November 12

This is a rerun of October 28. The results of the X rays are identical.

Today, after overlaying the flexion and extension plates, the surgeon is positively jocular. "I don't know who's looking after you," he says half humorously, half incredulously. "It looks like somebody is on your side."

"Can you see where they're fused?"

"No. We may never see where. But there's absolutely no movement, not a millimeter in any direction."

Now I am to discard the high collar except when travelling over dirt roads and abandon the soft one indoors much of the time. I am to begin gentle range of motion with my neck: up, down, and side to side. In OT/PT the therapists will gradually help me hold my head straight (I am still tilted to the left from all those weeks in the halo). As for the decreased sensation and function in my right hand and fingers, maybe I will get them back, maybe not. He will repeat the X rays in one month. Am I out of the woods? He will not say definitively.

That afternoon, Wendy, my PT, says that dealing with spinal cord injuries is like dealing with a death. The patient must go through the same stages of anger, denial, and so on, to acceptance of his or her limitations.

Nevertheless, she is quite adamant: "You will get it back, you will get it all back." She removes my collar, squats down in front of me and tells me to lift my chin. I do so, possibly an inch. Then, under instruction, I lower my chin, possibly two inches. But the side to side motion evades me.

"What's stopping you?" she asks.

"Terror," I reply. She assures me that my muscles will keep me from turning too far. Bone will not grind upon bone. It is perfectly safe to turn my head.

That evening I turn my head a little more. When I wake

toward dawn, I take the collar off. I still cannot turn on my side without considerable pain on the opposite side of my neck, but I remind myself how relatively comfortable this position is compared to the steady torture of the halo. . . .

April 23

Most afternoons when I climb the hill to pace my mile around the ring, I try to time my walk to coincide with Victor working Boomer under saddle, or my former carriage-driving navigator riding Deuter. I envy their easy posture as they flow past me trotting, looping in large circles, then picking up a canter. I'm torn between such jealousy that I almost wish I weren't here to watch and the deep pleasure I take in seeing my horses in action.

For weeks now I've been thinking about getting up on my horse. I don't have any big plans to ride him, but I have this dogged faith that just walking around while another person leads Deuter will help me reestablish my balance. After all, we're financial supporters of a local riding-for-the-handicapped program; we even donated an aging bombproof pony mare who could tolerate the lifting and positioning of a young patient on her broad back. Why not our own thera-peutic riding program?

Today the three of us enter into a conspiracy: with their steadying hands and the help of the mounting block I normally use to climb over my garden fence, I am going to sit on my horse.

Deuter stands like a rock while I shakily attempt to mount. It is very hard to get my right leg over his side; he waits while I take a handful of mane and, with Victor steadying me, haul myself into position. I look around me. I've been planning this for so long! I thought regaining my seat in the saddle would bring with it some sort of epiphany, a revelation of huge consequence. Instead, I feel merely at home. I am back in my peaceful kingdom.

From this new perspective, the crowns of the maples are just beginning to redden. One final pocket of snow along the brook catches the afternoon sun. The raucous calls of pileated woodpeckers sound from the shagbark hickories. They're getting ready to nest. The whole impetuous natural world is poised to burst forth. We begin our stately procession, Deuter obediently following Victor.

I close my eyes, let my hips absorb my horse's familiar cadence, let my torso follow the motion. I am letting myself believe I will heal.

from

WASTED

MARYA HORNBACHER

*Marya Hornbacher bounced between bulimia and
anorexia for 13 years, whittling herself down to 52
pounds before finally accepting the help she needed.
In this excerpt, she explains the day-to-day,
unromantic reality of her cure.*

From here on out things are very blurry. Sitting in my room with my roommate, who started to cry and said, Marya, I'm sorry, I called your parents. I was just so worried. It took me a minute to register. Then I picked up the phone, it was the middle of the night I think, and called my parents and said, I'm really sorry, but I've got to come home. I hope you don't mind.

They minded.

My father explains this minding, years later: "I had said to you for so long, 'You're not eating enough, you're looking deadly ill again.' We said it and said it and said it, you said, 'I'm fine, I'm fine, I'm fine,' you lied, you lied, you lied. When you wanted to come home, something in me said, 'She damn well better be sick.'"

If I put myself in my parents shoes, I can understand. After four years of watching your child play an infantile game of chicken, watching her stand at the edge of a cliff, teetering and laughing, almost falling and almost falling but never quite flinging herself over the edge, I can see how a worried audience might eventually get a little sick of this particular game. I can see how people might need to, for their own sanity and for simple reason's sake, let go.

And I can see, too, how a person's brain might refuse to accept that this time, she's actually gone over the edge.

My father flat-out did not want to believe that this was it. Neither did I. My own behavior at this point was entirely contradictory: I knew that I needed to get home, but I didn't want to admit that I was really sick. Like, really fucking sick. I lied about my weight and said I was just so stressed that I thought a short break from school would do me some good. My father suggested I work fewer hours. I was continuously hysterical, terrified that my one chance to get saved was out of my reach. The girl who cried wolf. I talked to my mother occasionally, incoherent, trying to get her to convince my father to let me come home, just for a break, I said. There was a lag time—a few days? a few weeks? time unravels in my head here—while my father and I argued in a series of phone calls about whether or not I should come back, my therapist pleaded with them, my roommate did. Then I just up and dropped out of school. I walked into my counselor's office and said I was an anoretic and needed a leave of absence. She was incredibly understanding and very supportive. She, too, called my parents and told them I—haha—visibly needed a bit of a rest. I packed my things and sent them home, quit my job, and hopped on a plane to Minneapolis.

Let us say that my reception was not exactly warm.

I can understand that. I think it would be unpleasant to look at your child and realize she is going to be dead very shortly. My father was furious and my mother was terrified into a chilling silence. The night I got home, my mother sat at the kitchen table with me while I ate several bowls of cereal in a row and then cried because I'd eaten too much, and she just said, Honey, oh, honey, don't say that. Lifting my head from the place mat, I looked at her, searching her eyes for an answer, and I asked: Mom, do you think I'm crazy?

There was an excruciating silence. The clock ticked. I was still wearing my coat.

She said, looking out the window, "I think you're very sick."

It took me a minute to realize that she'd just said: Yes.

I've never been so terrified in my life. I had registered, to some extent, that this was the end, that I was honest-to-God about to push my leaky little rowboat away from shore and really truly *die*. The idea began to sink in, more than it ever had, that I might be crazy, in the traditional sense of the word. That I might be, forever and ever amen, a Crazy Person. That what we'd suspected all along, what I'd been working so hard to disprove, might be true. I preferred, by far, being dead.

I spent the next few days sitting on the couch in a quilt, looking out the window, thinking about madness while my parents pleaded with me to go to the doctor, just to get a checkup.

I agreed to go. The night before I went, I drove—yes, drove—over to the university district to read in a café. I couldn't read, of course. I kept thinking about the fact that

I'd just eaten dinner, a bit of dinner, and it was making noise and jumping around in my stomach and I thought about throwing up but decided that as long as I was going to throw up I might as well throw up something besides the three bites of skinless chicken I'd eaten. I bought a few muffins and walked around eating them, the old familiar adrenaline rush pumping through me, propelling my legs into a Burger King, writing a check from an account that was empty, chewing calmly. Then I was off, running through the town, stopping here and there and eating and throwing up in alleyways and eating and blacking out and standing up and running and eating as I walked, impervious to the cold, hand to mouth and hand to mouth. I bounced checks worth $200 in a few hours eating and running and purging and finally getting into the car and stopping on my way home at a Perkins, my last supper, I thought. I ordered pancakes with whipped cream and bacon and eggs and hash browns. I threw up in the bathroom, bought a slice of pie, ate it in the car and threw up when I got home. I got into bed, too tired to do my exercises.

It was the worst night of my life. It is the only lucid memory of this entire time. I dreamed I was eating and eating in a dark, hellish restaurant, and everyone was staring but I couldn't stop eating and then I'd jerk awake and think it was real and panic and then remember it wasn't real. I hadn't really eaten, everything was okay, and then, horribly dehydrated, I'd take huge swallows from the bottle of diet orange soda I had by my bed, crash back into sleep, return to the restaurant, and keep eating, and wake, and panic, and drink, and sleep and dream, hours and hours of dream eating and the echo of people laughing as I ate and ate. When morning came I was essentially broken. I could hardly talk.

My father drove me to the hospital for my checkup. For some reason it didn't register with me that I was seen in the emergency room. For some reason, when I walked in, the woman at the triage desk took one look at me as I came through the door, picked up the phone, and said something I couldn't hear. Then there was a sound like a pummel of hoofbeats and someone's voice on the loudspeaker. There was a flurry of people. I was taken to a room. I lay down on the little bed and someone put a blanket on me. Someone came in and poked at me, then helped me sit up, handed me a little can of juice. It said BLUE BIRD APPLE JUICE. Apparently I was supposed to drink it. When the somebody left, I poured it down the sink, thinking, Why am I pouring this down the sink? What does this prove?

That thought was my downfall.

A doctor came in. She was brisk. She told me she was going to admit me. I said I had to go, I was meeting friends for breakfast, which was true. I'd been worried all morning about how I was going to get out of eating at breakfast, wondering if the restaurant had yogurt, and whether it was fat-free or low-fat, and I asked if I couldn't come back later? wondering if in the meantime I could gain enough weight to keep myself out of the hospital, something in the range of fifty pounds, and I was very tired and I lay my head on the pillow and closed my eyes for a minute. She waited. I pushed myself up from the bed and smiled and asked, Okay? I can go?

She said: You aren't going to make it down the block.

I thought about that for a minute.

I thought it was possible that she was right.

I asked if I could go have a cigarette while I thought about this. She humored me. I walked outside, holding the wall as I went. It was too cold to smoke, so I ground the cigarette out with my heel, turned, got dizzy, bent over, and waited. While I waited I counted my bones. They were all still there. Then I thought, my God.

I straightened up, held the cold brick wall while the dizziness came in waves and washed away. I walked very slowly inside, placing my feet carefully on the floor. I went to the desk and signed myself in.

I have not enjoyed writing this book. Making public what I have kept private from those closest to me, and often enough from myself, all my life, is not exactly my idea of a good time. This project was not, as so many people have suggested, "therapeutic" for me—I pay my therapist a lot of money for that. On the contrary, it was very difficult. I wrote in stops and starts, trying to translate a material object, a body, into some arrangement of words. Trying to explain rather than excuse, to balance rather than blame. The words came bitten-off, in quick gusts and then long ellipses. After a life-time of silence, it is difficult then to speak.

And even when you have spoken, you find your lexicon vastly insufficient: the words lack shape and taste, temperature and weight. *Hunger* and *cold*, *flesh* and *bone* are commonplace words. I cannot articulate how those four words mean something different to me than perhaps they do to you, how each of these has, in my mouth, strange flavor: the acid of bile, the metallic tang of blood.

You expect an ending. This is a book; it ought to have a beginning, a middle, and an end. I cannot give you an end. I would very much like to. I would like to wrap up all loose ends in a bow and say, See? All better now. But the loose ends stare back at me in the mirror. The loose ends are my body, which neither forgives nor forgets: the random half-hearted kicking of my heart, wrinkled and shrunken as an apple rotting on the ground. The scars on my arms, the gray hair, the wrinkles, the friendly bartender who guesses my age, smiling, saying, "Thirty-six?" The ovaries and uterus, soundly asleep. The immune system, trashed. The weekly trips to the doctor for yet another infection, another virus, another cold, another sprain, another battery of tests, another prescription, another weight, another warning. The little yellow morning pills that keep one foot on the squirming anxiety that lives just under my sternum, clutching at my ribs.

The loose ends are the Bad Days: my husband finding a bowl of mush on the kitchen counter, cereal I poured and "forgot" to eat, my husband arguing with me about dinner (No, honey, let's *not* have rice cakes with jelly). The loose ends are the nightmares of hunger and drowning and deserts of ice, the shivering jolt awake, the scattering of cold sweat. They are the constant trips to the mirror, the anxious fingers reading the body like Braille, as if an arrangement of bones might give words and sense to my life. The desperate reaching up from the quicksand of obsession, the clawing my way a little farther out, then falling back. The maddening ambiguity of "progress," the intangible goal of "health."

It does not hit you until later. The fact that you were essentially dead does not register until you begin to come alive. Frostbite does not hurt until it starts to thaw. First it is numb. Then a shock of pain rips through the body. And then, every winter after, it aches.

And every season since is winter, and I do still ache.

February 18, 1993. I am given a week to live.

Four years (approximately 169 weeks, 1,183 days, 28,392 hours) pass.

March 11, 1997. I am alive.

There will be no stunning revelations now. There will be

no near-death tunnel-of-light scenes, no tearful revelatory therapy sessions, no happy family reunions, no cameo appearances by Christ, M.D., no knight on a white horse galloping into my life. I am alive for very menial reasons:

1. Being sick gets singularly boring after a while.
2. I was really annoyed when told I was going to die and rather petulantly went, Well fuck you then I won't.
3. In a rare appearance by my rational self, I realized it was completely stupid and chicken-shittish of me to just check out of life because it ruffled my feathers.
4. It struck me that it was entirely unoriginal to be starving to death. Everyone was doing it. It was, as a friend would later put it, totally passé. Totally 1980s. I decided to do something slightly less *Vogue*.
5. I got curious: If I could get that sick, then (I figured) I could bloody well get unsick.

So I did. Am. However you want to put it. Obstreperousness, which as a character trait is extremely exploitable in the energetic annihilation of one's own body and individual self, is also very useful in other pursuits. For example, life.

My eating disorder was not "cured" the minute I rolled— was rolled, rather, in a wheelchair with an IV in my arm, head nodding and heart lurching in my chest—onto the eating-dis-

orders unit one bitterly cold day, February 18, 1993. It was
not cured during the three months I stayed there, or during
the years that have passed between then and today. I sit here
now, eating dry cereal from a bowl because going to the store
for milk seems somehow complex. It was not cured. It will not
be cured. But it has changed. So have I.

I am precisely twice the size I was then. Which means I
am still underweight. Which also means that in the mess of
the last four years, I did a few things right. I am three inches
taller than I was then, which means, maybe, that the body
surges upward toward light, like a plant seeking sun. I am
classified as (Axis I) 1. Atypical Bipolar II, cyclothymic,
hypomanic 2. Eating Disorder Not Otherwise Specified
(ED-NOS), (Axis II) 1. Borderline?, which means, essentially, nothing. I have scars all over my arms that were not
there in 1993, which means some sadness came alive as my
body did, and I, mute, etched it into my skin. It also means
that we do not keep razors in my house. I am married, which
means many things, including but not limited to the fact that
I've learned a thing or two about love, and patience, and
faith. It means I have a responsibility to stay here, on earth, in
the kitchen, in the bed, and not seep slowly back into the
mirror.

And I am all right. We will not deal here with words such
as *well*, or *recovered*, or *fine*. It took a long time to get all right,
and I like all right quite a bit. It's an interesting balancing act,

the state of all right. It's a glass-half-empty-or-half-full sort of place, I could tip either way. It's a place where one can either hope or despair: Hope that this will keep getting easier, as it has over the past few years, or despair at the infuriating concentration balance requires, despair at the fact that I will die young, despair that I cannot be "normal," wallow in the bummerish aspects of my life.

Blab blah blah. I'm sick of despair. It's so magazine-model-looking-apathetic-and-underfed-and-stoned-and-exactly-the-same-as-all-the-other-wan-sickly-models. Forgive me for being chipper, but despair is desperately dull.

So I guess what happened is that I got tired of being so dull.

This is what happened: I went to the hospital and stayed there for a very long time. I got out of the hospital and threw myself into life with precious few tools and made a big mess and broke a bunch of things. Learned to be more careful. I worked, made friends, had a messy love affair, moved into a crack house apartment downtown and got a cat. Learned that in order to live, plants need water. That girl cannot live by cereal alone, though I go back and forth on that one still. That friends are a good source of food and soul when one has not yet gotten the hang of cooking or living (as opposed to dying) alone. That nothing—not booze, not love, not sex, not work, not moving from state to state—will make the past disappear. Only time and patience heal things. I learned that cutting up your arms in an attempt to make the pain move from inside to outside, from soul to skin, is futile. That death is a cop-out. I tried all of these things. I shaved my head, attempted suicide in November 1994, got forty-two stitches in my left arm, which hurt like a sonofabitch, and decided that was enough of that. I wrote and published and read and researched and taught and went to school from time to time and drank a lot of coffee and had a lot of really macabre dreams and played Trivial Pursuit and went to therapy and found myself extremely wrapped up in the business of life. I learned, gradually, to just fucking *deal*.

There is, in fact, an incredible freedom in having nothing left to lose.

In my limbo period after leaving the hospital the last time, I was grasping at straws. If you do that long enough, you eventually get a hold of some, enough, anyway, to keep going. I no longer had anything that I understood or could believe in. The situation I was in then is not at all uncommon. The experts say, What did you do *before* your eating disorder? What were you like before? And you simply stare at them because you can remember no before, and the word *you* means nothing at all. Are you referring to Marya, the constellation of suicidal symptoms? Marya, the invalid? Marya, the patient, the subject, the case study, the taker of pills, the nibbler of muffins, the asexual, the encyclopedia, the pencil sketch of the human skeleton, the bearer of nightmares of hunger, the hunger itself?

It is impossible to sufficiently articulate an inarticulate process, a very wordless time. I did not learn to live by words, so I have found myself with few words to describe what happened. I've felt rather like I was dubbing in voices and adding Technicolor to a black-and-white silent film. This history is revisionist in that same way: I have added words, color, and chronology to a time of my life that appears to me a pile of random frames scattered over the floor of my brain. I am sometimes startled, now, when I stand up and turn to the door to catch myself in the mirror. I'm often surprised that I exist, that my body is a corporeal body, that my face is my face, and that my name has a correlation to a person I can identify as myself. But I suppose it's not so strange to create a collage of memory—clippings that substitute for a linear, logical narrative. I did a very similar thing with myself.

There is never a sudden revelation, a complete and tidy explanation for why it happened, or why it ends, or why or who you are. You want one and I want one, but there isn't one. It comes in bits and pieces, and you stitch them together wherever they fit, and when you are done you hold yourself up, and still there are holes and you are a rag doll, invented, imperfect.

And yet you are all that you have, so you must be enough. There is no other way.

I make it sound so simple: I say it got boring, so I stopped. I say I had other things to do, so I stopped. I say I had no other choice but to stop. I know all too well that it is not that simple. But in some ways, the most significant choices one makes in life are done for reasons that are not all that dramatic, not earthshaking at all—often enough, the choices we make are, for better or worse, made by default. It's quite true that there was no revelatory moment. Mostly what happened was that my life took over—that is to say, that the *impulse* for life became stronger in me than the impulse for death. In me, the two impulses coexist in an uneasy balance, but they are balanced enough now that I am alive.

Looking back, I see that what I did then was pretty basic. I took a leap of faith. And I believe that has made all the difference. I hung on to the only thing that seemed real to me, and that was a basic ethical principle: if I was alive, then I had a responsibility to stay alive and do something with the life I had been given. And though I was not at all convinced, when I made that leap of faith, that I had any sensible reason for doing so—though I did not fully believe that there was anything that could possibly make as much sense as an eating disorder—I made it because I began to wonder. I simply began to wonder, in the same way I had wondered what would happen if I began to lose weight, what would happen if I stopped. It was worth it.

It *is* worth it. It's a fight. It's exhausting, but it is a fight I believe in. I cannot believe, anymore, in the fight between body and soul. If I do, it will kill me. But more importantly, if I do, I have taken the easy way out. I know for a fact that sickness is easier.

But health is more interesting.

The leap of faith is this: You have to believe, or at least pretend you believe until you *really* believe it, that you are strong enough to take life face on. Eating disorders, on any level, are a crutch. They are also an addiction and an illness, but there is no question at all that they are quite simply a way of avoiding the banal, daily, itchy pain of life. Eating disorders provide a little private drama, they feed into the desire for constant excitement, everything becomes life-or-death, everything is terribly grand and crashing, very Sturm and Drang. And they are distracting. You don't have to think about any of the nasty minutiae of the real world, you don't get caught up in that awful boring thing called regular life, with its bills and its breakups and its dishes and laundry and groceries and arguments over whose turn it is to change the litter box and bedtimes and bad sex and all that, because you are having a *real* drama, not a sitcom but a GRAND EPIC, all by yourself, and why would you bother with those foolish mortals when you could spend hours and hours with the mirror, when you are having the *most interesting* sadomasochistic affair with your own image?

What all this grandiosity covers—and not very well, I might add—is a very basic fear that the real world will gobble you up the minute you step into it. Obviously, the fear is incredibly large or you wouldn't go to all the trouble of trying to *leave* it, and certainly not in such a long, drawn-out manner. The fear, too, is a fear of yourself: a completely dualistic and contradictory fear. On the one hand it is a fear that you do not have what it takes to make it, and on the other hand, a possibly greater fear that you *do* have what it takes, and that by definition you therefore also have a responsibility to do something *really* big. It's a little daunting, going out into the world with this state of mind. Most people go out with a general idea that they'll do something or other and that it will be okay. You go out with the certainty that you will be a failure from the outset, or that you will have to do something utterly stellar, which implies the potential for failure anyway. When I was growing up, I always felt there was an expectation that I would do one of two things: be Great at something, or go crazy and become a total failure. There is no middle ground where I come from. And I am only now beginning to get a sense that there is a middle ground at all.

I had to decide that whatever happened, I would be all right. That was the hardest decision I've ever made, the decision to protect myself no matter what happened. My entire life, I've turned on myself the minute something went wrong, even a tiny little thing. It is not an uncommon habit among women. Among those of us who see in all-or-nothing terms, it seems as if you have only two choices: either lash out at the world and label yourself as interminably hysterical, shrill, unstable, and otherwise flawed, or lash out at yourself. With eating disorders, that lashing out at yourself is unfortunately rewarded—temporarily—by the world and thus is all the more tempting. But then the whole thing goes sour.

My leap of faith was more a negative reaction against the idea of wasting my life than it was a positive, gleeful run into the arms of the world. I'm wary of the world, even now. But I would not say I am wasting my life.

There is a difficult factor in deciding to end the game, and that is that most women are playing it at some level of intensity or another—and all of those levels have sublevels of dangers, not just the over-the-top-mortality-star type of disorder. Eating-disordered people, for the most part, don't talk to one another. It is usually not a little sorority where it's all done in a very companionable way. It's usually intensely private. And when you decide you are tired of being alone with your sickness, you go out seeking women friends, people who you believe can show you by example how to eat, how to live—and you find that by and large most women are obsessed with their weight.

It's a little discouraging.

I can think, in retrospect, of all sorts of ways in which I might have avoided an eating disorder, and thus avoided the incredibly weird journey through the darker parts of the human mind that my life, essentially, has been. If I had been born at a different point in time, when starving oneself to death did not seem such an obvious and *rewarding*—Oh, you've lost so much weight! You look fabulous!—way of dealing with the world, of avoiding the inevitable pain of life. If I had been a different sort of person, maybe less impressionable, less intense, less fearful, less utterly dependent upon the perceptions of others—maybe then I would not have bought the cultural party line that thinness is the be-all and end-all of goals. Maybe if my family had not been in utter chaos most of the time; maybe if my parents were a little better at dealing with their own lives. Maybe if I'd gotten help sooner, or if I'd gotten different help, maybe if I did not so fiercely cherish my secret, or if I were not such a good liar, or were not quite so empty inside, maybe maybe maybe.

But all this is moot. Sometimes things just go awry. And when, after fifteen years of bingeing, barfing, starving, needles and tubes and terror and rage, and medical crises and personal failure and loss after loss—when, after all this, you are in your early twenties and staring down a vastly abbreviated life expectancy, and the eating disorder still takes up half your body, half your brain, with its invisible eroding force, when you have spent the majority of your life sick, when you do not yet know what it means to be "well," or "normal," when you doubt that those words even *have* meaning anymore, there are still no answers. You will die young, and you have no way to make sense of that fact.

You have this: You are thin.

Whoop-de-fucking-dee.

But when you decide to throw down your cards, push back from your chair, and leave the game, it's a very lonely moment. Women use their obsession with weight and food as a point of connection with one another, a commonality even between strangers. Instead of talking about *why* we use food and weight control as a means of handling emotional stress, we talk ad nauseam about the fact that we don't like our bodies. When you decide not to do that, you begin to notice how constant that talk is. I go to the gym, and women are standing around in their underwear bitching about their bellies, I go to a restaurant and listen to women cheerfully conversing about their latest diet, I go to a women's clothing store and the woman helping me, almost universally, will launch into a monologue about how these pants are very slimming, how lucky I am to have the problem of never being able to find clothes that fit, "Because you're *tiny*!" she'll squeal. I have to remind myself that it's not a conversation I want to get into. I refuse to say, "Gee, thanks." I don't necessarily *want* pants that are slimming, I don't want to look like the photos of skeletal models on the walls. Wanting to be healthy is seen as really *weird*.

So I'm weird. So what?

I want to write a prescription for culture, some sort of tranquilizer that will make it less maniacally compelled to climb the StairMaster right into nowhere, and I can't do that. It's a person-by-person project. I do it, you do it, and I maintain the perhaps ridiculous notion that if enough people do it we will all get a grip. I want to write about how to Get Well, but I can't do that either. I want to do a sidebar here with little pie charts breaking health down into statistical slices, showing the necessary percentages of therapy, food, books, baths, work, sleep, tears, fits, trials, and errors, and I can't. I find this maddening. If I were to describe the path between point A and point B, I would have to detail a convoluted, crisscrossed, almost blind stumble through a briar patch: the doublings-back, the stumbles into different, smaller rabbit holes, the sudden plunking down and howling with rage. In the end, I will have to point out that my stumble is specific to me. Your stumble will be different. You will avoid potholes I fell headlong into and find yourself tripping into quicksand I missed.

It is not a sudden leap from sick to well. It is a slow, strange meander from sick to mostly well. The misconception that eating disorders are a medical disease in the traditional sense is not helpful here. There is no "cure." A pill will not fix it, though it may help. Ditto therapy, ditto food, ditto endless support from family and friends. You fix it yourself. It is the hardest thing that I have ever done, and I found myself stronger for doing it. Much stronger.

Never, never underestimate the power of desire. If you

want to live badly enough, you can live. The greater question, at least for me, was: How do I decide I want to live?

That is a question I'm still working on. I gave life a trial period, six months, and said that when the six months were up, I could get sick again if I really wanted to. In that six months, so much happened that death seemed, primarily, inconvenient. The trial period was extended. I seem to keep extending it. There are many things to do. There are books to write and naps to take. There are movies to see and scrambled eggs to eat. Life is essentially trivial. You either decide you will take the trite business of life and give yourself the option of doing something really cool, or you decide you will opt for the Grand Epic of eating disorders and dedicate your life to being *seriously* trivial. I kind of go back and forth, a little Grand Epic here and a little cool trivial stuff there. As time goes by I take greater and greater pleasure in the trivial stuff and find the Grand Epic more and more dreary. It's a good sign. And still, every goddamn day I have to think up a reason to live.

Obviously I've come up with something.

I do not have a happy ending for this book. I suppose I could end it with my wedding—Former Anoretic Catches Man! Ex-Bulimic Saved from Gastric Rupture by Pretty White Dress!—but that would be ridiculous. I could end it with the solid relationship I have with my parents, but that seems less than relevant. I cannot end it with assurances of my own Triumph Over Adversity, because (1) we're a ways off from Triumph yet, and (2) the Adversity was, um, me. I cannot end it with my blooming health or stable weight because neither exist. I cannot sum up and say, But now it's over. Happily Ever After.

It's never over. Not really. Not when you stay down there as long as I did, not when you've lived in the netherworld longer than you've lived in this material one, where things are very bright and large and make such strange noises. You never come back, not all the way. Always, there is an odd distance between you and the people you love and the people you meet, a barrier, thin as the glass of a mirror. You never come all the way out of the mirror; you stand, for the rest of your life, with one foot in this world and one in another, where everything is upside down and backward and sad.

It is the distance of marred memory, of a twisted and shape-shifting past. When people talk about their childhood, their adolescence, their college days, I laugh along and try not to think: that was when I was throwing up in my elementary school bathroom, that was when I was sleeping with strangers to show off the sharp tips of my bones, that was when I lost sight of my soul and died.

And it is the distance of the present, as well—the distance that lies between people in general because of the different lives we have lived. I don't know who I would be, now, if I had not lived the life I have, and so I cannot alter my need for distance—nor can I lessen the low and omnipresent pain that that distance creates. The entirety of my life is overshadowed by one singular and near-fatal obsession. I go to great lengths now to compensate for a life of sadness and madness and a slow dance with death. When I leave my house, I put on a face and a dress and a smile and wave my hands about and talk brightly and am terribly open and seem to have conquered my monsters with great aplomb.

Perhaps, in some ways, that's true. But I often feel as though they have conquered me. As I write this, I am only twenty-three. I do not feel twenty-three. I feel old.

I have not lost my fascination with death. I have not become a noticeably less intense person. I have not, nor will I ever, completely lose the longing for that *something*, that thing that I believe will fill an emptiness inside me. I do believe that the emptiness was made greater by the things that I did to myself.

But to a certain extent—the extent that keeps me alive, and eating, and going about my days—I have learned to understand the emptiness rather than fear it and fight it and continue the futile attempt to fill it up. It's there when I wake in the morning and there when I go to bed at night. Sometimes it's bigger than at other times, sometimes I forget it's even there. I have days, now, when I don't think much about my weight. I have days, at least, when I see properly, when I look in the mirror and see myself as I am—a woman—

instead of as a piece of unwanted flesh, forever verging on excess.

This is the weird aftermath, when it is not exactly over, and yet you have given it up. You go back and forth in your head, often, about giving it up. It's hard to understand, when you are sitting there in your chair, having breakfast or whatever, that giving it up is stronger than holding on, that "letting yourself go" could mean you have succeeded rather than failed. You eat your goddamn Cheerios and bicker with the bitch in your head who keeps telling you you're fat and weak: Shut *up*, you say, I'm *busy*, leave me alone. When she leaves you alone, there's a silence and a solitude that will take some getting used to. You will miss her sometimes.

Bear in mind she's trying to kill you. Bear in mind you have a life to live.

There is an incredible loss. There is a profound grief. And there is, in the end, after a long time and more work than you ever thought possible, a time when it gets easier.

> *This is the Hour of Lead—*
> *Remembered, if outlived,*
> *As Freezing persons, recollect the Snow—*
> *First—Chill—then Stupor—then the letting go—*
> —Emily Dickinson

There is, in the end, the letting go.

THE LETTER WRITER

ISAAC BASHEVIS SINGER

*Sometimes we are unaware that we need to be healed
until someone or something changes our lives. Herbert
Gombiner is old and weak, living alone with his books
and his memories. It takes the advent of life-
threatening illness, coupled with the unexpected
arrival of a compassionate woman, to fully
wake him to what his life had
been and could be.*

Herman Gombiner opened an eye. This was the way he
woke up each morning—gradually, first with one eye, then
the other. His glance met a cracked ceiling and part of the
building across the street. He had gone to bed in the early
hours, at about three. It had taken him a long time to fall
asleep. Now it was close to ten o'clock. Lately, Herman
Gombiner had been suffering from a kind of amnesia. When
he got up during the night, he couldn't remember where he
was, who he was, or even his name. It took a few seconds to
realize that he was no longer in Kalomin, or in Warsaw, but
in New York, uptown on one of the streets between
Columbus Avenue and Central Park West.

It was winter. Steam hissed in the radiator. The Second
World War was long since over. Herman (or Hayim David, as
he was called in Kalomin) had lost his family to the Nazis. He
was now an editor, proofreader, and translator in a Hebrew
publishing house called Zion. It was situated on Canal Street.
He was a bachelor, almost fifty years old, and a sick man.

"What time is it?" he mumbled. His tongue was coated,
his lips cracked. His knees ached; his head pounded; there
was a bitter taste in his mouth. With an effort he got up, setting his feet down on the worn carpet that covered the floor.
"What's this? Snow?" he muttered. "Well, it's winter."

He stood at the window awhile and looked out. The

broken-down cars parked on the street jutted from the snow like relics of a long-lost civilization. Usually the street was filled with rubbish, noise, and children—Negro and Puerto Rican. But now the cold kept everyone indoors. The stillness, the whiteness made him think of his old home, of Kalomin. Herman stumbled toward the bathroom.

The bedroom was an alcove, with space only for a bed. The living room was full of books. On one wall there were cabinets from floor to ceiling, and along the other stood two bookcases. Books, newspapers, and magazines lay everywhere, piled in stacks. According to the lease, the landlord was obliged to paint the apartment every three years, but Herman Gombiner had bribed the superintendent to leave him alone. Many of his old books would fall apart if they were moved. Why is new paint better than old? The dust had gathered in layers. A single mouse had found its way into the apartment, and every night Herman set out for her a piece of bread, a small slice of cheese, and a saucer of water to keep her from eating the books. Thank goodness she didn't give birth. Occasionally, she would venture out of her hole even when the light was on. Herman had even given her a Hebrew name: Huldah. Her little bubble eyes stared at him with curiosity. She stopped being afraid of him.

The building in which Herman lived had many faults, but it did not lack heat. The radiators sizzled from early morning till late at night. The owner, himself a Puerto

Rican, would never allow his tenants' children to suffer from the cold.

There was no shower in the bathroom, and Herman bathed daily in the tub. A mirror that was cracked down the middle hung inside the door, and Herman caught a glimpse of himself—a short man, in oversize pajamas, emaciated to skin and bone, with a scrawny neck and a large head, on either side of which grew two tufts of gray hair. His forehead was wide and deep, his nose crooked, his cheekbones high. Only in his dark eyes, with long lashes like a girl's, had there remained any trace of youthfulness. At times, they even seemed to twinkle shrewdly. Many years of reading and poring over tiny letters hadn't blurred his vision or made him nearsighted. The remaining strength in Herman Gombiner's body—a body worn out by illnesses and undernourish-ment—seemed to be concentrated in his gaze.

He shaved slowly and carefully. His hand, with its long fingers, trembled, and he could easily have cut himself. Meanwhile, the tub filled with warm water. He undressed, and was amazed at his thinness—his chest was narrow, his arms and legs bony; there were deep hollows between his neck and shoulders. Getting into the bathtub was a strain, but then lying in the warm water was a relief. Herman always lost the soap. It would slip out of his hands playfully, like a live thing, and he would search for it in the water. "Where are you running?" he would say to it. "You rascal!" He believed there was life in everything, that the so-called inanimate objects had their own whims and caprices.

Herman Gombiner considered himself to be among the select few privileged to see beyond the facade of phenomena. He had seen a blotter raise itself from the desk, slowly and unsteadily float toward the door, and, once there, float gently down, as if suspended by an invisible string held by some unseen hand. The whole thing had been thoroughly senseless. No matter how much Herman thought about it, he was unable to figure out any reason for what had taken place. It had been one of those extraordinary happenings that cannot be explained by science, or religion, or folklore. Later, Herman had bent down and picked up the blotter, and placed it back on the desk, where it remained to this day, covered with papers, dusty, and dried out—an inanimate object that for one moment had somehow freed itself from physical laws. Herman Gombiner knew that it had been neither a hallucination nor a dream. It had taken place in a well-lit room at eight in the evening. He hadn't been ill or even upset that day. He never drank liquor, and he had been wide awake. He had been standing next to the chest, about to take a handkerchief out of a drawer. Suddenly his gaze had been attracted to the desk and he had seen the blotter rise and float. Nor was this the only such incident. Such things had been happening to him since childhood.

Everything took a long time—his bath, drying himself,

putting on his clothes. Hurrying was not for him. His competence was the result of deliberateness. The proofreaders at Zion worked so quickly they missed errors. The translators hardly took the time to check meanings they were unsure of in the dictionary. The majority of American and even Israeli Hebraists knew little of vowel points and the subtleties of grammar. Herman Gombiner had found the time to study all these things. It was true that he worked very slowly, but the old man, Morris Korver, who owned Zion, and even his sons, the half Gentiles, had always appreciated the fact that it was Herman Gombiner who had earned the house its reputation. Morris Korver, however, had become old and senile, and Zion was in danger of closing. It was rumored that his sons could hardly wait for the old man to die so they could liquidate the business.

Even if Herman wanted to, it was impossible for him to do anything in a hurry. He took small steps when he walked. It took him half an hour to eat a bowl of soup. Searching for the right word in a dictionary or checking something in an encyclopedia could involve hours of work. The few times that he had tried to hurry had ended in disaster; he had broken his foot, sprained his hand, fallen down the stairs, even been run over. Every trifle had become a trial to him—shaving, dressing, taking the wash to the Chinese laundry, eating a meal in a restaurant. Crossing the street, too, was a problem, because no sooner would the light turn green than it turned red again. Those behind the wheels of cars possessed the speed and morals of automatons. If a person couldn't run fast enough, they were capable of driving right over him. Recently, he had begun to suffer from tremors of the hands and feet. He had once had a meticulous handwriting, but he could no longer write. He used a typewriter, typing with his right index finger. Old Korver insisted that all Gombiner's troubles came from the fact that he was a vegetarian; without a piece of meat, one loses strength. Herman couldn't take a bite of meat if his life depended on it.

Herman put one sock on and rested. He put on the second sock, and rested again. His pulse rate was slow—fifty or so beats a minute. The least strain and he felt dizzy. His soul barely survived in his body. It had happened on occasion, as he lay in bed or sat on a chair, that his disembodied spirit had wandered around the house, or had even gone out the window. He had seen his own body in a faint, apparently dead. Who could enumerate all the apparitions, telepathic incidents, clairvoyant visions, and prophetic dreams he experienced! And who would believe him? As it was, his co-workers derided him. The elder Korver needed only a glass of brandy and he would call Herman a superstitious greenhorn. They treated him like some outlandish character.

Herman Gombiner had long ago arrived at the conclusion that modern man was as fanatic in his non-belief as ancient man had been in his faith. The rationalism of the present generation was in itself an example of preconceived ideas. Communism, psychoanalysis, Fascism, and radicalism were the shibboleths of the twentieth century. Oh, well! What could he, Herman Gombiner, do in the face of all this? He had no choice but to observe and be silent.

"Well, it's winter, winter!" Herman Gombiner said to himself in a voice half chanting, half groaning. "When will it be Hanukkah? Winter has started early this year." Herman was in the habit of talking to himself. He had always done so. The uncle who raised him had been deaf. His grandmother, rest her soul, would wake up in the middle of the night to recite penitential prayers and lamentations found only in out-dated prayer books. His father had died before Herman— Hayim David—was born. His mother had remarried in a faraway city and had had children by her second husband. Hayim David had always kept to himself, even when he attended heder or studied at the yeshiva. Now, since Hitler had killed all of his family, he had no relatives to write letters to. He wrote letters to total strangers.

"What time is it?" Herman asked himself again. He dressed in a dark suit, a white shirt, and a black tie, and went out to the kitchenette. An icebox without ice and a stove that he never used stood there. Twice a week the milkman left a bottle of milk at the door. Herman had a few cans of vegeta-bles, which he ate on days when he didn't leave the house. He had discovered that a human being requires very little. A half cup of milk and a pretzel could suffice for a whole day. One pair of shoes served Herman for five years. His suit, coat, and hat never wore out. Only his laundry showed some wear, and not from use but from the chemicals used by the Chinese laundryman. The furniture certainly never wore out. Were it not for his expenditures on cabs and gifts, he could have saved a good deal of money.

He drank a glass of milk and ate a biscuit. Then he carefully put on his black coat, a woolen scarf, rubbers, and a felt hat with a broad brim. He packed his briefcase with books and manuscripts. It became heavier from day to day, not because there was more in it but because his strength diminished. He slipped on a pair of dark glasses to protect his eyes from the glare of the snow. Before he left the apartment, he bade farewell to the bed, the desk piled high with papers (under which the blotter lay), the books, and the mouse in the hole. He had poured out yesterday's stale water, refilled the saucer, and set out a cracker and a small piece of cheese. "Well, Huldah, be well!"

Radios blared in the hallway. Dark-skinned women with uncombed hair and angry eyes spoke in an unusually thick Spanish. Children ran around half naked. The men were apparently all unemployed. They paced idly about in their overcrowded quarters, ate standing up, or strummed mandolins. The odors from the apartments made Herman feel faint. All kinds of meat and fish were fried there. The halls reeked of garlic, onion, smoke, and something pungent and nauseating. At night his neighbors danced and laughed wantonly. Sometimes there was fighting and women screamed for help. Once a woman had come pounding on Herman's door in the middle of the night, seeking protection from a man who was trying to stab her.

Herman stopped downstairs at the mailboxes. The other residents seldom received any mail, but Herman Gombiner's box was packed tight every morning. He took his key out, fingers trembling, inserted it in the keyhole, and pulled out the mail. He was able to recognize who had sent the letters by their envelopes. Alice Grayson, of Salt Lake City, used a rose-colored envelope. Mrs. Roberta Hoff, of Pasadena, California, sent all her mail in the business envelopes of the undertaking establishment for which she worked. Miss Bertha Gordon, of Fairbanks, Alaska, apparently had many leftover Christmas-card envelopes. Today Herman found a letter from a new correspondent, a Mrs. Rose Beechman, of Louisville, Kentucky. Her name and address were hand-printed, with flourishes, across the back of the envelope. Besides the letters, there were several magazines on occultism to which Herman Gombiner subscribed—from America, England, and even Australia. There wasn't room in his briefcase for all these letters and periodicals, so Herman stuffed them into his coat pocket. He went outside and waited for a taxi.

It was rare for a taxi, particularly an empty one, to drive down this street, but it was too much of an effort for him to walk the half block to Central Park West or Columbus Avenue. Herman Gombiner fought his weakness with prayer and autosuggestion. Standing in the snow, he muttered a prayer for a taxi. He repeatedly put his hand into his pocket and fingered the letters in their envelopes. These letters and magazines had become the essence of his life. Through them he had established contact with souls. He had acquired the friendship and even the love of women. The accounts he received from them strengthened his belief in psychic powers and in the world beyond. He sent gifts to his unknown correspondents and received gifts from them. They called him by his first name, revealed their thoughts, dreams, hopes, and the messages they received through the Ouija board, automatic writing, table turning, and other supernatural sources.

Herman Gombiner had established correspondences with these women through the periodicals he subscribed to, where not only accounts of readers' experiences were published but their contributors' names and addresses as well. The articles were mainly written by women. Herman Gombiner always selected those who lived far away. He wished to avoid meetings. He could sense from the way an experience was related, from a name or an address, whether the woman would be capable of carrying on a correspondence. He was almost never wrong. A small note from him would call forth a long letter in reply. Sometimes he received entire manuscripts. His correspondence had grown so large that postage cost him several dollars a week. Many of his letters were sent out special delivery or registered.

Miracles were a daily occurrence. No sooner had he finished his prayer than a taxi appeared. The driver pulled up to the house as if he had received a telepathic command. Getting into the taxi exhausted Herman, and he sat a long while resting his head against the window with his eyes shut, praising whatever Power had heard his supplication. One had to be blind not to acknowledge the hand of Providence, or whatever you wanted to call it. Someone was concerned with man's most trivial requirements.

His disembodied spirit apparently roamed to the most distant places. All his correspondents had seen him. In one night he had been in Los Angeles and in Mexico City, in Oregon and in Scotland. It would come to him that one of his faraway friends was ill. Before long, he would receive a letter saying that she had indeed been ill and hospitalized. Over the years, several had died, and he had had a premonition each time.

For the past few weeks, Herman had had a strong feeling that Zion was going to close down. True, this had been predicted for years, but Herman had always known that it was only a rumor. And just recently the employees had become optimistic; business had improved. The old man talked of a deficit, but everybody knew he was lying in order to avoid raising salaries. The house had published a prayer book that was a best-seller. The new Hebrew–English dictionary that Herman Gombiner was completing had every chance of selling tens of thousands of copies. Nevertheless, Herman sensed a calamity just as surely as his rheumatic knees foretold a change in the weather.

The taxi drove down Columbus Avenue. Herman glanced out the window and closed his eyes again. What is there to see on a wintry day in New York? He remained wrapped up in his gloom. No matter how many sweaters he put on, he was always cold. Besides, one is less aware of the spirits, the psychic contacts, during the cold weather. Herman raised his collar higher and put his hands in his pockets. A violent kind of civilization developed in cold countries. He should never have settled in New York. If he were living in southern California, he wouldn't be enslaved by the weather in this way. Oh, well . . . And was there a Jewish publishing house to be found in southern California?

The taxi stopped on Canal Street. Herman paid his fare and added a fifty-cent tip. He was frugal with himself, but when it came to cabdrivers, waiters, and elevator men, he was generous. At Christmastime he even bought gifts for his Puerto

Rican neighbors. Today Sam, the elevator man, was apparently having a cup of coffee in the cafeteria across the street, and Herman had to wait. Sam did as he pleased. He came from the same city as Morris Korver. He was the only elevator man, so that when he didn't feel like coming in the tenants had to climb the stairs. He was a Communist besides.

Herman waited ten minutes before Sam arrived—a short man, broad-backed, with a face that looked as if it had been put together out of assorted pieces: a short forehead, thick brows, bulging eyes with big bags beneath them, and a bulbous nose covered with cherry-red moles. His walk was unsteady. Herman greeted him, but he grumbled in answer. The Yiddish leftist paper stuck out of his back pocket. He didn't shut the elevator door at once. First he coughed several times, then lit a cigar. Suddenly he spat and called out, "You've heard the news?"

"What's happened?"

"They've sold the building."

"Aha, so that's it!" Herman said to himself. "Sold? How come?" he asked.

"How come? Because the old wise guy is senile and his sonny boys don't give a damn. A garage is what's going up here. They'll knock down the building and throw the books on the garbage dump. Nobody will get a red cent out of these Fascist bastards!"

"When did it happen?"

"It happened, that's all."

Well, I *am* clairvoyant, Herman thought. He remained silent. For years, the editorial staff had talked about joining a union and working out a pension plan, but talk was as far as they had got. The elder Korver had seen to that. Wages were low, but he would slip some of his cronies an occasional five- or ten-dollar bonus. He gave out money at Hanukkah, sent Purim gifts, and in general acted like an old-style European boss. Those who opposed him were fired. The bookkeepers and other workers could perhaps get jobs elsewhere, but the writers and editors would have nowhere to go. Judaica was becoming a vanishing specialty in America. When Jews died, their religious and Hebrew books were donated to libraries or were simply thrown out. Hitlerism and the war had caused a temporary upsurge, but not enough to make publishing religious works in Hebrew profitable.

"Well, the seven fat years are over," Herman muttered to himself. The elevator went up to the third floor. It opened directly into the editorial room—a large room with a low ceiling, furnished with old desks and outmoded typewriters. Even the telephones were old-fashioned. The room smelled of dust, wax, and something stuffy and stale.

Raphael Robbins, Korver's editor-in-chief, sat on a cushioned chair and read a manuscript, his eyeglasses pushed down to the tip of his nose. He suffered from hemorrhoids and had prostate trouble. A man of medium height, he was broad-shouldered, with a round head and a protruding belly. Loose folds of skin hung under his eyes. His face expressed a grandfatherly kindliness and an old woman's shrewdness. For years his chief task had consisted of eating lunch with old Korver. Robbins was known to be a boaster, a liar, and a flatterer. He owned a library of pornographic books—a holdover from his youth. Like Sam, he came from the same city as Morris Korver. Raphael Robbins's son, a physicist, had worked on the atomic bomb. His daughter had married a rich Wall Street broker. Raphael Robbins himself had accumulated some capital and was old enough to receive his Social Security pension. As Robbins read the manuscript, he scratched his bald pate and shook his head. He seldom returned a manuscript, and many of them were lying about gathering dust on the table, in his two bookcases, and on cabinets in the kitchenette where the workers brewed tea.

The man who had made Morris Korver rich and on whose shoulders the publishing house had rested for years was Professor Yohanan Abarbanel, a compiler of dictionaries. No one knew where his title came from. He had never received a degree or even attended a university. It was said that old Korver had made him a professor. In addition to compiling several dictionaries, Abarbanel had edited a collection of sermons with quotations for rabbis, written study books for bar-mitzvah boys, and put together other handbooks, which had run into many editions. A bachelor in his seventies,

Yohanan Abarbanel had had a heart attack and had undergone surgery for a hernia. He worked for a pittance, lived in a cheap hotel, and each year worried that he might be laid off. He had several poor relatives whom he supported. He was a small man, with white hair, a white beard, and a small face, red as a frozen apple; his little eyes were hidden by white bushy eyebrows. He sat at a table and wheezed and coughed, and all the while wrote in a tiny handwriting with a steel pen. The last few years, he couldn't be trusted to complete any work by himself. Each word was read over by Herman Gombiner, and whole manuscripts had to be rewritten.

For some reason, no one in the office ever greeted anyone else with a "hello" or a "good morning" on arrival, or said anything at closing time. During the day, they did occasionally exchange a few friendly words. It might even happen that, not having addressed a word to one another for months, one of them might go over to a colleague and pour out his heart, or actually invite him to supper. But then the next morning they would again behave as if they had quarreled. Over the years they had become bored with one another. Complaints and grudges had accumulated and were never quite forgotten.

Miss Lipshitz, the secretary, who had started working at Zion when she was just out of college, was now entirely gray. She sat at her typewriter—small, plump, and pouting, with a short neck and an ample bosom. She had a pug nose and eyes that seemed never to look at the manuscript she was typing but stared far off, past the walls. Days would pass without her voice being heard. She muttered into the telephone. When she ate lunch in the restaurant across the street, she would sit alone at a table, eating, smoking, and reading a newspaper simultaneously. There was a time when everyone in the office—old Mr. Korver included—had either openly or secretly been in love with this clever girl who knew English, Yiddish, Hebrew, stenography, and much more. They used to ask her to the theater and the movies and quarreled over who should take her to lunch. For years now, Miss Lipshitz had isolated herself. Old man Korver said that she had shut herself up behind an invisible wall.

Herman nodded to her, but she didn't respond. He walked past Ben Melnick's office. Melnick was the business manager—tall, swarthy, with a young face, black bulging eyes, and a head of milky-white hair. He suffered from asthma and played the horses. All sorts of shifty characters came to see him—bookies. He was separated from his wife and was carrying on a love affair with Miss Potter, the chief bookkeeper, another relative of Morris Korver's.

Herman Gombiner went into his own office. Walking through the editorial room, and not being greeted, was a strain for him. Korver employed a man to keep the place clean—Zeinvel Gitzis—but Zeinvel neglected his work; the walls were filthy, the windows unwashed. Packs of dusty manuscripts and newspapers had been lying around for years.

Herman carefully removed his coat and laid it on a stack of books. He sat down on a chair that had horsehair sticking through its upholstery. Work? What was the sense of working when the firm was closing down? He sat shaking his head—half out of weakness, half from regret. "Well, everything has to have an end," he muttered. "It is predestined that no human institution will last forever." He reached over and pulled the mail out of his coat pocket. He inspected the envelopes, without opening any of them. He came back to Rose Beechman's letter from Louisville, Kentucky. In a magazine called the *Message*, Mrs. Beechman had reported her contacts over the last fifteen years with her dead grandmother, Mrs. Eleanor Brush. The grandmother usually materialized during the night, though sometimes she would also appear in the daylight, dressed in her funeral clothes. She was full of advice for her granddaughter, and once she even gave her a recipe for fried chicken. Herman had written to Rose Beechman, but seven weeks had passed without a reply. He had almost given up hope, although he had continued sending her telepathic messages. She had been ill—Herman was certain of it.

Now her letter lay before him in a light-blue envelope. Opening it wasn't easy for him. He had to resort to using his teeth. He finally removed six folded sheets of light-blue stationery and read:

Dear Mr. Gombiner:

I am writing this letter to you a day after my return from the hospital where I spent almost two months. I was operated on for the removal of a spinal tumor. There was danger of paralysis or worse. But fate, it seems, still wants me here . . . Apparently, my little story in the *Message* caused quite a furor. During my illness, I received dozens of letters from all parts of the country and from England.

It so happened that my daughter put your letter at the bottom of the pile, and had I read them in order, it might have taken several weeks more before I came to yours. But a premonition—what else can I call it?—made me open the very last letter first. It was then that I realized, from the postmark, yours had been among the first, if not the very first, to arrive. It seems I always do things not as I intend to but according to a command from someone or something that I am unaware of. All I can say is: this "something" has been with me as long as I can remember, perhaps even since before I was capable of thinking.

Your letter is so logical, so noble and fascinating, that I may say it has brightened my homecoming. My daughter has a job in an office and has neither the time nor the patience to look after the house. When I returned, I found things in a sorry state. I am by nature a meticulous housekeeper who cannot abide disorder, and so you can imagine my feelings. But your profound and truly remarkable thoughts, as well as the friendliness and humanity implicit in them, helped me to forget my troubles. I read your letter three times and thanked God that people with your understanding and faith exist.

You ask for details. My dear Mr. Gombiner, if I were to relate all the facts, no letter would suffice. I could fill a whole book. Don't forget that these experiences have been going on for fifteen years. My saintly grandmother visited me every day in the hospital. She literally took over the work of the nurses, who are not, as you may know, overly devoted to their patients—nor do they have the time to be. Yes, to describe it all "exactly," as you request, would take weeks, months. I can only repeat that everything I wrote in the *Message* was the honest truth. Some of my correspondents call me "crackpot," "crazy," "charlatan." They accuse me of lying and publicity-seeking. Why should I tell lies and why do I need publicity? It was, therefore, especially pleasing to read your wonderful sentiments. I see from the letterhead that you are a Jew and connected with a Hebrew publishing house. I wish to assure you that I have always had the highest regard for Jews, God's chosen people. There are not very many Jews here in Louisville, and my personal contact has been only with Jews who have little interest in their religion. I have always wanted to become acquainted with a real Jew, who reveres the tradition of the Holy Fathers.

Now I come to the main point of my letter, and I beg you to forgive my rambling. The night before I left the hospital, my beloved grandmother, Mrs. Brush, visited with me till dawn. We chatted about various matters, and just before her departure she said to me, "This winter you will go to New York, where you will meet a man who will change the direction of your life." These were her parting words. I must add here that although for the past fifteen years I have been fully convinced that my grandmother never spoke idly and that whatever she said had meaning, at that moment for the first time I felt some doubt. What business did I, a widow living on a small pension, have in far-off New York? And what man in New York could possibly alter my existence?

It is true I am not yet old—just above forty—and considered an attractive woman. (I beg you not to think me vain. I simply wish to clarify the situation.) But when my husband died eight years ago, I decided that was that. I was left with a twelve-year-old daughter and wished to devote all my energies to her upbringing, and I did. She is today good-looking, has gone through business school and has an excellent position with a real-estate firm, and she is engaged to marry an extremely interesting and well-educated man (a government official). I feel she will be very happy.

I have since my husband's death received proposals from men, but I have always rejected them. My grandmother, it seems, must have agreed with me, because I never heard anything to the contrary from her. I mention this because my grandmother's talk of a trip to New York and the man I would meet there seemed so unlikely that I believed she had said it just to cheer me up after my illness. Later, her words actually slipped my mind.

Imagine my surprise when today, on my return from the hospital, I received a registered letter from a Mr. Ginsburg, a New York lawyer, notifying me of the death of my great-aunt Catherine Pennell and telling me that she had left me a sum of almost five thousand dollars. Aunt Catherine was a spinster and had severed her ties with our family over fifty years ago, before I was born. As far as we knew, she had lived on a farm in Pennsylvania. My father had sometimes talked about her and her eccentricities, but I had never met her nor did I know whether she was alive or dead. How she wound up in New York is a mystery to me, as is the reason for her choosing to leave me money. These are the facts, and I must come to New York concerning the bequest. Documents have to be signed and so forth.

When I read the lawyer's letter and then your highly interesting and dear one, I suddenly realized how foolish I had been to doubt my grandmother's words. She has never made a prediction that didn't later prove true, and I will never doubt her again.

This letter is already too long and my fingers are tired from holding the pen. I simply wish to inform you that I will be in New York for several days in January, or at the latest in early February, and I would consider it a privilege and an honor to meet you personally.

I cannot know what the Powers that be have in store for me, but I know that meeting you will be an important event in my life, as I hope meeting me will be for you. I have extraordinary things to tell you. In the meantime, accept my deepest gratitude and my fondest regards.

I am, very truly yours,
Rose Beechman

Everything happened quickly. One day they talked about closing down the publishing house, and the next day it was done. Morris Korver and his sons called a meeting of the staff. Korver himself spoke in Yiddish, pounded his fist on a bookstand, and shouted with the loud voice of a young man. He warned the workers that if they didn't accept the settlement he and his sons had worked out, none of them would get a penny. One son, Seymour, a lawyer, had a few words to say, in English. In contrast with his father's shouting, Seymour spoke quietly. The older employees who were hard of hearing moved their chairs closer and turned up their hearing aids. Seymour displayed a list of figures. The publishing house, he said, had in the last few years lost several hundred thousand dollars. How much can a business lose? There it all was, written down in black and white.

After the bosses left, the writers and office workers voted whether or not to agree to the proposed terms. The majority voted to accept. It was argued that Korver had secretly bribed some employees to be on his side, but what was the difference? Every worker was to receive his final check the following day. The manuscripts were left lying on the tables. Sam had already brought up men from the demolition company.

Raphael Robbins carefully put into his satchel the little cushion on which he sat, a magnifying glass, and a drawerful of medicine. He took leave of everyone with the shrewd smile of a man who knew everything in advance and therefore was never surprised. Yohanan Abarbanel took a single dictionary home with him. Miss Lipshitz, the secretary, walked around with red, weepy eyes all morning. Ben Melnick brought a huge trunk and packed his private archives, consisting of horse-racing forms.

Herman Gombiner was too feeble to pack the letters and books that had accumulated in his bookcase. He opened a drawer, looked at the dust-covered papers, and immediately started coughing. He said goodbye to Miss Lipshitz, handed Sam a last five-dollar tip, went to the bank to cash the check, and then waited for a taxi.

For many years, Herman Gombiner had lived in fear of the day when he would be without a job. But when he got into the taxi to go home at one o'clock in the afternoon, he felt the calm of resignation. He never turned his head to look back at the place in which he had wasted almost thirty years.

A wet snow was falling. The sky was gray. Sitting in the taxi, leaning his head back against the seat, with eyes closed, Herman Gombiner compared himself to a corpse returning from its own funeral. This is probably the way the soul leaves the body and starts its spiritual existence, he thought.

He had figured everything out. With the almost two thousand dollars he had saved in the bank, the money he had received from Morris Korver, and unemployment insurance, he would be able to manage for two years—perhaps even a few months longer. Then he would have to go on relief. There was no sense in even trying to get another job. Herman had from childhood begged God not to make him dependent on charity, but it had evidently been decided differently. Unless, of course, death redeemed him first.

Thank God it was warm in the house. Herman looked at the mouse's hole. In what way was he, Herman, better than she? Huldah also had to depend on someone. He took out a notebook and pencil and started to calculate. He would no longer need to pay for two taxis daily, or have to eat lunch in a restaurant, or leave a tip for the waiter. There would be no more contributions for all kinds of collections—for Palestine, for employees' children or grandchildren who were getting married, for retirement gifts. He certainly wouldn't be paying any more taxes. Herman examined his clothes closet. He had enough shirts and shoes to last him another ten years. He needed money only for rent, bread, milk, magazines, and stamps. There had been a time when he considered getting a telephone in his apartment. Thank God he had not done it. With these six dollars he could manage for a week. Without realizing it would come to this, Herman had for years practiced the art of reducing his expenditures to a minimum, lowering the wick of life, so to speak.

Never before had Herman Gombiner enjoyed his apartment as he did on that winter day when he returned home after the closing of the publishing house. People had often complained to him about their loneliness, but as long as there were books and stationery and as long as he could sit on a chair next to the radiator and meditate, he was never alone. From the neighboring apartments he could hear the laughter of children, women talking, and the loud voices of men. Radios were turned on full blast. In the street, boys and girls were playing noisily.

The short day grew darker and darker, and the house filled with shadows. Outside, the snow took on an unusual blue coloring. Twilight descended. "So, a day has passed," Herman said to himself. This particular day, this very date would never return again, unless Nietzsche was right in his theory about the eternal return. Even if one did believe that time was imaginary, this day was finished, like the flipped page of a book. It had passed into the archives of eternity. But what had he, Herman Gombiner, accomplished? Whom had he helped? Not even the mouse. She had not come out of her hole, not a peep out of her all day. Was she sick? She was no longer young; old age crept up on everyone . . .

As Herman sat in the wintry twilight, he seemed to be waiting for a sign from the Powers on high. Sometimes he received messages from them, but at other times they remained hidden and silent. He found himself thinking about his parents, grandparents, his sisters, brother, aunts, uncles, and cousins. Where were they all? Where were they resting, blessed souls, martyred by the Nazis. Did they ever think of him? Or had they risen into spheres where they were no longer concerned with the lower worlds? He started to pray to them, inviting them to visit him on this winter evening.

The steam in the radiator hissed, singing its one note. The steam seemed to speak in the pipes, consoling Herman: "You are not alone, you are an element of the universe, a child of God, an integral part of Creation. Your suffering is God's suffering, your yearning His yearning. Everything is right. Let the Truth be revealed to you, and you will be filled with joy."

Suddenly Herman heard a squeak. In the dimness, the mouse had crawled out and looked cautiously around, as if afraid that a cat lurked nearby. Herman held his breath. Holy creature, have no fear. No harm will come to you. He watched her as she approached the saucer of water, took one sip, then a second and a third. Slowly she started gnawing the piece of cheese.

Can there be any greater wonder, Herman thought. Here

stands a mouse, a daughter of a mouse, a granddaughter of mice, a product of millions, billions of mice who once lived, suffered, reproduced, and are now gone forever, but have left an heir, apparently the last of her line. Here she stands, nourishing herself with food. What does she think about all day in her hole? She must think about something. She does have a mind, a nervous system, She is just as much a part of God's creation as the planets, the stars, the distant galaxies.

The mouse suddenly raised her head and stared at Herman with a human look of love and gratitude. Herman imagined that she was saying thank you.

Since Herman Gombiner had stopped working, he realized what an effort it had been for him to wake up in the morning, to wait outside for a cab, to waste his time with dictionaries, writing, editing, and traveling home again each evening. He had apparently been working with the last of his strength. It seemed to him that the publishing house had closed on the very day that he had expended his last bit of remaining energy. This fact in itself was an excellent example of the presence of Godly compassion and the hand of Providence. But thank heaven he still had the will to read and write letters.

Snow had fallen. Herman couldn't recall another New York winter with as much snow as this. Huge drifts had piled up. It was impossible for cars to drive through his street. Herman would have had to plow his way to Columbus Avenue or Central Park West to get a taxi. He would surely have collapsed. Luckily, the delivery boy from the grocery store didn't forget him. Every other day he brought up rolls, sometimes eggs, cheese, and whatever else Herman had ordered. His neighbors would knock on his door and ask him whether he needed anything—coffee, tea, fruit. He thanked them profusely. Poor as he was, he always gave a mother a nickel to buy some chocolate for her child. The women never left at once; they lingered awhile and spoke to him in their broken English, looking at him as if they regretted having to go. Once, a woman stroked Herman's head gently. Women had always been attracted to him.

There had been times when women had fallen desperately in love with him, but marriage and a family were not for Herman. The thought of raising children seemed absurd to him. Why prolong the human tragedy? Besides, he had always sent every last cent to Kalomin.

His thoughts kept returning to the past. He was back in Kalomin. He was going to heder, studying at a yeshiva, secretly teaching himself modern Hebrew, Polish, German, taking lessons, instructing others. He experienced his first love affair, the meetings with girls, strolls in the woods, to the watermill, to the cemetery. He had been drawn to cemeteries even as a youngster, and would spend hours there, meditating among the tombstones and listening to their stony silence. The dead spoke to him from their graves. In the Kalomin cemetery there grew tall, white-barked birch trees. Their silvery leaves trembled in the slightest breeze, chattering their leafy dialect all day. The boughs leaned over each other, whispering secrets.

Later came the trip to America and wandering around New York without a job. Then he went to work for Zion and began studying English. He had been fairly healthy at that time and had had affairs with women. It was difficult to believe the many triumphs he had had. On lonely nights, details of old episodes and never-forgotten words came to him. Memory itself demonstrates that there is no oblivion. Words a woman had uttered to him thirty years before and that he hadn't really understood at the time would suddenly become clear. Thank God he had enough memories to last him a hundred years.

For the first time since he had come to America, his windows froze over. Frost trees like those in Kalomin formed on the windowpanes—upside-down palms, exotic shrubs, and strange flowers. The frost painted like an artist, but its patterns were eternal. Crystals? What were crystals? Who had taught the atoms and molecules to arrange themselves in this or that way? What was the connection between the molecules in New York and the molecules in Kalomin?

The greatest wonders began when Herman dozed off. As

soon as he closed his eyes, his dreams came like locusts. He saw everything with clarity and precision. These were not dreams but visions. He flew over Oriental cities, hovered over cupolas, mosques, and castles, lingered in strange gardens, mysterious forests. He came upon undiscovered tribes, spoke foreign languages. Sometimes he was frightened by monsters.

Herman had often thought that one's true life was lived during sleep. Waking was no more than a marginal time assigned for doing things.

Now that he was free, his entire schedule was turned around. It seemed to happen of itself. He stayed awake at night and slept during the day. He ate lunch in the evening and skipped supper altogether. The alarm clock had stopped, but Herman hadn't rewound it. What difference did it make what time it was? Sometimes he was too lazy to turn the lights on in the evening. Instead of reading, he sat on a chair next to the radiator and dozed. He was overcome by a fatigue that never left him. Am I getting sick, he wondered. No matter how little the grocery boy delivered, Herman had too much.

His real sustenance was the letters he received. Herman still made his way down the few flights of stairs to his letter box in the lobby. He had provided himself with a supply of stamps and stationery. There was a mailbox a few feet from the entrance of the house. If he was unable to get through the snow, he would ask a neighbor to mail his letters. Recently, a woman who lived on his floor offered to get his mail every morning, and Herman gave her the key to his box. She was a stamp collector; the stamps were her payment. Herman now spared himself the trouble of climbing stairs. She mailed his letters and slipped the ones he received under the door, and so quietly that he never heard her footsteps.

He often sat all night writing, napping between letters. Occasionally he would take an old letter from the desk drawer and read it through a magnifying glass, Yes, the dead were still with us. They came to advise their relatives on business, debts, the healing of the sick; they comforted the discouraged, made suggestions concerning trips, jobs, love, marriage. Some left bouquets of flowers on bedspreads, and apported articles from distant places. Some revealed themselves only to intimate ones at the moment of death, others returned years after they had passed away. If this were all true, Herman thought, then his relatives, too, were surely living. He sat praying for them to appear to him. The spirit cannot be burned, gassed, hanged, shot. Six million souls must exist somewhere.

One night, having written letters till dawn, Herman inserted them in envelopes, addressed and put stamps on them, then went to bed. When he opened his eyes, it was full daylight. His head was heavy. It lay like a stone on the pillow. He felt hot, yet chills ran across his back. He had dreamed that his dead family came to him, but they had not behaved appropriately for ghosts; they had quarreled, shouted, even come to blows over a straw basket.

Herman looked toward the door and saw the morning mail pushed under it by his neighbor, but he couldn't move. Am I paralyzed, he wondered. He fell asleep again, and the ghosts returned. His mother and sisters were arguing over a metal comb. "Well, this is too ridiculous," he said to himself. "Spirits don't need metal combs." The dream continued. He discovered a cabinet in the wall of his room. He opened it and letters started pouring out—hundreds of letters. What was this cabinet? The letters bore old datemarks; he had never opened them. In his sleep he felt troubled that so many people had written to him and he hadn't answered them. He decided that a postman must have hidden the letters in order to save himself the trouble of delivering them. But if the postman had already bothered to come to his house, what was the sense of hiding the letters in the cabinet?

Herman awoke, and it was evening. "How did the day pass so quickly?" he asked himself. He tried to get up to go to the bathroom, but his head spun and everything turned black. He fell to the floor. Well, it's the end, he thought. What will become of Huldah?

He lay powerless for a long time. Then slowly he pulled himself up, and by moving along the wall he reached the bathroom. His urine was brown and oily, and he felt a burning sensation.

It took him a long time to return to his bed. He lay down again, and the bed seemed to rise and fall. How strange—he no longer needed to tear open the envelopes of his letters. Clairvoyant powers enabled him to read their contents. He had received a reply from a woman in a small town in Colorado. She wrote of a now dead neighbor with whom she had always quarreled, and of how after the neighbor's death her ghost had broken her sewing machine. Her former enemy had poured water on her floors, ripped open a pillow and spilled out all the feathers. The dead can be mischievous. They can also be full of vengeance. If this was so, he thought, then a war between the dead Jews and the dead Nazis was altogether possible.

That night, Herman dozed, twitched convulsively, and woke up again and again. Outside, the wind howled. It blew right through the house. Herman remembered Huldah; the mouse was without food or water. He wanted to get down to help her, but he couldn't move any part of his body. He prayed to God, "I don't need help any more, but don't let that poor creature die of hunger!" He pledged money to charity. Then he fell asleep.

Herman opened his eyes, and the day was just beginning—an overcast wintry day that he could barely make out through the frost-covered windowpanes. It was as cold indoors as out. Herman listened but could hear no tune from the radiator. He tried to cover himself, but his hands lacked the strength. From the hallway he heard sounds of shouting and running feet. Someone knocked on the door, but he couldn't answer. There was more knocking. A man spoke in Spanish, and Herman heard a woman's voice. Suddenly someone pushed the door open and a Puerto Rican man came in, followed by a small woman wearing a knitted coat and matching hat. She carried a huge muff such as Herman had never seen in America.

The woman came up to his bed and said, "Mr. Gombiner?" She pronounced his name so that he hardly recognized it—with the accent on the first syllable. The man left. In her hand the woman held the letters she had picked up from the floor. She had fair skin, dark eyes, and a small nose. She said, "I knew that you were sick. I am Mrs. Beechman— Rose Beechman." She held out a letter she had sent him that was among those she found at the door.

Herman understood, but was unable to speak. He heard her say, "My grandmother made me come to you. I was coming to New York two weeks from now. You are ill and the furnace in your house has exploded. Wait, I'll cover you. Where is your telephone?"

She pulled the blanket over him, but the bedding was like ice. She started to move about, stamping her boots and clapping her hands. "You don't have a telephone? How can I get a doctor?"

He wanted to tell her he didn't want a doctor, but he was

too weak. Looking at her made him tired. He shut his eyes and immediately forgot that he had a visitor.

"How can anyone sleep so much?" Herman asked himself. This sleepiness had transformed him into a helpless creature. He opened his eyes, saw the strange woman, knew who she was, and immediately fell asleep again. She had brought a doctor—a tall man, a giant—and this man uncovered him, listened to his heart with a stethoscope, squeezed his stomach, looked down his throat. Herman heard the word "pneumonia"; they told him he would have to go to the hospital, but he amassed enough strength to shake his head. He would rather die. The doctor reprimanded him good-naturedly; the woman tried to persuade him. What's wrong with a hospital? They would make him well there. She would visit him every day, would take care of him.

But Herman was adamant. He broke through his sickness and spoke to the woman. "Every person has the right to determine his own fate." He showed her where he kept his money; he looked at her pleadingly, stretched out his hand to her, begging her to promise that he would not be moved.

One moment he spoke clearly as a healthy man, and the next he returned to his torpor. He dreamed again—whether asleep or awake he himself didn't know. The woman gave him medicine. A girl came and administered an injection.

THE LETTER WRITER

Thank God there was heat again. The radiator sang all day and half the night. Now the sun shone in—the bit of sunlight that reached his window in the morning; now the ceiling light burned. Neighbors came to ask how he was, mostly women. They brought him bowls of grits, warm milk, cups of tea. The strange woman changed her clothes; sometimes she wore a black dress or a yellow dress, sometimes a white blouse or a rose-colored blouse. At times she appeared middle-aged and serious to him, at others girlishly young and playful. She inserted a thermometer in his mouth and brought his bedpan. She undressed him and gave him alcohol rubs. He felt embarrassed because of his emaciated body, but she argued, "What is there to be ashamed of? We are all the way God made us." Sick as he was, he was still aware of the smoothness of her palms. Was she human? Or an angel? He was a child again, whose mother was worrying about him. He knew very well that he could die of his sleepiness, but he had ceased being afraid of death.

Herman was preoccupied with something—an event, a vision that repeated itself with countless variations but whose meaning he couldn't fathom. It seemed to him that his sleeping was like a long book which he read so eagerly he could not stop even for a minute. Drinking tea, taking medicine were merely annoying interruptions. His body, together with its agonies, had detached itself from him.

He awoke. The day was growing pale. The woman had

383

placed an ice pack on his head. She removed it and commented that his pajama top had blood on it. The blood had come from his nose.

"Am I dying? Is this death?" he asked himself. He felt only curiosity.

The woman gave him medicine from a teaspoon, and the fluid had the strength and the smell of cognac. Herman shut his eyes, and when he opened them again he could see the snowy blue of the night. The woman was sitting at a table that had for years been cluttered with books, which she must have removed. She had placed her fingertips at the edge of the table. The table was moving, raising its front legs and then dropping them down with a bang.

For a while he was wide awake and as clearheaded as if he were well. Was the table really moving of its own accord? Or was the woman raising it? He stared in amazement. The woman was mumbling; she asked questions that he couldn't hear. Sometimes she grumbled; once she even laughed, showing a mouthful of small teeth. Suddenly she went over to the bed, leaned over him, and said, "You will live. You will recover."

He listened to her words with an indifference that surprised him.

He closed his eyes and found himself in Kalomin again. They were all living—his father, his mother, his grandfather, his grandmother, his sisters, his brother, all the uncles and aunts and cousins. How odd that Kalomin could be a part of New York. One had only to reach a street that led to Canal Street. The street was on the side of a mountain, and it was necessary to climb up to it. It seemed that he had to go through a cellar or a tunnel, a place he remembered from other dreams. It grew darker and darker, the ground became steeper and full of ditches, the walls lower and lower and the air more stuffy. He had to open a door to a small chamber that was full of the bones of corpses, slimy with decay. He had come upon a subterranean cemetery, and there he met a beadle, or perhaps a warden or a gravedigger who was attending to the bones.

"How can anyone live here?" Herman asked himself. "Who would want such a livelihood?" Herman couldn't see this man now, but he recalled previous dreams in which he had seen him—bearded and shabby. He broke off limbs like so many rotten roots. He laughed with secret glee. Herman tried to escape from this labyrinth, crawling on his belly and slithering like a snake, overexerting himself so that his breathing stopped.

He awakened in a cold sweat. The lamp was not lit, but a faint glow shone from somewhere. Where is this light coming from, Herman wondered, and where is the woman? How miraculous—he felt well.

He sat up slowly and saw the woman asleep on a cot, covered with an unfamiliar blanket. The faint illumination came from a tiny light bulb plugged into a socket near the floor. Herman sat still and let the perspiration dry, feeling cooler as it dried.

"Well, it wasn't destined that I should die yet," he muttered. "But why am I needed here?" He could find no answer.

Herman leaned back on the pillow and lay still. He remembered everything: he had fallen ill, Rose Beechman had arrived, and had brought a doctor to see him. Herman had refused to go to the hospital.

He took stock of himself. He had apparently passed the crisis. He was weak, but no longer sick. All his pains were gone. He could breathe freely. His throat was no longer clogged with phlegm. This woman had saved his life.

Herman knew he should thank Providence, but something inside him felt sad and almost cheated. He had always hoped for a revelation. He had counted on his deep sleep to see things kept from the healthy eye. Even of death he had thought, Let's look at what is on the other side of the curtain. He had often read about people who were ill and whose astral bodies wandered over cities, oceans, and deserts. Others had come in contact with relatives, had had visions; heavenly lights had appeared to them. But in his long sleep Herman had experienced nothing but a lot of tangled dreams. He remembered the little table that had raised and lowered its front legs one night. Where was it? It stood not far from his bed, covered with a pile of letters and magazines, apparently received during his illness.

Herman observed Rose Beechman. Why had she come? When had she had the cot brought in? He saw her face distinctly now—the small nose, hollow cheeks, dark hair, the round forehead a bit too high for a woman. She slept calmly, the blanket over her breast. Her breathing couldn't be heard. It occurred to Herman that she might be dead. He stared at her intently; her nostrils moved slightly.

Herman dozed off again. Suddenly he heard a mumbling. He opened his eyes. The woman was talking in her sleep. He listened carefully but couldn't make out the words. He wasn't certain whether it was English or another language. What did it mean? All at once he knew: she was talking to her grandmother. He held his breath. His whole being became still. He made an effort to distinguish at least one word, but he couldn't catch a single syllable. The woman became silent and then started to whisper again. She didn't move her lips. Her voice seemed to be coming out of her nostrils. Who knows? Perhaps she wasn't speaking a known language, Herman Gombiner thought. He fancied that she was suggesting something to the unseen one and arguing with her. This intensive listening soon tired him. He closed his eyes and fell asleep.

He twitched and woke up. He didn't know how long he had been sleeping—a minute or an hour. Through the window he saw that it was still night. The woman on the cot

ISAAC BASHEVIS SINGER

was sleeping silently. Suddenly Herman remembered. What had become of Huldah? How awful that throughout his long illness he had entirely forgotten her. No one had fed her or given her anything to drink. "She is surely dead," he said to himself. "Dead of hunger and thirst!" He felt a great shame. He had recovered. The Powers that rule the world had sent a woman to him, a merciful sister, but this creature who was dependent on him for its necessities had perished. "I should not have forgotten her! I should not have! I've killed her!"

Despair took hold of Herman. He started to pray for the mouse's soul. "Well, you've had your life. You've served your time in this forsaken world, the worst of all worlds, this bottomless abyss, where Satan, Asmodeus, Hitler, and Stalin prevail. You are no longer confined to your hole—hungry, thirsty, and sick, but at one with the God-filled cosmos, with God Himself . . . Who knows why you had to be a mouse?"

In his thoughts, Herman spoke a eulogy for the mouse who had shared a portion of her life with him and who, because of him, had left this earth. "What do they know—all those scholars, all those philosophers, all the leaders of the world—about such as you? They have convinced themselves that man, the worst transgressor of all the species, is the crown of creation. All other creatures were created merely to provide him with food, pelts, to be tormented, exterminated. In relation to them, all people are Nazis; for the animals it is an eternal Treblinka. And yet man demands compassion

388

from heaven." Herman clapped his hand to his mouth. "I mustn't live, I mustn't! I can no longer be a part of it! God in heaven—take me away!"

For a while his mind was blank. Then he trembled. Perhaps Huldah was still alive? Perhaps she had found something to eat. Maybe she was lying unconscious in her hole and could be revived? He tried to get off the bed. He lifted the blanket and slowly put one foot down. The bed creaked.

The woman opened her eyes as if she hadn't been asleep at all but had been pretending. "Where are you going?"

"There is something I must find out."

"What? Wait one second." She straightened her nightgown underneath the blanket, got out of bed, and went over to him barefooted. Her feet were white, girlishly small, with slender toes. "How are you feeling?"

"I beg you, listen to me!" And in a quiet voice he told her about the mouse.

The woman listened. Her face, hidden in the shadows, expressed no surprise. She said, "Yes, I did hear the mice scratching several times during the night. They are probably eating your books."

"It's only one mouse. A wonderful creature."

"What shall I do?"

"The hole is right here . . . I used to set out a dish of water for her and a piece of cheese."

"I don't have any cheese here."

"Perhaps you can pour some milk in a little dish. I'm not sure that she is alive, but maybe . . ."

"Yes, there is milk. First I'll take your temperature." She took a thermometer from somewhere, shook it down, and put it in his mouth with the authority of a nurse.

Herman watched her as she busied herself in the kitchenette. She poured milk from a bottle into a saucer. Several times she turned her head and gave him an inquiring look, as if she didn't quite believe what she had just heard.

How can this be, Herman wondered. She doesn't look like a woman with a grown daughter. She looks like a girl herself. Her loose hair reached her shoulders. He could make out her figure through her bathrobe: narrow in the waist, not too broad in the hips. Her face had a mildness, a softness that didn't match the earnest, almost severe letter she had written him. Oh, well, where is it written that everything must match? Every person is a new experiment in God's laboratory.

The woman took the dish and carefully set it down where he had indicated. On the way back to the cot, she put on her house slippers. She took the thermometer out of his mouth and went to the bathroom, where a light was burning. She soon returned. "You have no fever. Thank God."

"You have saved my life," Herman said.

"It was my grandmother who told me to come here. I hope you've read my letter."

"Yes, I read it."

"I see that you correspond with half the world."

"I'm interested in psychic research."

"This is your first day without fever."

For a while, both were silent. Then he asked, "How can I repay you?"

The woman frowned. "There's no need to repay me."

Herman fell asleep and found himself in Kalomin. It was a summer evening and he was strolling with a girl across a bridge on the way to the mill and to the Russian Orthodox Cemetery, where the gravestones bear the photographs of those interred. A huge luminous sphere shimmered in the sky, larger than the moon, larger than the sun, a new incomparable heavenly body. It cast a greenish glow over the water, making it transparent, so that fish could be seen as they swam. Not the usual carp and pike but whales and sharks, fish with golden fins, red horns, with skin similar to that on the wings of bats.

"What is all this?" Herman asked. "Has the cosmos changed? Has the earth torn itself away from the sun, from the whole Milky Way? Is it about to become a comet?" He tried to talk to the girl he was with, but she was one of the ladies buried in the graveyard. She replied in Russian, although it was also Hebrew. Herman asked, "Don't Kant's categories of pure reason any longer apply in Kalomin?"

He woke up with a start. On the other side of the window it was still night. The strange woman was asleep on the cot. Herman examined her more carefully now. She no longer mumbled, but her lips trembled occasionally. Her brow wrinkled as she smiled in her sleep. Her hair was spread out over the pillow. The quilt had slid down, and he could see the bunched-up folds of her nightgown and the top of her breast. Herman stared at her, mute with amazement. A woman had come to him from somewhere in the South—not a Jewess, but as Ruth had come to Boaz, sent by some Naomi who was no longer among the living.

Where had she found bedding, Herman wondered. She had already brought order to his apartment—she had hung a curtain over the window, cleaned the newspapers and manuscripts from the large table. How strange, she hadn't moved the blotter, as if she had known that it was the implement of a miracle.

Herman stared, nodding his head in wonder. The books in the bookcases did not look so old and tattered. She had brought some kind of order to them, too. The air he breathed no longer smelled moldy and dusty but had a moist, cool quality. Herman was reminded of a Passover night in Kalomin. Only the matzos hanging in a sheet from the ceiling were lacking. He tried to remember his latest dream, but he could only recall the unearthly light that fell across the lake. "Well, dreams are all lost," Herman said to himself. "Each day begins with amnesia."

He heard a slight noise that sounded like a child sucking. Herman sat up and saw Huldah. She appeared thinner, weak, and her fur looked grayer, as if she had aged.

"God in Heaven! Huldah is alive! There she stands, drinking milk from the dish!" A joy such as he had seldom experienced gripped Herman. He had not as yet thanked God for bringing him back to life. He had even felt some resentment. But for letting the mouse live he had to praise the Higher Powers. Herman was filled with love both for the mouse and for the woman, Rose Beechman, who had understood his feelings and without question had obeyed his request and given the mouse some milk. "I am not worthy, I am not worthy," he muttered. "It is all pure Grace."

Herman was not a man who wept. His eyes had remained dry even when he received the news that his family had perished in the destruction of Kalomin. But now his face became wet and hot. It wasn't fated that he bear the guilt of a murderer. Providence—aware of every molecule, every mite, every speck of dust—had seen to it that the mouse received its nourishment during his long sleep. Or was it perhaps possible that a mouse could fast for that length of time?

Herman watched intently. Even now, after going hungry for so long, the mouse didn't rush. She lapped the milk slowly, pausing occasionally, obviously confident that no one would take away what was rightfully hers. "Little mouse, hallowed creature, saint!" Herman cried to her in his thoughts. He blew her a kiss.

The mouse continued to drink. From time to time, she cocked her head and gave Herman a sidelong glance. He imagined he saw in her eyes an expression of surprise, as if she were silently asking, "Why did you let me go hungry so long? And who is this woman sleeping here?" Soon she went back to her hole.

Rose Beechman opened her eyes. "Oh! You are up? What time is it?"

"Huldah has had her milk," Herman said.

"What? Oh, yes."

"I beg you, don't laugh at me."

"I'm not laughing at anyone."

"You've saved not one life but two."

"Well, we are all God's creatures. I'll make you some tea."

Herman wanted to tell her that it wasn't necessary, but he was thirsty and his throat felt dry. He even felt a pang of hunger. He had come back to life, with all its needs.

The woman immediately busied herself in the kitchenette, and shortly she brought Herman a cup of tea and two biscuits. She had apparently bought new dishes for him. She sat down on the edge of a chair and said, "Well, drink your tea. I don't believe you realize how sick you were."

"I am grateful."

"If I had been just two days later, nothing would have helped."

"Perhaps it would have been better that way."

"No. People like you are needed."

"Today I heard you talking to your grandmother." Herman spoke, not sure if he should be saying this.

She listened and was thoughtfully silent awhile. "Yes, she was with me last night."

"What did she say?"

The woman looked at him oddly. He noticed for the first time that her eyes were light brown. "I hope you won't make fun of me."

"God in heaven, no!"

"She wants me to take care of you; you need me more than my daughter does—those were her words."

A chill ran down Herman's spine. "Yes, that may be true, but—"

"But what? I beg you, be honest with me."

"I have nothing. I am weak. I can only be a burden . . ."

"Burdens are made to be borne."

"Yes. Yes."

"If you want me to, I will stay with you. At least until you recover completely."

"Yes, I do."

"That is what I wanted to hear." She stood up quickly and turned away. She walked toward the bathroom, embarrassed as a young Kalomin bride. She remained standing in the doorway with her back toward him, her head bowed, revealing the small nape of her neck, her uncombed hair.

Through the window a gray light was beginning to appear. Snow was falling—a dawn snow. Patches of day and night blended together outside. Clouds appeared. Windows, roofs, and fire escapes emerged from the dark. Lights went out. The night had ended like a dream and was followed by an obscure reality, self-absorbed, sunk in the perpetual mystery of being. A pigeon was flying through the snowfall, intent on carrying out its mission. In the radiator, the steam was already whistling. From the neighboring apartments were heard the first cries of awakened children, radios playing, and harassed housewives yelling and cursing in Spanish. The globe called Earth had once again revolved on its axis. The windowpanes became rosy—a sign that in the east the sky was not entirely overcast. The books were momentarily bathed in a purplish light, illuminating the old bindings and the last remnants of gold-engraved and half-legible titles. It all had the quality of a revelation.

ACKNOWLEDGMENTS

We gratefully acknowledge all those who gave permission for written material to appear in this book. We have made every effort to trace and contact copyright holders. If an error or omission is brought to our notice we will be pleased to correct the situation in future editions of this book. For further information, please contact the publisher.

Excerpt from *Anatomy of an Illness* by Norman Cousins. Copyright © 1979 by Norman Cousins. Used by permission of W.W. Norton & Company. ❖ Excerpt from *My Year Off* by Robert McCrum. Copyright © 1998 by Robert McCrum. Reprinted by permission of W.W. Norton & Company. ❖ "Broken Vessels" from *Broken Vessels* by Andre Dubus. Copyright © 1991 by Andre Dubus. Reprinted by permission of David R. Godine Publishers. ❖ Excerpt from *Ordinary People* by Judith Guest. Copyright © 1982 by Judith Guest. Reprinted by permission of Penguin Putnam Inc. ❖ Excerpt from *Bless Me, Ultima* by Rudolfo Anaya. Copyright © 1972 by Rudolfo A. Anaya. Used by permission of the author. ❖ Excerpt from *Drinking: A Love Story* by Caroline Knapp. Copyright © 1995 by Caroline Knapp. Used by permission of

ACKNOWLEGMENTS

The Dial Press/Dell Publishing, a division of Random House, Inc. ✤ Excerpt from *The Patient Who Cured His Therapist* by Stanley Siegel with Ed Lowe. Copyright © 1992 by Stanley Siegel and Ed Lowe. Appears by permission of the publisher, Marlowe & Company. ✤ "Elliott" from *The Measure of Our Days* by Jerome Groopman. Copyright © 1997 by Jerome E. Groopman. Used by permission of Viking Penguin, a division of Penguin Putnam Inc. ✤ Excerpt from *An Anthropologist on Mars* by Oliver Sacks. Copyright © 1995 by Oliver Sacks. Reprinted by permission of Alfred A. Knopf, a Division of Random House, Inc. ✤ Excerpt from *Inside the Halo and Beyond* by Maxine Kumin. Copyright © 2000 by Maxine Kumin. Reprinted by permission of W.W. Norton & Company. ✤ Excerpt from *Wasted: A Memoir of Anorexia and Bulimia* by Marya Hornbacher. Copyright © 1998 by Marya Hornbacher-Beard. Reprinted by permission of HarperCollins Publishers, Inc. ✤ "The Letter Writer" from *Collected Stories* by Isaac Bashevis Singer. Copyright © 1982 by Isaac Bashevis Singer. Reprinted by permission of Farrar, Straus & Giroux, LLC.

BIBLIOGRAPHY

Anaya, Rudolfo. *Bless Me, Ultima.* New York: Warner Books, 1994.

Cousins, Norman. *Anatomy of an Illness.* New York: Bantam Doubleday Dell, 1991.

Dubus, Andre. *Broken Vessels.* Boston: David R. Godine, 1991.

Groopman, Jerome. *The Measure of Our Days.* New York: Penguin Books, 1998.

Guest, Judith. *Ordinary People.* New York: Penguin Books, 1982.

Hornbacher, Marya. *Wasted: A Memoir of Anorexia and Bulimia.* New York: HarperCollins Publishers, 1999.

Keller, Helen. *The Story of My Life.* New York: Bantam Books, 1990.

Knapp, Caroline. *Drinking: A Love Story.* New York: Bantam Doubleday Dell, 1996.

Kumin, Maxine. *Inside the Halo and Beyond.* New York: W.W. Norton & Company, 2000.

McCrum, Robert. *My Year Off.* New York: Broadway Books, 1999.

Sacks, Oliver. *An Anthropologist On Mars: 7 Paradoxical Tales*. New York: Vintage Books, 1996.

Siegel, Stanley and Ed Lowe. *The Patient Who Cured His Therapist*. New York: Marlowe & Company, 1999.

Singer, Isaac Bashevis. *The Collected Stories of Isaac Bashevis Singer*. New York: The Noonday Press, 1991.